s. m. i. l. e.

s. m. i. l. e.

Kevin Reeves

Cushite Press
Chicago, Illinois

Published by Cushite Press
thesmilestory.com

ISBN: 978-0-9728581-9-9

For Maya

Acknowledgments

I am thankful for the love of all my family and friends. You believed in me and supported me long before I began writing. I love you all. I will be there with you when it matters.

There were many instances along my apprentice journey where a word was given that lifted me. Writing, while having to make a living, while taking on the fullness of life, is hard. These instances of encouragement were grace. Thank you to those that spoke excitedly about my early writings and ability. Thanks to the spirit that compelled you.

Specifically, there are those who engaged my early work fully, encouraging me in extraordinary ways: Thank you, Jamaica Kincaid, for seeing my talent and helping me believe I could become an artist. Pierre, my brother, before the pen and with it in hand, thank you for the long walks and conversations talking about art. Our relationship is a blessing. Deangelo, your powerfully inspiring words alone were a blessing, but your friendship is even greater. Shawn, thank you for your remark during spring break our senior year and then, much later, your declarations during and after reading *Son of the City*. You are a great friend. Rodney, you may not remember a certain contrary look that you gave me when I felt like all was lost, but I am thankful for it and much later you defending my path and my gift. Mama (Sheilah) Seymour, for loving reading the way you do and for taking my early writings seriously, as if I were a known author, thank you. Malika, thank you for believing and, despite my stubbornness, convincing me to meet your mother. Dr. Graham, aside from my wife, your devotion to my work has been unmatched. Thank you for your support and for allowing me to meet great artists. Taii, we began this journey around the same time. Thank you for your ear and your understanding. Andrae, thank you for listening while I talked on and on about this work well before I had written a word of it. Also, thanks for giving me the opportunity to read my first short story to you and Myehla. Edward P. Jones, you did not have to read and comment extensively on *Son of the City*. Your attention and compliments helped lift me. Granddaddy, if not for your gift of oratory and your love of telling stories, this may not have been. You continue to inspire me; thank you for influencing me to dream. Daddy, thank you for understanding my artistic sensibility, once an artist always an artist, for reading my work, encouraging me, and engaging me openly about it. Mama, you introduced me to the wonders of reading. What would I be without your love? Brandy, you have read and listened to everything I have written since we came together. No one has believed like you.

Special thanks to Marona Graham-Bailey and Joanne Asala for helping me edit the story. Also thanks to Willie, Xavier, Benny, Brandon and Eunice for your invaluable input during this process.

Part I

Chapter 1

Aisha Star Bowerman-Johnson and Aaron Jamal Benjamin met across the river, on the athletic side of the Charles. From this beginning, their relationship stretched nine years, mostly from afar. Mostly, these years were filled with great fondness and affection for each other, certainly friendship, although there was a fracture that required mending. When it had, in the last days of 2005, Aaron flew one way from New York to Chicago.

On New Year's Eve, with many of Aaron's bags still unpacked and his boxes sealed, the two sat on Aisha's couch, cuddling. They planned to celebrate the holiday alone; had promised each other that nothing would distract them from doing so. The old apartment building where Aisha lived was built solidly, so noises above and below would be of no concern.

Slowed and with time, they held each other, sharing soft, unhurried kisses. Feeling each other's touch, something seized them, something alien and wonderful. It had their hearts jumping all around in their chests, their stomachs sinking. Tingling on their lips, in their mouths, their throats, traveling down to the tips of their toes and back again to their lips. They felt light, as though they were not sitting on the couch at all, but in the air, floating, borrowing a piece of secluded sky.

To their left, radiators lined the wall, hissing. The releasing steam sounded an eternal "yes," and as Aisha and Aaron caressed their spirits said it, too. *Yes, at last, this feels right. I'm afraid, thrilled. I love you, yes. This is love, yes.*

The TV was on but turned down. There may as well have not been a TV in the room. What mattered was each other's embrace, their conversation and Aaron's antics, him explaining why he was cool *before* the cash. All that mattered was their laughs, their silence. The wonderful silence. It was no longer empty, but filled, overflowing.

They fell asleep intertwined that night. Aaron covered Aisha in his arms, the two looking into each other's eyes until sleep set in. They saw the sleepiness there and the pace, not the power, of their kissing slowed. Struggling to stay awake, they were determined to remain in the moment until both realized that this time was unlike before. There were going to be many more nights just the same. He was not going away. She was not going away.

Chapter 2

Aaron and Aisha spent the winter months with only each other, comfortable solely with each other's company outside of work. Despite all their differences, compromising came easily. Indeed, all concessions came easily, except for the matter of Aaron's wardrobe. Mostly, Aisha pursued the issue with tact. His shoes were off limits. She knew not to bother them, would not even mention them. But his clothes she could work on. Item by item, she worked to decrease his collection, covertly removing this piece and that piece, giving them away in small quantities. Aaron was observant, but he did not notice the small reductions. This pleased Aisha. She was even happier the day that Aaron willingly gave away armfuls of his own clothes. He thought this would satisfy her but it only made her more determined.

One Saturday morning, as the two lay thinking about rising and appreciating the calm of lying together before another busy day, Aisha turned her head toward the bedroom closet. She stared curiously at Aaron's side of clothes. His portion still drastically overwhelmed her modest collection. Blinking as though to make sure her vision was accurate, she turned over to Aaron.

"Let's go to the Goodwill after you pick me up today."

"Uh, uh, you're not going to start that this morning. You think I'm going to lie here and listen to that?" Aaron slid out of bed, talking to Aisha and to himself, and headed for the kitchen. Aisha got up and followed him.

"But AJ, you still have too many clothes. You don't even wear half of them."

She stopped, opening the hallway closet. "Look at this. It looks like nothing has even changed!"

Aaron had a taste for pancakes that morning. He took out the mix, an egg, milk, and a bowl and started to prepare the batter. As he worked at his station, Aisha joined him in the kitchen.

"It's not my fault you picked this joint without good closet space."

"It does have good space. It was built for people with the right amount of clothes."

Aaron started whipping the pancake batter. "What people? You ain't talking about me. I got the right amount."

"AJ, you have enough clothes to start a chain!"

"Hell yeah, Jamal's or Mal's. 'Where you get that?' 'Mal's, dog.'"

Aisha took a grapefruit out of the refrigerator then grabbed a knife to cut it. Her back was turned to Aaron.

"It doesn't take that many clothes to look good."

"Why doesn't it?" Aaron said, sitting the batter down. "What you want me to do, Superstar? Give away *all* of my clothes?" At this, Aisha smiled and turned around.

"Yes, so I can have you all the time, all to myself, bare."

"Here you go. If I'm gone be bare, you better believe it's about to go down. I'll get bare right now if you say you're ready. Say you ready." Aaron acted as if he was about to strip his t-shirt and shorts off.

Aisha blushed. "AJ."

"Uh huh, see. Don't let your mouth get you in trouble. I know you want me." Aisha smacked his arm.

"You do, don't front. I know you be getting that feeling. Don't let this thing I'm doing fool you. As soon as you're ready, I'm ready. For real. I could be downtown in the middle of a big day. You hit me saying you're ready, I'm headed home. 'Um, y'all can handle this. Isaac, I'll holla.'" Aaron acted out the movements of coming home, much to Aisha's delight.

"Yeah, so don't go talking about me being bare if you ain't ready for me to be bare. You know me. We can get it on here on this kitchen floor right now!" Aisha smiled and turned back to her grapefruit.

"Right. Back on the clothes, right?"

"Are you going to make your pancakes? Because I'll wait to fix the rest of my breakfast."

"Fix? You don't have nothing to fix. I'm done talking if you're done."

"So we'll be able to take some of your clothes to the Goodwill today?" Aisha said, turning around.

"See, you ain't done. Star, I'm black. And black folks gone look good."

"AJ, don't say that."

"What? I ain't black now?"

"No. Being black has nothing to do with it."

"Hold up. Black folks don't like looking good?"

"Why are you generalizing?"

"Generalizing? You're the one that told me the first thing black folks did after Emancipation was go buy the best buggy, the big buggy sitting on chrome."

"Some of them. That hardly gives you the authority to say that."

"Authority? You trippin'."

"No, I'm not. You're wrong!"

"How you figure? Walk around here; go back to my old block and see what's happening. If they ain't getting it, they trying to get it, and if they ain't trying, it's because they've accepted they just can't. Shid, but I can!"

"AJ, that's terrible!"

"No, that's real. Superstar, you are not the norm. You're an outlier. You better believe most black folks want to look good before anything else and if it ain't clothes, it's something else."

"You're completely generalizing. I don't agree. Skin color has nothing to do with it."

"Yes it does. You know what I'm talking about. I'm 'bout to fix my breakfast. I ain't messing with you."

"Let's see if you can do this—" Aisha brought her hand close to her face and made as if it were Aaron's mouth opening and closing. "—and fix your food at the same time."

"Yeah, uh huh. Naw, I'm going to stand right here and make my case while you tryin' to change me."

"AJ, don't say that. I wouldn't; you know that."

"Then I'm keeping my gear. Why switch it up now, act like I don't like it? I do. You acting like you don't like it."

"I don't!"

"Yes you do. Yes you do. You know you like how your boy come through. Oooo wee! That boy cold."

"Whatever, AJ. The way you dress is the last thing—"

"But it's part of it. You know it. Say you weren't checking my style back in Boston." At this, Aisha smiled.

"Uh huh, I know when I'm right." Aaron glanced at the clock on the wall. "We're not going to have time for me to fix the good *hot* breakfast I wanted before you started harassing me."

Aaron covered the pancake batter and placed the bowl back in the refrigerator. Looking in it for something else to eat, he pulled out a grapefruit and some cream cheese then moved to the counter to untie a bag of bagels.

"You want one of these?"

"Half," Aisha said, moving to the kitchen table with her grapefruit and a glass of water. After Aaron finished preparing his portion, he joined Aisha at the table with two handfuls of food.

"Nah, but for real it's going to be good to give away some more of my clothes. Someone is going to get hooked up."

"Good!"

"Psych!"

"AJ!"

"Ah, you remember that?" Aaron said, laughing. "I didn't know y'all used to say it in the 'burbs. 'Psych your mind your booty shine, your mama smell like turpentine.' We used to say that and half of us didn't know what turpentine was or what it smelled like, but it sounded like something you didn't want yo mama to smell like and it rhymed! We were creative in the 'hood."

"Well, I was creative in the *'burbs.*"

"Yeah, because it was just you and your mama, but you weren't like us. We had to come up with some stuff!"

"I shouldn't have said anything. You're not going to drag me into another city versus suburbs debate."

"Nah, I'm off that. It ain't where you're from, it's what you do. But for real though," Aaron continued, "I got something for you that you can't dispute. And I got numbers; been taking random samples."

"When have you had the time to take random samples?"

"Every day. You're going to feel me on this."

Aisha sighed.

"A'ight. Man! Been meaning to rap with you about this; what happened to my sistas?"

"Huh?"

"The South Side. My South Side sistas." Aaron's face grimaced. He stood up from the table.

"Like all of them…" He made an arc with his hand over his stomach and then quickly sat back down, taking a quick bite of his grapefruit. "Big. Bellies. Back fat. Like everyone."

"Stop. What is with you this morning?"

"What? Naw, I'm serious."

"People all over the country are struggling with weight. Not just black women on the South Side, AJ."

"Yeah, I feel you, for real. All these fat-ass kids. Having to tell kids to go outside and play. What kind of shit is that? People are fucking these kids up!" Aaron shook his head and took an angry bite of his bagel.

"AJ."

"Naw, it's true. Just letting the shorties do whatever. Pop Pop tore my ass up!"

"I didn't get hit and I turned out fine."

"You know what I'm saying. But don't get me on another tangent. Forget the rest of the country. What about my South Side sistas, damn? And you can't say nothing about a segment because I've been taking random samples."

"That's ridiculous."

"Naw, straight up. I'm talking about young to old, coming from all parts of the South Side, working downtown, school, shopping, hopping on to go to work in the 'burbs, all that—"

"Are you finished?" Aisha said, about to stand up. "I'm going to get ready."

"Nah, Star, hold up. For real. I ain't even got to my point."

"I don't know why you're making such an issue about it."

"'Cause I been seeing it every day for the last few months. And now that the big winter coats are starting to come off…I'm telling you it wasn't like this in New York. I don't know. Maybe I just wasn't around it out there like I am here. Maybe that's it. Coming back, I'm realizing how hella divided the Chi is. The South Side got, like, two diverse neighborhoods. It's funny, I haven't told you this yet, but it happened again yesterday after work. The weather's getting warmer and it keeps happening. Did I tell you about this? The white people messing up and getting on the wrong bus?"

"No."

"Okay, I can't believe I haven't told you this. By accident, they get on the Jeffery Express downtown, going south. They just be riding along, sometimes sitting down, but most times standing up right by the back door. You know, trying to look casual. But you know they got to feel a certain kind of way with all the black people on the bus. Got to. Just like if a black person walked on an all-white bus, you're going to feel something. Anyway, they just be riding along until we pass that last stop on Columbus, right around the museum campus. After that, I'm checking them out to see their reaction. I know I'm going to see some comedy, for real. Most times, as soon as that bus gets on Lake Shore Drive, speeding along, you can see it on their faces. 'Oh, man, I'm on the wrong bus. Where is this bus taking me? What am I going to do?' It's all on their faces. Hilarious. They're looking around at all the black people on the bus and they're realizing their mistake more and more. If it's a group, a pair, which most of the times it is—I kind of feel sorry for the solo traveler, they be looking real scared—but if they're in a group they'll start whispering to each other. 'Damn, we messed up. What do we do?' Then some nice person gets their attention and tells them how to put their life back in order when the bus gets to 67th street. Been happening a lot. Crazy. A whole side of the city, one race.

And a whole helluva lot of white people that think everywhere on the South Side other than Hyde Park is a straight war zone. But yeah, in the mornings and on the way home, I'm looking at the sistas like no! What happened? I promise you, back in the day it wasn't like this. Of course, you had your big mamas, but it wasn't like this! I was a young freak and I don't remember all these bellies like this on my black beauties. It's like everyone! I see a flat stomach or even a little pudge and I'm straight applauding, 'Yeah!' Even on the teenagers, the teenagers! Their metabolism is supposed to be going like this." Aaron started making his hands go up and down fast as if they were pistons.

"Okaaay."

"What? I know you're not getting upset."

"No. Not at you. But what's the use in talking about it?"

"Somebody got to start talking about it, because, man, it's out of control."

"You don't understand. It's harder for women, black women."

"Why?"

"I'm not going to get into this with you."

"Why not? Is it harder for them to fill up that fridge with some fresh fruit and vegetables? Take some walks? Hell, I struggle with eating right too, but damn!"

"You make it sound so easy. It's not that simple, AJ."

"Really? Why isn't it?"

"It just isn't."

"What? Is it some psychological thing because most black men like thickness and the women know that? So they just let themselves go because it's all right at first and then they just get thicker and thicker until it's out of control? And then black men still accepting it, what?"

"Is it all about a man? Really, AJ?"

"I'm a man. What you want me to do? You're not helping me out. Star, you're going to tell me that women don't think about men? Black women don't be thinking about black men? You open up any of these magazines, listen to any conversation; hell, I listen on the bus all the time. And a lot of the time you're going to hear talk about me up in there, a man. That's why I took it there. But I mean, just overall, humans, our body ideals, are shaped by the cultures we come up in. Since you're making me break it all down like you don't know me. I don't like when you do that."

"I know. I know. Let's not argue."

"We're not arguing."

"I know. But AJ, yes, that may be a part of it, but only a small part. It's more complex than that."

"Well, what's up then?"

"Neither one of us has the time. And even if we did, I'm not going to sit here like I have all the answers. Books could be written about it. You don't have it all figured out, either."

"Yes I do."

"You think you do. Look, it's something I'm sensitive to. Okay? It's a problem. All facets of health aren't being actively practiced in many communities of color. But I'm there every day, working. It is easy to talk about, but hard doing the work trying to affect change."

"Yeah, I feel that. You are. I feel you. But I don't know? I feel like it's really not that hard. People make it hard. Know what I'm saying? Living up to ideals. I ain't asking the sistas to go out and try to look like a runway model. That's stupid. All I'm saying is, be your best. Why not? Look at all the benefits. Look, I'm out of shape now, been so busy downtown I don't have time to work out and I eat far worse than you. But I got that switch. Know what I'm saying? And I'm not going to let myself fall too far off. But even beyond that, my genes are different. Yours are different. Both of us build lean muscle quicker, easier, but I'm not saying folks should kill themselves to alter their DNA. Do you know what I'm saying? Be happy how God made you. But I don't care what nobody says; God didn't mean for everybody to have big ass bellies and back fat."

"Oh, so now you know God?" Aisha asked curiously, glad that Aaron was finished. It was time. She could not let her students arrive before her. They liked coming early.

"Yeah, you haven't noticed? That's my man."

Chapter 3

Aisha's mother died at the beginning of her freshman year of college. She spent all of that first year recovering, at its end reaching the point where she felt almost normal in uncontrolled social situations and something like her normal self outwardly. Fortunately, her friend Kaii was there for her in the earliest days.

Every night during dinner, Kaii would walk food from Annenberg Hall, across Harvard Yard, to Grays Hall, and up four flights of stairs to Aisha's dorm room. Sometimes Kaii ate with her and at other times, when she had already eaten with others, she'd stay with Aisha and talk. Aisha tried not to depend on these visits, but because they happened so faithfully, she could not help but depend on them. She could not help falling in love with her new friend, the way Kaii cared for her, how caring Kaii was. Or the way she expressed herself, giving Aisha all the updates on what fun things were happening on the yard and along the river, telling her of those people she found interesting, likable, and those she'd rather not spend her time around again.

Aisha learned of Aaron in this way, except at the time she and Kaii were talking in Holworthy, Kaii's dorm, which was on the other side of the yard directly opposite Aisha's dorm. Aisha had walked back and forth from Grays to Holworthy so many times she had come to know how many steps it would take. In a similar way, after Kaii saw Aaron for the first time at a party, which sparked her incessant conversation about him, he was no mere upperclassmen, her pretending he were her boyfriend, making Aisha laugh with all their imaginary rendezvous, Aisha knew almost exactly what Aaron looked like before ever seeing him in person.

Months would pass before Aisha finally saw Aaron for herself. When she did, it happened on the track in Gordon Field House, one of the few places she could be seen out. Kaii was there, supporting Aisha from the stands and watching Aaron's every move in the infield, him raking the long jump pit then wondering why he was doing it, deciding someone else should be doing it, looking around, seeing a worthy replacement, calling for the replacement, and handing the unlucky underclassman the rake. He then moved to joke with the elder athletes. In the middle of his joking, Kaii saw Aaron spot Aisha. She watched his forehead wrinkle and his head tilt to one side. He removed himself from his conversation and gave full attention to watching Aisha. He watched her warm up, stretch, at the starting line, through the race to the finish, and her victory walk back. On the walk back, Aaron approached her. Kaii couldn't believe her eyes. It was not because her imaginary boyfriend was talking to her girlfriend, but because of the way Aisha dismissed him.

A little while after the encounter, when Aisha went to greet Kaii in the stands, Kaii let her know exactly how she felt about the situation.

"Um, why did you treat my boyfriend like that?"

"I wasn't mean to him."

"Star, you didn't even open your mouth."

"But I wasn't mean."

"You know I don't care if you date him, right?"

"What? What are you talking about? That was nothing."

"Um, yes, it was. You don't have the eyes right now. Use mine. He went *out of his way* to speak to you."

"Yeah, and he was in my way."

"Look, girl, I'm with you. I get it, the whole 'don't mess with me when I'm competing' thing, but, yeah, despite all of that, I haven't been stalking him for the last three months for my health. I could be living vicariously through you!"

"Kaii, I got to go."

"Okay, but you got to come out and play at some point…"

Aaron continued to approach Aisha at each home track meet. And Kaii continued to watch every approach, each one making her more determined to have Aisha go out on a date with Aaron. Kaii resolved she at least needed to hear what he had to say. "At least if he turns out to be a jerk, then I can stop making up these fantasies about him. They're no good anymore anyway! They can't compete with the real-life drama! Star, do it for me! No, but seriously, it's time for you to start socializing outside of the dorms with people other than me and your roommate. I don't mean to sound harsh, but it is. I'm tired of you. No, you know I'm just playing about the tired part. I love you. But go out with the boy just once!"

Eventually, mostly because of Kaii's unwavering insistence, Aisha did agree to see Aaron. One night, after all her work was complete, she opened her school's e-mail database, searched for Aaron's address, and sent him an e-mail.

Hi Aaron,

I will meet you for lunch at your dining hall. I am free this Thursday from 12:00–1:30. Let me know if this works for you.

Until then.

The lunch went well. Aisha found Aaron to be interesting and much different than she expected. Somehow, he made her laugh. They were both from Chicago, in Aisha's case, the Chicagoland area.

When Aisha returned the favorable report to Kaii, telling her she had agreed to meet Aaron again for lunch, Kaii started dancing on the spot. It was a made-up dance she called the matchmaker shaker and each time Aisha came back with an Aaron report—because the lunch dates in Quincy dining hall continued—Kaii would do the dance, adding variations and naming them as she went along.

After one such meeting, Aisha agreed to see Aaron's dorm room. Aaron coaxed her with jokes about his unworthiness and seriously interjected that he wanted to introduce her to Isaac, whom he had brought up frequently in their dining hall conversations.

Isaac was not there on the first trip, but Aisha met him on her next visit back to Aaron's dorm room. During this time, Aisha told Aaron little about her personal life, never once alluding to her mother's death. She was able to control the conversations and remain in control in a manner close to her typical personality. She was quiet and selective about when she spoke.

After walking into Aaron's dorm room for the first time, coming to sit on the edge of his bed, him at his desk, her noticing all of his Michael Jordan posters on the walls, the Michael Jordan "Wings" poster stretched out on the wall to her back, her first words were, "You have a lot of shoes." By the sight of them spilling out of the closet, she figured he must like shoes and it was a good way to set the tone. Because they were meeting in a more intimate environment did not mean she would open up any more than she already had.

Aisha's conversation starter helped Aaron to relax. He did like shoes. Bending over and going into his closet, he pulled out a pair of sneakers. They were his first pair of Air Jordans, the Air Jordan IIIs, the most beautiful shoes he had ever seen. Aaron did not get them when they debuted. He bought them when they were rereleased in 1994. "I found out quick that Harvard paid bank for work study. My homeboys were trippin' when I told them how much I was getting paid for what I was doing. Yeah, and I'm still on it. Most of that money goes into the market and my shoes, as you can see." Aaron spoke while holding the prized pair of shoes flat on one palm. Before he set the shoes down on top of his desk, Aisha noticed a flash of something in his eye. Aaron did not tell Aisha then what prompted the flash. Instead, he began to tell her about his affection for the Air Jordan line in general.

He told Aisha his family did not have much money and his grandfather, whom he called Pop Pop, refused even considering the idea of getting him a pair of Air Jordans. He always had some pithy comment about how the shoes would not make Aaron jump any higher and certainly would not make him any smarter. But that mattered little to Aaron. They were the shoes to have. Young men would line up on the shoe's release date as though they were at a concert waiting to gain access to an arena to see their favorite artist. The shoe's progenitor was their favorite artist. Aaron's friend Wayne got a pair each time the shoe was released. Aaron's friend Biggums was like him; his mother could not afford to buy him a pair. Biggums and Wayne were his best friends coming up and every time Wayne got a new pair of Air Jordans, Aaron and Biggums gazed admiringly at their freshness. They would gaze even when the shoes had become less fresh.

In his dorm room that day, he told Aisha about the time he almost had himself a pair. A local drug dealer everybody knew as LD used to get lively watching Aaron develop on the basketball court. Pacing back and forth alongside it, he hooted and hollered and bet money that Aaron, who at the time was hardly into his teens, would do something with the basketball to embarrass opponents twice his age. Once, after Aaron did just that, LD said, "Lil Jam, you got some go, but what up with them muthafuckin' shoes?" Going into his pocket, LD pulled out a thick roll of money. Sweeping his thumb back and forth over it, he casually put five hundred dollar bills into Aaron's hand. He did it so easily the hundred dollar bills seemed like change, something Aaron would go to the corner store with and buy a pickle. "Go get you some new kicks, shawty."

A short while later, Aaron did, buying his own pair of Air Jordans. What a great feeling it was, a feeling that was short lived. Pop Pop made him take it all back, get all the money back, and give every cent back to LD. He went along with Aaron for every step. In confronting LD, Pop Pop said, "Don't give this boy here no more money!" The confrontation came in front of a crowd of LD's people. Aaron feared for Pop Pop, but nothing happened. LD did nothing, even when Pop Pop concluded, saying, "Stay away from my boy!"

Aaron's anger for having to give up his Air Jordans gradually lessened. He respected Pop Pop. They had been through much together.

In his dorm room, Aaron did not tell Aisha what he and Pop Pop had been through, the memories of first seeing the Air Jordan IIIs. The first time came at a community talent show where his grandmother performed with her two friends in a gospel trio. The three singers all wore bright green sequined dresses that did not fit them the same anymore. There in attendance was a young man with a Jheri curl that reached down to his shoulders. His greasy hair rested on his crisp gray and white Nike jogging suit, which was accented by a gold rope chain and completed at his feet by the Air Jordan IIIs. Only days after the talent show, Aaron saw the shoes again on Ben's feet.

Ben was also one of the first that Aaron saw wearing the stair step box cut. He did not live on Aaron's block, but Shequanita, who everyone called Nita, did, and Ben dated her. Aaron fantasized about one day having Nita. He fantasized all the time about having her when she was with Ben. Nita was seven years older than Aaron was and Aaron had just reached the seventh grade, but he felt sure he could get her. Eventually, he did, but it came long after Ben was shot to death.

Ben being shot caused Pop Pop to start their neighborhood watch program. The shooting was not a common occurrence on their block. It was a singular event. Before that fateful evening, with the sun almost gone from the sky and Aaron and Pop Pop getting ready to go to a basketball game, even the mildest discord was rare on their block. But that evening, four shots rang out.

After hearing the shots, hesitating for the shortest time, Aaron dashed out of the house to see the shape of things left. Pop Pop ran after him, concerned and furious that the boy would do such a thing. He had yet to remove all the habits Aaron had gained living with his mother. Aaron had learned it was better to face fear, to see what the object of his fear looked like, to be properly prepared for it. If he did not, the object of his fear had a better chance at doing more to him than making him afraid. He had to face it. Often he did, seeing things a child should not see, things no one should have to see. Finding Ben lying there with blood coming out of his chest, bleeding everywhere, and without his shoes, was one of these moments.

All the blood and the look on Ben's face haunted Aaron. The sight of it stayed with him, yet Aaron's most lasting image of Ben lying there was of his shoeless feet. At some point, Aaron's eyes locked on Ben's bright white socks. They were the whitest-looking socks he had ever seen.

After Pop Pop called the police and Ben's body was removed, he gave Aaron a whipping and cursed him to his room. Aaron rested on his bed, listening to music from the radio his mother had bought him. He thought about Pop Pop no longer being physically strong enough to give him real pain from whippings. Then, for the rest of the night, he pictured Ben's shoeless body lying in the street.

It would not be until much later that Aisha learned about Ben's death, though not in detail. Aaron rarely ever talked about his dark moments in detail. Still, in his own way, he told Aisha in a way that she would know.

Chapter 4

The first time Aaron visited Aisha and her family at their northwest suburban home, he didn't eat meat for two days. He felt proud that he was able to mask his disappointment at the food offerings. Still, he wondered why Aisha didn't save him. Was she trying to get back at him? She never once offered to run him around the corner for fast food. The closest he came to meat was a joke Robert's wife Susan made about cooking a steak. Susan still liked meat.

When Aisha dropped Aaron off on the South Side, he immediately asked Pop Pop to take him to a burger place on east 71st. Pop Pop agreed.

Upon arriving, Pop Pop was surprised to find that the business was black owned. They served turkey burgers, which was good; beef really didn't agree with his system. When he and Pop Pop returned home and sat down at the kitchen table, Pop Pop took a few bites of his burger and said to Aaron, "Yeah, this good. They can get my return business."

Aaron remembered each of his last visits with Pop Pop well. After that Chicago visit he would only see Pop Pop three more times.

Aisha had only been back in the states for a few months during that time, having lived in Senegal for a year. With the beginning of her last semester of college near, she little expected to get a call from Aaron before leaving campus for winter break. When he did call, he asked her if she was going home for the break. When she replied yes, he asked could he come see her.

Aisha had only heard from Aaron twice during her yearlong stay as an exchange student in Senegal. Initially, she wrote him often. In Aaron's first letter, he told her he wouldn't be able to write her back much. He wasn't good with words and Wall Street had him very busy.

Still, he told her he would read everything that she sent. With each letter she wrote, Aisha imagined what Aaron's response might be. Not being able to write her back much meant one letter for every four of hers, right? No, she had thought wrong.

Over time, under the African sun, surrounded by so much new culture, both in her studies at Cheikh Anta Diop University and outside of it—especially outside of it—around all the shiny-faced, bright, smiling children she loved, romance found her and the idea of Aaron was sent to the back of her mind.

The young man, Jawara, who so much enriched her experience, was nothing like what she thought was her type. He was skinny with bug eyes and slightly bucked teeth. She liked hair that was faded on the sides and wavy on the top. Jawara's hair was clumped on top and beaded up into tiny, nappy balls on the sides. Yet he had an innocent spirit. Though some of his ways were slick, it was a childish slickness, a naivety that comes with having never known harsh reality. His skin was beautiful and he spoke five languages, all beautifully. His voice was deep and melodic and he was not intimidated by her looks or that she was an American. Jawara took her around Dakar, giving her access to new worlds with such ease, making it feel like it was always hers. With their feet touching as the ocean's tide drifted underneath their bottoms, pulling the sand away and pulling them closer to the sea, she thought she was in the deepest love. She was even willing to marry him to allow him an opportunity to come to the United States. It would allow them an opportunity to let their love continue and flourish after her time in Senegal was up. They were ready, very close to him leaving his homeland and coming to live in Cambridge with her. It would be easy. Harvard was liberal. No one would have to know but her roommates and they could keep quiet. She had a single so she and Jawara would not be in the way. But Aaron came back. He got in the way. She received a simple letter from him. It read:

Hey Superstar,

I know I haven't written in a while, really ever. I've had a lot going on in New York and I'm doing well. I've never stopped thinking about you, even when your letters stopped. I did read everyone. I know you're coming home soon and I was hoping that I could see you. I might be up for Harvard/Yale this year, maybe then? I hope you're healthy. Don't come home with no diseases or nothing. I hope you've been safe. I hope you are all right.

After finishing the letter, she sat it down. She then picked it up and read it again, then once more before finally folding it back up and placing it back in the envelope. She looked at his name on the envelope, Jamal Benjamin, and knew her feelings for Jawara were not as strong as she had thought. She could not marry him. He could not come back with her.

Telling Jawara this was hard for her, for both of them. The breakup became extra difficult because around the same time she did get a disease, malaria. It was as if the continent was getting back at her for breaking the heart of one its sons.

While recovering from her sickness, Aisha wrote a passionate love letter to Aaron. She envisioned him receiving it and being so moved that he'd fly to Chicago to meet her in the airport. He'd lift her off the ground in an engulfing hug, swing her around, and tell her how much he had missed her. It was going to be the coming together of true love. But none of that happened. She didn't hear from Aaron until the phone call came to her dorm room.

Aaron took a week off around that time. It was the holiday season and the first vacation of any kind he'd taken in his three years working on Wall Street. He had not missed a single day of work and he wouldn't have taken that week if his mentor, Bill Long, did not suggest it. So Aaron flew back to Chicago and home with Pop Pop.

Aaron and Pop Pop talked to one another everyday over the phone while they were apart and this partly made up for Aaron not being able to come home but for a few quick weekend trips, each in those first few years out of college. Together that holiday season in Chicago, Aaron and Pop Pop fell into an inseparable groove. The two spent every minute together. They got up and ate breakfast together, talking about the local news in the paper. Pop Pop asked Aaron about how he felt certain events would affect the market. He became fascinated with capital markets as soon as Aaron did. Initially, it was his interest and encouragement— "Boy, that's what you need to be doing; that's why you're there"—that motivated Aaron to learn as much as he could, grabbing at Isaac's brain, who happened to be his freshman roommate, and going back for more.

Aaron went along for Pop Pop's morning walk around the neighborhood. When he found himself bumping into Pop Pop's pistol bag, he decided to walk on his left. Earlier, when Aaron asked him about the unfamiliar presence of the gun, Pop Pop had replied, "I'm an old man, son. And the neighborhood is changing. No, it's fine. It's all right. Don't worry about me. I just take it along with me on my walks."

During the day, they would go together on Pop Pop's rounds to see his old friends that Aaron grew up knowing: Joe, the alley mechanic, who retired from Ford at sixty-five, but still fixed neighborhood clunkers out of a vacant lot. Walter, who had been the maintenance man for the same building he lived in for forty years. He used to date all the young women that moved into the apartment, until one day he met his match. Johnny, Pop Pop's fishing buddy, who refused to stop driving even though his license was revoked for getting caught too many times speeding drunk on the highway. For some reason, he liked beat up vans with only two seats in front and lots of junk in the back. Aaron looked at Johnny's balding head and remembered him having a little more hair on it and how he would turn around with a beer in his hand, laughing at Aaron as he was tossed side to side along with the junk as the three of them drove north of Chicago for good fishing. Finally, they visited Paul, who was a retired postal worker. Paul lived in a convalescent home. Out of all the friends, Paul's children had the most professional success as adults, so, more than the others did, he questioned Aaron about his affairs in New York. To everything that Aaron said, Paul added that he should get in touch with this one or that one of his children, followed by him muttering that this one or that one of his children were ungrateful. While at Paul's bedside, Aaron turned to look straight at Pop Pop. Pop

Pop understood.

Pop Pop's friends were still full of life but Aaron could see how age had worn them. But not Pop Pop; Aaron thought Pop Pop looked like he'd live forever. He was the same man that had taken him away from terror so many years ago.

After their rounds, the two would take naps at the same time. After rising from their beds, they'd go downstairs to watch Pop Pop's favorite public access channel. Pop Pop argued at the screen. Aaron watched and listened. During the evenings, they ate at Pop Pop's favorite South Side restaurants. In each, the wait staff and management received him like an old friend. Pop Pop pointed at Aaron, exclaiming, "This my boy. That's right, that's the one."Aaron would nod and Pop Pop would continue, "Tell 'em what you want son, they already know what I'm having."Most nights they'd come home from dinner to watch Pop Pop's old Western movies. Aaron had bought him many of the classics since he'd graduated from college, often replacing Pop Pop's favorites on VHS with DVDs. It tickled Aaron to see how masterfully Pop Pop had learned to work the DVD player and his excitement about the extra features. He liked the interviews and the historical perspectives, telling Aaron which ones he liked most of all while he loaded each night's movie.

One night, Aaron and Pop Pop traveled to Hillside to watch the Proviso West High School holiday basketball tournament. Aaron was surprised to see Pop Pop wear the pair of Air Jordans he had sent home as a joke. The shoes looked brand new, as if it were the first time he had ever worn them. Pop Pop's Harvard baseball cap, however, had faded to an entirely different shade and had a small tear on the left side of the brim. He had to get Pop Pop another one. Maybe Aisha could pick one out and send it to him?

Aisha met Aaron and Pop Pop at the basketball game. Sports had been as much a part of her life as it was for Aaron. Her father had indoctrinated her at a young age.

Out of the many exuberant basketball fans, Aisha spotted Aaron quickly, recognizing the way his body moved when he became excited. A player had just dunked the basketball and out of all the fists pumping in the air, she saw him. She was so stupid. Why was she so attracted to him? Why did her heart want him to give her more of what he clearly could not? She knew she was young, but she felt mature, ready. He wasn't ready and he might never be for her.

Heads turned to admire her as Aisha walked to where Aaron and Pop Pop were sitting. It didn't matter that she wore the plainest, most unrevealing clothes. Not baggy, certainly not tight and not dull, but certainly not bright. No-name clothing. Her hair was up in her customary curly puff ponytail. This was the style that she had been wearing for years, having discovered it as a little girl when her mother hadn't quite learned to deal with her grade of hair. It was the style that she had abandoned for straightening in later years, but came back to not because the natural look had come back into style, but because it was most convenient for her. In her young womanhood, she did not like wasting energy on things that weren't important to her. She wasted little time considering the reasons for people's looks. She had spent much too much time as a child worrying about people looking, pointing at her and her family, thinking about the hurtful things they said, the names she was called because of her appearance, their appearance, how it triggered the thoughtless conditioning in people. Kids could be terribly cruel, products of their parents' pointing. After a while, it, and the chaos within her home, which complicated the pointing, made situations worse, more confusing, caused her in her early years, right around the time her father left, to point at herself, to look within and stay there. She learned to give meaningful attention only to the substance of true beauty; often she found it within herself, so she was happy alone. It made her weird to the world. When her appearance became what was universally accepted as beautiful, the favorable looks and the new kind of pointing didn't reach her. She didn't get it, like most everyone else did. She enjoyed looking at herself in the mirror. What she saw was pleasing to her, not because of what the turning heads at the basketball games saw, but because when she looked in the mirror she saw her true self, from what she learned from the inside, for constantly learning herself from the inside and not from the characterizations of the outside world.

Like some who watched her walk by the sideline of the basketball court, many had attributed her look, the way she walked in her own world, to her owning her looks, to them defining her, to her knowing that it automatically placed her in a different position in society, that she knew how to use it, to get things, get places, get her way, that she was used to having her way.

Yet her look was something that came about through a need to survive. It was just her. Though she could not, then, explain the reasons for it. As she sat down between Pop Pop and Aaron, she wished, however, that she could understand why Aaron was the way that he was. She let him in for a reason. He was special, but he acted as though he was unaware that he was her first love. Or if he knew, he did not know what to do with her heart.

After the game, she watched Aaron shake Pop Pop's hand and ask him if he would be okay driving home alone, to which Pop Pop replied, "Boy, I've been driving these roads the same way since Daley had them laid. Alone or with someone makes no difference."

"I see you've lost some weight," was the first thing Aaron said to Aisha when they were sitting alone in her car with the engine running.

"Yeah, I'm just getting my figure back. I contracted malaria right before I was about to leave."

"You sure that's all?"

"What are you trying to say?"

"I mean, did you get tested for everything?" Aisha looked at Aaron and saw a strange seriousness in his eyes. A haze of darkness, mixed in with light. It was the same seriousness she had seen in his eyes when she first came to his dorm room three years before. She felt uncomfortable not knowing what made him look that way and in the way he was implying that she might have some sort of sexually transmitted disease.

"Aaron, I'm still a virgin. I don't care if you don't believe me. Also, you should know that Africa isn't only some A.I.D.S. ravaged place. It's a beautiful place."

"A'ight, Superstar, don't get hype on me; my fault." There was silence and then Aaron continued."Did you enjoy the game?" Aisha paused before answering him. She had to collect herself, get a grip on her emotions. She felt she could have easily continued berating him. Why did she get like this around him? The only other person in the world that could make her lose her composure and get the same sort of emotional rise out of her was her mother. She turned to look at him. He smirked, waiting for her answer, the small light of his cracked smile melting her coolness by the second. His eyes still showed truth. Whatever he was doing in New York, however rough and way off from what she felt for him he was, however much at times she wished she could contain her feelings for him or lock them away and launch them into outer space, she knew he genuinely cared for her and they had a connection. If only she could better understand their situation. It frustrated her. Figuring problems came easily to Aisha. She rarely had trouble gaining clarity with issues of her life. Schoolwork had always been fun. Atop a mountain of books, the air wasn't thin for her, but abundant, fresh, and she loved the view. She had stopped running track in a snap, easily putting away her winged shoes. And she no longer was confused about her race, her place. Yet there were a few things she couldn't understand, like why her father never reached out to her. She knew nothing until the letter her Grandmother Johnson sent her. Why did her mother have to die so young, before Aisha could even become a woman? And why did she love this smirking boy so much, when he hadn't even given her his whole heart?

"Yes, I had a good time. It was exciting."

"You should have been there back when we played! Man, I swear we were balling better. Talent goes in cycles."

Chapter 5

Wednesday was a special day. One of Aaron's best boyhood friends, Ronald T. Biggums, would be visiting with the couple. After school, Aisha began getting the apartment together. She turned on some Senegalese music while she cleaned. They both were clean people, although they had the tendency during the week to let things go. Aaron had once suggested, half-serious, half joking, that they should get a housekeeper. "She'd be the first cleaning lady in this neighborhood since the white folks left." The moment popped back into Aisha's mind, making her smile, as she bustled around picking up Aaron's pile of underwear in the bathroom. She gathered and hung up her blouses that she had draped over her favorite reading chair in the bedroom, picked up any miscellaneous garments lying around, and straightened out the bed. She moved to the second bedroom, which Aaron called the library because of the bookcases filled with books lining the walls. They were her most valued possession. Some of them were scattered on the little desk, along with some of her teaching materials, so she straightened, replaced, and ordered. She stopped for a moment to look out the window and admire the lake. She could only see a sliver of blue because of the position of her building and because her apartment stood on the second floor, but it was enough for her. She loved water. Perhaps it was because some of her earliest and most pleasant memories were of her and her parents at the beach or them driving across the Golden Gate Bridge with her pointing out the window, asking questions. Her own best friend lived on the West Coast, where Aisha was born. Although Kaii lived in Los Angeles, not the San Francisco Bay Area, where she was from.

In recent years, Aisha had fleeting thoughts of returning west, back to the Bay Area, though she knew little of it aside from her happy childhood memories. If it weren't for her students and her work in the school's neighborhood, her impulse would have been stronger. The idea of a fresh start appealed to her. Like Aaron at one time, she began to feel the heaviness of her history with the Chicagoland area. She had also reached a point where her appreciation for family, familial love, and aging made her think daily of her future. If she moved west, she could be closer to her mother's brothers. One uncle lived in Oregon and the other Montana. She had not seen them much when her mother was living, and after her mother died she had seen them only once. Even then, it was hard for her to communicate with them. Though they were family, they hardly knew each other. But she had her own kind of family developing in Chicago, not by blood but by loyalty. She loved her students and Raven and Kiki were good girlfriends. Her relationship with her stepfather, Robert, was improving. She began to allow herself to open to him. And when Aaron decided to come back there was no doubt about her staying. She'd give them one final shot. This one felt like the winning one. She'd remain in her cozy apartment, which was grouped in a few four-story buildings two blocks from the South Shore Cultural Center, now a rehabbed relic. Gone were the structure's days of distinct privilege and its members who lived as though their lives of better living at the exclusion of others were a birthright.

Coming home early from work, Aaron entered, momentarily stopping Aisha's cleaning.

"Uh huh, cheating on me again, thinking about Ja Rule," Aaron said, coming to where Aisha was cleaning and giving her a kiss on the cheek.

"Jawara. And every time I'm listening to this music I am not thinking about him."

"How could you not?"

"AJ! Shut up and start helping me clean."

"For what? Biggums? You should see how that man lives." Aisha continued to move around, straightening. Aaron followed her, smirking.

"C'mon, help me. He's our guest."

"He ain't no guest. He family."

"Ugh!" Aisha gasped. "You have a comeback for everything. Just help me."

"Only if you give me a better kiss. That old leaning over cheek thang ain't gone get it."

"Go collect your shoes at the door."

"Where's my better kiss?" Aisha smiled, stopping what she was doing, and walked up to Aaron. He wrapped his strong arms around her and they shared a passionate kiss, stopping before they both became too aroused.

"I love you," Aaron said.

"I love you, too."

◆　◆　◆

Biggums came with food. He clutched two big sacks in his large meaty hands. Walking into the apartment, he nodded to Aaron and Aisha and found the table, setting the food down as if he had done it before.

"What, you just gone walk in and not show us no love?" Aaron said. Biggums moved toward Aisha with his arms outstretched.

"My, you're beautiful. It's so wonderful to finally meet you." Aisha blushed and smiled in Biggums's embrace.

"Ay, aight, hands off my woman, you big ol' ugly bear." With those words, Biggums excused himself from Aisha and snapped around with his fists in the air.

"Dude, a lot's changed since you been gone, man," Biggums said, circling Aaron as if in a ring.

"You ol' ugly bear. Ain't nothing changed but your weight." At that, Biggums threw a quick jab. Aaron dodged it and landed a light body blow. Biggums made an "O" sound and started laughing. They locked hands and hugged.

"Man, about time you got over here."

"What? You know where I stay. You ain't been to my spot, either—"

"Yeah, you're right. It's on both of us," Aaron said.

"This time," Biggums replied. "C'mon, let's eat. I'm hungrier than a hostage. Where y'all plates?" Aisha pointed to the right cabinet and then walked to open it when Biggums could not tell which one she had pointed to.

When all the plates, cups, and drinks were set on the table, the three sat down to eat. Biggums noticed Aisha had only fixed herself a small portion of cabbage, baked macaroni and cheese, and candy yams, without meat.

"Don't be shy, Star. There's plenty chicken and ribs. Help yourself."

"I'm a vegetarian."

"Ohhh. Well I'm an everythinganarian."

"She can see that."

"AJ, I think he looks fine."

"Thank you," Biggums said, nodding gracefully to Aisha.

"No you don't," Aaron said. "Stop lying, this nigga needs some vegetarianism in his life and some jogging in a gymnasium type shit in his life on top of that."

"Ronald, you look fine to me," Aisha said, turning to Biggums.

"Thank you," Biggums returned, grinning.

"Y'all can cheese all y'all want. You didn't know this man growing up. And you're sure warming up quick to this old hobbit foot."

"I know your insect feet ass ain't talking."

"I'd rather be tall with little feet than short with big hobbit feet."

"Nigga, you ain't tall. Star's taller than you!"

"No she's not!"

"Uh oh, Ronald, you've touched a sensitive place," Aisha said, smacking Aaron's hand lightly and smiling.

"I know. I know. This dude, swearing he's tall, always wanted to make it into the six-feet somethings. See, I accept my shortness. You need to finally accept your shortness, homie. You in the five-foot club."

"Nigga, I don't know what you talking about. I'm six feet."

"It's okay, AJ, five-eleven is above average height for a man," Aisha said, rubbing his hand and smiling.

"Naw, don't touch me," Aaron playfully pulled his hand from under hers. "Y'all can gang up on me if you want, but I know I'm six."

"Okay, dude, you're six," Biggums said, giving a winking look to Aisha. Aaron ate his food with a pouting, defiant look, causing Aisha and Biggums to laugh.

"Ay, I'm sorry," Biggums continued, pointing a half-bitten chicken leg toward the direction of the living room. "But I can't play it off anymore. Who is this dude singing? Are y'all kidding me? Y'all be listening to this?" Aisha and Aaron's heads almost hit the table, they began laughing so hard. The African rhythms filling the apartment air had become one of the soundtracks to their secluded lives.

"It's Youssou N'dour," Aisha said.

"You stole my what?" Biggums replied.

"He's singing in Wolof. He's a Senegalese singer."

"Um, I don't know no Senegalese, so can you please put something on that we can all sing along to?" Aisha laughed and blushed, lowering her head some.

"I'll DJ," Aaron said, saving Aisha from a potentially neurotic moment and allowing him to put some of his music on. "Dog," Aaron continued as he headed out of the room, "I couldn't take it at first, either, and I joke with Superstar about Juwanna Man, her African boyfriend. But I can't front; this dude is kind of tight."

"Aight, I'll take your word for it."

Biggums continued to scarf down his food. It was so delicious he forgot he was in the presence of a lady. He asked Aisha to excuse his table manners and proceeded to question her about her time in Africa. No one he had ever known personally had been to Africa.

He had figured it was Aisha's music. Biggums knew about Aisha, knew of her, since Aaron first met her in college. Aaron came home to Chicago on a break talking about her. Since that first time, Aisha was discussed or at least mentioned in every one of Aaron and Biggums's conversations. Even during the time Aaron and Aisha were not speaking to each other, when Aaron refused to bring her up, Biggums spoke of her. Though he had not met her and had only talked to her on the phone once or twice, he liked her, liked her for his friend.

While Aaron set his music player up, Biggums found out that Aisha spoke French. Flirtingly, he asked her to say something to him using the language. Aisha thought for a moment, then said, "AJ, *t'aime comme un frère. Tu es son frère.*" Aaron came back into the kitchen as she finished. Now Tupac Shakur's voice rang out through the apartment.

"Ay, don't be sharing that with this man," Aaron said.

Biggums flinched at Aaron as if he was going to hit him, then looked to Aisha for the translation. "What did you say?"

"I said, 'AJ, loves you like a brother.'"

"Why you lying to him? I don't like fat people."

"AJ, stop being mean," Aisha said, turning to Biggums and rubbing his arm on the top of his bicep. Biggums's face went calm. Her touch distracted him from the comeback he had prepared to deliver.

"He has an athletic build," Aisha continued.

"Yeah, under fifty pounds of fat," Aaron said. Biggums's face remained at ease because Aisha still had her hand on him, now his shoulder.

"He used to have a little speed." With this comment, Aisha took her arm away from Biggums and moved her chair back, closer to Aaron.

"I'm still fast."

"Yeah, right."

"I can beat you."

"Nigga, you ain't never beat me. How you figure you can do it now?"

"Let's go outside and prove it," Biggums said, standing up abruptly.

"Bet," Aaron said, doing the same.

"Nah, nah, I don't feel like embarrassing you in front of your woman."

"Uh huh, that's what I thought."

"Whatever, nigga. Ay, why you put this on?"

"This is Pac!"

"I know who it is. I can't listen to Pac no more."

"What! You tripping. Pac don't get old."

"Nah, I'm not saying that. Pac's a legend."

"Then what you saying?"

"Nah, I don't know. It's sad. Listening to Pac now gets me sad."

"Sad! Then stop listening to 'So Many Tears' then, nigga. Pac ain't sad."

"I didn't say he was sad, I said…forget it." Aisha studied Biggums's face after she saw that he was serious about what he was saying.

"Ah," Aaron said, waving at Biggums. "You trippin'. This is the same man that rolled around all summer, in a bucket, with a face pull off, your old blue Corsica, playing 'Wonda Why They Call You Bitch' on repeat. Every time I got in this man's car, he had that song on. Had me humming in lecture when I went back to school and everything." Aaron saying this seemed to pick Biggums up; he raised his shoulders back up some.

"I did use to roll to that, didn't I?"

"Whole summer."

"Yeah, man, that was a minute ago."

"Superstar, let me tell you about this man and women," Aaron said, shaking his head and turning to Aisha. "I told you the story of how we met, right?" He had told Aisha the story, many times, but he liked telling it so he began to tell it again.

"This dude was the most proper speaking fool on the South Side. 'Hello, I'm Ronald T. Biggums, pleased to meet you.'"

"My mama," Biggums muttered.

"Right, and we all straight trippin' off how the dude is talking. But then, he gone follow that up with, 'Excuse me, but do you happen to know where Lashonda Barrett lives?' Baby, we like, ten, eleven, twelve, out there playing ball, doing dumb shit. We thinking about girls, but not all like that. You know? This man comes in the neighborhood speaking proper as hell, asking about—of all people—my little play girlfriend at the time—"

"How many times you gone tell this story! Star, you've heard this story, haven't you?" Biggums said, turning to Aisha. With a smile she nodded her head yes.

"Uh uh, I'm getting to my point. So I tell him where she lives. I don't care she was just one of my little girlfriends in the neighborhood, and somehow from there we got cool. Cooler than all the rest of those fools

I was hanging with. Now, through all these years I done seen this man, all because he's a sucka for women, get mad at his sweet mama, move out, join a gang, change his name to Ronnie Mo', drop out of school—"

"I was stupid."

"But the whole time he's still the same proper-speaking, good dude."

"Just dumb."

"Right, and you got some good sense back, but you're still on that dumbshit. Forget these hos!" Aaron looked at Aisha, a plea for forgiveness. His emotions had gotten the best of him. He tried not to talk like that around her. She didn't look disturbed.

"I feel you. I feel you," Biggums said.

"Know what I'm saying!" Aaron returned.

"It's still going on, too. But let me tell y'all. Let me tell y'all what's been happening."

It began with Biggums getting an upgrade on his cell phone in the Southwest Loop off Roosevelt road. It was one of his favorite stores to go to because all the attendants were cute to him. He liked petite, pretty, barely legal-aged women. He found reasons, therefore, to hang around the store, flirting, looking at gadgets hanging on the walls, flirting some more. He'd find various reasons to come back to the store, like a change of battery, phone cover, to pay his bill, etc., none of them necessary. He had other locations around the city that he would frequent with cute clerks. There was the home improvement store in South Holland, where he worked as part-time security or the convenience store off of 95th and Ashland, where one of his favorite clerks worked. He'd buy candy from her, all with the same end result as the cell phone store. For his efforts he received batting eyelashes and giggles. They took his compliments but didn't give him their numbers. Or they gave him numbers that were wrong, or that were never picked up when he called. Still, Biggums continued.

In this mode, on a break from flirting, he happened to look outside the store window and caught a shape and a profile of a face that excited him. He calmed himself and in his mind said, "If she walks past this window again while I'm in this store, then I'll go talk to her." She did. Biggums excused himself from the clerk whose face he was in and skipped out the door after her. He admired her tiny figure and round behind as she walked in front of him. When she was almost to the intersection ahead, he began to lose heart. He said to himself, "If that light turns red and she stops, it was meant for me to talk to her." It did. Biggums made it to her at the light and turned the fullness of his charm on. To his surprise, validating the fake fate games he played in his head, she was receptive to him. She gave him her number and actually picked up the phone when he called. She was twenty-two, but spoke, to him, in a manner that was beyond her years. They had interesting, mature conversations. While they talked, he pictured her tiny waist and round backside on his lap. She found out that he loved children, beaming about his little niece as he did, and soon brought her two-year-old daughter around him. Within weeks, they began to spend every free minute together, the three of them. Biggums would pick them up from the housing project she stayed in whenever she wanted to run errands. The baby's car seat became a fixture in his car. He took them to the children's play place and for walks in the park. Biggums, being a good cook, cooked for them. Once, the baby called him "Daddy." His heart melted, her eyes sparkled.

Every time Biggums was alone with her in his basement apartment, he would initiate intimacy. She'd kiss him, but only so much. She'd let him rub on her behind, but only so much and only with pants on. She never took her pants off for him, although she did allow him to go under her shirt and rub her tiny breasts a couple of times, but never for long. Her expression would often be blank when he involved himself with her in this way. He attributed it to the hard life that she had lived. She opened up to him, which he liked, telling him tales of dysfunction and molestation. He believed her. It wasn't a revelation.

She worked as a hostess at a restaurant downtown. He'd been there to visit, watching her zip around making an honest living. She was trying to make her situation better. That's why her baby didn't live with her; she had to get herself together first. Biggums accepted all of this, although he didn't like the fact that she never answered his calls at night. He said to her, "You should answer your phone when you get off. I want to make sure you're all right. You know, make sure you get home safely." She told him she would, but never did.

Biggums decided to increase his affection. More romance would work. He hadn't been with a woman in a very long time, fearing as he left his young man years he'd end up like his father, whom he called "his sperm donor." He stopped counting siblings after his grandmother reported the thirteenth illegitimate child being born. He wanted to end this cycle so he turned to God, going to church and paying his tithes, but things with that didn't work fast enough. So when he got a job working as a correctional officer in Chicago's county jail, he moved to a friend of the family's basement apartment and, still fearing of being like his father, satisfied himself with pornographic flashes on the computer screen. The internet brought a wonderland of smut with the click of a button, but after a while, it wasn't enough to sate his hunger. Being with his new friend, he was able to give her all he had pent up. The only thing left was for them to have sex.

Biggums bought concert tickets to the upcoming Jill Scott concert and on the night of the concert invited her to his basement early. He had cleaned his entire place up and had spread hundreds of rose petals on the floor, beginning on the steps and descending into the apartment. He lit fragrant candles and played the sultry soul music he loved so much. On the way to pick her up, he could barely contain his excitement. She was going to love it and he was finally going to have sex again. He would be able to touch the soft skin of her naked, plump behind.

Upon arriving at the apartment, he anxiously opened the door. "I asked you over here early because I have a surprise for you." He took her by the hand and led her down the stairs, not looking at her face until they had reached the center of the living room. Filled up with the romantic musings of his childhood, the music, and the moment, he looked at her face. There was nothing there. Her face showed the same flat look it did when he rubbed her over her clothes. Then she said, "Why did you do all this?"

They didn't end up going to the concert that night. Biggums called Aaron for advice and to see if he and Aisha wanted the tickets, but no one picked up the phone. And she wanted to go home. He was devastated. They were through. What else could he do? What else could his heart give? But a couple of weeks later she began coming around again and he put aside his hurt. Maybe all she needed was more time.

A couple of days before he visited Aaron and Aisha, he had visitors come see him at work. They were the girl's mother and the mother's boyfriend. They said they hated to see him being manipulated the way that he was. He was a good person and she was playing him. Biggums questioned their motives. She had told him about them and their ways. The mother and boyfriend could see this on his face so they offered up information on her that he did not know. They directed him to a website to look at. "Check it out," they said. "Bet you she didn't tell you about that."

Having finished the story, Biggums asked Aaron and Aisha if they would like to see the website to see what he found. They nodded their heads yes. When Biggums turned, Aaron looked at Aisha and shook his head side to side.

Biggums found his way to the computer like he did the dinner table upon first coming in. Aisha and Aaron followed behind him.

"This is what I found," he said as he pulled up the low-rate escort site with blurred faces and naked bodies. "There she goes right there," Biggums said, pointing to the girl who had given him so much excitement and disappointment.

Aaron couldn't help but look at her behind first. Although Biggums felt an instant kinship with Aisha, he didn't tell the story in her presence as he would if it were just he and Aaron. In the version he shared with the couple, he did mention the roundness of the girl's bottom. Knowing Biggums, Aaron could infer the rest. Aaron fixated on that region and was slightly disappointed that it didn't live up to what he had imagined. It did not come close to the best of what he had already seen for himself.

Aaron's attention was taken away from the screen when Aisha asked Biggums, "Why isn't her face blurred like the rest?"

"I dunno," Biggums replied, looking dejected.

The exchange made Aaron smile. He stood there with the two people dearest to him in the world. One, a part of his precious past, the other, integral in his grand future. Both in that moment made him realize how happy he was with his decision to come back to Chicago. He certainly didn't feel the haunted, lonely feeling that he feared so much after Pop Pop died. Everything in Chicago felt new, full. He was living an entirely different life. He felt different, a fuzzy feeling of familiarity with the wash and whirl of spontaneity. There he was, looking at smut on the screen again with Biggums, the person who had introduced him to pornography when they were boys. Biggums's uncle, Bobby, had a trunk full of comic books, nude magazines, and pornographic VHS tapes, each with its own orderly section. Aisha knew the stories of the boys sneaking into Bobby's room to drool in front of the screen. When Aaron asked could he take a tape, Biggums said no, because his uncle knew every one of them by memory. Once, Bobby caught them. But he didn't mind. He sat down for a moment and watched it with them, saying, "Don't y'all be comin' in here messing with my shit without me knowing it," before getting up and leaving out the room.

The three stood there, Biggums in the middle, Aisha to his left, and Aaron to his right. Biggums mouthed words to Aisha that Aaron couldn't focus on, sad, nonsensical words. Instead, he focused on Aisha's face, so caring and so understanding without having full understanding. She had that way. She didn't have to experience something herself to have deep empathy for the person. Aaron was sure that, standing there crouched by the computer screen, it was the first time she had seen such a thing. He could tell by the innocent fascination in her eyes, by his accounting of her experiences. He didn't know all that she had ever done and couldn't break down her life by each singular defining moment, however large or small, as she could. But he did know her truth. It excited him to learn new things about her, like how she sat there looking at an escort page and listening to Biggums sadly drone on. The revealing never surprised him. He knew her deeply, from her expanding core.

"—so I'm done with her ass," Biggums said, turning away from the computer. Aisha turned away too. They all went to sit in the living room.

"You sure don't sound like it," Aaron said, fully involving himself in what Biggums was saying once again. "You sound like her explanation is going to keep you there."

"I mean, her people are shady and I don't like that she lied to me, but…"

"But what? Either you done with her or you're not. And I don't want to hear some bull shit about 'everybody hiding something,' either."

"Dog, it's true."

"So, you don't have to accept that shit!"

"Biggums," Aaron continued, "what you expect? Huh? You picked this chick up off the street. Nigga, you can go out the door right now and pick up ten women by the way they looked and all ten of they asses got a good chance at being fucked up. And you taking that home with you every time, dog! I mean damn, you can't go about it like that."

"How am I supposed to go about it then?"

"I don't know. You got to find your own way, but it ain't like that. Ain't shit good out there waiting for you on the street, straight up."

"But the little baby? I feel sorry for the baby. Look, she be sending me pictures." Biggums held up his phone and showed Aisha the images. Aaron didn't look.

"Man, c'mon, Biggums, you ain't stupid. She is really trying to play you for a sucka. And you letting her! Using her damn baby! How transparent is that shit?"

"I know, but the baby."

"Fuck that! It's not your child."

"But I can help her."

"Dog, you barely helping yourself. You can't help nobody until you all the way good."

"I just feel sorry for the baby."

"Look, you can't save everybody. This chick might not even be consciously trying to get you, but this is what she knows. Hustling. Surviving. So she gone use that. And I know your ass. You want to get some booty again, too. Fine, get some, but don't do it how you doin' it, and don't be putting it all on 'I just want to help the baby.' Yeah, you like the baby, but you also thinking about your little wee wee."

"Ahhh, you bogus!" Biggums laughed and threw his fists back in the air. The two slapboxed for a bit, laughing the entire time.

"Man, look, you in your early thirties now and completely by yourself, no kids. You've done a'ight up to this point; you might as well do it right."

For the rest of the night they caught up on the current state of their lives, reminiscing about old times and happenings in the worlds they knew. Back and forth from one topic to the next and back to old times, then laughter, then serious conversation, and laughter again. Aisha and Aaron had to rise early for work the next day and the fact that it was getting very late crossed their minds, but neither of them made mention of it. Biggums was the first visitor to come by their little place by the lake, but more than that, it felt like family reuniting and the night kept flowing. Aisha eventually opened bottles of wine. All three got tipsy for the first time in months. They laughed more and just when the night's life seemed like it was fading, Biggums noticed a Scrabble board under the end table in the corner and all three jolted alive again. Biggums bragged that he was the best Scrabble player in the land, but he never had anyone to play with. Aisha, in her own way, expressed the same sentiment. Aaron, like a prize-fighting promoter, exalted both of their qualities that would make the games a good match.

In a friendly way, Aaron eventually called the night to an end. He stood up and said, "A'ight, dude, let me walk you to your car." Biggums hugged Aisha and ensured her that he most certainly wouldn't forget about their Scrabble game and walked out the apartment door with Aaron.

"Ay, man, Star's a beautiful woman," Biggums said as he and Aaron exited the building.

"I know. I'm lucky."

"Look at you. I haven't seen you like this in a minute!"

"I know, dude, it feels good. The night was good. You straight to drive?"

"I'm straight. Hey, you about to do your thing when you get back, ain't you?"

"Nigga, why you still asking about my action? You need to get you some pussy."

"I do. But nah, I know it's different with her and everything, but y'all getting down, right?"

"Not yet."

"Whaaat! Still! How does she do it? Hell, how the hell you doing it!"

"For a long time I didn't. But it's cool now. I'm with it."

"For how long?"

"For however long, and I'm not jagging either." Aaron smiled at Biggums.

"Stop playing."

"Nope. Trying something new."

"And you getting on me! Nigga that ain't human! You gone have sperm coming out of your pores or explode from non nut bust build up or something, damn!"

"For real. The shit is hard, but I'm seeking that next level. Can't stay stuck on the same stuff." Biggums pressed his lips together and made a sound.

"Shid, I can stay stuck in some pussy for the rest of my life."

"True. True. But then that might be all you ever get."

The two had made it to Biggums's car. Biggums took his keys out with one hand and with the other shook Aaron's hand. When Biggums tried to separate, Aaron would not let his hand go.

"Ay, I'm here for you, dog. Things are going to be different."

On the walk back to the apartment, Aaron pondered the reality of Biggums's inquiry. He had been candid with his friend, but those few words did little to convey the trials of his abstinence. He couldn't remember a period of more than a few weeks since he lost his virginity at thirteen to a sixteen-year-old girl in the neighborhood, where he didn't have sex. When he realized that coming to Chicago to be with Aisha was the right thing, he began slowly eliminating sex partners in New York. In his last few months in the city, he had scaled it down to one stable friend and those he might take home for one night. But the opportunities for both were limited due to his increased phone conversations with Aisha in the night hours. His loins tugged at him and his call waiting tempted him, but he would not end his connection with Aisha until they were both mumbling on the phone. It felt like the right thing to do. Still, when their phone calls ended, sometimes his libido would conquer his fatigue and Aaron would lie in bed, recalling past fantasies.

But from his first day in Chicago he had gone without anything. When Aisha heard his plan, he could see she wanted to believe but knew she was skeptical. She had a right to be. She knew his appetite and elements of his history. He knew hers. After complete dismissal came cynicism, then shock, followed by rejection, and finally acceptance. She made him a believer. Aisha was unlike any woman he had encountered. No flesh had ever been in her, anywhere, no hand but hers had rubbed her private places. The authenticity of her actions, over a long period of time, her unwavering consistency, baffled him. One day she finally revealed part of her secret; she, in her freshman year at Harvard, discovered—out of curiosity more than burning desire—what two of her fingers could do, in the shower, lying on her bed, developing an immature mastery of loving herself, pleasing herself. This helped him have a better understanding. Although he could never, even in his abstinence or even with her mother entreating her to make the first time right, fully understand how she did it.

Aisha's skepticism, as when anybody doubted him, was like rocket fuel. Her agreeing to give up her long habit to match his effort—so they were each giving up something—solidified his decision.

The first two months were nearly unbearable. His withdrawal included sleepwalking, hovering over Aisha until he came to the realization that he was not dreaming and could not have her; incessant sexual dreams that occasionally became wet, an embarrassment that fascinated Aisha; having to sleep against a body pillow to blockade contact with her backside; and finally, perhaps the worst of all steamy images, flashbacks that crept into his mind during the workday. Yet, recently, something had changed. All the symptoms of withdrawal had gone. The arousal still came, but it was more like a baby boy in a bathtub. And like a two year old, he felt a bountiful surge of energy. He could not remember when his head was so clear, when he felt such peace. He didn't know how long he would feel that way and he didn't share his feelings explicitly with Aisha because he didn't want her to get any Gandhi-like ideas. Through it all he felt a pure love. It felt like being brought to his knees while still standing taller than he ever had.

When the men left the apartment, Aisha went back to her room. She swooned. Laying face up on the bed, the ceiling spun. She giggled at the wine and the drunken happiness that came even before the intoxication. She had heard so much about Biggums and he turned out to be exactly how she had imagined him.

From time to time, when Aaron wasn't home, she'd look at his small brown photo album. She'd imagine herself growing up in his neighborhood, them being sweethearts from the start. What would her life have been like had she grown up in the city? She knew a story about every face in the album. Aaron went through it once, narrating. Aisha didn't forget even the faces of lesser significance. Aaron put the album together after Pop Pop died. He told her he thought it would be the closest he would ever get to home again. In it were boyhood pictures of Aaron, Biggums, and their friend Wayne Alexander. The boys called themselves BBA. They were known as such around the neighborhood until the influence of the Blackstones became too great and part of Biggums's and Wayne's loyalty left BBA and went to the "Mos." None of them ever took fully to gangbanging. They had better dreams. They all could see beyond the neighborhood, which had much to do with how close they were.

Wayne took his own life around the beginning of the previous year, right around the time Aaron and Aisha started talking again. When Biggums informed Aaron of it, Aisha became like a counselor to

Aaron. He told her that Wayne had always been sensitive and the world they lived in really couldn't understand him. He didn't seem to fit, but he couldn't see himself fitting anywhere else. Ultimately, Aaron thought the pressures of Wayne's struggles with the mother of his children—something Aisha was quite familiar with growing up and with the parents of her own students—led him to pulling the trigger.

Throughout the night Aisha searched Biggums's eyes for signs of pain, especially after he mentioned being sad. If Aaron was affected, she was sure Biggums had to be. At the start, she did see pain, but as the night went along his eyes smiled more.

Aisha closed her eyes and curled up on the bed. The spinning room was beginning to make her nauseated and thoughts of her past life, a reoccurring nightmare, sprung to her mind. She hated the dream. At first she hoped she'd outgrow it. When it continued, and she and Aaron began living together, she hoped their love would take it away. But nothing took it away. She had dreamt it at least a few times since Aaron moved back to Chicago.

In the dream, her father beat her mother in front of her and then turned to her with tears in his eyes, his hands out, palms up, no words spoken. She was sure she had never lived the dream, so she was unsure about its meaning. It was about the only secret she held from Aaron. He knew about her mother being abused, but he didn't know about the dream. When the time was right she would tell him.

Aisha felt Aaron's warm, wine-smelling breath on her cheek first, then his lips. She told him she loved him without changing the position of her body. He returned the expression and readied himself to go to bed. She could feel him positioning the body pillow against her backside. Soon, the body pillow would no longer be necessary. More than ever, she felt the right time was near, it was then. Like the dream, she only had to wait for the right moment.

Chapter 6

The morning after Biggums visited, as always, Aaron stood waiting at the bus stop right in front of Aisha's apartment building on the northeast corner of 72nd and South Shore Drive. He would take either the 6 or the 26 to 67th and Jeffery, where he would catch the 14 and take it downtown. Standing there, he thought about how wholly different his life was just a year ago, how a common conversation between him and Biggums the year before opened his eyes to the inevitable economic crisis ahead. Aaron's awareness had peaked at the right time and, if his strategy was properly executed, he and Isaac stood to make a tremendous amount of money. No one was paying attention. No one could see it coming. He would not have seen it, either, if Biggums had not mentioned Mookie.

In early January of 2005, Aaron made his first trip back to Chicago since Pop Pop died. He chose to stay at the Drake Hotel. He and Aisha were getting along well again and he did not want to be in the same place as her at night. She might want to cuddle with him in bed and he could not cuddle. How could she be content only cuddling, kissing, and talking? Amazing. He knew himself; knew better, he could not take that. He would not put himself through that kind of frustration again. He was too used to having his way with women. Where there was mutual attraction and close, comfortable quarters, he would have his way. And out of all the women he had ever met or been with, Aisha attracted him the most. Yet, he chose to stay at the Drake specifically because of Pop Pop. Before Grandma Benjamin died, Pop Pop was proud that he was able to take her to the hotel for the weekend. After their stay, they came home and told Aaron all about it, which he never forgot. He arrived at the Drake and was impressed, but no more impressed than other fine hotels he had been in around the world. Hotels of its caliber had become normal for him. It was the memory of how happy Pop Pop was to stay there that made the place special.

Aaron only stayed at the Drake for the weekend. He had dinner with Isaac and his wife Katie that Friday evening and partied with Biggums the rest of the night. The other part of the trip he spent with Aisha. In between his dinner with Isaac and Katie and partying, Biggums met him at the hotel's bar.

After a few drinks at the bar, Biggums brought up Mookie.

"Yo, guess who I bumped into, who was asking about you?"

"Who?"

"Mookie."

"Ahh, what that fool talking about?"

"Man, I told him how you were doing big things and he said he was too." Aaron swirled his drink and chuckled to himself, then spoke.

"Man, that nigga ain't on shit," he said, taking a sip of his drink.

"He said he's going to catch you."

"Catch me? Please, a whole lifetime of hustling—" Aaron cut himself off and took another sip of his cognac. The statement wasn't even worth finishing.

"He said he's making one fifty. And it looks like it, too. He showed me a picture of his crib and his car on his phone."

"First of all, he's lame for taking pictures of his shit and walking around with it and you a lame for looking." Aaron turned to look directly at Biggums. "Dog, I wipe my ass with one fifty. He better stop worrying about me and start worrying about getting locked up." Biggums laughed at this.

"Straight up, that's what I was thinking. I'd be seeing him in the County. But, nah, he's legit now."

"Legit? Doing what?"

"He's getting people into houses. Said he couldn't wait until the summertime because he was going to make more money than that."

At the time, Aaron did not make much of their conversation about

Mookie. But upon returning to New York and reflecting on his Chicago weekend, the conversation stood out. Aaron had gone through high school with Mookie. He had always talked big, but the biggest thing about him was his mouth. He was always into something, always some scheme, working some angle, cooking up some hustle. He was hard working, but only in finding the next move to get over on others. And he was only smart enough to see what was right in front of his face. The more Aaron thought about Mookie making the kind of money Biggums reported, bringing in business for some lender, the more he thought something had to be wrong. Aaron had not gone so far that he couldn't see making one hundred and fifty thousand dollars a year was a good living. It was a good living that should not come easy. It was coming easy if Mookie was into it. Something had to be wrong.

Aaron worked in fixed income since his start on Wall Street. Back on the job, he began to take a look at what was happening around him. Was something there? He would come home from work and obsess over the numbers, spending entire weekends in, hardly eating while analyzing more figures. Something was there and the more he found the more he could not believe what was before him.

Still, he had to make sure. Before he approached Bill Long about it, he had to be certain. He went in again and again for more thorough analysis, trying to become expert on the situation in a matter of months. When he finished, he was supremely confident in his findings. It was backed by his qualitative instinct, him knowing Mookie. Surely there were plenty other Mookies across the country, profiting easily on people's dreams of owning a home, all in an honest rush to arrive, signing home loans they could not afford, that would eventually upend them. But Aaron's confidence was supported most by his quantitative analysis. His industry had created the financial instruments that enabled the Mookies of the country to thrive.

When Aaron approached Bill Long with his information, his mentor replied, "No, no, you're being naive…It's all too established… Stop being a data dick." The man who had taught Aaron so much, who gave him the early opportunities in the business that most did not get, would not believe him after he had worked so hard. His findings were so clear. Aaron shared some of his findings with Isaac and Isaac believed.

In the ten years since they had graduated from Harvard, Isaac, who had been Aaron's roommate all through school, had turned his dorm room trading operation into a formidable business. His Colossus group had just over two billion in assets under management. At its inception, Aaron had the opportunity to be co-head of it.

Aaron and Isaac became great friends in four years. In that time, they also found out that they worked well together. Isaac had introduced Aaron to capital markets in their freshman year and by their senior year he was so impressed at how adept at dorm room trading Aaron had become he often loaned Aaron money to trade with. Isaac felt Aaron joining him was an easy decision. He saw greatness in their future together. He planned for the two of them to graduate, return to Chicago, and become partners of the audaciously named group. But Aaron had a different view. He and Pop Pop could not see turning down the lucrative offers the big New York banks offered him for uncertainty. The big New York banks offered him over double what Pop Pop had made at the peak of his earnings. Pop Pop said to Aaron, "Isaac's a smart boy, but there ain't no guarantee for success. White folks get a better shot, but that don't mean they don't mess up. If you mess up with him, it's going to take you longer to get back. That's just the truth, son. His people got money. And you don't need to be back here in Chicago. Go on. Them banks offering that money now. Take it. I don't want you coming back here. See what's there for you in New York."

Aaron knew Isaac better than Pop Pop, knew how sharp he was, his drive, and his love for the market. It was Isaac's budding love that spawned his own and he never doubted that his roommate would be successful, but he agreed with Pop Pop. He would take the money the big banks offered him, what felt like a small fortune to him then, and write his own story. He did not know where he would be led in New York; really, in New York there was more uncertainty. He did not know he would meet an unlikely mentor, Bill Long, and that every morning Bill

Long would make Aaron buy him coffee with Aaron's own money, two creams five sugars, or how Bill Long knew after one sip if he'd forgotten even one packet of sugar and how he would call him every epithet in the English language for the mistake and for his mistakes during the day. Color came up twice. "Aaron's stupid black ass." The first time Aaron gave him a look that said, "What did you just say? Do not say it again." The second time Aaron responded ferociously, standing eye to eye, prepared to lose his job and maybe more than that. Bill Long smiled and told him he had said it on purpose to see how Aaron would react. "Only the idiots care about race. I care about making money." He saw that Aaron learned quickly, regardless of their differences, like Aaron's speech. The way Aaron spoke actually endeared him to Bill Long. When others on the desk felt differently, he stood up for Aaron. They wanted to make Aaron take speech classes. "Idiots. Assholes. Everyone has a fucking accent; yours is just different. I told them they were all assholes. You're a fucking Harvard graduate. Who gives a fuck if you don't sound like everyone else? Can you make money?"Bill Long showed Aaron how to make money.

When Bill Long left to start his own group, Aaron took over his position on the desk and did better than Bill Long did when he was there. Later, he left the bank to go work with Bill Long. They made a lot of money together, but it had to end. When Bill Long would not believe him, Aaron left to go work with Isaac, in Chicago.

Aaron had never doubted his decision to go to New York after college until he moved in with Aisha. What might it have been like? He couldn't say. Things seemed to turn out all right the way they went. He did know for certain he would have more money had he gone with Isaac from the start, but he did all right for himself in New York. He had been no lightweight.

Presenting the essence of what he found to Isaac, the two discussed his claims and him coming on. When Isaac balked at Aaron's proposition, hard negotiations began. It was a heated back and forth with Aaron finally saying, "You ain't about to get me on the cheap. I can't believe yo ass! You're trying to do me? Me! It's me! Fuck being friends, right? Right. It's about the business at hand and you clearly not seeing what I'm seeing, dog. This Colossus thing giving you a name, but you believing your own hype! You and none of the muthafuckas you got working for you see what I see. I'm going to save your ass and make both of us a shitload of money! I've been studying this shit for months! And no one will fucking believe me! You know me. Dub, I'm telling you this is going to be big. It's all about to collapse and if you just drop your sack and agree to my terms, we'll be crazy paid on the other side of it." Later, they moved forward in agreement.

Aaron felt he could not lose in Chicago. Every day he took the 6 and the 14 buses to get downtown, getting to the office and getting to know all the Colossus employees. He observed their work habits and personalities, what moved them to perform. He and Isaac talked serious strategy, actionable sessions that gave rise to Aaron already recruiting a few new guys to the group. After the work day, he and Isaac would sometimes reminisce about how they used to argue about the market and basketball, how equally impassioned they were about both, but looking back how, in the beginning, their knowledge of basketball far surpassed their knowledge of the market. But that was their gestation period, early and unfounded cockiness, the feeling that they already had minds like Warren Buffet. It encouraged daring and long hours of studying the market, skipping classes, and having to cram to avoid being asked to leave for a year after both were put on academic probation.

There were drunken nights, stumbling through the yard holding one another up, and drunken nights riding the T with the football players who somehow hung upside down like bats from the stability bars, others sliding across the T floor on their bellies, shocking pedestrian riders though not in fear. They were clearly Harvard students. They had the look and in between their cursing something intelligent blurted out, expressions that didn't seem to fit the spectacle they created. There were nights throwing balls into plastic cups filled with beer, raising their arms in celebration, and kissing the new girl by their side. They'd both bring new girls back to their dorm room. And dorm room parties, Aaron taking Isaac to the black parties, him laughing at Isaac's drunken rhythm less side-to-side move, rubbing against some black girl who didn't have much rhythm herself. She tried hard anyway. Most of them tried hard enough to dance in a way that came easily to those from Aaron's neighborhood. Aaron danced effortlessly, whispering words into his dance partner's ear. And them bringing more new girls back to the dorm, waking in the morning and waiting for the new girls to leave. Once gone, it was time to share the past night's fun. Breakfasts allowed storytelling, telling the tales nearly as good as living the adventure. They joked and laughed and greedily stuffed food in their mouths, laughing, letting food fall out of their mouths, falling on each other.

Times had changed. Now they laughed with food in their mouths with their significant others—Aaron with Aisha and Isaac with his wife Katie and their newborn. Isaac often demanded that Aaron and Aisha come by the house because Katie craved adult conversation after going "gaga goo goo" half the day and the other half speaking intelligently to the baby. Now there were mouths to feed, a whole other reality, great responsibilities, a business that had to remain viable in an increasingly unstable market, and a strategy that would keep them relevant for years to come.

After work that day, Aaron decided to walk from 67thstreet. He had been neglecting his body so the walk felt good. Thoughts of his love for Aisha, of seeing her soon, were on his mind. She had him on her mind, too, for looking down at his phone he could see she was calling him. He was arriving home later than usual and the spontaneous walk made the time he was away longer. When he told her he had decided to walk and would be home soon, she made sure everything was all right before hanging up. She called back minutes later, saying, "Where are you? Are you here yet?"

"I'm almost there, baby," Aaron responded, picking up his pace and eventually breaking out into a jog. They remained on the phone with each other, laughing at how out of breath Aaron became.

Chapter 7

Every Saturday Aisha and Aaron shared Aisha's red SUV. Aaron would drop Aisha off at school and go downtown to his office. On occasion, he did not go downtown at all, but remained at school to help Aisha in her program.

The idea of Aaron helping came to Aisha one night while she read in bed. Abruptly, she stopped reading and turned to Aaron, asking him if he would be willing to help her some Saturdays. He responded, "Yeah, I'll read with the shorties." But Aisha had a different idea. Her program centered on literacy, but if Aaron was willing to help, she had to use his mathematical mind. She could adapt a part of the morning so the students could benefit from his love of numbers. Did he still remember the math games Pop Pop used to play with him? Of course he did; he remembered everything. And Aisha remembered everything about Aaron's life that he had shared with her; particularly sharp were her memories of the times he opened up about his early days because those times were rare. So they started there.

In order to maintain structure and in the interest of planning, Aisha went over the games with Aaron only days later. She also presented him with other mathematic games she found, allowing him to select which he liked best.

When Aisha shared her idea with her principal, she expected Dr. Haywood would want her to explain her thought process and plan, which she did. Dr. Haywood trusted her. Aisha created the Saturday literacy program three years before Aaron arrived, adjusting it over time for improvements and the growing demand of students who were interested. Still, there was proper protocol and Aisha was thankful that Dr. Haywood demanded that everything done at Richard Wright conformed to it. Not for the sake of protocol, but for the sake of the students.

Before Dr. Haywood arrived, Aisha taught under an apathetic school leader. The school suffered because of it. Aisha also suffered, almost quitting after her fourth year. Though she liked the full autonomy the former principal's negligence allowed her, and the inside of her classroom ran well, she could not take seeing a school that needed so much from its leaders receive so little. The principal's attitude was infectious and it stuck to everyone like sinister sap of a diseased tree. And the students suffered the most. Seeing it every day, and only having so much power, it beat Aisha's spirit down. But Dr. Haywood's arrival gave new life to the dying school. She brought with her a turnaround spirit. At the start of Aisha's program, her inviting Raven and Kiki to help was a part of its momentum.

Raven and Kiki met Aaron for the first time on Aaron's first day working in the program. At the right moment, they cornered Aisha.

"Bitch," Kiki said, almost in a whisper. "Why didn't you tell us your man was so damn fine?" Raven did not speak, just nodded her head with a smile and gave Aisha a shove.

"I might could see now why you hold on to the coochie like you do," Kiki said, then quickly added, "Naw, ain't no nigga that fine. I got needs." With that, she and Raven shared a laugh, high-fived, and walked back to the children as though none of it had just happened.

The Saturday after Biggums's visit was one that Aaron remained to help. It humored Aisha to see Raven and Kiki playfully flirting with him. If Aaron looked like he needed something and one of them happened to be in his vicinity—which, despite the divisions in the math and literacy groups, they made it a point to—they'd say, "I'll get it for you, Aaron," singing his name in high-pitched, soft voices.

The students had fully warmed up to Aaron by then, so much so that by the end of the day Aisha was peeling two little ones off his legs. They had wrapped themselves around him as if he were playground equipment. Aaron walked with them, taking giant steps for effect, saying,

"Aw, Ms. Bman's ruining our fun." Aisha didn't mind them playing, but her program had to remain organized, even in the lax atmosphere. She well understood the needs of the little ones, for it was them that she taught, but she knew certain things were in her control and others were not. There is a level of affection that should go with instruction in the learning atmosphere. If done right it helped tremendously. That is where her influence was. It was what she could control.

Leaving the school, Aaron and Aisha walked out into sunshine. It was a beautiful spring day. After they both were settled in Aisha's truck, Aaron in the driver's seat, Aaron turned to Aisha and said, "C'mon, let's go buy me a car."

"Really? Now?"

"Yeah, you didn't have any plans, did you?"

"No, but you hadn't said anything about wanting a car now."

"I wanted to surprise you. It's time. This ain't New York. Plus, you trying to get me to be all frugal and shit like you."

"AJ, no I'm not."

"Yes you are. You ain't slick. I gotta be real. I can only abstain from so much." He squeezed Aisha's thigh and smiled. A somber look came over Aisha's face.

"Don't get all serious. I'm all good with what we're doing. You give me that good balance, for real. But I can't lose me. Know what I'm saying?" Aisha nodded her head.

"So, smile for me…C'mon, you don't have no reason to be all frowned up." Aaron shook Aisha's thigh in his grip. She still kept the somber look. Smiling, he loosened his grip from her thigh and began moving his hand slowly toward her crotch. Aisha remained firm, but couldn't take it when he got close.

"AJ, stop playing around." She smacked his hand away, smiling.

"Uh huh, I knew that would get you to smile. I know one thing; I'm going to be smiling when I'm there." Aaron nodded to the place his hand just was.

"So will I."

"Yeahhhh, that's what I'm talking about," Aaron said, starting up the truck. "So let's do it in my new car."

"AJ…"

"For real, do you know how many people got their first piece in a car? It'll be like we're teenagers again."

Aaron drove down Wolcott and hit Garfield Boulevard, making a right.

"Where are we going? What kind of car are you going to get?"

"Aw, trying to change the subject, huh? Up around Lake Forest, I've been looking at this Maserati online."

Aaron continued on Garfield, crossed King Drive, and entered Washington Park. He passed the DuSable Museum, then the ice skating rink in the mall across from the University of Chicago. Aisha couldn't help smiling each time she passed it now, remembering Aaron falling and unsteady, expecting to be perfect his first time. He constantly blamed the dullness of the blades, yelling to Aisha to wait on him when she skated off, laughing. They crossed Stony Island, seeing ahead the pond at the backside of the Museum of Science and Industry, then rode around to the museum's front side. On Lake Shore Drive, Lake Michigan sparkled in the sunlight to their right, waves rippling at its bluest of blue. The early spring runners, bikers, and walkers were out taking advantage of the day, moving steadily along the bike path. Aisha turned to Aaron and said that they would have to get out there soon. He nodded. She patted his stomach.

"Don't even trip. I still got it," he said.

"Some of it," she said. "But it doesn't matter; I love you," Aisha said, teasing.

"Okay, keep on," Aaron said. "Don't forget I use to roll, too." Aisha remained quiet, smiling at the lake.

"Uh huh, I might get out there and feel good. Keep on. You'll be looking at my back."

"No, no. We're going to run together," Aisha said, reaching over, kissing him on the cheek and then over to his ear, grabbing his lobe in her mouth.

"Get off my spot! What you…ahhh! That's one of the reasons I'm going to get this car!" Aisha resumed her position with a contented look on her face, gazing at the lake. They were passing McCormick Place and the marina after it. Aaron glanced over at it. Soldier Field was next, now a fused mass of old and new architecture. With the road bending, they passed the museum campus with The Field Museum, Planetarium, and Shedd Aquarium. Lake Shore Drive straightened out again and the traffic began to congest. Grant Park and Buckingham Fountain were to their left. Aaron and Aisha both looked over. The fountain's water had not been turned on yet, but Aaron imagined it at night, spouting high in the air and changing colors.

"Chicago's a beautiful city," Aaron said. "We're going to be down here a lot in the summer."

Aisha placed her hand on Aaron's leg. They had been imagining nearly the same scene. Although in Aisha's mind, her stomach was pressed against the fountain's rail lightly from Aaron's weight enwrapping her from behind. She could feel the sprinkles of water on her face from the light breeze and Aaron's light breathing on her neck. They were silent in her vision, as they were in the car. Both the real and imagined moments warmed Aisha. She knew the car Aaron was going to get would be showy, but this time she didn't care.

They passed Navy Pier with its grand Ferris wheel circling the air. At one time, a construction like it in Chicago was a marvel, the first of its kind. When Kaii came to visit Aisha one summer, they rode the Navy Pier Ferris wheel together. As they reached the top for the first time, Kaii told Aisha she had read about the World's Fair of 1893 and how Ida B. Wells-Barnett boycotted it. Instead of participating in the grandeur of the event, which displayed American innovation, Chicago architecture, and many new spectacles of wonder, she passed out pamphlets that detailed the unjust treatment of blacks in the country and the horrors of lynching, speaking on what she believed motivated the lynchings. Aisha was happy to get the information. Kaii always shared little facts with Aisha. She knew Aisha appreciated it. She had been there when

Aisha anguished over deciding to be an African American Studies concentrator or a History and Literature concentrator. Her anxiety was heightened by the recent loss of her mother. Her mother loved books, too.

As a television and screenwriter, Kaii didn't use much, if any, of the African-American history she learned in her work. But the knowledge remained with her, useful at times, like at the top of Ferris wheels.

Aisha taught herself black history. The more she read through books on the subject, the more she felt she learned about herself, how the world saw her, and why. When she was younger, she tried to situate her existence during slavery and reconstruction. Her existence, in the way she came to be, would have been quite rare, almost non-existent. If it did happen, she and her mother would have lived like ghosts, outcasts, fugitives. Her father would have hardly been able to be seen with them, even in the most liberal parts of the country. Her mother was white. Aisha could not pass for white. Her hair was too curly, her skin not quite light enough. It would have been different had her mother been black and her father was white. That combination worked from the moment African women slaves were herded on the ships to cross the Atlantic. The peculiarity of this contradiction made complete sense for those in power and, as in all times, it made sense to most everyone else. Many of the minority that did not accept it kept quiet, for they valued their lives and their families. Those that were loud were brave, unafraid of death. Aisha saw herself as brave, but she had the hardest time placing herself in that time, picturing herself being brave back then. She tried so hard, at one point she became unreasonably frustrated. Her emotions didn't arise solely from the difficulty in setting and seeing her genetic makeup during the early parts of her country's history. There, too, was frustration because, at that time as a modern teenager, though there were more people who resulted from similar coupling, she struggled extra hard to reconcile her humanity with the society she lived in.

In the car with Aaron, Aisha was comfortable, the musings of her makeup, in any time period, no longer was an issue. Kaii's words materialized differently than in Aisha's mind that day. At the top of the Ferris wheel, it came as good information to know. In the car with Aaron, she pictured Ida B. Wells-Barnett passing out the pamphlets. It was not difficult for her to see the grounds at the World's Fair. It took place right around where she and Aaron ice-skated. And she knew well Ida's iconic pose. She could see the eagerness, the fire in Ida's eyes. She could hear her voice strong, articulate, clear, so much so that it drew people near. Many that approached still rejected the pamphlets, some accepted them though they were illiterate, and eventually threw them on the ground. Many of the literate who accepted pamphlets ended up throwing theirs on the ground as well. Aisha saw Ida watching the people eating Cracker Jack or hamburgers for the first time. She saw them appreciating the music of Scott Joplin at the fringe of the fair, the twinkle in their eyes and the involuntary tap of their feet, a few unawares, stomping her very pamphlet in the ground.

Aisha turned to Aaron and shared her reverie with him. Once he had enough information, he got into it, adding to her daydream. He talked about the poor kids that infiltrated the fair, running around and getting into mischief, being chased by the fair's security, and running for their lives and laughing when it was over and they were safe. Then he broke off his thoughts when he felt he had nothing more to add and laughed, asking her the latest on Kaii. Aisha came alive again. She loved how Aaron listened to her, how he responded to her quirky ways. After she updated him on Kaii, Aaron began talking again.

"I didn't know all that stuff about Ida B. You know there used to be projects named after her?"

"Aren't they still there?"

"Yeah, but they're as good as gone."

"Oh, yeah."

"I use to hang around there, playing around. That's what probably made me think of the boys running around the fair, her name and all that." Aisha was quiet again. She had taken her seatbelt off and found a way to lay her head on Aaron's lap.

"The kids wore you out, huh?"

"No, I just like laying on you."

"I like that you like it." He combed her hair with his free hand, looking down at her for a second then returning his eyes to the road.

"AJ, what's a Maserati?"

They arrived at the luxury motors dealership to friendly smiles. An older man with a full head of silver gray hair walked up to them and introduced himself. Aaron sized him up. The salesman was about six feet, three inches tall and looked like he was at least in his sixties. He had warm eyes and a pleasing, easy, serving demeanor, though he didn't wear a look of servitude. When Aaron told the salesman that they were cash-paying customers and were ready to buy that day if they found the right car and the right deal, he noticed the salesman pepped up, though he remained poised. He asked them whom the car was for. Aaron said, "It's for me, but it'll be both of ours. I'm thinking about a Maserati. This is one of the places that I've been looking at."

While Aaron listened to the salesman go on about each car, Aisha was having a moment. Her hand brushed lightly over arbitrary parts of the cars that Aaron and the salesman stopped at. She was taken with the cars in the showroom. What was it? Why couldn't she dismiss the experience like she did Aaron's clothes and other extravagances he talked about? Did it have to do with him saying "ours"? There was something about Aaron saying "ours" to the salesman, something about the way it rolled of his tongue without effort or hesitance, leaping into her ears to rest inside of her. What a strange place to have that feeling!

A smile came to Aisha's lips as she came to terms with her excitement. The salesman, getting a greater sense that Aaron was a serious buyer, had worked them over to the Ferraris after Aaron didn't like how the Maserati looked in person.

"You know what?" Aaron said, staring at the Ferrari in front of them. A Spider is what the salesman called it. He turned to Aisha. "Isaac has a Ferrari; I think the Enzo." The salesman interrupted. "Oh yes, we don't have an Enzo in right now, but it's a beaut."

"Yeah, it's smooth, but I don't want the same car as him."

"Of course, we have other models."

"Nah, I don't want a Ferrari." The salesman paused, looked at Aisha, and then back to Aaron and said, "You two, I think I have the perfect car for you."

The salesman led them over to the dealer's Bentley section, walking specifically up to a black model.

"This is the Continental GT. It's last year's model, an '05 with very low miles. The previous owner loved this car, but his wife made him trade it in. He already had a sports car and she refused for her car to be the only car to take the kids around in. You see, it seats four, but the space in the back leaves something to be desired; the only minor flaw, really. Do you have children?" They shook their heads no. Aisha grabbed Aaron's hand and squeezed it tight, an effort to prevent him from blurting out something inappropriate. Feeling the pressure, he smiled.

"Well, good," the salesman continued. "Hop on in and get a feel." He opened the door for Aisha. Aaron waited until Aisha was seated and went around the car and got in. Once Aaron had settled, the excitement in Aisha's eyes was all he had to see. He asked the salesman if they could test drive it. He nodded, asked for Aaron's driver's license, and went away to get the keys.

The test drive sold Aaron. During the ride, Aisha stopped trying to mask her excitement. This act was the final selling point for Aaron. After some easy negotiations, he drove the car off the lot, Aisha following behind in hers.

In the car, Aaron immediately called Aisha. His mouth moved as fast as the Bentley's spinning wheels. He drove it as if he owned the road, slowing only after Aisha admonished him, saying, "I'm going to hang up. I'm not going to listen until you stop going so fast!" The car slowed while Aaron's mouth kept going the same speed. Anything that came to his mind came out: how the Bentley emblem, the letter "B" with wings, symbolized how they both were going to fly, them both having the letter "B" in their last name, to how he used to make fun of her hyphenated name because she was the first person he ever really knew that had a hyphenated name. *What's up with the two last names?* Then he talked about Pop Pop and how he wished he were there to see him riding so clean and happy. He wished they were riding together. How he wished Aisha were in the passenger seat and not on the phone, and how he wished he could go pick up Wayne when they got back home, or how they would pick up Biggums and go to dinner. Was that okay with Aisha? Good. He knew it would be. They were going to go to Joe's Stone Crab on Rush Street. Before he left New York, a client of his told him the food was good there. "See if you were riding with me, I wouldn't have to hang up to call these restaurants. Let me call them and I'll call you right back, baby, my star. We're doing it! I love youuuu! Okay, let me call. I'll be right back." Their reservations were made and he was back on the phone with Aisha, talking about old times, and times to come, what he and Isaac were about to do at Colossus. Then he hung up with Aisha, calling Isaac and speaking to him in the hyped moment in the hyped tones that Isaac was used to. After finding out that Isaac and Katie were at home, he told them that he and Aisha were going to stop by, but only for a little while; they had some other things to do. Calling Aisha back, he told her to follow him. They were going to say "what's up" to their friends.

It was late afternoon when Aaron and Aisha left visiting with Isaac and Katie. Before leaving, standing in the foyer of their home, Aaron told his friends that he and Aisha were going to Museum Park next to look at the newly built condominiums. He quickly turned to look at Aisha, for he knew it was another revelation for her. With words and playful gestures, he attempted to smooth things over. Aisha wanted him to be open. Overtime, their roles had reversed. And he had just then informed her about looking for a new place to live, and it came in front of others. But these were surprises, good ones. And they were not just any others, it was Isaac and Katie. Such things you had to be mindful of in relationships, like timing and the other person's feelings. He joked about the moment amongst the four, the thought process change, and the changing habits of living with someone you love. With that look, turning to Aisha, how he quickly tried to smooth it over, Isaac knew none of that ever happened with Aaron and women before. But it was happening then. Aaron acted it all out in his boisterous way. Isaac and Katie laughed; Aisha merely smiled.

Because of that smile, Aaron knew he needed to explain further. Getting back into the car, he called Aisha and told her that he would surprise her every once in a while, that all could not be shared, and he did not feel that all was supposed to be shared. They still were individuals, but she made him better. He knew this. She was his mirror, but maybe he could be her mirror, too. He knew she loved her little apartment, but from the time he moved in it was too small for the two of them. She had to know change was coming. Didn't she? She did.

High up, going building to building in Museum Park, Aaron looked for the same face on Aisha that he saw inside the Bentley. Slowly, he saw her begin to open to the idea of new possibilities.

On the way up to a large three-bedroom apartment, the building's realtor said, "Wait until you two see the view from this place. It's stunning."

It was true. As soon as Aisha stepped into the open area of the apartment the view pulled her directly to the floor to ceiling windows facing the lake. Aaron turned his head to watch her, so the realtor stopped speaking and held out her hand as if to say, "Please join her." He did. He took Aisha's hand in his hand and kissed her on the cheek. Aisha turned to him, put her hand on his face, and then rested her head on his shoulder.

◆　◆　◆

Biggums lived in the basement apartment in the house of his deceased aunt's mother-in-law. The remnants of others who had lived there and left or lived there and died were still in the basement. For Biggums it was a museum of memories. His aunt's big fish tank with no fish, which never had fish, as far as Biggums could recall. The baby bed in the corner of the living room; he used it to hang his uniform on. The set of encyclopedias from the seventies, whose buyer he didn't know and was sure no one ever read them. He sure didn't as a boy, or now as a man. The two bedrooms with mounds of memories piled so high there was no room for Biggums. He preferred sleeping on the couch, anyway.

When Aaron and Aisha walked in, they found Biggums trying in vain to tidy his place up. Air freshener in one hand and a carton of fried chicken bones in the other, he told the two he had been taking a nap when they called and didn't realize they would be there so soon.

"A nap at night?" Aaron said

"Yeah, I'm nocturnal."

"Nigga, you need to be more cleanly. This shit don't make no sense." Aaron pointed to the big piece of cake on the cocktail table.

"Ain't no woman going to want to come down here."

"Aisha, please excuse the mess. It's wonderful to see you again." Biggums flashed a charming smile.

"Your proper-speaking ass needs to take out this trash and save that shit for someone else."

Aaron avoided a liquid substance on the top of the garbage, found a dry spot, compacted the trash, and tied it up.

"C'mon, y'all," Aaron said, picking up the bag. "Our reservation is for seven thirty."

Aaron had not told Biggums about his new car. Walking outside and seeing the car, it appeared Biggums might just elongate his mass and do a back flip.

"Dayyyum! This is you?!"

"Yep."

"My boy didn't play, got the Bentley on them? Joe this thing is ca-cold!"

"Look at this!" Biggums continued, his voice going high, circling the car gracefully in a happy hop and making it to the driver's side. He looked hard at the interior then out to Aisha and Aaron, at the interior again and back to the two, as if to say, "You see this?" Of course they had, which made his antics even funnier.

"I'm gone let you push it, but later," Aaron said. "I'm starving; let's go. Oh, the back is a little tight, dog."

"What? What you say? Man, I'm hardly hearing you. This dude snapped off! Man, I'd sit in the trunk. That mug is probably plush."

Biggums found a way to sit comfortably in the back and the three headed downtown.

Dinner enlivened Biggums even more. He aptly demonstrated the best of etiquette that his mother had drummed into him, which he never saw use for or little reason for growing up. Back then, it made him feel like an outsider, but in the restaurant with his two friends and a succulent meal in front of him, he felt at home. He piled his plate high with crab, getting two orders. Who knew when the next opportunity like that would come?

After dinner, with the dinner party of three in the car, Biggums spoke up.

"I hate to break up our party, but Star, is it all right with you if Jam and I go out?"

"Sure. You don't have to ask me, Ronald."

"Yes, I do. And my mama is the only one that calls me Ronald, but you're so beautiful you can call me whatever you want."

"Easy, fat boy," Aaron said.

"Ay, ay y'all listen," Biggums said, positioning his head in between the front seats. "You know I don't even mind being the third wheel with you two. Y'all my people. This feels good, for real. My man is back and Star, I'm glad y'all together. Thank you for bringing me along, getting the old boy out of the basement."

"C'mon, dude. You don't got to say none of that. I told you I'm back, homie." The three went quiet, taking the moment in, listening to the quiet hum of the ride. Then Aaron spoke.

"You trying to go to a strip club, ain't you?"

"Huh?" Biggums said, taken aback.

"C'mon, man. I know you," Aaron said looking in the rearview mirror.

"Me and Star talk. She don't care," Aaron continued.

Biggums paused, considering his response. Then he stole a sheepish glance at Aisha, whose head was turned slightly, a pleasant smile on her face, waiting to hear what he had to say.

"Oh, y'all open like that?" Biggums paused again, thinking about Aisha's image of him. "Well, yeah. That's what I was thinking about doing." The three started laughing. Then Biggums broke in.

"Hold up, though, but Star you don't have to worry about Jam hanging with me."

"I know Ronald, you're fine."

"Man, he know everything is cool," Aaron said. "He ain't even going to be thinking about me when we get up in there."

"Dog," Aaron continued, looking in the rearview mirror at Biggums again. "I tried to get Star to go once. She's never been. But always asking me questions." Aaron looked over at Aisha then reached his hand over and rested it on her thigh. "So I'm like, 'c'mon baby, let's go check it out.' No interest." Aisha didn't respond, but silently agreed. She was curious, but Aaron had given her enough information for her to experience it without having to go.

"Yeah, everything ain't for everybody. I use to not be with it, remember that?"

"Hell yeah! Main one chasing girls in the neighborhood, fighting his mama over girls, changing his life over girls—"

"Okay," Biggums said.

"—then when we all get up in one for the first time he's as shy as you, Star. I thought he'd jump right in, but nope."

"I warmed up after a while though."

"I never doubted it."

"But Star, when Jam was in New York, I stopped going completely for a minute."

"What made you start going again?" Aisha asked.

"Got tired of being by myself," Biggums said.

"Yeah," Aaron said, speaking up, "and that cyber booty is a gateway drug."

The strip club that Biggums directed Aaron to was in the southern suburbs of Chicago. Pulling up to it, a look of disgust came over Aaron's face. The place looked like a shack with big bright letters atop it.

"Why you pick this spot?" Aaron said, parking the car next to a black Cadillac truck.

"Five-dollar head."

"Rubber head?"

"Yep."

"That's wack."

"Not to me."

They both got out of the car and walked in the direction of the club. Aaron fished in his pocket and gave Biggums a hundred dollars.

"Here. Have fun. I can't believe you picked this wack-ass spot."

"Thanks, man, but I got money." Aaron gave him a look.

"Aight, then. I appreciate it. And you gone see, the spot's cool."

After they were patted down, Biggums went in his pocket to pay for admittance but Aaron quickly stepped in front of him and paid for both of them, and they entered.

There were at least a hundred men packed in the tiny, stuffy place. The music pounded; Biggums perked up, bobbing his head. Aaron surveyed the place. It was a full-nudity club, which Aaron figured, after Biggums informed him of his motivations for going. A skinny girl with a tattoo of a panther on her thigh danced on a miniscule stage. Surrounding her were throngs of men packed tightly together with lifeless-looking eyes. Hardly anyone that Aaron could see was spending money. No money being thrown at the stage; no money in hands, wiggling, waiting for the right moment to be placed in between the garment and sweaty, heavily perfumed flesh or smacked and rubbed on the fleshly backside to stick for a moment before it fell off. This was all common, the proper way of things in the strip club, but Aaron saw none of it.

"Man, I'm not standing up," Aaron said. "Ask dude if there are any tables." A server came by shortly, informing Aaron of the drink minimum for a table. Aaron nodded. The server led Aaron and Biggums to a small, square table in the corner and asked what they wanted to drink. Aaron told her what type of vodka he wanted and the mixers. When she went away, he turned to Biggums and said:

"What's up with you, dude?"

"Huh? What you mean?" Biggums said, not looking at Aaron, his eyes alive, hungry.

"Look at all these niggas. And where are the strippers?" Aaron pointed at the small stage.

"Look at that shit—an empty stage! I ain't never seen an empty stage for this long at a strip club. Look, it's still empty; where are the chicks?"

"My man said some girls took off," Biggums said.

"On a Saturday! You crazy," Aaron said, looking at Biggums, who hardly paid him any attention.

"Go on, man," Aaron said, "I'm cool. You don't have to entertain me." With that, Biggums shook Aaron's hand and lost himself in the crowd.

Shortly after Aaron was seated at the table, the server brought the drinks. She gave him an enticing look as she set everything up and continued it up until the moment she turned to leave. Not long after the server left, a stripper made her way to the table.

"You want your dick sucked?"

"No."

"Why?"

Aaron looked at her, looked through her until she got the idea and left. He had caught on by then. The place that Biggums disappeared to was where everything happened. He spotted other strippers taking men from where they were standing against the walls, leading them to the back. Instead of giving lap dances in the back, they were putting faces in laps. Before the stripper approached Aaron, he had seen her callously proposition others.

Aaron felt like he stood out, but to her he wasn't special. The stripper was strictly about her business; quantity over quality. He watched her go from man to man, ultimately rejected by each one until she made it to him. Were they rejecting her because she was so thirsty?"Her thirsty ass," Aaron thought. Had they already been back there? Why just stand there, looking like that, waiting for a tired stripper to perform an uninspired routine? He would not have been there had it not been for Biggums. All of this was behind him. From the moment he left Aisha, she had not left his mind.

While playing in parlors of lust, far away from Aisha, with the farthest emotional distance ever between them—a deep chill—occasionally Aisha came to Aaron's mind. He remembered these places. They were antithetical to the dead and dirty building where he sat waiting for Biggums, wanting to be home, considering the magnitude of the chasm now between him and his old friend. They were bewitching places: in New York, in Las Vegas, in Atlanta, in foreign countries with their own rules; places of nakedness where the workers—the women—and their beautiful bodies, eroticize speaking to primal nature, bringing about the rise, hardly discernable from the real rise, all in the heat of propped-up paradises powering exalted fantasies. Transporting Aaron, the seeker, momentarily taking him and the seekers away from their reality. Back then, on rare occasions, in the smallest gaps of space—which were quickly crushed closed by conquest, orgasm, and alcohol—Aaron thought of Aisha.

Feeling as though Biggums had been out of his sight for long enough, together with his loathing of the place and its poor ability to even mildly stimulate him, Aaron searched the club with his eyes. Where was Biggums? Turning to look in a new direction, he spotted a stripper who looked, he figured, something like himself in the wretched place. She did not belong there. Where did she come from? As she walked, every other man who was crammed against the wall, sitting at the outer tables near the stage, pulled at her, groped her, came to life as though they were men cursed to statues and her walking past was the spell that reanimated them. She had a short hairstyle with a piece of hair that made a fancy curl on her forehead. Her facial features were symmetrical, pretty, like a doll. Her brown skin was unblemished, unmarked, silky; her curves round, perky, tight. Aaron could not take his eyes off her until he saw she was walking toward him. He feigned interest in the stripper on the tiny stage until she was right up on him.

"Hey, sweetie, would you like me to dance for you?"

"What are you doing in here?" Aaron couldn't help asking.

"I'm new, just started." She smiled at him. A pretty smile, too? Aaron didn't respond. She moved closer to him, putting her hand on his shoulder, swaying subtly to the music, allowing Aaron to see her, examine all of her up close. She could see his eyes liked what he saw. And when Aaron felt the blood begin to pulse, he spoke.

"You know what?"

"What?"

"You banging, girl, for real. But, nah, I don't want a dance." Aaron pulled out some money. "Do me a favor, though," he said, coolly placing the money in her hand. "Go find my man. He's a short, chunky dude with a friendly face. He's in here somewhere. He'll see you when you see him. Get him out of there and dance for him."

"Okay," she said, leaning over and giving Aaron a kiss on the cheek. She walked away smiling, half turning her head around to see Aaron admiring her.

It bothered him that the men grabbed at her, but she looked like she knew how to handle herself. What would become of her? She wouldn't be in that place for long, Aaron thought. She was new, just beginning. She probably lived in the neighborhood and needed the money. She would find another place that fit her and her ambition, a place where she could make better returns for less effort. Maybe she would find some man with money that would put her on his payroll. She deserved better. Why did she deserve better? He knew nothing about her. How many like her had he already seen? And aside from her looks, wasn't she like every other stripper in the place? Did they deserve better? Did he not think of them because they were already worn, tattooed, some scarred from C-sections, fights? They had children. Didn't their children deserve better? What in the hell was he thinking about? Who the hell cared? Living with Aisha. He would have never had these thoughts before. Still, it was not all Aisha. To get in that place where he could accept her he had to become less cynical, less hard, trust her with his vulnerability. That is what mattered. All that surrounded him did not matter. There would always be sex to sell and always buyers for it. From five-dollar, two-minute fellatios in cloudy, funky-smelling backrooms to five-thousand-dollar girlfriend experience, two-day excursions. None of it mattered. All that mattered now was Aisha, home.

As agreed upon, the girl led Biggums by the hand, moving through the crowd of envious eyes toward Aaron. She ostensibly danced for Biggums, sitting her backside in his lap for a time then coming up, making eye contact with Aaron. Aaron tipped her handsomely. Pay her for all the times you will not be in places of this kind anymore, he thought. You know what they do to you.

After the dance, Aaron stood up, motioned to Biggums, and walked out.

In the parking lot, there were two men admiring his car. As Aaron walked up to it, they spoke to him.

"This you, fam?"

"Yeah."

"This muthafucka cold right here."

"Thanks."

"For sho, I gots to get me one of these."

Aaron hopped into the car, started it, and watched the rearview mirror for Biggums or whatever else. Eventually, Biggums sauntered his way out and into the car.

"Ay," Biggums said. "I know you don't want it, but that stripper wanted me to give you her number." Aaron returned a look.

"I know. Had to ask. You know I'm gone call her. She was so damn sexy!" Biggums started to gesticulate in his seat.

"Get your hormones in order in my ride, man…So you had a good time?"

"Hell, yeah! But you didn't. Did you? I could see it in your face."

"It's all good. I'm out with you. It's been too long."

"For real, homie. It ain't back in the day no more, huh?"

"Nah, not anymore."

On their ride home, Biggums began talking about his job at Cook County Jail. It paid good money, but he was getting tired of it. It didn't challenge him. The only challenge he had was denying that he knew inmates every once in a while when they recognized him from coming up in the same areas. "You don't know me; lock up bitch." Aaron didn't say a word, just smiled and listened to his friend spewing everything that was in his heart, much like he had done on the phone earlier with Aisha that day. While Biggums talked, Aaron thought about his computer sitting between mounds of mess in the basement. It looked out dated, slow. He would get himself a new one only if he agreed to think seriously about starting school. One class at a time; he didn't care, as long as he went back, as long as he got started, as long as he kept at it.

Chapter 8

Amonth of Saturdays after Aaron bought the Bentley, it was stolen. The possibility had crossed Aaron's mind, given the neighborhood that Aisha lived in. When you crossed South Shore Drive going west, the area changed quickly. The South Side was that way. But this thought had been fleeting. The apartment complex Aisha lived in had permit parking in a gated lot that stretched alongside the four buildings. On the other side of the buildings there was a dead-end side street, which abutted a high gate, leading to boulders and then to the lake. Permitted spots were also available on this street. Aisha parked her truck on the dead-end side street and Aaron parked the Bentley in the gated parking lot alongside the building, and everything was fine.

Having seen Aaron's car a few Saturdays before it was stolen, some of the students had asked Aaron for a ride in it. On that particular day, he told them that he and Ms. Bman had to leave, but the next Saturday he returned he would surely take them for a ride in it. The following Saturday he did not go to the program. But that morning, the Saturday the car was stolen, he left downtown early, excited about the day. His car was clean and he rode comfortably in it, wearing a jogging suit and a pair of his Jordans.

Arriving at Aisha's school, he parked his car and exited. The sun hung brightly in the air, just above the rooftops of the neighborhood buildings. Aaron stretched. The homes directly across from the school made him think about Pop Pop and his old neighborhood. He smiled. Pop Pop would be proud. The kids loved the same mathematic games he raised Aaron on.

Aaron entered the school and climbed the stairs, thinking that maybe some of the students in the Saturday program would one day need more challenging mathematic games. Hopefully, they would find good teachers, a good teacher like he did, like Mr. Weidel. He needed Mr. Weidel. How instrumental he was, helping Aaron and his peers. Mr. Weidel could have taught or been anywhere else, but he was right in Aaron's freshman math class, right in the inner city, right in the middle of it all. He got right in Aaron's face when Aaron got tough with him, thought he was smarter than Mr. Weidel was, the old goofy-looking white man. He was right there all four years, at all of Aaron's games, right there being nosy at one summer league game, a summer tournament, directing the gentleman from the Ivy League, with the Ivy League polo on, the shield over his breast, taking his attention from the player he was recruiting in the same tournament and directing him to Aaron. Coach Hughes. Mr. Weidel was right there, introducing Coach Hughes to Pop Pop. Then he was right there in their living room, a recruiter himself, before Coach Hughes came, telling him and Pop Pop about the Ivy League. Do they even play ball in the Ivy League? Yes, they do. Mr. Weidel was an Ivy League grad, the first in his family to go to college, the first in a neighborhood of German immigrants to go to such a prestigious university. He first challenged Aaron in the classroom, then challenged him to do what no one expected him to do. Go to Harvard. "If you can get in, you must go." He came up with every example of professional athletes that had come out of the Ivy League. Unbeknownst to Harvard, Mr. Weidel, Harvard's best recruiter, was telling Aaron he could be the first to take Harvard to the tournament. He would be on TV and everyone would talk of his talent and his mind, and it would give him exposure. But there was nothing like the exposure he would get every day at Harvard, so he must go, though his standardized tests were low, his verbal score bringing it down—but not down so low he had a problem getting into other schools. His marks were high enough where he never even considered his grades, never considered the possibility of sitting out a year like some of his city rivals, then city all-star teammates did, high enough that he would be easily admitted into Illinois state schools on academic merit alone. But things worked differently at Harvard. It was a difference Aaron cared little about. He did not want to go that far from home, that far from Pop Pop. But Pop Pop liked everything that Mr. Weidel said. Aaron hated that Pop Pop had to pay when he did get in, even if the amount was small. It hurt that there would be no need for a pen, no place set up for him to declare and put on his school's hat, but despite that, it looked like his fate was resigned to that place. He would go to that place to put a smile on Pop Pop and Mr. Weidel's faces. To make them proud, he would destroy the Ivy League and still go pro. He would still play in the summer Pro- Am, still play against guys he used to destroy in the state who went to the big schools, the schools he once saw himself at, but he would still go pro. He would go pro from that place that made Pop Pop and Mr. Weidel happy.

But he did not go pro. Things changed. Changes, like Harvard, that he never saw coming. Maybe some of Aisha's students, who really liked the math games, maybe something like what happened to him, would happen to them. Change that they could not see, higher learning, higher learning curves, starting at the bottom because it was new, strange, the unseen change, but jumping, jumping up the curve to being able to see through liquid markets, derivatives, and credit. One day he would be able to set it so his children would have an easier time, at an earlier time, imagining anything, any possibility. It could happen to Aisha's students too and he'd be a small part of it and Pop Pop, too, because, like him, it all started with math games and strictness, Pop Pop being hard on him like Aisha was on them.

Inspired by these thoughts and with good feelings surging through his body, Aaron burst into the classroom yelling, "Ahhh!" The smaller kids ran to him, attaching themselves to his legs, had him do the giant walk again. Aisha smiled, shook her head, and allowed the disruption to persist for a little while.

When it came time to leave, Aaron agreed to play basketball with some of the older boys in the program. Skipping down the stairs with little feet skipping behind him and going outside, the sun still bright, inviting, directly overhead, they made their way to the parking lot where the basketball courts were. Aaron looked to where his car once sat and saw nothing. Where his car once was there was only empty space, a damned empty space. His heart dropped and his hands began to twitch. The boys around him started asking where his car went, then one pushing another and pointing to Aaron's face, telling his friend to shut up, can't you see he's getting mad? Aaron didn't hear them. He stood there, looking at the empty space. They all stood there, not saying a word. One of the boys thought to himself how he wouldn't be able to get the ride Aaron had promised him. He watched Aaron suddenly burst from where he was standing, dashing back into the school. Aaron ran up the stairs to Aisha's classroom where Raven, Kiki, Aisha, and some remaining children were packing up.

"Star, give me your keys!"

"What's the matter? What happened?" Aisha said, fishing in her pockets.

"Somebody stole the fucking car!" Aisha held the keys in her limp left hand and Aaron snatched them. He turned around, running, yelling, "Call the police!"

"Wait, AJ where…" but he had already gone.

Raven dialed emergency and told the police about the theft. She described the car and the scenario perfectly, her voice rising in excitement as if the car were her own. Aisha looked to Kiki for support, a clue of what might be happening. Picking up her phone, she called Aaron. When he didn't answer, she began to worry. As calmly as she could, she told the remaining children to stay in the classroom, that she would be back to walk them down in a minute. She walked out the classroom with Kiki following her. As soon as she left the view from the doorway, she burst into a run down the stairs. Kiki matched her speed. Maybe she could catch Aaron before he pulled off? But when the two made it outside, Aaron was nowhere in sight. Some of the little boys were still there. They saw in Aisha's eyes what she wanted and told her that Aaron had pulled off and went in that direction, pointing west. She thanked them and told them that everything would be fine and it was time to go home. They didn't move and Aisha raised her voice. "Boys, go home." Kiki helped her. "Did y'all hear Ms. Bman? Get on." "That's okay, Kiki. Boys, we'll be fine. Go on home now; we've called the police." At that, the boys slowly walked away. Aisha called Aaron again and this time he answered. Getting an earful of profanity—incongruent phrases of rage barely comprehensible to Aisha—she learned that Aaron was driving around, looking for the culprits. In one clear moment, he asked whether they had called the police. Aisha said that they had called, and pleaded with him to turn around, telling him she was scared. Aaron didn't respond to her concern, but began cursing again. Aisha held the phone, listening, hoping he'd get it out of his system with her in the moment and come back. Just come back. Why was he doing this? She wished she were there with him. She could get him to turn around if she were there.

Raven came outside with the rest of the children. Seeing that Aisha was on the phone, she started the children toward home. Watching the children's backpacks get farther and farther away, Aisha nearly screamed, "AJ, come back here!" Raven and Kiki watched her with wide eyes; their children, Raven's son, Norrell, and Kiki's daughter, Tyeisha, both age nine, were by their sides. After her yell, she heard nothing else from Aaron. He had hung up on her. Her spirit sank and tears welled up in her eyes. Then she saw, coming from around the corner, her truck speeding toward the school. But Aaron didn't stop. He made some motion with his hands that appeared to her like he was saying he was going to circle the block.

At least she saw him; he was near, Aisha thought. She wiped her eyes. Raven and Kiki, pulling their children gently along with them, moved closer to her to give her a hug. After minutes of Aisha contemplating, hoping for the best, talking to Norrell and Tyeisha, shielding them and cheering herself up through the innocent looks of their eyes, seeing the concerned look in the eyes of their mothers, Aaron finally pulled in front of the school.

"The police ain't here yet?" Aaron said, jumping out of the truck. His eyes glowed wildly. He couldn't stand still.

"Who called?"

"I did," Raven said.

"What did you tell them?"

"I told them 'bout yo car. Everythang; what kind of car it is, the color, year, school's address, how long ago it was…"

"How long ago did you say it was?"

"I said it just happened. She said she dispatched a car."

"They ain't here yet! I'm about to knock on these doors to see who saw something. Somebody saw something. Shit!" Aaron looked at Aisha with his glowing eyes and walked away from her again. Aisha felt powerless. She didn't really know what was going on. It was terrible that the car was stolen, but why was Aaron acting this way? The car was insured. She had never seen him so upset, not even when they had their biggest argument.

The three women watched Aaron go house to house, up and down the block, talking to people and looking more upset each time he stepped away. Eventually, Raven and Kiki began talking between themselves, offering what they felt to be plausible explanations. Norrell and Tyeisha, sensing the tension but no immediate danger, occupied themselves with some object on the ground.

After Aaron had gone to every house and apartment building in the general vicinity of the school, he came back and sat down on the curb. Aisha moved to sit down next to him. She rubbed the back of his head up and down, saying, "It's going to be okay." He didn't respond, just stared out toward homes on the opposite side of the street. Aisha saw Aaron's eyes calming and she began to feel better. After a while, two police cars pulled up. Two officers stepped out. Aaron stood up quickly. The policemen were both white men who looked to be a few years older than Aaron.

"Are you the ones that called?" one of the policemen said, looking Aaron up and down, the other by his side.

"Yeah, that was over forty minutes ago."

"Listen, sir, we didn't ask you that. Calm down."

"How the hell am I supposed to be calm? Someone ever stole your car?"

"No. Look we're here to help. Relax."

"Yeah, y'all a little too relaxed, while muthafuckas riding around here in my shit." Aisha reached for Aaron's arm, but sensing it, he moved away, a step closer to the police officers.

"Hey, watch your language," the other officer said, speaking up. "That's uncalled for and there are children around."

"What? Y'all funny."

"Listen, what happened?"

"I came outside and my car was gone! I rode around looking for them in my woman's car and been up and down the block questioning the people in the neighborhood. But of course don't nobody know shit!" People from the neighborhood began to come outside to watch the spectacle. Some sat on their porches, the very same porches that Aaron had gone to. Some came all the way down to the edge of their lawns. A teenage boy looked on from the corner, sitting on a bike.

"Listen, all we need from you is for you to tell us information pertaining to your stolen vehicle."

"What do you think I'm doing?"

"Sir, I'm not going to tell you again; ease your attitude." The police officers' posture changed and so did Aaron's. He seemed to be getting angrier by the minute. Aisha watched it all, wanting to speak up, step in, and diffuse the situation, but she didn't have the words. Why wouldn't the words come? It was no time to be reserved. Speak up, she told herself. Something is happening. Raven and Kiki could see it, too; Kiki whispered to Raven, "Look at Aaron…"

"What type of vehicle was it?" the other officer asked again.

"What? A Bentley coupe. You didn't get that over the radio?"

"Don't tell us how to do our jobs. You just answer the questions we ask you. What do you do for a living, sir?"

"What? What the hell does that have to do with my car being stolen?"

"By the way you're acting, everything."

"Y'all real funny. I'm going to report this," Aaron said, staring at their badges.

"Report what?" both policeman asked.

"Report you! Asking about my job? Y'all doing a terrible-ass job!"

"We have to know if it were some type of vendetta. We have to know what we're getting into with you."

"What! I co-head a hedge fund. What the hell are y'all talking about?"

"Sir, this is the last time I'm going to tell you about the language."

"He's telling the truth," Aisha said, finally able to break the seal on her silence.

"Listen, miss, stay out of this."

"Don't talk to her like that!" Aaron said. "Look at you. I'm a black man in a situation you can't comprehend!" He was screaming. "You don't even know what a hedge fund is, do you? Do you? What? Oh, I'm a drug dealer? That's how I got my car? Me helping at this school is a front? Huh?"

"Sir, calm down. No one said any of that."

"What? You didn't have to say it! Your dumb asses don't know the difference between a victim and the criminal."

"That's it." One of the officers approached Aaron. "Now you've done it. You're under arrest for disturbing the peace."

"What?!" Aaron responded, taking a step back from the approaching policemen.

"Officer, really this is all a big misunderstanding," Aisha said.

"Miss, stay out of this!"

"Get away from her!" Aaron screamed at the policeman who addressed Aisha. When he turned, the other officer grabbed his arms and buckled his knees from behind so that Aaron hit the ground. Aaron tried to scramble to his feet and take his hands from the one cuff, but the officer that had addressed Aisha quickly shifted positions, slamming his knee into Aaron's back. When Aaron fell, the officer put his club to the back of Aaron's neck. All three women screamed Aaron's name. He continued to struggle, hate churning in his belly and vitriol spewing from his mouth. He spit out blades of grass then looked up and saw something in Aisha's eyes. The sight brought a calm over him. He laid his face in the dirt and submitted. The cuff's cold steel tightening painfully around his wrist felt strange. What a strange feeling. He looked over to the people watching the scene, and back to Aisha, saying "I'm sorry" as they lifted him up and put him in the squad car.

Aisha went to the police station to pick up Aaron. While waiting for him to be released, she asked the police officers in the reception area about the status of the car. The two officers whom she directed the question to had no information about the theft, but found an officer who did. He was one of Aaron's arresting officers. The officer approached Aisha, looking differently than he had outside the school, almost apologetic. He said to her, "We have officers alerted about the car. A car like that isn't hard to find. I'm surprised they got away with it. We'll find it. We'll get 'em."

Aaron came out looking solemn. Aisha wanted to wrap her arms around him, but it didn't feel right in the moment. In her car, Aisha focused all of her energy on Aaron sitting beside her in the passenger seat. Neither of them spoke. Aaron rested his head on the headrest, closed his eyes, and didn't utter a word the entire ride home.

Inside the apartment, Aaron went right to the bedroom and lay down. Aisha followed, her energy still concentrated on him, trying to clear her thoughts of all that happened and just be present, supportive. But she didn't speak, couldn't speak. What would she say? She needed him to know that all she cared about was how he felt right then. She lay down beside him. They faced each other, though Aaron didn't look her in the eyes. Aisha touched his face with her hand and was zapped. It was as if all the feelings she ever had for Aaron, all their moments together, including her seeing him face down in the grass, raced through her hand and her body. Her eyes began to well up and she brought her lips to his. He kissed her back, softly, looking at her teary eyes. While her lips rested against his, sharing his breath, Aisha took Aaron's hand and placed it on her chest. They remained that way for a time, holding each other, kissing occasionally until the passion in Aisha's kisses picked up; she grabbed the back of his neck, pulling herself close to press against him. He caressed her chest then removed his hand and wrapped all of him around her. Their lips remained, searching each other's for new truths, higher levels of love. Their tongues tussled freely, without hesitation, wild, touching the roof of mouths, slipping over the teeth, then retracting, while their lips worked to communicate in new ways. They removed their lips from each other only when they felt the wetness of one another's tears. Aisha, first kissing his eyes then all over his face, appreciated every moment that her lips found a new place. She wanted his lips on her. Yes, now. She began furiously removing her top. Aaron understood. He helped her, but didn't rush. Aisha stopped, letting him do what she just madly went about. She relaxed, allowing herself to be fully in his power, feeling every bit of his touch as garment after garment was removed. He removed his as he removed hers, synchronizing the disclosing of their flesh until they were completely naked. Aisha felt Aaron against her. Softly, he kissed her lips. She didn't know what to do, but that didn't matter. *Let him lead, he'll show you, he'll take care of you. He loves you, how he loves you, it's true, it's so true.* His hands rubbing her body on her hips, now over her backside, then up her back, running his fingers up her spine, then her neck, over her shoulders, turning her around, on her breasts. His fingers traipsing over her nipples lightly, a gentle squeeze, his lips now on her breasts, his hands, too, working in tandem, massaging, moving, suckling, sending rush after rush through her, one of his hands now under her back, strong and pressing up, bringing his mouth more firmly against her breast. He hungered for her. *He loves me.* Their lips back together warm and more wise, wet, soft, whimpers, whimpering faintly into each other's mouths, clutching each other's hands, as if holding on for life, their lives in each other's hands, and him back down, kissing every part of her on his descent. Covering her body with kisses, at her navel, licking it with a rhythmic reluctance, pausing as if he were unsure but every sensation feeling like certainty. Then, moving again, his hands running along her inner thighs, his mouth kissing where his hands left the trail, on her knee caps, her shins, her calves, her ankles, her feet, his hands going under her and gripping her behind, his mouth back on her inner thigh, near her middle, so close to her middle, but not there, kissing everywhere but not there, so close, ooo, ooooo, trembling, trembling? She knew this feeling, but she didn't. She hadn't touched herself. He hadn't touched her. But she was shivering ecstasy in his hands, so true, so new, how beautiful. She lived in his arms.

Aaron held Aisha close, their legs wrapped around each other's. He brought his lips to her cheek each time she trembled, each orgasmic aftershock that continued to come to her rumbled in him, made him feel the wonder of the moment. Everything but her, there in his arms, had gone away. He held her tight, imagining how she would feel around him, how it would feel inside of her. He was ready, yet he, too, felt unsure. He desired Aisha's body with such anxiousness, such expectation, and she was in his arms, ready for him to take her. But alongside his impulses, there was something else. Strangely, he felt virginal, innocent, a man-child having lived former lives with the instincts of great lovers he had yet to discover. Be patient. They had only just begun, and for the moment, Aisha, naked in his arms, them kissing intermittently, was enough. Looking each other in the eye like they never had before, returning each other's gaze, unblinking, blinking, then coming right back, speechless but understanding everything in each other completely, was enough.

Aisha awoke not remembering falling asleep. Aaron slept soundly, still holding her. She surveyed his muscular, naked body laying so close to her. The sight of him aroused her. She wanted him to wake. They could sleep another time, later. The time had come and she felt it still, all of it. Her body begged for him to touch her again. The fortress walls she had built high and solid over the years to control that particular need, the ones her hormones knocked savagely against at night, at the sight of a fine man and his scent, lay in ruin. Rubble was all that remained. Aaron smashed her guard to pieces with the force of his heart. She wanted him now. Her heart pounded in her chest so hard she thought Aaron must feel its pressure. Refreshed from sleep, she directed all her energy, her thoughts, all of her laying there, toward this sleeping man next to her, her man. An overwhelming feeling to shake him furiously, to say "wake up!" came over her. She had to gain control. Could she? Should she? She lay there wondering what would be the best way to wake him. After pondering a few different scenarios she decided she would go down on him.

It occurred to her that she had no skill whatsoever with the technique. Still, she was not the teenage girl who had just discovered herself in the shower anymore. She had not participated, actually, but her mind had been in preparation. In all the years of being around women's sex talk, listening to Kaii's stories, entering into Raven and Kiki's world, listening to their stories, observing, giggling, accepting some things for herself, completely rejecting others, all the things she didn't have the chance to talk about with her mother, she had learned some things. Hearing other women's conversations about their sexuality freed her, gave definition to feelings she felt in her body, clarity to situations she had thought about but had not acted on. It gave her additional comfort in her strangeness, for in comparison to most, she was strange. Men interested her, were beautiful to her, but as she ventured through life, other elements of the world always seemed more beautiful, seemed to have more satisfaction in them and less chance for letdown. She had never loved any boy or man enough to allow herself to be given over, to be entered. Giving herself only to things she loved seemed to always work well, fulfilling her, even when that love turned into hatred, as it did with her running. She wondered where her mother felt safe to talk about her sexuality. Whom did she say raunchy things around? Did she have a private circle where those things could comfortably come out? Aisha had never seen her mother talk on the phone or go out with girlfriends. But she had to let it out, didn't she? Or did it happen before her? Maybe she had it before her and maybe it changes with age? Maybe it didn't need to be talked about anymore because it's been lived so much, sexuality known so well that talking about it was no longer necessary, except for maybe a rare mention, something subtle, an innuendo, resulting in a chuckle, then going on with other conversation. She wanted to discover all of that, and some parts of life you could only learn by doing.

Aisha moved herself from under Aaron and to his middle.

Aaron awoke from a dream seemingly into another. He blinked, trying to make sense of what he was feeling and seeing. Aisha just kept concentrating on not hurting him, getting more and more aroused by Aaron's baffled moans, and stuttering words as his brain caught up with his body.

When Aaron did gain clarity, he stopped Aisha. Taking her in his arms, he brought her back to the bed and patiently began loving her toward total submergence.

It surprised Aisha that she began to enjoy the act right away. She had heard only unpleasant stories about the first few times. But this was not the case with her and Aaron. It was instant ecstasy, them making love over and over proving the illusory quality of time. Their moments flowed seamlessly from love to love, to the most wonderful pillow talk to love, to food, their choices already chosen, no friction, just flowing in love. Leaving the bedroom and making love all over the apartment, finding and figuring out which places on each other brought forth the giddiest groans, the most pleasurable pulses. They took pride in learning each other in that way, paying attention to reaction. Treating each other's bodies better than their own, and then realizing happily that the other's body was their own, *mine, this breast is mine, this bicep, this earlobe, mine, these shoulders, mine, ours.*

They made love on both of Aisha's favorite reading chairs and after finishing for the moment on the chair in the second bedroom, surrounded by all her books, Aisha looked at Aaron and said, "It's the perfect fit." Aaron delighted in the little saying, the perfect fit. It was.

At some point Aaron realized that it was Monday morning. During their revolution there was no need or desire to look at the clock, but when he did happen to turn and see it, thinking momentarily how strange the little object with little glowing red numbers looked, it dawned on him that he should call Isaac to tell him that he would not be coming into work. Aisha's spring break had started, but what was the name for what they were in?

Holding Aisha, Aaron asked, "Do you know what time it is?"

"What day is it?" Aisha replied.

They both giggled. "For real."

"Baby, hold up, I got to call Dub."

"Noooo."

"Naw, it's all good. Don't trip, I'm staying right here with you."

Aaron dialed Isaac. Aisha snuggled closer to him, as if she were making sure their connection remained while they invited the outside world into their haven. Once again she noticed the sound of cars passing outside, rumbling buses, their TV left on some channel that had watched them while the couch temporarily became their bed. When Isaac picked up the phone they talked straight, as only best friends can. Aisha heard the entire exchange.

"Calling in sick?" Isaac said with a smile in his voice.

"Love sick, Dub. Star and I are making love. Well, not now. We just finished, but you better believe we gone be at it again." Aaron turned and smiled at Aisha.

"Really! That's awesome! I was starting to worry about you."

"Yeah, all it took was me getting my car stolen."

"Huh? You're joking."

"Nope, I would have bought a dope ride and set it in the 'hood years ago if I knew that's all it took." Aisha hit Aaron playfully.

"Wait, Jamal, is your car really gone?"

"Yep."

"All right. I guess I'll hear about it when you come back in."

"You know it."

"When are you coming back?"

"I can't say, but it's on when I do get back."

"Cool, positive carry?"

"Like we've never seen."

Aaron took the next week off. He and Aisha went on long walks along the lakefront, holding hands, sitting on the embankment, looking out at the rippling water. One morning they got out of bed early and walked to watch the sunrise over the lake.

During the day, they mostly lied around, made love, and played around. They watched movies and told each other new stories, the ones reserved especially for that time. Aaron washed Aisha's hair with her special shampoo, the kind that she said worked best on her hair, the kind made by those who must have understood her blended hair grade. Aaron ran his hands through her hair as they bathed together, joking that his shampooing got her naps out.

The police calling to tell Aaron that his car had been totaled in a brief, high-speed chase didn't bother him at all. The call came while Aisha read to Aaron from a book she had been really enjoying. He had not thought about the car and the incident since speaking to Isaac. He made light of it to Aisha, "I'd rather roll with you anyway. We must not be meant to be apart."Aisha responded, trying to talk in trading terms, trying to fashion some response, saying it would be his only loss and smiling at how silly she sounded. Aaron appreciated her encouragement, her keen interest in him, which largely included the moves he made in his business and how he had to think about his business incessantly. Aisha participated. Not just then, because they were living together, but since the beginning. She was consistent, caring, never wavering in her character. It was why her students loved her and how she was able to win over some of her blind and stubborn parents. In situations where he would have cursed people, Aisha internalized the hurt and exhaled more love. After being around her long enough, her quiet, enigmatic nature drew people to her, made them feel like she was a friend, a good friend, even if it was not the case. He had to protect her, make sure he was always there for her, and that no harm that he could control would befall her.

The last time Aaron had these kinds of thoughts he was a too-mature little boy, looking at his grandparents after they had shown him who they really were. They showed him they wanted nothing but to be there for him, to rehabilitate him, rescue him from the way he viewed the world with their love. But his thoughts of Aisha had a higher level of intensity and understanding. He had feared losing Pop Pop at one time. He thought of losing Aisha in that moment and it left him, momentarily, in shambles.

Aisha read it on Aaron's face and asked him what was wrong.

"Nothing… Superstar," Aaron said, smiling at Aisha. "You and the homeboy, God, are my greatest gains forever."

Chapter 9

Aaron started working long hours again the week after their break. So Aisha decided to visit Raven and Kiki one day after school. The building where they rented a big, four-bedroom apartment together was not far from the school.

Raven and Kiki grew up in Englewood and had never left. With their apartment, they created the space that they always talked about as little girls. Both were raised in homes that had too many struggling people packed inside. There were too many struggling people and not enough awareness that developing little girls are often prey in such environments. So both little girls were touched improperly.

While walking home together from school one day, Kiki expressed her disgust with her particular situation. She was not loud about it or particularly animated, but the closer they came to being home the more Kiki huffed her breath and sucked her teeth. Her head gradually hung lower, her shoulders slumping, her feet dragging. Raven noticed the change in her friend's demeanor, asking her the reason behind it. Kiki told her. Raven believed her. She shared her story with Kiki. They had been enduring similar mistreatment. The instinct that gave them the feeling that something was wrong—this touching, it was not right—was bolstered by both girls sharing how they felt with each other.

They began to support one another, teaming up. Against their mothers' rules and wishes, they learned to stay out and sneak out of the house when their mothers were away working multiple jobs to support them and grown borders, among them the violators of their bodies. They learned to fight by talking about fighting. They showed each other fighting moves, how to fight hands off them, moves that they had drawn from their minds, from TV shows, cartoons. Moves that they never used, but in the acting out, in talking about being bold, cursing and talking tough, as if they were men on the street corner, they developed armor. Its strength brushed back the offenders and anyone else who even thought about taking the chance, taking them for weak. And they had one another. They went through it all with each other and it made them extremely close.

They shared this part of their past with Aisha in the year she taught their children as first graders. In the beginning of that year, their children, Norrell and Tyeisha, came home beaming about their new teacher, Ms. Bowerman. They also came home weighed down with work. Slipping their backpacks off and letting them drop to the floor with a loud thud, they insisted on getting to work right away. Ms. Bowerman wanted them to make sure they had their homework done. When Aisha sent letters home inviting her students' parents to open house, Raven and Kiki were ready. They had to see who this teacher was who gave their children homework packets as though they were in college. At least it seemed that way to them, for neither one of the mothers had been to college. They knew it was more work than they ever took home in high school and that didn't seem right. They were glad that their children liked the teacher and were eager to do their work. Unlike many of the teachers they had coming up, this Ms. Bowerman seemed to care, however crazy she was. But did she really care or was she some loony that wanted to work their children like slaves to keep them busy? What was her plan? What was she up to?

The pair had already planned to be more involved in their children's schoolwork that school year. Their children were not going to stay in Englewood like they had and this Ms. Bowerman had given them a good opportunity to get started. But they had expected something much different, a teacher with a style they were accustomed to or perhaps a white girl, naive, bright and enthusiastic, someone that wouldn't last. They had seen white teachers rotating in and out of their neighborhood, but not one of the faces they saw became static. Two years, maybe three, and they were gone. The same went for one new black teacher. They knew who was new to their neighborhood, knew those who did not really want to belong.

On the night of the open house, Raven and Kiki left Norrell and Tyeisha with Raven's mother, bringing along with them the big, thick packets, as though they were exhibits in a trial. They were the first in the classroom. Aisha greeted them with a smile, found out whose parents they were, and asked them if they wanted to first see where Norrell and Tyeisha sat. After that, she showed them the children's work that hung from the walls.

Aisha had to prepare herself well beforehand to speak so openly, so much, to adults. To involve her children's parents, she had to go beyond her comfort level. As they moved around the classroom, Aisha noticed that both women carried one of her homework packets. She pointed it out, saying, "I see you've brought a power packet!" The expression brought a smile to Raven and Kiki's faces. Their children would come home with the same inflection in their voices. "These are power packets!" Norrell would flex his muscles to show power. He knew the packets didn't work on that kind of power, but he didn't know how to show his brain flex. The packets must have worked, though, because he could surely feel his brain get tired.

As Aisha explained the principle behind her power packets to Raven and Kiki, gradually, more parents made their way in. Aisha took that time to have all of the parents sit down so she could give her formal introduction. Then, in a move that had not been in her plans, she motioned to Raven and Kiki and the packets in front of them. Picking one up so the rest of the parents could see it, she said, "I'm sure you all have questions about our Power Packets. I was just speaking to Ms. Nelson and Ms. Gates about them..." Aisha then went into a part of the open house that she had practiced: her ideology and goals for her students' first-grade education. She talked about how the student's foundation, the child's earliest years, might be the most important. She wanted the students to get accustomed to high standards and hard work and believed that each one of her students could work toward and achieve whatever they desired most in life. It was her job to present them with as many alternatives as she could, even while they couldn't really understand it. But career choices, the field trips to colleges and museums, were complimentary things, not as fundamental to her everyday classroom routine as the basics: phonics, reading, math, independent thought, dreaming, focus, commitment, and consistency.

At some point, caught up in the passion of the moment and in the intent eyes of Raven and Kiki, who had locked in on Aisha like overachieving students in her classroom, Aisha's plans to demonstrate a lesson morphed into her conducting herself as though the morning bell had rung and her students were all in their seats. She began drawing all sorts of things with the marker on the dry erase board, turning to the parents for their feedback. She transitioned as if she were teaching. She picked up the current read-along book and read with such expression Kiki said "keep going" when she was about to stop. So Aisha continued, to the chagrin of one parent who got up and walked out. Aisha saw her leave but kept concentrating on the text and the interested parents' eyes, particularly Raven and Kiki, until she came to an appropriate ending.

Through the course of that school year, Aisha grew closer to Raven and Kiki. They were her most involved parents, though it went beyond that. Raven and Kiki opened up to Aisha. They felt they could trust her. And, about midway through the school year, they told Aisha that they were having trouble with Norrell and Tyeisha acting like kissing cousins. They had caught them a few times playing "house," touching each other inappropriately. They told Aisha this as she sat in their apartment, continuing on with parts of their lives and describing how the inappropriate playing troubled them more because of the trouble they endured as little girls. They asked Aisha if she would watch their behavior in class and in the hallways, gave her permission to separate or discipline them in her own way, and asked her to report to them what she saw, if anything.

Aisha never saw anything of the sort of behavior Raven and Kiki conveyed that night in their apartment. She did, however, call home to report the good news of their son and daughter's achievements and to compliment them on their efforts to help them at home. It showed in the classroom. Out of these calls, school meetings, and field trips, the three became friends.

Pulling up to their apartment, Aisha thought how fortunate she was to have them as friends. They entered her life right after Dr. Haywood had re-inspired her, nourishing her educational spirit, and a part of her own spirit, back to health. It also was the time loneliness began to grip her greatest. She and Aaron had begun talking again, but it was sporadic and she couldn't trust it, wouldn't trust it, though her heart ached to want to believe.

Aisha lifted the big bag she used for school from the passenger seat of her truck and lugged it to the front door of Raven and Kiki's apartment. If she were going to hang out, she had to grade her student's work while doing it. Raven and Kiki were accustomed to it. She rang the bell. Kiki's voice sang out over the intercom and when Aisha identified herself, the door buzzed.

Stepping into the apartment, she was greeted by Norrell and Tyeisha, who ran up to her and hugged her.

"Ooo, ooo, can we help you grade?" they said after seeing the bag they had come to know years ago as her students.

"Have you finished your homework? Hey ladies..." Aisha said, smiling at Raven and Kiki, who were both sitting in the front room. Kiki had some of her styling tools out and stood above Raven, curling her hair.

"Yes!" both children said.

"What's up, girl?" both of their parents said.

Aisha opened her bag and took out some packets so the children could start grading.

"Uh uh, Star," Kiki said, motioning with her hot curler, "y'all take her bag to the back. We got grown folks business to talk about."

Norrell slung Aisha's bag off the ground, nearly spilling one of the packets out, and he and Tyeisha hurried to the back.

"You know where my grading pens are," Aisha raised her voice to the children, who had made it to the back in a flash. "And ask me if you have any questions. Raven, only smiley faces and exclamation points. Keep the praise consistent."

With that, Aisha sat down on the leather couch and took a look around. Unlike her, her friends had so much style. Each time she came by, she enjoyed looking on what new touch they had added. This time she noticed a different fake plant a few feet from their entertainment center and a new piece of artwork that hung on the wall behind the couch.

"So tell us, bitch, what you an' Aaron do last week?" Kiki said.

"She glowing; look at her," Raven said, smiling at Aisha.

"Uh hem, I seen it when she came in the door."

Aisha blushed and didn't say anything. Her eyes sparkled.

"Uh, uh, no you didn't?" Kiki said.

"Hell naw, this record-breaking bitch done finally gave up the coochie!" Kiki said, stepping away from Raven's hair stomping, running in place around and around in a circle.

Kiki had a running joke with Aisha that she would end up in some book for the oldest virgin alive. When Kiki first established the joke, Aisha almost fell down from laughter. Not only because of the way Kiki said it, but also because it caused Aisha to imagine herself in one of those books about facts and great fact feats she liked reading as a little girl. The taunting about her virginal status also came in different names at different times: "Here comes the coochie clamp champ" and "I know sister-saving-herself don't have nothing to say about it." Or "don't look at me like that, Ms. Pussy Pure" and "this bitch don't eat meat AND she don't get no dick, ain't *that* some shit?" Aisha enjoyed it all, as she did them, watching their shoulders heave up and down over the realization that she had given herself fully to Aaron.

"Look, Raven, I ain't even gone ask her how it was. I know she ain't gone to tell us," Kiki said after she had settled.

"Tell us," Raven said, looking eager.

"It was, I don't know, I guess like I dreamed. I know that sounds corny, but it's true."

"Well, damn! Then, girl, I'm happy for you," Raven said.

"Where can I get some of *that* dick? I can't even get on you no more. Can I? You's a woman now…You's a woman now…You done took the chains off the chastity belt. Did the rust fall up in it, girl? Did your stuff work right? Tell us how Aaron's fine ass slid up in there," Kiki pointed her curling iron down at Aisha's mid-section.

"Ooo, you so nasty!" Raven said.

"Hey, look," Kiki said, taking one of the curlers once again to Raven's head, "I want to know details."

Aisha told them enough to satisfy, but not so much that her and Aaron's privacy was compromised. She told them, in her way, and she found that she enjoyed having something to say on the subject of sex.

Aisha went home after leaving Raven and Kiki's apartment. Instead of sitting in her reading chair with her book, as she normally would on Aaron's late nights, she climbed in bed instead and read. She figured she would be able to stay up. She had spoken to Aaron and he said he was on his way. But sleep overcame her.

Again, she dreamt of her father. The same dream—his hands out, pleading, tears streaming down his cheeks. It woke her. She found Aaron lying next to her. She sat up and in a loud, clear voice said, "AJ, I've been dreaming about my father." But Aaron did not respond. Aisha remained sitting up for a moment, watching Aaron sleep, then thought, "That's it. I've said it. It's out there. The next time he'll be awake and we'll talk about it."

Chapter 10

As April turned to May and May to June, Aisha and Aaron learned new routines, the difficult balance of actively working at two great loves, for someone, for something. They managed well, however, for both had been without the other for long enough to truly appreciate how extraordinary their relationship was. Unlike fleeting romance, passionately hot ordeals that flame bright for a time then burnout quickly, or shiny relationships that sparkle big and bright until the luster rubs away, they had a real love.

During the passing months, Aaron often paced around the apartment with figures in his head, sometimes not hearing Aisha when she spoke to him. On nights Aisha did not want to be alone, she would meet him downtown in the office, reading in the conference room, out of his sight so as not to distract him, until he had exhausted himself. As he made sure Colossus's strategy to fully capitalize on the market on its decline was foolproof, he also had been working on another surprise for Aisha.

On a sunny Saturday in mid-June, Aisha had planned for them to drive out to the suburbs to see her stepfather, Robert. He had been protesting about never seeing her, telling her how the baby was growing and of everything that she missed out on. So when Aaron downplayed the need for delaying their plans, saying he had to take care of some business first and he did not know how long it would last, but that he did need her to come with him, Aisha became frustrated. She wanted to see Robert, Susan, and the baby and she wanted it to be on her time. It was about an hour's drive to the suburbs and they did not have all day to be messing around with Aaron's clients. They were beginning to get imbalanced—work, work, work—and that was not good.

Yet on the drive to wherever they were going, she grew calm. She could not stay upset with him for long and was thankful they were together. Aaron pulled Aisha's truck off Lake Shore Drive and seemed to be driving to Soldier Field. They parked near a marina and Aaron said, "This guy I'm meeting is here with his yacht. It's the only way I could catch him." The two walked around the marina. Aisha admired the different styles of yachts while the rhythm of the current bumping up against the vessels' hulls lulled her into a trance. Suddenly, Aaron stopped near one of the yachts, looking perplexed.

"Well, he said he'd be here at this time," Aaron said, resting his arm on what Aisha assumed to be the man's vessel.

"Where is this cat?" he continued, taking a step away from the yacht. He was smiling.

"You don't seem too upset," Aisha said, still in a sort of a daze, lost in the spell of the lake."Normally, you can't stand when people are late."

"Yeah, but this dude is cool. Let's jump on." Aaron reached out his hand.

"AJ, no! Wait on him. You don't know him well."

"Yes I do, c'mon."

Aaron hopped on the boat and extended his arm for Aisha to join him.

"You've never told me about..." She was about to speak about Aaron's relationship with the man when her eyes caught the lettering on the stern. It read *Aisha Star* in big, black letters. Aisha stood silent for a moment, her arm involuntarily raising and pointing at her name on the yacht. Her eyes met Aaron's; he was grinning ear to ear. He hopped back off the yacht to the dock where Aisha still stood, planted, smiling in disbelief.

"Chi summer is here, baby!" Aaron said, looking at Aisha staring at her name. It shamed her to think it, but her name on it looked like it belonged there against the glare of the yacht's whiteness.

"I had to get it for us. First Chi summer of many to come. And since right now I don't have time for us to take vacations, I figured we could take weekend ones on our own cruiser." At these words, Aisha turned from her name and leapt into Aaron's arms. He caught her and swung her around and around, both laughing gaily.

When Aisha's feet were back on the ground, Aaron said, "Let's go aboard."

Once on, Aaron changed his tone of voice and the manner of his speech.

"As you can see, there's plenty of room and seating available in bridge deck. Have a seat; try it out. Isn't it comfortable? Yes, comfort and plenty spacious for family and friends to enjoy a pleasant day along the water. Here's your wet bar, fridge, and ice maker. A camper enclosure for all your miscellaneous items." Aisha followed, thrilled by their yacht and tickled by Aaron's latest transformation describing it. He would spring into them at home on rare occasion as if, for the moment, he were tired of being himself. All his transformations made Aisha laugh, all but one.

It had happened in Aisha's apartment, when Aaron started talking in a flamboyant gay man's voice, capturing all the requisite antics, lip smacks, eye rolls, and sashaying. That part was funny to Aisha. What was not funny was when he seemingly dropped the transformation and became himself again. He took her hands in his hands and told her that he liked wearing her underwear to work, saying, "As a matter of fact, I have some on right now." At first, Aisha laughed it off, dismissing it as another transformation. But Aaron kept going, never once cracking a smile, which was uncharacteristic of his transformations. He could never hold them without showing a hint of how much he enjoyed his own routine. At that moment, he looked coldly serious, especially when he said, "We share everything. And I felt like the gay man routine would be a good segue into telling you that I like wearing women's underwear under my clothes sometimes." He entered into an elaborate and believable story of how it began. He used to go into Grandma Benjamin's room as a boy when Pop Pop wasn't around and put on her bra and panties. Later, he'd take the women's undergarments that he dated and would wear them.

Upon feeling that this was not a transformation, Aisha stood up from the couch and walked away from him. She felt as if her whole world were falling into a black hole. She did not know him. She did not know the man she thought she knew well and loved. All the wonderful things about their relationship had been a lie. How could she have been wrong about the time, the transparency and openness they had? She felt light, as if she were about to faint. She wanted him out of her home at once. Could she deal with this fetish of his? Was it only that? Only the women's clothes? No, it had to be more. What more? She felt as though breath were leaving her chest. It was.

Aaron followed her into the bedroom, seeing that he had indeed taken the transformation too far. He began apologizing profusely, smiling and convincing, having to work far harder to steer her from the fabricated story than he did in creating it. He was proud of the fabrication until he saw how much it hurt her. He didn't mean for it to hurt her the way it did. But seeing her and reflecting on the moment, he could see how it was a big mistake. He felt terrible. He told her this, stripped down to his underwear and showed off his boxer briefs. Told her men's underwear was all he had ever worn. He swore. He had thought of the stupid women's clothes thing in the moment and went with it. And he should not have because it hurt her and was now hurting him terribly. He loved her and was true, had always told her the truth. Everything about him, even some of the things she maybe should not know. But she could take it and was not judgmental. So he told her, told her most everything that he felt she needed to know about him. He wanted her to know him. From the beginning, she was unlike anyone he had ever met. The connection they had from the beginning was unlike anything he had ever felt and time bore it out, made it realer, stronger, yes, better. And he was so sorry he hurt her. It was all a lie, a terrible lie that went too far. She knew he was crazy, knew how he came up, the things he saw, but he never did what he just pretended to do and had always told her the truth. She knew him. He would never do it again and he learned from it. "Forgive me, baby. Please forgive me. I'm sorry, man, it was stupid. I'm learning. I was trippin'. I was really trippin'."He cradled her, told her she knew that when he was younger he had thought he would be an actor. Before Pop Pop rescued him, he would pretend that he was Arnold on *Diff'rent Strokes*. His dark side had manifested in the wrong way. He was still learning him and still learning her; please forgive him.

Aisha looked into Aaron's eyes in that moment and saw truth, contrition for what he had done. The cold look that hurt was gone. She had not been wrong. She did know him. With him touching her then, it felt right. She looked into his eyes and saw the man she knew, a man flawed, but beautiful, hers to love and grow with. Somehow, the hurt that he caused made her feel closer to him. He continued to apologize, petting her and kissing her, saying he was stupid, it was a stupid joke and he'd never do it again. He smiled at her and said, "There are some cats out there with crazy fetishes, but that ain't me, baby."Aisha turned over in the bed, looked at him, and said, "I know."

"Here's your engine hatch, good power there, and oh, I forgot to show you your anchor…as you can see, there's extra chain to stay comfortably way out there… Now if you would follow me into the cabin." The two walked across the deck and down the yacht's stairs. Aaron continued, "To your right you'll see a full galley. Have a feel of these counter tops. The cabinets are cherry. And have a look at these hardwood floors. You can leave your home on land and come to one on the water. To our left back, there's an aft guest stateroom. Let's have a look. You see, there are twins that can convert to a queen size. Spacious, isn't it? Okay? Back out in the saloon you have a leather sectional, television, and other lovely furnishings. Now, let's move to the forward cabin stateroom. Isn't this pedestal queen bed lovely? Some good action can happen in here." At that remark, Aaron could not hold the transformation any longer. He started laughing and Aisha tackled him on the bed. They kissed and held one another. Then Aaron said, "C'mon, let me show you the rest of it."

He took her to the bridge and, in his normal voice, showed her all the instrumentation, explaining what they were used for. Bill Long had taken him out many times on his yacht, letting him take control and discussing techniques of a helmsman with him. Aaron was no expert, but he was proficient.

Showing Aisha around excited him. She had done so much already, it was nice to see the surprise and newness on her face. Still beaming, he began to go over the safety precautions with her. He showed her where the fire extinguishers and life vests were and they put them on each other. He talked about man overboard procedures and said they would drill it once they pulled out of the marina. He talked to her about the moorings, the dock lines, the spring lines, and their respective usages.

As they were about ready to cast off, Aaron, having said and gone over all he felt was important, was slapped by Aisha on the arm.

"Why didn't you tell me about all this?"

"Ah," Aaron laughed, "I told you I was gone get you."

"When did you get it all done?"

"On Saturdays."

"So, you weren't working?" Aaron gave Aisha a look that said, "Now, c'mon now. You know me."

"Then when?" Aisha said.

"After I left the office I had to hustle, shift gears, and bit by bit get things done so you wouldn't know."

Aisha hugged him. "You did a great job. I love you! I love it!"

After the skippers casted off, they took the yacht out on the lake to get a feel for its handling, first Aaron and after him Aisha. When they were comfortable, Aaron set a course to meet Isaac and Katie at Oak Street Beach within the breakwater.

The *Aisha Star* entered the Oak Street Beach area. As they approached Isaac's yacht, they could see Katie with their baby in her arms, taking the infant's little hand and waving it to them. Aaron cut off the engine and brought the yacht in steadily, close to Isaac's yacht, which was named *Colossus Jr.* There were at least twenty other yachters already gathered in their vessels, talking, laughing, drinking, enjoying the beautiful day and the beginning of Chicago's most celebrated season.

Spring lines connected the *Aisha Star* to the anchored *Colossus Jr.*

so that the two vessels touched. Isaac jump from the *Colossus Jr.* onto the *Aisha Star,* barking out a remark about modern-day pirates of the eastern shores of Africa, saying, "I'm commandeering this vessel and all that's on it." To which Aaron replied, "Ah, yeah? You ready to die? Must be, we don't play that on the *Aisha Star.*" At this, Isaac smiled and stuck out his hand. Shaking hands, the two men laughed and shared an aggressive hug. Isaac then hugged Aisha and said, "I think Katie wants you to hop over. Alls she's been talking about is you two getting together again." Aisha smiled. She enjoyed Katie's company, too. She turned and saw Katie alone with the baby, waiting for her. She gave Aaron a look, turned, took some steps toward a good jumping point, and with an athletic leap hopped onto the other boat. Aaron caught Isaac admiring the jump and joked with him about looking at his woman. They gave each other a happy, knowing look.

On the *Colossus Jr.,* Aisha and Katie immediately fell into full conversation. They talked about the baby; they talked a lot about Aisha's teaching and her school. Both Katie's parents were high school English teachers, so she grew up loving books, like Aisha did. They talked about their ambitious and competitive men and all they had to put up with. At some point, they settled into the comfortable conversation that long friends have where any subject is open, appropriate, and comfortable, where the conversation flows and the time passes without regard.

Isaac and Katie met at Harvard, too, but unlike Aaron and Aisha, they'd been together without break since their sophomore year. Aisha had exchanged pleasantries with Katie the times she had come to visit Aaron in his dorm his senior year. Neither of them knew then that casual conversation with one another in a dorm room would lead, somehow, to them relating and relaxing on the calm waters of Lake Michigan. Aisha felt that they were on the way to becoming good friends. She had told Kaii about Katie the last time she and Kaii spoke on the telephone. For the first time, she could see a stable family life for her in the future.

When the sun had almost set, the two women said their goodbyes and promised to get together soon. Aisha leapt back to Aaron and Isaac to Katie. The skippers of both vessels coordinated their cast offs and guided their vessels in opposite directions.

After some time, Aisha noticed that Aaron was not returning home, instead going farther out into the lake. When she asked him what he had planned, he said, "I want to leave the city lights behind, tonight. Let's make our own light." The serene look on his face, the drone of the motor, and the water crashing against the hull as the yacht cut through the lake, soothed Aisha. She kissed Aaron on the cheek and sat down next to him, watching them make their way to the center of themselves.

The farther they traveled, the more the sky seemed to open up and shine its lights at them. When they reached the point where they felt as if it were just them in the whole world, Aaron cut the engine off and asked Aisha to help him anchor them in the deep.

With the boat secure, he took Aisha's hand and led her to the cabin. He set her down at the galley table and produced placemats, silverware, and candles from one of the cabinets.

"Are you going to cook for me?" Aisha said.

"Now, this is supposed to be a special night. Ain't nothing special about me trying to cook."

"I'll love whatever you do."

"That's why you're my Superstar." Aaron went in the refrigerator and pulled out two aluminum containers.

"Dishes from our two favorite restaurants." He held one container out. "A vegetable medley of goodness and pasta for you." Bringing that container back and putting the other one forward, he said, "And some succulent steak, spinach, and rice for me." Aaron turned the oven on and placed the dishes in it to warm. He lit the candles and sat.

"So I did a'ight?" Aaron asked.

"Better than all right."

"Yeah, I try to do what I can," Aaron said, rubbing his hands together in a cocky way.

"I love all of it. I love you."

"I love you, too."

"Oh, AJ, wait! I forgot to call Robert."

Aisha stood up to see if her phone was on her. She had forgotten where she put it, forgotten about the little object entirely. When she did find it, she saw that she had missed calls from Robert. She called. Aaron watched her. When Robert picked up, Aisha told him the news of the surprise and the time they were having. She said she would have him, Susan, and the baby along for a ride as soon as they could. But they would also be sure to come and visit them in the suburbs soon.

"He's excited."

"I heard."

"Did you hear him say he wants to make sure you're taking care of your money?" Aisha smirked.

"Dude be nagging, don't he?"

"I know, but he means well."

"Well, next time we see them, I'm going to pull him aside and tell him I'm good. Man, it trips me out how much that dude looks like an accountant. You know? What comes first, people looking like their profession or their profession making them look like their profession?"

"You're silly."

"You know I don't look like what I do."

"Oh, stop."

"Okay, I'll spare you tonight. This night isn't about me; it's about you on your maiden voyage on the *Aisha Star!*"

"We should make a toast. Where's the wine, AJ?"

"Not yet."

"What's going on? I saw Isaac had some beers, but not you?"

"I know. C'mon, let's go out on deck. We'll come back down here when the food is warm."

Bright stars embedded in the clear night sky greeted them as they stepped from the cabin and onto the deck. They both sat down. Neither of them spoke for a while. Aisha noticed a change in Aaron's demeanor. He looked pensive, somber.

"Are you okay?" she asked. Aaron nodded.

"I know I've said this before, but I want to say sorry for us not talking for those couple of years after Pop Pop died."

"It's okay."

"I know, but listen, I want to say sorry for everything I ever put you through. I feel like I had to go through it. We had to go through it to get us here, but I still want to say I'm sorry. It hurts me now to think about how you must have felt. All those letters you wrote me from Africa, how long you stuck by me, supported me when I was trying to figure things out. When I didn't have a clue how beautiful you are and how right we are together." Aaron took Aisha's hand.

"Even recently, that stupid joke. I'm a mess, Star, you know that, but I'm working on it and you help make me a better person. Sometimes, I try to understand why you are the way you are. How you got to become this way and how… why… I am blessed to benefit from it. But the whys aren't so important. It's the now. These months with you have been the happiest times of my life."

Aaron moved away from Aisha. Still holding her hand, he put one knee on the deck's floor. He dug in his pocket for a second and pulled out a black box. He opened it. The ring shown brilliantly even with just the illumination of the boat's light and faint stars. "I made sure they weren't conflict stones…Aisha, I want you to be my wife and I want to be your husband, forever. I love you so much." Tears were in Aaron's eyes; Aisha wrapped her arms around him and hugged him tight.

They remained there like that, Aaron setting the ring box down and wrapping his arms around Aisha. For a long time they sat, just holding each other, words not coming from their mouths, but their spirits singing hymns of love to each other, through each other. They kissed and Aisha tried on the ring. It slid easily on her finger and remained there, firm and beautiful. She was not into jewelry and things that shined. Aaron could have said the same words with a piece of circular cloth and she would have felt the same way. But the significance of the diamond was not lost on her. She loved it. It came from him, from his heart, from his heart's deep, from deep in the earth, a symbol of creation and transformation, a proud, bright, element, one small piece in the plan of eternity. And somehow, with it on her finger, Aisha felt connected with the scope of its existence. She could not stop looking down at it. She thought about how hard Aaron had worked to keep the night secret, while he worked inexhaustibly hard at his passion, at loving her the right way. What a magnificent feeling. At that moment, she understood all the love in the universe.

Chapter 11

Aisha did not want to have a wedding. She arranged it so that they would be married by the court the same afternoon they closed on their new home. This way, they moved into their new apartment married, which didn't matter to Aisha as a matter of principle or rule, but she thought the idea of it was nice.

Eventually, Aaron acquiesced. Initially, he envisioned something large, an event where all the people that he had even the slightest moments of significant interaction with in his life—people from his old neighborhood, people from high school, people from Harvard, people from New York City—would be invited. It would be the grandest wedding the South Side had ever seen, rivaling all the best weddings in all of Chicago, even ones bought by old money. He could see the grand ballroom, Bill Long at one of the tables with his glass of Scotch in his hand. He could see Biggums and Isaac standing with him, but at that point, he understood what Aisha meant and ceased to imagine the large affair. He would not, however, go downtown to be married in anything he had in his closet and Aisha would not, either.

The Friday before the closing, Aaron asked Aisha to meet him downtown after school. She protested this request. She knew his intentions and did not feel it necessary, but eventually she gave in.

When Aisha arrived downtown, they left the financial district, driving north of the river and parking just west of Michigan Avenue. Leaving the parking garage and walking east toward Michigan Avenue, Aaron skipped backwards, smiling at Aisha.

"You're going to hit someone doing that," Aisha said. Aaron glanced over his shoulder then turned back to Aisha.

"C'mon, Superstar, get your face together, why you acting up?"
"I'm doing this for you."
"Uh huh, and we're about to do it to death!"

Aaron made sure to start shopping for Aisha first. He did not intend on getting all that much for himself, anyway, and he had been waiting for the opportunity to take Aisha shopping.

Aaron made the occasion known to the sales associates upon entering each store and each boutique. He even got Aisha's reluctance out in the open, which, each time, evoked either subtle, strange looks from the associates or quick and flirty "well, I'm not like her. You can shop for me anytime" looks. Aaron found all these moments hilarious. Aisha did not. After leaving one store, having already gone to a number of them unsuccessfully, Aisha chided Aaron.

"AJ, stop telling them I don't want to shop."
"Nope. Not until you see the value in what I'm doing."
"Well, I don't."
"Then I'm going to keep putting you on blast."
"Well, I'm going to just find something in the next place we go."
"Good. Anything you put on you'll make look good, anyway, Superstar. Give me a kiss." Aisha kissed him and then went right back to her look of protest.
"I bet you wouldn't be like this if we were in Italy."
"What's that supposed to mean to me, AJ?"
"A'ight, when we go, I'm leaving your butt at the hotel. Give me another kiss."
"No."

Aaron kept up his act in the next boutique they entered. But that time, the associate showed no sign that she found Aisha's behavior strange. She looked at both Aaron and Aisha the same, turning to Aisha with a genuine look of warmth and understanding. "How is she pulling this off?" Aaron thought. Aisha studied the woman's face and for the first time looked like she would be open. Aaron did everything he could to stop from smiling, but Aisha saw him. Still, it did not sway her mood. The sales associate was the consummate professional. Seamlessly, she moved Aisha in and out of couture, bringing a smile to her face in the different looks she made up. Leaving the store, Aisha clutched two handfuls of bags, walking with a contented stride. Aaron said nothing, only observed and enjoyed.

♦   ♦   ♦

The closing went well. Aaron used Isaac's real estate attorney, a thorough and funny guy who told jokes as he gave an overview of each document that Aaron and Aisha signed. With their sets of new keys in hand, they hurried home to shower and change clothes. Biggums, Isaac and Katie, Robert and Susan were supposed to meet them downtown.

When Aaron and Aisha arrived at the courthouse, they found everyone there. They had planned on making introductions, but by the looks of their friends, everyone was already acquainted. They had been passing stories along to one another. Later, together, they all stood before the judge and witnessed Aisha and Aaron married under law.

Isaac and Katie treated the marital party to an exquisite meal at one of their favorite restaurants downtown. Unlike other times, when they were in each other's presence outside of the office, Aaron and Isaac did not discuss the market or anything remotely close to business. They talked about good times past. Isaac recounted the first time that Aaron came home to Quincy House with his eyes wide, talking about the beautiful freshman who paid him no attention. In Aaron's pursuit of Aisha, Isaac learned new aspects of his friend that had not been revealed in all the time they roomed together. He told of a time when Aaron walked into his single with the most dejected look on his face. Isaac was in a nostalgic mood with the ending of college near and was listening to his Nirvana CDs. Speaking up, Aaron had said, "Dog, she just won't let me in."

"Well, Star," Isaac said at the restaurant table, raising his glass. "You've let him in now and when you do that he's a hard man to get rid of. Not that you would want to. I wish you both much happiness and prosperity."

"Hear! Hear!" Biggums said in a loud, full-throated voice, which set everyone to laughing and toasting their glasses.

After dinner, everyone hugged one another as if they were old friends and said they looked forward to seeing each other again. Robert and Susan said they had something for the newlyweds at the house, but they were going to make them come out to the suburbs to get it. Aaron responded, saying, "Since y'all got a gift for us, I guess we can make it out there." Biggums handed Aisha a card while Aaron joked further with Robert and Susan outside. Everyone waited on the valet. Biggums's car pulled up first and when he reached in his pocket to pay for it, Isaac wouldn't have it. He waved him off and gave the valet money for each of the wedding party's cars, pointing each person out to make sure there would be no trouble. Biggums shook hands and hugged Aaron then Aisha and drove off. Shortly after, Robert and Susan did the same. When Isaac and Katie's car arrived, they motioned for Aisha and Aaron to come toward it. Isaac pulled out a well-packaged, rectangular object that appeared to be a painting and handed it to Aaron. The couples hugged again, half hugs for Aaron who held the painting, and said their goodbyes.

Aisha could not wait to open the painting and Biggums's card when they got home to the apartment on South Shore. First, she opened Biggums's card. She figured he had handed her his first, so they would go in that order. Biggums wrote to the couple in very small print to fit the spaces of the card. Aisha read it aloud; it began this way:

I was going through an extremely tough time when Jam first came back. When I didn't really hear from you both for a while it made it harder, lonelier. Wayne was gone, no way of getting to him and you all were here and it seemed that it was no way to get to you. I've been just trying to figure out life. What's the good life for me? When I did start coming around, when we all started hanging out, your love for each other inspired me. I know your story, been there at a distance for all of it. Sometimes I feel sad when I'm around you, wishing I had what you have, but most times I feel so blessed to have friends like you that are in so great a love and show much love towards me. So I guess what they say is true. God may not always be there when you call him, but he's always right on time . . .

After finishing his card, Aaron reported to Aisha that Biggums was still messing with the girl that he had showed them on the computer screen. Aisha comforted him, saying, "Ronald is smart. It's just a phase; he'll be okay." Aaron gave her a look that said, "How are you so sure?" But Aisha did not respond. Keeping the energy upbeat and forward, she directed Aaron's attention to the painting. They opened it together, taking their time so they would not damage the package's contents. When it was unveiled, Aaron turned to Aisha and said, "I like it, but who is it?" "AJ, it's an original! It's Jacob Lawrence! Isaac and Katie are so cool! I love it! I love our friends! I love our gifts!"

"Hey!" Aisha continued. "I have an idea. Let's move in tonight."

"Tonight?" Aaron said. "The movers are coming tomorrow."

"I know. It'll be fun. It'll be like camping. We can bring my sleeping bag and sleep on the floor."

"A'ight. I'm with that."

"Great! And we can make s'mores!"

"S'mores? The stuff on TV?"

"Not just TV, AJ. You're so silly. Stop acting like such a city boy."

"But that's what I am, Mrs. Benjamin. I'm a son of the city. What I know about camping? Boy Scouts of America didn't come through my 'hood."

"Well, tonight will be your first time, sort of," Aisha said, giggling. "And we'll bring my flashlight and tell ghost stories! Let's go!"

Before going to their new home, the two stopped at the grocery store to buy marshmallows, graham crackers, and chocolate bars. They also had to buy batteries for Aisha's flashlight. Aaron collected some snacks and looked at Aisha and said, "Hey, it's our wedding night," as if to excuse them from deviating from the pledge to stay fit together.

Entering the lobby of their new home, the two were greeted by a tall, bald-headed, black man with glasses sitting at the reception desk. He looked to be in his early forties.

"How are we doing tonight?" he said, getting up and reaching to shake hands with Aaron.

"Very well, thank you," Aisha said, waiting for her turn to shake hands. "It's a great night, my man," Aaron said as he shook the gentleman's hand. "We were just married. I'm Jamal and this is my wife, Aisha."

"I'm Carl. Congratulations! So where's the party at? You're visiting tonight?"

"Nope," Aaron said. "We live here now."

"Right on!" Carl said. "Glad to have a brother and sister here," he continued after sensing that this statement would not be offensive to either of them. It was the way Aaron shook his hand, the way Aisha looked at him.

"Yeah," Aaron said. "Good to meet you, Carl. We'll rap, gotta roll now."

"Oh, oh, I'm sorry for holding y'all up. If ever you need anything, just call Carl. This is my shift. And welcome again."

Aaron had already begun walking away, pulling Aisha along. She felt it polite to remain still, hearing the rest of Carl's words. Aaron knew why she remained and pulled her anyway. Carl continued talking to them, talking to himself, in an excited tone as they entered the elevator.

Aisha never saw any of the luxuries that Aaron had added to her life being for her. But as they walked into their new apartment with its large floor-to-ceiling windows, high up, with a view of the illuminated Chicago Skyline North and the black vastness of the lake to the east, she was struck. There were no radiators in their new place, but she still heard the "yes" sounding. It was louder and clearer than ever, even in a place that she never saw herself being, among things that she did not think were for her. It was for her because she was with Aaron and they had gotten it together. It was new, a new start together. He liked it so she embraced it. Aaron helped to stretch her perspective. Expensive things did not have to be ostentatious.

Aisha was so consumed with her thoughts she didn't hear Aaron talking to her. He had taken a quick tour of their new home, jogging around it and saying things that Aisha was not focusing on. He came jogging back into the kitchen area where Aisha was standing and stepped on one of the grocery bags Aisha had set down.

"AJ, you're going to break the graham crackers before we even make them." With a smile, Aisha reached down and grabbed the bag off the floor, reaching in with one hand to pull the contents out and put them on the counter. When her eyes met Aaron's, she set the bag down and went to him. While interlocked in a passionate kiss, Aaron lifted her onto the granite, causing the bag to fall to the floor. Their clothes did not fall to the floor at first, just the quickest access to become one.

Eventually, they ended up on the floor. His back pressed against the hardwood floors, Aaron caught a distorted glimpse of himself in the reflection of the refrigerator as his head turned in ecstasy. He looked at Aisha on top of him. She knew better what to do now, although that did not matter much to Aaron. Every time they made love was uniquely beautiful to him. Aisha could have remained the same lover she had been on the first night, unsure and inexperienced, and it wouldn't have bothered him. He had already made peace with those thoughts, the fact that he had begun early and had known many lovers. He had done everything he had wanted that turned him on and nothing that didn't. Some, he began realizing when he and Aisha started reconnecting, his former life in stark contrast with the energy he felt in their early conversations, made him feel ashamed. Some of it she knew, but not all. She would never know all, no need. All had been washed away. He committed himself fully to her, the purging and purifying. He was innocent again, which he thought he could never again retrieve. There was no going back. But he had, by taking a step forward, coming back to Chicago and back to Aisha and her beauty, her goodness, her love, their unbelievable love. It came through faithfulness, before he even left New York. He couldn't see how it would happen but he believed. He believed and it worked out, came together. It rescued him from the path to everything and nothing, extravagant emptiness. Through faithfulness, listening to the voice that said believe. It looked like no way, but things began happening and he gradually let go and let himself be guided only by love.

Aaron and Aisha climaxed, shuddering against one another on the kitchen floor. They smiled happy, drained and fulfilled smiles, the afterglow of love's spontaneity upon them. It remained on them after they showered together, both soapy, sponging each other down and around over the smooth surfaces and hard-to-get places. They enjoyed the feeling of each other's hands. Rinsing and kissing softly, they toweled off hard and played around in their new bathroom, joking about the old bathroom and how rich they were now. Pointing at the fixtures, they laughed at how important they must be, talking in mock bourgeois voices. Aisha's laughter stopped her voice. But Aaron, as always, continued in the voice as if it were his own until Aisha slapped him playfully, telling him she wanted his voice back.

Fully dressed, they moved back to the kitchen. Aaron opened a chip bag and began munching, watching Aisha arranging the graham crackers, chocolate, and marshmallows. When she was ready, she asked Aaron to turn off the lights so the burners would feel more like mini campfires. With the lights off, Aisha turned the opposite burners of the stove all the way up. She jumped up on one side, sitting, and instructed Aaron to jump up on the other. She handed Aaron his skewered marshmallow and proceeded to roast hers.

"Bring it closer to the flame, AJ."

"Naw, I don't want mine burnt like yours."

"It's supposed to be like that, silly. It's better that way, trust me. Bring it closer." Aaron listened and moved his stick closer. When both of their marshmallows were nice and crispy, Aisha set hers hanging off the counter so it would not fall, but also so the marshmallow would not be smashed. She took Aaron's marshmallow and slid it off its stick in between two graham crackers. She then took off the top and placed a chocolate piece on the marshmallow and handed it to Aaron, waiting for him to bite it before she prepared hers.

"Damn, this is good! This is what I missed out on camping, huh?" Aisha laughed lightly.

"Yeah, and the sounds of the forest, all the creatures. And ghost stories! Ghost stories are next!"

"Who's going to tell them?" Aaron said with a mouthful of his s'more.

"You are. You'll be good," Aisha said, preparing her sandwich and taking a bite.

"A'ight, then I'm going to tell some 'hood ghost stories."

Before story time, Aaron fixed himself another s'more. They rolled out the sleeping bag in their new bedroom. First Aisha slid in and then Aaron, exclaiming, "This is a big-ass sleeping bag." Aisha replied, saying it was her father's. This brought silence. Aisha reached for the flashlight, turned it on, put the light under her chin, and said, "It's story time!"

After Aaron was done telling stories, he changed his voice to his version of a monster's. "Will you let the monster have you? Monsters need some, too. How come they don't ever show us monsters getting none in the movies? What's wrong with us? Always creeping up on other people doing it. We be killing y'all because y'all won't let us get none. Can the monster get some, damn!" He kept it up until Aisha started laughing, and before Aaron could fully transform back into himself he was into Aisha.

As they were falling asleep in each other's arms, the last thing they each thought about, each in his or her own way, were their fathers.

Something in the night made Aisha stir, making her realize that Aaron was no longer pressed up against her in the sleeping bag. Where was he? Aisha slid out of the sleeping bag then put on her panties and one of Aaron's t-shirts. She left the bedroom. Rounding the corner to the living room, she found Aaron standing, still naked, his head resting against the window. Aisha tiptoed behind him and stuck her arms underneath his armpits and placed her hands on his chest. She turned her head and rested it on his back.

"Hey there, Mrs. Benjamin," Aaron said, lifting his head from the glass, but not turning around. He reached one arm back and rubbed Aisha on the hip.

"Hi, Mr. Benjamin." The two were silent for a moment then Aisha spoke.

"How long have you been out here?"

"Not long. I really just got up. You felt me gone?"

"Yes. What's wrong?"

Aaron waited then asked, "Did the mother and father thing on the marriage license bother you?

"A little, you?"

"Yeah, a lot. I didn't show it though, didn't think it was going to hit me like it did."

"What happened?"

"You know, again, all in my face. 'You don't know who your father is.' You know? It hit me hard. Something about that moment. I don't know. It's like I'm almost an orphan. I mean, I barely knew mama before she died. We didn't have a lot of time. Pop Pop used to tell me a lot about her...I know you've heard all this before...it's different now, though..."

"No, AJ, go on." Aisha softly kissed Aaron's back.

"Star, we're going to have a family. We really are. And it's going to be healthy because we're going to see to it, know what I'm sayin'? Our kids are going to be smarter than us and they're going to have a better chance of being anything they want. We probably won't see a billion; maybe close. You never know. But our kids, they'll have a better chance than we did. Know what I'm sayin'? They'll only hear 'no' when they need to. Like you're always talking about, they'll dream big from the start. Family. A solid foundation. You know, I read a little bit of *Anna Karenina.*"

"You did!"

"Yeah, I heard one of the guys on the desk saying something about Tolstoy, some quote Tolstoy said about war. I can't let these cats be up on stuff I could know. I ain't never read Tolstoy, but I knew you had it. So one day I skimmed *War and Peace* a little then put it down and picked up *Anna Karenina* to get a feel of that, since it was next to it on the shelf. And you know, that first line in it is the truth. He had it right. All happy families are alike. We're going to be a happy family, Star. Ain't gone be no prolonged unhappiness in our house, uh uh. I was born into an unhappy family. Really wasn't a family, just me and mama. And he's right, all unhappy families are all different. That's all I saw growing up, all types of different unhappiness. It was regular, and we had fun in it! That's all we knew, know what I'm sayin'? Looking back, knowing what I know now, I don't know how I came out of it. What kind of person do you become when you come to see unhappiness as a way of life, an everyday thing? Look at me. You never see me. I've been trippin' off that. You know how much I've moved. Like these innocent shorties dying right now, all around where you teach. Burying their classmates is what they know. That's life for them. Just stuck, trying to get out. Getting used to funerals for your friends. We were just shorties. That was my life. And now it's their lives. It's still going on. And I'm scared for you over there in Englewood sometimes, you know? Sometimes I think you should just quit before some shit happens. I know I shouldn't think like that. And I know you won't quit no matter how large I get...You're doing the right thing, the stuff that most of us don't do. Don't even think about. And I just got to believe you'll be okay. All the shit that I been through, I turned out okay. But how? That's what I've been trippin' on. Why did I make it? How? And like this? Look at us, Star. I never thought about nothing like this growing up. Family? Drunk, pimpin', hustlin', gun-totin', gang-bangin'-straight-gangster-nation uncles. Smooth, slick-talkin' uncles thinking they on it, teaching you the wrong shit. Drugged-up mamas, mamas living off their children, mamas working crazy hours for pennies and watching their kids get ate up by the streets. Everybody chasing something, all the wrong shit. No love, mama's there but gone and Daddy's long gone. Never there. None of my friends lived with their father. Not one. And only a couple daddys even came around, but if they did, they weren't on anything positive. They were like just another dude in the neighborhood. Daddy just in name, know what I'm sayin'? But kids used to be happy just to say it when their daddy came around. 'My daddy.' Just feel happy to feel that they got a daddy, even if he ain't on shit. You know how lucky I was to have Pop Pop? He was the daddy for most of the neighborhood. I remember going to basketball tournaments and seeing a few real fathers, like, coaching their sons and rubbing them on the head and stuff, and looking at them like they were a myth. You know? I didn't really see Pop Pop as my father until I got older. The older I got, the more I appreciated him. He beat out a lot of my bad habits. And I hated him at first. But he loved me. And I started seeing it and I started loving him back. And when I lost him…I mean, what made me so different? Why did Pop Pop break through with me and not Mama? Did he change? Was it me? Was it mama? Why me, you know, like this, with you? Look at us. I know I've worked hard and all, but there's a lot of people that work hard. So what made me so different? I worked hard, but I also got lucky a lot. Or was it luck? And if it's not luck, why don't others get it? You know why I was so mad that day the Bentley got stolen?"

"No, why?"

"I'm just now figuring it out myself. I had to think back on my mood, what was on my mind at the time. And I was in your Saturday school thinking all of these kids can go on and be outstanding in their own way. I was feeling real good about the shorties in the neighborhood and then I come outside and the car is gone. And then the police were all nonchalant, like it's just expected in that neighborhood. Like that's just the norm and no change is even close. Like that's what I get; that's what I deserve. The muthafucka didn't even know me, but he looked at me like he knew my whole history. Could just sum me right up. But even in all that unhappiness in the 'hood, when I was growing up there was so much talent, so many distinct personalities. You know all my stories. All the dudes in the 'hood I grew up with. These cats had color and they were brilliant in their own way. I was always good at math and a lot of my homies could hardly add or read a lick in the classroom, but you get them on the street and they would come up with some shit! I mean, you talking about ghetto inventions, deductive reasoning, figures, figuring stuff out, but it all went to the wrong place. And like now, it's worse than ever. Daddy's still gone, more gone, it's like middle class gone now, even muthafuckas with money. Kids only knowing one parent. Like that's what's up! It's like everyone just accepts it. Just being the same. And I'm not in the 'hood like I use to be; haven't been in a long time and for real, Star, I'm troubled by the struggle to stay there in some way. Look at where we are now—Soldier Field, the lake, the *Aisha Star* somewhere down there, me and Isaac about to pull this thing off. This stuff is far away from where I grew up. It's just down the street, but psychically, you know? It'll pull you away."

"If you let it. You can't let it."

"But baby, you're special. Nobody has what you have or they don't want to have it and that's what I'm saying. Everybody wants to be the same. You're different. Everybody wants what they think everyone else wants. Like these shorties; they're losing their personalities. They all want to be Jay-Z. And I understand. Hip hop helped keep me sane comin' up. We both love it. But it's just one thing. It's so much out there. But they're not paying attention. No one is paying attention. Even the so-called sophisticated folks, they want to be that nigga, too. But I ain't never heard none of them talking about my song! Don't nobody talk about 'Meet the Parents.' That's one of dude's greatest songs and don't nobody *ever* talk about it. This dude rapped how it all break down in the 'hood and issued the realest challenge and nobody heard it! He rapped my life! My homies' lives! All of us could have been staring down the barrel of the gun like that. We did stare down it; some of us just didn't get shot, but we still affected! Look at Biggums; he's making it better than most, but that nigga still strugglin'. I was saved by Pop Pop and Grandma Benjamin. How come nobody focusing on that? But I don't care. Let's do us. This is real. You help me stay real. I got stay..." Aaron turned around and faced Aisha for the first time.

"You will. We will," Aisha said.

"I love you, Star."

"I love you, too."

"Dang, I was just going, huh?"

"I'm glad."

"I just have so much on my heart, man. Things are happening so fast. I want to be so much. I want to be a good father, but is that the only thing? Should I just work on our family? How to keep it balanced? I don't know?"

"You don't have to. I don't, either. We'll figure it out together."

Chapter 12

Aisha nearly told Aaron about her desire to see her father on their wedding night, while Aaron vented pressed against the window. Though the mood seemed right, she knew the moment could not contain her adding her feelings. She did, however, bring up her feelings about her father a few days later as she and Aaron watched TV together. The sharing was a continuation. She had already told Aaron about the dreams. And from the dreams she moved to the things she had held back for so long.

When she dreamed the dream again, she stirred, waking Aaron, prompting his concern and awaiting ear. She told him about the letter she received from her Great Grandmother Johnson not long after her mother's death. What a great betrayal. It was all too much. And she took her hurt, her confusion, out on Robert because he was the only one in on it who was there. But it was not about Robert, it was about her mother, who was her biggest believer and her best friend, gradually becoming so after their battles after her father left. All those years her mother knew her father's whereabouts. And her father's grandmother had known, this woman who wrote to her as if she knew her, as though the subterfuge could be excused in the wake of her mother's death. No. How could they? They never told her.

Reading the letter, Aisha discovered that her mother had been in secret communication with her Great Grandmother Johnson. It had been going on since she was a little girl. At once, she demanded that Robert show her all record of this cloaked relationship. Following behind him to their bedroom, she watched as he went into her mother's nightstand and pulled out a stack of letters. How had she not discovered them before, in such an obvious place? Yes, there all the time, in her face. She had jumped up and down on that bed, hung her head down to the floor, lay her head right next to the nightstand and dangled her feet by it while reading many times before. Never once did she think to look in it. She thought she knew all there was to know about her mother. They were together all the time and her mother was predictable and plain, especially after marrying Robert.

Aisha summarized the contents of the letters for Aaron. She had read each one twice, right after her mother's death, and, a short time later, furiously denied the existence of the letters and Grandmother Johnson. The letters were left in their place until she returned from Africa. Robert seemed to be getting serious about Susan, so she took possession of the letters, keeping them with her from then on but never reading them again. The words and the woman—her so-called grandmother who seemed to write only about God and the Bible and some of her activities in some small town in Missouri, no gossip, nothing deeply personal, never mentioning her father, just what the Bible says and advice to her mother—did not matter to her.

That is how Aisha remembered it as she reported to Aaron. And there remained questions, like the dreams, which would not go away and only grew in urgency, more bothersome over time. Even as she went away and was transformed by her experience at Harvard, where she grew and flourished, getting along well after her mother's death, accepting life on its terms and adapting well, the questions remained. Why did her mother never tell her about this link to her father? Why did she lie? Who was this woman that her mother felt the need to consult? How was it they seemed to never discuss her father in the letters? Did her father also know where Aisha was all along? Was he somehow in on it, too? Did this woman, her grandmother, tell him? If so, she never mentioned it in any of the letters to her mother and he didn't care, anyway. He never tried to contact her.

After Aisha opened up to Aaron that night, she decided to write her Great Grandmother Johnson. She pulled one of the letters from the old stacks she had stored away to get the address and mailed off a letter to Haveton, Missouri. Eight days later, she received an excited response back from Grandmother Johnson. It read in that all-too-familiar script, that familiar tone. She found out her father was still living and not far from Grandmother Johnson. Come to find out her father always talked about her. Grandmother Johnson saw him often and thought it would be a good idea if she came to see him. Aisha agreed.

She let Aaron read the letter. When he finished it, he looked at her and said, "When you feeling it, let's go!"

Chapter 13

Aisha surprised Aaron with news that she would be teaching as a part-time faculty member at Malcom X College. She wanted to overcome her fear of speaking to adults, especially ones she did not know. She found herself more and more giving impromptu teaching lessons to her students' parents. Why let her personal shyness around adults limit her from using her skills as an educator and helping them if they were open to it? So, at the beginning of the summer, she began teaching two free noncredit courses, Adult Basic Education and Literacy. Though she did not have a Ph.D. or Master's Degree in English, her Master's degree was in education, her undergraduate curriculum at Harvard and the Hoopes Prize she won for her thesis "The Transformative Child in the Works of Toni Morrison" enabled her to teach a credited class to associate degree seeking English students. She called that course dessert. Each summer night after Aaron returned home and had his bowl of cereal, he would listen to that day's story in higher education. With so many personalities, now including adults, Aaron never tired of hearing the stories, especially because Aisha told them with passion. He liked when she'd come to life and speak without breathing. Normally, he was the one of the two who would speak that way. Aisha opened up the most with him, more than she ever had with anyone else.

Aisha's sense of style also surprised Aaron. She always talked about how stylish Raven and Kiki were, but without consulting them, she had outfitted their apartment in a stylish décor. She even surprised herself. In her free time from teaching enrichment classes during the week at Richard Wright, and her college courses Monday through Saturday, Aisha searched all over the city, and for some pieces online, to add feeling, character, and warmth to their new home. The only items she had kept from the apartment on South Shore were her two reading chairs, her clothes, and her books. Out of all her outfitting, the building of her new bookcases excited her the most. She spent a long time finding a contractor to match her excitement. When finished, she had more space to add new books. New books to read—the summertime was perfect for that.

Chicago summers are a beautiful time. The city comes alive; the expectation, the build up and all that release in three months of heat. By the lake, there is peace: jump in, swim, splash around, play around, volleyball and throwing balls, playing on the sand, in the sand, sand castles, laying out on it. Look at all the people, up and down me, by me, free. Walking, running, skating, biking, boating, motoring along, spending long summer days anchored. Shirts off, shoes off, skin exposed, and the smells that enter the nose. Cooking out, barbeque, and the sounds that enter your ears. Soulful sounds that you hear, coming from sound systems, coming from chatter, coming from children's laughter, as they chase one another around trees, around cars, over legs and hands, around the sizzling grills, accidental spills on the grass, Mother Earth drinking it up. And the reprimanding, though it doesn't sting. Pausing and running again, mouths open, swallowing the summer air.

Have a drink by my bars, Rock 'n' roll sounds of the summer. Have drinks from personal bars, coolers, stashes in the trunks of cars, crisp beers in hand, reminiscing with those that love you most. Laughing with them, living in the moment with those that you love most, or most in that moment, liking, fleeting, loving and liking. Summer fun, tension rising, tension undone. See strangers coming together, big problems, then no problems. Problems by me, why would there be? There is no place for blues by my blue, under the blue sky, under the yellow rays of the sun, always making life possible. Summer time in Chicago is when life is most livable.

Living and loving fully, Aisha and Aaron spent most of their time by the lake, with friends on the South Side or with friends on the North Side. All the things they had imagined doing with someone they loved, they did. Aisha shared with Aaron her fantasy come true as they walked and stopped by Buckingham Fountain on a quiet night, with its spout of water and colors in the night sky, the wind blowing sprinkles in their faces.

Along with exercising and relaxing along the lake, going for rides on it, spending weekends on it, Aaron and Aisha watched movies in parks around the city. Movies they had not seen or all-time favorites, spread out on their blanket, gazing up at the screen along with other families, other couples in love, some loners, and some who were alone for the time, who did not mind seeing movies by themselves; parks on the West Side, parks on the North Side, parks on the South Side; favorite or curious films bringing a Northsider to the South side, Southsiders and Northsiders to the West Side. They dined in the many restaurants across the city, popular fancy restaurants and tucked-away small neighborhood gems. Occasionally, Aaron left Museum Park to go deeper on the South Side, back to 71st, for some Harold's fried chicken. Grease and brown bits would be left on his lips as he chomped away and teased Aisha about what she was missing. The two often walked to Millennium Park to rest on the grass in Pritzker Pavilion and enjoy the symphony; once they went to Ravinia to see a virtuoso, once to Lollapalooza to see three rappers, two of which were from Chicago, one of which was quickly becoming Aaron's favorite and internationally known. Once they went to the Art Institute because Aaron had never been, once to a night club to meet a few of Aaron's Wall Street friends in from New York, Biggums joining in, once to the Printers' Row book fair, once to a new comedy club in Bronzeville, where Aisha and Aaron falling against each other in laughter. Once they stayed in and hosted an event themselves, their housewarming.

The housewarming was a success. They managed to get such an eclectic bunch to mingle and have a good time. From Dr. Haywood, to Isaac and Katie, to Raven and Kiki and their children, to Robert and Susan with Justin and Biggums, who competed all night for Raven's affection with a young trader from Colossus, and other Colossus traders and other faculty members from Richard Wright and other persons from Aaron's dealings here and there, all had a good time.

When the housewarming night drew to a close, only Robert, Susan and Justin, Raven, Kiki, their children, and Biggums remained. Seeing that the numbers were good, Aaron suggested they all take the *Aisha Star* out on the lake. If they hurried, they could catch the fireworks at Navy Pier. All eagerly accepted and before long two carloads of the Benjamin's and their guests pulled up to the marina.

Aaron and Aisha led everyone to the yacht. On the way, Aisha leaned over to Aaron and whispered, "AJ, I should pilot tonight." Aaron turned, holding a strange look on his face that gradually changed to understanding. He was drunk.

"You're right. You're right," he said. "Can you handle her?"

"I handle you."

"You gone handle me tonight?" Aaron replied with a smile. Aisha turned to see if any of their guests had heard him, because he had spoken loudly. She saw that none of them were paying attention to them. Norrell and Tyeisha were making "ooh" noises and pointing and the rest of the adults, in a more adult way, were doing the same.

"You not gone answer my question?" Aaron said, smiling, lightly pulling at Aisha's hand.

"C'mon," Aisha said, "and help me get everyone on." Aaron gave her a quick and light smack on the behind; Raven and Kiki caught him, and so did Tyeisha, now that the group had caught up to them. Aaron bent down and said, "Ty Ty, she's my wife. Husbands get certain privileges. Remember that." Aisha gave Aaron a look.

"What?" Aaron replied. "I'm putting her on game early…Okay, y'all welcome to the *Aisha Star*. You are our first group of guests and we are happy to have you come aboard with us. Before we step on, I'd like to introduce you to the skipper, Mrs. Benjamin. She will be piloting the vessel for us all tonight. She's a mighty fine pilot. I can vouch for her competence. I'm going to be in charge of safety and entertainment, but I need two helpers." Norrell and Tyeisha shot their hands up.

"Okay, got 'em. My helpers have to wear lifejackets. Anyone else who cannot swim, I'd suggest once we're on the cruiser you put on lifejackets, too. It's nighttime and we don't want any accidents. Biggums, your big butt will float, so I ain't worried about you, I—"

"All right," Aisha said, cutting Aaron off. At that, Aaron closed his mouth and helped Aisha get everyone aboard.

Aaron got the children's life vests on and gave more instructions, this time more brief because he realized he was being longwinded. Aisha pulled out from the marina and into the lake.

Each of the guests explored the yacht on their own. Aaron had grown tired of talking. He went to the bridge. Aisha was at the helm, putting them in position for a good view of Navy Pier and the fireworks.

Below, Norrell and Tyeisha chased each other through the cabin, nearly knocking Robert down. They pointed and called on things, "Bingo. That's mine. That's my room." Raven and Kiki called to them to slowdown, but not in a very forceful way, for they were just as enchanted with the interior of the yacht. Robert and Susan settled onto the couch and admired the scene. Biggums, who had already been on once before, sat too, admiring Raven.

After a short time, Aaron joined the group in the cabin. He had attempted to distract Aisha with kisses, touches, and talk of a quick lovemaking session. Aisha, remaining focused, lovingly bumped him away.

With Aaron returning below deck, all the guests complimented him on the yacht. Aaron graciously received their compliments, saying thank you. He began setting out refreshments, which Norrell took to right away. Tyeisha, now in a posture much like her mother's and for the moment done running around, sat and observed with a calm, mature look, calling Norrell greedy. In response, Norrell happily nodded his head, lifted his free arm, and flexed it.

Aaron continued to get the others more comfortable, showing them extra features below, and then he began telling them his version of how he covertly bought the yacht and detail for detail about the day he proposed to Aisha. It did not occur to him that he had already shared the same story with Robert and Susan on his and Aisha's recent trip to visit them in the suburbs. He could not tell by their expressions, for everyone listened to him as though it was their first time hearing it, even Biggums.

When Aaron finished the story, Biggums pulled him to the side and quietly said he would like to speak with him privately. Aaron looked around at everyone else. Seeing that things were fine, with Robert and Susan engaging Raven and Kiki in conversation and Tyeisha back to being a little girl again playing with Norrell, Aaron motioned for Biggums to follow him.

Aisha was nearly in position and Aaron shouted to her, "Mrs. Benjamin, you ready to drop anchor?"

"Yes," she responded.

Aaron motioned to Biggums again, saying, "C'mon help me drop this anchor." Aaron yelled up to Aisha again for the depth, when she responded he got the ratio for the scope and the amount of rode he needed in his head. He gathered the nylon line and handed Biggums the short length of chain.

As they maneuvered to the foredeck, Aaron explained the process of anchoring to Biggums, adding, "Listen, man, because I'm gone let you take her out with a honey one day. And you better not fuck my shit up. Got to get all the lessons in you can."At this, Biggums's mood changed, as did the need to talk to Aaron. He felt somewhat ashamed. What had he been thinking? Typically, he would not be self-conscious about his weight or the expressions that Aaron threw at him, but earlier, when Aaron made the joke about him floating, he did. At the time, he felt the comment belittled him and portrayed him in a bad light. It may have damaged his chances with Raven. Did he see her laugh at the joke? But watching Aaron and Aisha work hand signals in the dark, Aaron commenting how they came up with them together, the two together a short time later dropping the anchor below, waiting for the dig and hold, and it holding, he realized Aaron was being who he had always been. He had changed, but then he had not. Aaron was the same person who stood up for him when Carnella Jones tried to alienate him in front of everyone, saying he spoke like a white boy, especially in front of a girl he liked at the time. He was the same person around the same time that had warned him about joining the Black Stones, but did not treat him any differently when he did anyway. He was the same person that Wayne had referred to before he took his own life, saying, "Ronnie, stay with Jam, mayne, stay with him. He on some other shit right now, but he got love for us, for real."And he knew how Aaron acted when he drank.

"So, what did you want to talk about?" Aaron said, laying down on the foredeck and motioning for Biggums to do the same. All the other guests had come from the cabin and were sitting on the deck, marveling at the glow of the skyline. Aisha had come from the bridge to join them.

"Ah, I know. Your ass want to talk about Raven, don't you?" Aaron said.

"Yeah," Biggums responded.

"I peeped that. She too old for you, ain't she? Your chester ass. She 'bout ten years older than how you like 'em."

"I know. I know."

"And she got a shorty."

"He's a cool little dude."

"Yeah, Lil Rel is my little homie. So what's up?"

"Nothing. I'm just feeling her."

"A'ight, cool. Have some confidence, dude. I keep telling your ass, women love confidence." Aaron reached out his hand for Biggums to shake it. "You're golden, dog, remember that. Fat as hell, but golden."

Biggums nodded his head and the two got up to join the others.

The rest of the night Biggums got less attention from Raven then he had at the party. Though his efforts were solid, natural and unforced, she didn't seem interested, her mind in a different place. So he backed off. It bothered him for a brief time, seeing Robert and Susan, Aaron and Aisha, but when the fireworks began going off, illuminating the sky with bright colorful, fantastic flurries, a calm feeling came over him. For the first time in a long time, he felt content with his life, with living.

Chapter 14

Late in the summer on a Friday, not long after the housewarming, it occurred to Aisha that the entire summer had passed and she had not sought out her father. The new school year would begin soon, which meant there was little time to do so.

She had thought of it often. When to go? But the allure of summertime in the city with Aaron, great weekends, her college courses and her regular students, pushed the idea of the trip to the back of her mind each time the thought arose. As she was on her way to meet some of her continuing education students for dinner (they invited her in appreciation, in the reluctant celebration of their class's end), she felt she had to go find him that day, especially if Aaron was to go with her. At the dinner, she could hardly enjoy herself, such was the overwhelming feeling that she had to go.

It was nine o'clock by the time she arrived home. Aaron arrived a little over an hour later. He and Isaac had met for drinks at a bar on Rush Street. Upon greeting him, in his embrace, Aisha found that his breath didn't smell much of liquor and his eyes were clear and wide.

"You didn't drink much?" she asked.

"Nah, I had a couple drinks, but that was earlier in the evening. I got caught up talking with Isaac and really didn't have a taste for liquor after that."

"Are you okay?"

"Yeah, I'm all right."

"No, you're not. What happened? Did you and Isaac get into another argument?" Aisha said, walking with Aaron to the couch and sitting down with him. Before answering, Aaron paused, kicked off his shoes, and put his feet up on the ottoman. Once again, it took everything in

Aisha not to blurt out what was on her mind in his moment.

"Nah, just a heated discussion about the market, about my strategy. He's getting gun shy, you know? I kind of understand; it's his group, he got it to this point. But what I've brought is going to take it to the next level. I mean he knows the numbers. But it didn't come from him, so he doesn't trust it all the way. He has to go big. Know what I'm saying? This is big. If we play it right, the money will be crazy. Might be a once-in-a-lifetime opportunity." Aisha began massaging Aaron's shoulders. She hoped her hands could somehow communicate her heart before her mouth spoke it. She hoped he could hear her, feel her through her touch.

"Star, sometimes I think me and Isaac aren't meant for the long haul. You know? Like, I might have to start my own group." Aisha didn't respond; she stopped massaging him and looked in his eyes. What should she say? What could she say? Her emotions were in conflict. She said nothing.

"What do you think?"

"It's hard to say."

"Huh?"

"I mean, AJ, I believe in you. Whatever you choose to do I'm with you."

"Uh huh… Now, what's up with you, sounding all funny?"

"I'm sorry; I've been listening. It's just," Aisha hesitated. "I think tonight's the night we should go see my father."

"Tonight?"

"Yeah, I mean this weekend's the best weekend, the only weekend."

"What? Why?"

"Well, school starts in a couple weeks and I need all of next week to prep. And also I forgot next Sunday Raven, Kiki, and I are meeting with some parents in the neighborhood."

"That's cool; but why not leave in the morning?"

"I thought of that, but it's a seven-hour drive and that wouldn't give us much time down there."

"Star, that doesn't make sense."

"I know. I know it doesn't, but I just think we should go now."

"Star, four hours isn't going to make that much of a difference. We've both had long days."

"I know, okay, you're right. In the morning. You're coming with me, right?"

"Naw, Superstar, I'm staying here," Aaron said sarcastically.

"Okay, thank you." She kissed him. "I love you," she said moving toward him for another kiss. That kiss motivated the stripping of clothes and them making love on the couch.

Lying together naked, neither was drained by their lovemaking session but felt energized. Feeling adventurous all of a sudden, Aaron turned to Aisha.

"C'mon, let's go right now."

"Really? Right now?"

"Yeah, I'm ready."

Aisha laughed and said, "No you're not, you're naked."

"And I'm ready. I'm gone go like this. Meet Grandma J like this. 'Hey Mama J, pleased to meet cha!'"

"You're so silly."

"Nah, but seriously, you got the directions and stuff already?"

"Yes."

"Then let's go."

"Really? Are you sure? We don't have to."

"Let's roll baby. Pop Pop used to tell me all the time how he used to drive from Mississippi to Chicago through the night. He liked riding like that better. So, it's in my blood and I've never done it." Aaron started moving, as if readying himself to get up. "C'mon, if I get tired we'll just switch or pull over." Aaron stood up and began putting his underwear on.

"AJ, at least shower first."

"Okay, c'mon in there with me," he said, walking in the direction of the bathroom.

"AJ…" Aisha said, smiling.

"Girl, we just washing together to be fast. My turn around time ain't like that."

"I could get you going."

"You can, huh? Now who's being nasty? Look what I've done."

They had made it to the bathroom.

"Uh uh," Aisha said, turning the water on. "It was always there."

"Then you fooled the hell out of me."

"You couldn't see that I was waiting for you?"

"No more waiting."

"Yes, no more."

Aisha had already packed their bags. After Aaron took a quick look in the mirror, he grabbed the bags and went to the kitchen to grab two bananas and two apples. They left the apartment. Making it to the ground floor, the doorman, Carl, greeted them as they left. He asked where they were going. Aaron said, "Taking a road trip, man. We'll holla at you when we get back."

They drove Aisha's SUV north on Indiana, making their way eventually to Interstate 57.

From the time they pulled out of the garage, Aaron talked non-stop, from his different voices to genuine, regular excitement over what they would discover. At some point, he began questioning aloud. How were Grandmother Johnson and her father, really? How did they live? What was the small town like? What did Aisha think she'd say when she saw him? Taking glances at Aisha, he could see that his questions weren't having a good effect on her. She was not matching Aaron's enthusiasm anymore and was kind of stammering through his questions, not really answering them at all. A weary look began to come over her. Aaron decided to be quiet. They had been on the road for about an hour and a half.

"Are you all right?" Aisha asked in a weary voice.

"Yeah, I'm cool. I'll let you know if I'm not." At that, Aisha reached over and rubbed the back of his head and fell asleep.

As he drove, Aaron's mind continued to race about Aisha's father.

Aisha told him that her father had once, for some years, been a player in the National Football League. Aaron recalled then, as he sometimes would, the feelings he had once held so close about playing professional sports, his love for basketball. He used to dribble the basketball everywhere and the court was hallowed ground. Everything in his world went away once he stepped foot on it. He saw nothing but triumph on it and alone the net's string music was the sweetest sound. With others, in quick competition, the yells and shit talking, the feel of pure exertion and something about his deep devotion for it ever since he received his first ball as a boy, the honor in it, starting on the playground but moving beyond, it helped save him. He and Isaac connected early because they saw in each other that understanding, though their worlds and their athleticism could not have been more disparate.

Aaron was content with his place in life, but there remained the curiosity of how it would be to play at the highest level, matching up daily with the athleticism at that level, pitted against the best minds in the game. A level playing surface, man versus man and the grandiosity of that stage, the feel of its rush. So many thousands watching and cheering in person, millions more from their homes, all that fanfare, people putting their hopes in you, heroic nights, many remembering you all their lives. Making a good living doing something you had done since childhood, dreamed about since childhood, acted and reenacted magical moments that could be manifested under the brightest lights, on the greatest of fields. How did that feel? Still, there was the comedown correlation. It came to Aaron again. He had first thought of it in a pulled-back moment in New York, partying with some NFL players in the V.I.P. section of a nightclub. He could work in his business for the rest of his life. They could not. That inevitable coming down from that high up, he also would not ever know about. What was it like for Star's father coming down? Maybe someday his son would understand what it meant to be him, while he grew and worked to make himself his own man. He would make it so all his son's questions were answered. His son would not have to imagine what his dad's life was like. There would be no fantastical imaginings and destructive dismissals, leaving great craters that never would be filled, even in driving down. His son would not have to drive anywhere to get to know him. He would be there, always, real, however real life became, no matter what.

As the road grew darker, with just them on it, it seemed to Aaron that the road would disappear, as if he were driving on nothingness. He pushed steadily along for hours, fueled by his thoughts. Thinking of Pop Pop motivated him. Pop Pop was looking down on him, proud of what he had become. Aaron remembered all of his stories and on that dark road, he happily replayed them in his mind. He replayed the times Pop Pop described his mother, in her happy days. He could only vaguely remember happy days by himself with his mother. Full days of happiness were hard to come by, but he liked to believe there were once happy days. Pop Pop told him stories about his mother as a little girl, how things Aaron did reminded him of her when she was younger, how smart she was. She was independent, too. He had a favorite story that Pop Pop told about his mother trying to cook the family breakfast when she was five. She had gotten out of the bed before everyone, stacking telephone books to get her ingredients from the high parts of the refrigerator. She crawled deep into the cabinets to get the pots and pans she needed, being quiet and not banging at all for fear of waking her parents. She, again, used the phonebooks to stack them near the stove, grabbing a third phonebook because she needed more elevation over the stove to cook her masterpiece. She determined it best, however, to prepare her ingredients on the floor. She dumped the ingredients in the pan and looked at the stove to figure out how she would get above it. With her cooking station set up, she proceeded with her plan. She cracked eggs and whipped them with pieces of shell floating around in the egg yolk. She let that sit. Then she pulled out the bacon and put it in a pan. She lifted herself onto the phone book and turned the pilot on, lighting it as she had seen her mother do so many times. She got back down off the phonebook and grabbed the skillet with the bacon inside it and lifted herself up, holding it with one hand as she had imagined. The heavy skillet wobbling in her other hand was nearly vertical to the ground, but the bacon stayed, although one piece curled toward the bottom; she hoisted the skillet over her eye. She looked at the egg yolk, with the pieces of shell floating in it, but knew it wasn't time for that yet. Next were the homemade biscuits.

From his bed, Pop Pop said he smelled bacon cooking. When he looked over and saw his wife still sound asleep, he leapt up from his bed and went downstairs to see what was going on. He found his little girl, with a mess of batter scattered on the floor, on her hands, on her nightgown and on her face, the eggs still on the floor waiting to be cooked, the bacon cooking. She looked up at him and said, "I'm cooking a good breakfast, Daddy." Indeed she was. He did not spank her, though he told her it was wrong and she should never do it alone again. He helped her finish the meal and when Grandma Benjamin woke up, she woke up to breakfast in bed.

Aaron liked that story the most. He liked imagining his mother as the little girl by the stove. Many of his happy times were with his mother in the morning, her cooking him breakfast. She never failed to do that.

Aaron looked over at Aisha. She slept so soundly. How beautiful she was. This trip must be a lot on her. He began to grow tired and the nothingness feel of the road occurred more often. He kept pushing on, determining he would pull over if it got too bad. He wanted to surprise Aisha with the progress he had made and impress Pop Pop with his stamina. He drove on with his eyes heavy, squinting, and slowing down because the lines began to blur, the nothingness even greater. Then he looked over at Aisha again and thought of the family they would have. He'd tell his children about this trip one day, how he and their mother popped up and decided to go look for granddad. He decided it was time to pull over. When he looked back to the road, he could see a faint line of pink on the horizon. The sky was lighting up. The sunrise was near and in that moment, he didn't feel tired anymore.

Aisha waking. Rolling. Tossed hard against something. Aaron!

I am sitting on the ground. Where am I? How did I get here? My truck. Upright. Aaron still in the truck. His arm hanging out the window.

He needs help. A woman in front of me, looking at me, concerned. She's in a white uniform. My face hurts. My head hurts. Why is she not helping Aaron? Her face is round, white. I must go help him. Stand up. Walk to the truck to help him. She's stopping me. Why is she stopping me? Why is she not helping Aaron? Aaron's hand is out the window. Look. He needs me. She's in front of me. "Remember him like he was," she says. I stop. Her eyes. What is that in her eyes? What is this?

It's morning. There are fields. This is a road. I am standing in the middle of the road. People around. Aaron's arm is hanging out of the truck. He's not moving. The truck is upright. The woman said *remember* him. Blood on me. Touching my face. Blood on my hands. "WHAT—IS—THIS! WHAT—IS—THIS! WHAT—IS—THIS!" It's not real. We were on the way to see my father. We were going from Chicago to Missouri to see my father and everything was fine. I was asleep and Aaron was driving. Aaron. What happened? "WHAT—IS—THIS!"

Her hands shaking, screaming, a voice she's never heard. Not her own. Who was she? This is not my life. Not this. This cannot be my life. It is. It is what? It is what? No. How? Please, no.

They were leaving me alone; now they are asking me to move. These people, the woman with the round white face. Paramedics. They are leading me to the ambulance. I am following. They want me to leave Aaron. Aaron. I'm leaving you. In an ambulance. They are asking me questions about family. Was there anyone? Please, miss, we must tell his family.

Part II

His cleft lip makes him look kind. He is kind. The cleft lip makes him look as he is. He's a slim man, white. He seems to be quiet, like me. He's been so kind to me. Caring, gentle, good care. He's giving me good care. He told me they would not be able to fix my face here because they don't have any plastic surgeons. My hand and face are bandaged. So is my arm. Everything else is fixed, though, he says. The MRI showed my brain was okay. It's the most I've heard him say. They can't fix my heart. He's a kind man.

Where is Aaron? Where have they taken him? He's not him anymore, but where have they taken him? Where is he in this place? Is he here? I'm uncomfortable in this bed, things sticking in me. I am lonely. I am not loved. There is no love. There is no one to love me. Alone, so alone, the room to myself. No one but the kind man coming in sometimes. He's a kind man. He said Ronald is on his way. I hope he gets here soon. I need him to be here. What time is it? How long will it take him? Where is he on his journey? I need him. I'm so lonely. Where am I? Somewhere in Illinois. I don't think we made it to Missouri. We. Aaron. Aaron, I'm sorry. I'm sorry. I'm sorry. I'm sorry. I'm sorry. I'm sorry. I'm sorry. I'm sorry. Aaron, I love you. I love you so much. Where are you? Where have you gone? I can't feel you. You're not here with me. Where are you? AJ, I'm sorry. I love you. Where is Ronald? Please come, Ronald. Please hurry; I'm so alone. I'm not loved. No love. Only the kind man. Why did this happen to me? Why did I feel like I didn't want to die before, all the flashing lights and them wheeling me around? "I want to live! I want to live! Aaron! Aaron! I want to live!" But I don't feel like that now, what was wrong with me? I don't want to live now. This is not living. Aaron you are not here and there is no love. I cannot go on. Ronald, please hurry. The clock. How long would it take for him to get here? I'm sorry.

Aisha continued looking at the clock, dozing off and looking at the clock again. When the nurse came in, she'd try to smile for him to show him she appreciated his kindness.

At some point, she looked over and Biggums was sitting beside her. The look on his face she had never seen before. It was serious and somber and sad and caring. How strange everything was. Sadness shrouding everything. Biggums was there by her side.

He told her that he called Robert and Susan and that they were on the way. He was called first because he was the last person who had called Aaron. Aaron's cell phone still worked. Hers didn't. He couldn't get in touch with Isaac, but he had left a message.

Biggums had left work right away. For some reason, he checked his cell phone when he usually wouldn't. If he was playing cards or joking with the other correctional officers or talking tough to the inmates or talking straight to the inmates, there normally was little need to check his cell phone. There was so little, but so much, going on in the jail. And his cell phone didn't get good reception in the jail, anyway. But he saw a number he didn't know, checked it, and left the jail right away. Crying and praying and cursing and silent, mostly silent, driving a hundred miles an hour the entire time, not worried about police. They didn't matter and he had a badge and gun. Always with his gun; he wasn't the police, but he could carry one. But that didn't matter. If he got pulled over he didn't know what he would do. What would he say? What happened? Nothing mattered; just get there. He drove all five hours with no music. It was on when he first got in the car but the sounds seemed wicked, not right. This situation wasn't right. He was not supposed to be getting that call. All was happy. They were all happy. He had begun feeling happiness again after so long.

Biggums didn't say anything to Aisha, just sat there by her side. Aisha was the first to speak. She asked if Biggums were comfortable sitting in that chair. He looked uncomfortable. This affected Biggums, made him think of better days, of Aaron and why he loved Aisha so much. But he didn't show Aisha this. He maintained his look and said, "I'm fine. Don't worry about me. Just rest, Star." He didn't speak or utter a sound again until Kaii called the hospital room.

Aisha was glad to hear Kaii's voice. Kaii told her that Robert and Susan found her number and called her, but that's all she said. Aisha did not want Kaii to feel so bad. No one should feel the way she was feeling. No one should ever have to feel that way. Aisha began talking a little. She didn't talk much. She talked about what was in front of her—Biggums sitting there, keeping her company. He was wearing a knock off, designer t-shirt that reminded her of Aaron, one of his jokes about Biggums. She told Kaii this and laughed, but Kaii didn't laugh and neither did Biggums. Aisha wanted them to laugh with her. She was surprised that she could laugh, had laughed. Where did it come from? They did not laugh with her. Biggums tried, his lips parted and he chuckled, but Aisha could see it was forced, the same look still on his face. She could laugh.But moments later, the laughter, as though it had never come out of her mouth, was gone.

Chapter 16

Biggums was familiar with funerals. Since his first funeral at the age of eight, his uncle's, he had gone to at least a few funerals a year for the next twenty-some-odd years. When he was fourteen, he went to eleven funerals in a two-month span. With so many funerals taking place at the time, he figured, if he were going to attend, he might as well go in the proper attire. So he bought himself a suit with the money he had saved from odd jobs. The suit came from the Salvation Army store. The prices of suits at other stores were too high. After realizing this, Biggums reluctantly ventured to the place his mother used to take him to shop. He loathed those trips. But finding a suit there, a suit that fit him and looked good on him, removed most of the stigma he had attached to the place.

Through the next wave of funerals, when his tear ducts no longer produced water and something began to change inside of him, he began noticing the pretty women in attendance. He felt a mixture of shame and shamelessness. Maybe they might notice him in his suit? Death and pretty girls; he only looked at the pretty girls without tears in their eyes.

Around that time, along with thinking about which girl he would pursue that month, whether it was a continued effort at one that eluded him or a new one, Biggums also thought about how death would come. Who would it come to? Strangely, he never thought about his own death. He never thought it could happen to him, despite most of the funerals being for young people from his neighborhood. There were many times where he did not know the deceased personally, but he always knew of them through a reputation or the friend of so and so or what's his name's cousin, so he had to pay his respects.

Biggums, Wayne, and Aaron attended a good number of funerals together. They befriended one another in a more innocent time just before a particularly bloody time. The bloody time lasted all through adolescence.

When Wayne took his own life, his mother could hardly function. Wayne was her sweet child. Putting aside his own grief, Biggums helped Wayne's mother through the proceedings. He was by her side at almost every step in the week after his death. He even slept at her home for a few days on the couch, refusing the bed. At night before going to sleep, he would look at the familiar things in the living room and remember when they were boys, Wayne bragging about how he was the best at kissing with his tongue. Or the time Wayne held on to a firecracker too long, it exploding in his hand and him calling himself the Juggernaut because he was left unharmed. "I'm the Juggernaut. Ahh! I'm the Juggernaut!" Wayne came up with BBA, its code of conduct and its mission to be the smoothest and get all the girls, and how Wayne joined the Black Stones because he didn't want Biggums to go in alone, him and Aaron fighting about it.

Now there was Aaron's funeral. He would coordinate it with the funeral home, spread the word, and eulogize his best friend. That was his plan. He worked at it as though all the spirits gone prematurely from his neighborhood were at his back, propelling him, Aaron especially making things easier from the grave. He had talked with Aisha about where the funeral would be. He spoke to her every day.

On that particular day, he had mentioned to her that he was going to the funeral home, telling her the time but not at all expecting her to show up. He talked mostly about details with her so she had some idea of what was happening and to fill the deathly silence on the other end of the phone. At the end of each of their calls, he assured her that everything was being taken care of and that she should rest.

But Aisha disregarded Biggums's order for her to rest. Unbeknownst to Robert and Susan, having taken the commuter line downtown, then multiple buses to the South Side of Chicago, somehow arriving at her destination, Aisha showed up in the reception area minutes after Biggums had arrived. Walking up, the sight of her alarmed the attendant sitting at the entrance of the funeral home. Aisha remained heavily bandaged, a big bandage on the left side of her face, her head wrapped like a turban and a soft cast on her right arm. It wasn't the dressings that disturbed the attendant so much, not Aisha's slow gait or the cloud of sadness that came in the door with her and filled the room. Knowing it was there, Aisha tried to smile to disarm people. She did to not want the sadness that was overcoming her to affect those in her presence. She tried to be strong, to appear not to be broken so they would not have to worry, though she needed them, needed the caring and loving expressions she received. But the smile didn't work on the attendant. She didn't see it. She only saw Aisha's eyes. The blood from her head injuries had begun to drain and it caused Aisha's eyes to darken to a deep, full red. The attendant thought surely, by the look of this woman, she should not be at her desk asking about Aaron Jamal Benjamin's funeral arrangements. She should be somewhere in bed.

But she did her job, greeting Aisha then leading her to the funeral director's office where Biggums and the director sat talking. Biggums shook off his initial surprise to help Aisha to a seat, introducing her as Mrs. Benjamin to the funeral director. The large man returned a look of sympathy, plus kind words that were stock but said with care. He began to tell Aisha what he had been discussing with Biggums.

Aisha did not hear much of the details in the meeting. What were these things they were talking about? Was there anything she wanted to place in the casket? She could not respond, just sat, looking. Where is Aaron? This strange man is going to take care of Aaron's body. Where are you, Aaron? Can you see this strange man? He is a great big black man, still with all of his hair. He has rings on both of his hands. Look at the ring you gave me; it's beautiful. So pretty, this ring you gave me.

Biggums remained composed throughout the meeting. Aisha's coming in helped him to focus. It made him realize whom he was being strong for. Turning some, he stole furtive glances at Aisha. She had not asked one question, just sat staring with those eyes that Biggums could hardly stand to look at. Seeing her eyes shocked Biggums out of the automatic way he had been moving. Even as he planned Aaron's funeral, the days after the accident moving by, it did not feel like Aaron was gone. It seemed as though Biggums could get a phone call from him at any moment, Aaron fussing with him and telling him what he thought he should be doing. But when Aisha walked into the room, when he looked into her deep-red eyes, which a few days ago had looked so clear and full of life and happiness, there was no uncertainty. He knew for certain his friend was gone.

After the meeting, Biggums led Aisha to his car. As he helped her in, he thought about how he would fix his words to speak to her. Though he did not know the ultimate responsibility Aisha felt, he knew she had to feel ultimately responsible for attending to her husband's funeral. He knew she felt she had to do something. That's why she made the long journey from the suburbs to the South Side. Robert and Susan were helping her make all the phone calls. He and Isaac had already worked everything out. Now he had to reassure Aisha as best he could.

As they drove, Aisha received the essence of Biggums's words, but none of the detail. She existed then only in movement, pushed along it seemed only by pain, that of her heart, pumping pulses of living pain throughout her body. A feeling of no feeling, hollow, soulless, the pain of living death, walking, sitting, lying, rising, the pain always there as though it had always been there, as if that was how her life had always been. How well she existed in this state. But why, what was the point? Aisha did not think this, but felt it ever so vaguely. She hadn't felt life since the hospital, since she was closest to death. After she had laughed, life left her. Only the pain remained. So each time she received a person's expression, those closest to her speaking directly to her, other details, people, things, did not register. A desk may as well have been a doorknob; strangers were not there unless they touched her. Things came to her through their essence, some comprehension filtered through the channels of pain. Nothing worked the way it once had.

But as she listened to Biggums, it occurred to her that she had come down there for something, but what? Yes, she wanted them to play "Precious Lord, Take My Hand." She had found the song in a fleeting moment of lucidity, something coming to her not of her own volition. She found herself reading about Coretta Scott King, who had died when it was cold and she and Aaron were newly living together. She remembered. And yes, she thought as every fifth word of whatever it was she was reading registered, I at one time enjoyed reading the books with her stamp on it to my students. My students? This song was played at King's funeral. Aaron was my king. With some curiosity, a vestige of what once was, yet still just moving in pain, Aisha looked up the song, finding Thomas Dorsey's story. He had created it from pain. He had lost his spouse, too.

Nothing about God, in the Dorsey story or the King story that lead her to Dorsey, registered with Aisha. To her, God was and was not. She did not feel God as she did not feel anything else. Just pain. So the words of the song meant nothing. She only knew that something felt like she should have it played. Things were being taken care of. Those close to her were taking care of things, telling her to rest, but what was rest? There was no rest. Biggums was saying the same thing to her in the car and her saying to him okay, still not receiving it fully. She said she wanted the song played. He said okay. They arrived back at the house that reminded her of her mother, where she and her mother once lived. My mother. AJ.

Biggums drove back to the South Side thinking he would have to return to the funeral home and tell them there would be a change in the program. Who could he have sing the song? In an instant, it came to him. He picked up his phone and dialed. The moment gave him a feeling of happiness in the sadness, a feeling of productivity in chaos.

◆　◆　◆

Isaac did not make it to the hospital to see Aisha. When he checked his voicemail and called Biggums, hoping he had heard Biggums's words wrong while the phone was ringing, some sick joke, Biggums told him to stay in Chicago. All the tests were done and Aisha had been cleared to leave at any time. Their medicine could do nothing more for her; her healing could be done at home. Isaac should just wait to see her at home because she would be there soon.

Isaac was the executor of Aaron's estate. Aaron had approached him about it after his second month living with Aisha. He had it setup before they consummated their relationship. He believed. Isaac did not. Isaac understood setting up the first will when you planned to start a family or even before in other circumstances, but he had advised Aaron to wait. They had only been living together for two months and they hadn't really seen each other in years. What if they didn't work out and something happened? Nothing was going to happen, of course, but, in principle, what if it did? Everything would go to her except for a portion to his friend Biggums? He wasn't saying that Aisha wasn't a nice girl. He knew Aaron was crazy about her since he first met her, but that was a long time ago and things happen and their business was tough on relationships. You had to make sure you had the right woman. Aaron said to him, "Dub, listen, there are things I haven't told you about me and Star. Things that are hard to explain to your friends, to anybody, if you're not there. You really have to be her or me. Know what I'm saying? Listen, I feel a hundred times more certain about Star than I do about the market and you know how strongly I sold you on that." Isaac's face changed; Aaron laughed and continued. "It's going to work, trust me. You have to trust me, man. With me and Star, there is no right or wrong. We just are, for real, and have been for a while. It just took me a while to see it."

Isaac did not understand where Aaron was coming from, and did not spend much time trying to. He had his own home to be concerned about and a business, much of it now hinging on a bodacious plan. So he accepted it. As time passed and he spent more time around Aisha and Aaron, he felt better about Aaron's decision, even better when they got married and he saw the way they looked and interacted with one another. He knew that look.

Now, how would he explain the terms of Aaron's will, the business, and their agreement to Aisha? Surely, she knew how much money they had or at least had some idea. But the future. How the hell was he supposed to talk about the future with her? Was he even supposed to? He had to. This was not the way…Why? Damn it. Why?

Discussing the plans and the provisions set forth with Biggums wasn't especially difficult, somewhat awkward, but not terribly difficult. Yet he dreaded his inevitable conversation with Aisha. He was not ready. How could he talk to her without all his emotion pouring out or not seeming too cold, having stuffed it all deep inside? He was more comfortable with the latter, but he didn't want to show that side to Aisha. She deserved better than that and it wasn't how he truly felt. How would he show her how much Aaron meant to him with all else? He had to talk to Katie. She'd help him sort things out. He had been hugging her more tightly after the accident.

Chapter 17

Kaii flew in from Los Angeles to Chicago around noon the day before Aaron's funeral. Though Susan had prepared the guestroom for her, she felt herself falling asleep in bed with Aisha. The abrupt silence there made Kaii aware that she was no longer talking. Since she got there, she had been talking nonstop, pausing only when she walked in and remembered Ms. Bowerman greeting her for the first time. Aisha and Kaii had met at a pre-frosh weekend and Kaii, being from Indianapolis, drove to visit her new friend and future Harvard classmate for a weekend. They had such an instant connection. Their strangeness fit, a truly compatible weirdness, unlike the fit with the other weird and talented future Harvard students that were there that weekend. Walking in, Ms. Bowerman stood watering a plant that then hung from the ceiling off to the left in the entryway corridor. The plant was no longer there, but she could see the circular impression from the base once screwed in. Ms. Bowerman immediately began talking to Kaii, which made Kaii realize that Aisha didn't get her seemingly silent nature from her mother.

Kaii looked at Aisha fading away to sleep, eyes still open a little though not looking at Kaii. She hadn't ever looked straight at Kaii while she listened, but now her look was distinctly away from her. A house in mourning, but Kaii had walked through the door with the same easy stride as she had over ten years ago. She looked over at her laptop, although now she wondered why she had even brought it in the room. She had no desire to write and probably would not the entire trip. She hoped that her toting it around, setting it on the dresser near the bed did not upset Aisha. She was just trying to be as natural as she could. The same went for her incessant talking. She hadn't seen Aisha in a long time, longer than normal at least, her being with Aaron, and Kaii, thankfully, being so busy in L.A. Aisha liked hearing about her Hollywood stories and all of her "I'm a black woman that Hollywood doesn't know how to handle." She had been talking that way since they met, making people choke on their contradictions. Aisha seemed to be listening intently with a gaze. Although not directly at her as usual, similar to the look Kaii was used to. But Aisha probably was not hearing her like normal. How could she? Still, Kaii talked on.

She had decided during the ride from the airport, with Aisha occasionally giving her gentle sad smiles, that she could not remain silent her entire time there. Aisha's stepparents could go along with it, but she couldn't. She would speak up, speak some life into the dead and deep quiet that struck her as soon as she stepped in from the noise and business of the airport, right after Robert asked the customary, "So, Kaii, how was your flight?" After she answered, offering a little more than the question demanded, it set in. Aisha was her dearest friend and now she understood loss. Though her experience was different from Aisha's, she would draw direction from it.

A few years after graduation, a year or so after graduating from USC film school, she lost her big brother. He was more like a father to her, given the gap in their ages, and the fact that her father did not know what way he wanted to be in her life. She would draw from her favorite aunt and her mother's best friend. Though her mother did not take her brother's death as hard as Kaii thought, maybe because they all had time, her favorite aunt, Stella, still greatly helped her mother. She was herself, prancing around with her squeaky voice and little frame, the frame Kaii often wished she had. She got her father's body—a body Hollywood didn't like—and with her gender and skin color, it left her with no chance. So she made the beautiful characters speak for the way she would have liked had she been able to be in front of the camera, had she looked like Aunt Stella or Aisha. Aisha never expressed any interest in that sort of thing and Kaii loved her for it. Her silence and unassuming humility had power.

As sleep began to take over Kaii, causing her to lie down next to

Aisha, whose eyes were now all the way closed, she wondered whether her talking had the power that Aunt Stella's had over her mother. Was it helping? Should she be silent with her friend, too? When her brother died, Aisha had sent her letters with funny drawings by her students and her descriptions. She listened to Kaii talk many nights, sometimes all night about her brother and how he always encouraged her, told her she was beautiful and gave her advice on men that she seemed to never take. Why didn't she take it? Her brother had been a late-blooming ladies' man, a ladies' nightmare. He had all of the charm and sweetness of a good guy, but with a new, unquenchable appetite for variety, new flavors. The transition was shocking to her and her mother. "You should see me and know better, Kaii," he'd say. Aisha listened to it all. She was always there to listen about the hellish kids that Kaii was nanny for, her wondering how the parents could be so cool, together, but their kids so bad. Aisha listened as Kaii wondered about getting her break and getting it and being happy, but sad her brother couldn't celebrate with her. Aisha was there to celebrate with her. How could she be there for Aisha? She hoped the talking was okay. Kaii gently rubbed Aisha's arm above the soft cast, rubbing softly until she fell asleep.

Chapter 18

For Aisha, Aaron's funeral and the week that followed opened her to love again and moved her away from it.

It began with her waking up from a deep sleep and, for the moment, not feeling the weight of her world and knowing where in the world she had awoke. She looked at Kaii and blinked. It all came back. It all moved fast, that morning, that day. Mostly, Aisha went along in the same way she had been since her feet walked her away from her hospital room, taking those precious steps from the site where all her hopes and dreams were taken in an instant. There was no separating the former from the present, her from Aaron. They were one, and now, alone, she lived as if she had died. Only her shell remained with a small piece of soul inside of her, not leaving, waiting for something, losing the battle to the living death and the pain.

She saw those close to her getting ready, saw herself getting ready, saw them leaving. She saw the passing sites on the highway out the window of Robert and Susan's minivan, a blur of colors, language she seemed to once know on big boards. She saw the funeral home, Biggums, him seeing Kaii for the first time, then Raven and Kiki, all making gestures to one another and to her, then leading her into the building and walking to the front. There were people there, then more people and then more. They sat in the front, the casket closed, Isaac and Katie with their baby, Ryan, her smiling at Ryan, her feeling infantile like Ryan, wake and funeral blended, all the same to Aisha. She saw and did not feel anything but that which she had been until a stranger walked up front, a woman, black, stout. She started to sing.

Aisha recognized the words, but not the sound, not the woman making the sound. Who was this woman making this beautiful sound, singing the words of the song that had come to her? In her ear now, slowly moving, moving and rubbing to life, moving, moving? So much life and sorrow filling the air. Who is this woman singing with the want of raising the dead, something coming out of her that felt not from her, disturbing Aisha?

I know her, but I don't know her name. She's from Aaron's past. I know Aaron's past, all of it. I wasn't there, but I know, I feel all of it. It is a part of me. He gave me all of him. I know him and I know her and her singing, this feeling, so beautiful I am feeling. I am here. Why did this happen?

She began to cry. Tears flooded from her eyes, overcame her, and wetted the top of her blouse. She lay against Robert, shaking, asking why did this happen, feeling her mother on Robert and her uncontrollable shudders and tears, squeezing Robert's arm so that her repaired arm hurt. She could feel the pain, a different pain, Robert holding her.

The woman had finished singing, but Aisha's tears did not stop streaming. Through her watery eyes, her head not leaving Robert's shoulder, she saw Biggums walk to the podium. She felt the words coming from his mouth and his own uncontrollable tears keeping him from being able to finish. She wanted to help him, hold him like Robert did her, but she could not move. Every part of her was paralyzed except her eyes. But she could feel. She felt Isaac rise up from his seat, place his hand on Biggums's shoulder, and take the tear-soaked sheets from Biggums's hand. Isaac stood and read with fervor, unerring, as if he had read it before, as though he knew the words by heart. Biggums, his head down, shoulders occasionally going up and down, leaned against Isaac. Aisha felt it all.

With the service at an end, she moved with those closest to her. They guided her to receive the people in attendance, standing by her side like guardians. She could not comprehend the words people said to her, so deafened was she by the enormity of the moment, so loud was the coming to life and death, but she felt the love they passed on. It came from those she recognized outwardly, like Bill Long, and some of Aaron's former Harvard basketball teammates and Jaysil and Doug,

Aaron and Isaac's former block mates from Harvard. Aaron's favorite high school math teacher, Mr. Weidel, and his favorite park district coach, some traders from Colossus, and Dr. Haywood and many teachers and parents from Richard Wright and some of her former students, Retita, Marcell, Kenyatta, Paris, Felicia, L'Terrick, Eliot, Portia, Kayln, Dwain now eighth graders, all came to pay their respects. Then so many more without names, who gave Aisha their names and their relation and a hug and she felt the many, many more in her spirit.

♦ ♦ ♦

During the next week, Kaii and Susan, and immediately following the funeral and the day after Raven and Kiki, consoled and coddled Aisha, putting salve on the scabs throughout her head and painting her fingernails and toes. They filled the home up with happy chatter, girl talk that had not been heard there since Aisha's prepubescent days, before things changed. From time to time, Aisha tried to remember the names and faces of Aaron's people she did not know, who said such kind things to her after the funeral. Once the week was over, she ceased trying to remember their faces and instead tried to hold on to the feeling of her girlfriends' laughter, the hearty sound of spontaneous love covering all the hurt. Everyone had gone on living, back to their lives: Kaii to California, Raven and Kiki back to Englewood, Susan and Robert working and raising little Justin. Aisha realized that it had to be, but it saddened her, made her realize the fullness of the great sadness in her and the pain, though changed in its character, was more pronounced.

Chapter 19

Aisha lived with Robert and Susan for a month after the funeral. In the beginning, she could judge the quality of her days by how much she dressed. Most days she never bothered to change out of the clothes she had slept in. The old porch swing that her mother used to sit on to read still remained on the front patio. Many days Aisha would sit out on the patio in the brightness of the day in her pajamas, reading and rocking. She read some of the favorite books she had left at the house and, though they did not move her in the way they once had, they took her to a different place, allowing her to exist in a place that was sure and familiar.

As her physical wounds healed completely—her eyes clearing up, the staples removed from her arm, new skin filling in the lacerations on her head and new hair poking out under the old hair that covered the cut marks—Aisha began to think actively again. She began to observe the world she had come to inhabit for the time being, starting with the room she spent much of her youth in. How much smaller it seemed. Her entire world used to take place in that room and she found herself in the same position, but a completely different place. She felt as though she had lived lifetimes only to be reborn in the same room that she had grown up in, looking at the same awards decorating every wall. She had once placed each award, the academic and athletic, with such pride. But there, sitting on her bed, staring at all the adornments, the accolades that once had great meaning in her life, all seemed insignificant, as though she were staying in the room of a stranger. Somewhere in Aisha's mind, she knew she had done those things. Now, tucked away in a small place, something would signal her that, yes, this was your life. You traveled the world as a child, you, your mother, and your minds making a way. You had pen pals in Sweden, Nicaragua, and Argentina. You lived in Senegal,

Africa, for a year, those pictures of shiny, dark, clear-faced children you once played with and learned new things from. Those medals you won running fast, faster than anyone in your school ever had, faster than most in the state ever had. You were told you would run in the Olympics one day, but you gave it up because it was not your dream.

Hate bubbled up big from a small place each time she recognized the dream that was not hers, until she remembered Aaron. Running, and the hateful conflicted feelings she felt for her father, led her to the moment she met Aaron on the track at Gordon. Each time she looked at the track medals, the love she had for Aaron and for that innocent time momentarily overcame the new hate she felt. She remembered them walking along the Charles River in the springtime. Long walks and long conversations, the beauty of the light bouncing off the Charles, the peace of those alongside it, rowers occasionally going down it; Aaron teased her for quitting running, saying she was trying to be like him when she did not even know him, did not even know he had also given up his sport in his freshman year for another path. They walked along the same path together with bright hopes for the future. Even with all the hype surrounding her, he somehow understood her walking away, even with her saying so little. They were special. He was special and now gone. Where was he? She could not feel him anymore.

After a few weeks, Robert gradually began asking Aisha about her finances. At the moment, Aisha cared nothing about fiscal responsibility, the frugality of her former self. However, the first time Robert questioned her, during a rare moment where all in the house were sitting together in the family room, the TV on, she answered him in clouded and unfeeling responses: She would be okay for money. Everything was on automatic bill pay. Aaron had taken care of things. Uttering Aaron's name stopped the conversation, causing her to stand up and walk back upstairs to her room.

Along with all the other bills that Aisha paid no attention to, the next month's cellular phone payment was deducted from her account. She had not used the service once since the accident. In fact, she had not bought a new cell phone or even thought to buy one. The only time she dialed the phone, which was the house phone, was to hear Aaron's voice still on his voicemail. She had done it a few times, but each time it grew more painful, a mix of joyful reverberations at the sound of his voice followed by the stark reality of why she could not hear it in person. So she did not call it anymore.

People kept up with Aisha. Kaii called every day to check on her and Raven and Kiki as well, though less frequently. Biggums had not called since the funeral.

A former high school friend and teammate came by to visit one day while Aisha lay in her bed, staring at the ceiling, thinking about the relief she would have if she did not exist anymore. The way she was living, could see herself living going forward, was not living at all. So why live? As she began thinking actively again, along with other thoughts about the world that she could see, thoughts of her end became more regular. Why was life worth living? The ominous threats of these thoughts, which Aisha had not yet grown comfortable with, caused her to cease writing in a journal, an old habit she decided to pick back up in an attempt to make sense and sort out the dark and nihilistic thoughts she had. But the writing brought awful things out of her mind, making them more real and increasing her burden, adding to her confusion. Kill yourself. There is no way out. The sadness will consume you. She should give in, stop fighting the futile fight. What was she fighting for, anyway? Where was the fight coming from?

While she was in this spirit, the doorbell rang and Susan called up to Aisha, happily, saying that she had company.

A part of Aisha wanted to tell Susan to tell whoever it was downstairs to go away. Yet another part of her was curious and yet, even another part of her, the part she had the least amount of understanding of, told her to get up and stop thinking those thoughts. So she rose and went downstairs.

When Aisha reached the bottom of the staircase, she saw Susan sitting on the couch, entertaining someone she had never seen, both women eagerly engaging each other to ward of any awkwardness that loomed. Aisha saw this and saw that her old friend Cindy was the woman that Susan made conversation with.

Aisha quietly joined the two women sitting on the couch. She said hi to Cindy, offering the slight smile that she had not been using, and waited until Susan finished talking. Recognizing this, Susan quickly wrapped up her conversation, saying she would let the two catch up, then went into another part of the house.

Cindy spoke first. Aisha put on the best face she could. Cindy remembered Aisha's quiet nature and had come over knowing what Aisha's situation was. She wanted to reach out and offer support, so she began talking. She complimented Aisha on how well she looked and took her hand, saying she was sorry to hear about everything. There was silence, so Cindy began talking about her life. She had gotten married right out of college, but was recently divorced. She had moved back in with her parents, too, she added. But realized that saying the "too" might not have been the best thing to say and tried to quickly clean it up. Her parents had told her about what happened and she decided, since she was back in the neighborhood, she would come over to see how Aisha was doing. It had been a long time.

It *had* been a long time. They had not seen one another since graduating from high school, and really, since they had stopped being friends their sophomore year of high school. They were once the closest of friends in junior high. They both played the violin in the orchestra. To start, they were the fiercest competitors—who would sit first chair?—and they both liked running. In the innocent days after the cruel elementary school days and before the sectioned-off high school years, there was a time when Aisha told Cindy everything. Cindy knew her mother. She knew about her first crushes on boys and how boys began to look at Aisha as she began to blossom. The junior high years were all friendly, race and cultural status not as important as fun and similar interests.

But arriving in high school, things began to change. As they aged, society's rules became more important. They became more aware of them, aware of the importance of fitting in. Aisha began taking her running more seriously while Cindy, her social life.

Shifting the conversation, Cindy began talking about track and Coach Reiss, how she should not have quit and how she still loved running today. She had been running to relieve the stress of her divorce. Aisha did not respond. Her running life was not her life. Her life was sadness. She could appreciate Cindy coming over to see her. She could see how Cindy was hurting. Her senses for pain had become acute. She could feel all the pain in the world.

She did appreciate Cindy talking about Coach Reiss. He had been like a father to her, and his passion for running became hers, beating for a time her conflictions about running for her father's dream. Coach Reiss had run against Steve Prefontaine and had wonderful stories about his running days. He fully accepted Aisha for who she was, for he was sort of an outcast himself. Not very popular in faculty circles, he wore his hair long, a mustache and beard covering his face, and taught history as it was. He lived life as he once ran and coached Aisha the same.

He was upset with Aisha when she told him she was going to stop running. She was not able to give him a good answer, other than the surface level academic answer, for she could not articulate all that had been there about her father. She and Coach Reiss hadn't talked about the past, just the future. They didn't talk for a while as a result of her quitting, but they made up during spring vacation of her sophomore year in college. Aisha worked out with the team all week. After practice, she and Coach Reiss had wonderful conversations, more mature ones.

He died suddenly while she was in Africa and she had not been able to come back for the funeral. She was comforted by Jawara. He had almost been her husband. But now, she had no husband anymore. Aaron was gone. Who could comfort her now? Cindy, sitting across from her, suffering, them separated by a society that teaches separation, that loves limitation. All was bad.

In this spirit, with Cindy having nothing more to say, and with Aisha responding only through slight, increasingly strained smiles, the visit ended and Aisha returned to her room.

Chapter 20

September passed into mid-October and other than the oval scar on the left side of Aisha's face, none of her physical wounds could be detected. Yet the improvement of her appearance did not coincide with the betterment of her spirit. Everything seemed dark. Even rocking and reading now bothered her. It was October. Why did it still feel warm? Where was the cool Chicago fall breeze? She should have a jacket on, not be fine in shorts still. This was Chicago, city of distinct seasons, but everything had changed. Even the weather did not remain the same. She had noticed it before. For a few years it had been that way; there were some on television discussing the subject, in journals and periodicals, passing people on the street obliviously embracing the warmer weather without question. "Ah, what a beautiful day!" Warm in November, warm in December; it never happened when she was a little girl or even a teenager. It would start getting cold in mid-October and continued getting colder until March. But even in March, winter always seemed to get the best of spring. What a short outdoor season they used to have. Often in the heart of spring the temperature was so frigid she would need to quickly put back on her sweats after a race to stave off the shivers.

Sitting and swinging in that unfamiliar October warmth was a constant reminder of her madness; even nature had lost her normalcy. She could no longer stand to read and rock outside, which was the only thing that had suspended the weight from her, for a time, stopped its depress, its gradual, day-by-day pulverizing. When she thought she knew what it felt like to bear the full weight, it got heavier. Now she could no longer read outside and inside Robert seemed to be forgetting how she came to be in her condition.

He started commenting on her improved appearance, but with each compliment, Aisha saw the softness, the tenderness with which he tended to affairs mere days after the funeral, a side of him she had never seen, begin to fade. Though Robert had always taken great interest in Aisha, it had been in a very matter-of-fact way, never perfunctory, but certainly not affectionate. Her affection came from her mother and in high school her mother and Coach Reiss, him hugging her after tough workouts and races, hugging her with affection he would let only Aisha and his family see. Living at Robert's increasingly reminded Aisha of them both, all the pictures with them both, all of the awards because of them both. And though her mother's gardens were gone, the rows of perennial flowers finally ceasing to break through the soil a couple of years past, when Aisha would swing in front she could swear she could still smell the scent of her mother's garden in the air. Sometimes she would imagine her mother there, crouched over, without gloves, proud of her peasant hands, talking to Aisha but not looking up from what she was doing.

The images that once brought slight comfort began to haunt her. What could she do with these ghosts? And the small room she grew up in, surrounded by all her former triumphs, how strange they looked now and how little they meant. It all began to suffocate her.

Robert, and to some extent Susan, though she still came in Aisha's room every night to sit by her silently for a time without either of them speaking, except to say goodnight when she rose from the bed, were back to the business of their lives. For Robert, this meant his focus on finance, an emphasis he every so often began directing toward Aisha. He and Aaron had not been able to meet to discuss Aaron's financial wellbeing or how he was managing his money, an event that Robert had eagerly looked forward to, reminding the couple of it each time he talked to them.

Aaron used a reference from Isaac to set up the estate. All of this Robert wanted to know. He asked Aisha, how was the estate set up? Was she sure she was protected? What were her plans? Financial plans were important to long-term, healthy living. "I know things are hard on you right now, but I don't think it would hurt to begin considering your financial future."

By mid-October, these types of insistent approaches, on occasion fought off by Susan, began to bother Aisha. All that Robert said may have been logical, this she realized vaguely in some place where logic used to make sense to her, and he had always been that way, but she could not stand it anymore. His questioning made her think of things she did not want conjured up in her mind and the derivatives of such thoughts. The thoughts did not make her feel better. She did not know if she even wanted to feel better. She did not know if she even wanted to live. How would she live? Even still, this talk of finance gave her a nothing feeling that made her feel worse.

Even if Aaron had not left her any money, she had her own money. Just under one hundred thousand dollars, the combination of what her mother left her and what she herself had saved. A paltry sum compared to what Aaron left her, but she was fine and she hated that Robert made her unconsciously think of it all. These big numbers, what did they mean? They took away no pain, just added to the sadness.

The day Robert asked her about thinking about getting plastic surgery to remove the scar on her face—"You're a pretty girl, Aisha, and you have a lot of life to live yet"—she knew for certain it was time to go back home. What did he know about her life? Living could not fix the pain, only death.

Susan asked her to stay, explaining Robert's meaning, and how he loved Aisha and most nights in bed would not stop talking about her. Maybe she should have intervened more, she would, if Aisha would just stay. Justin loved her, too. Despite this, Aisha continued to pack and in a short time Robert, Susan, and baby Justin were driving Aisha back to Chicago, to the South Loop and Museum Park.

Out in front of her building, Robert helped Aisha wheel her suitcases to the entrance. He gave her a long hug and said, "Come home whenever you want; your other home." Aisha nodded. The softness had returned to Robert's eyes.

Robert would have helped Aisha up to their apartment, but he saw Carl, the doorman, walk from behind the reception desk and stand patiently at a distance that did not intrude. With pressed lips, Robert gave Carl a nod, which was returned. Aisha saw this gesture and turned to see Carl. She hugged Robert one more time and without saying goodbye reached down to grab one of her bags with her strong arm. As if it were his cue, Carl came over to help. "The sun has risen. I've been waiting for you, Mrs. Benjamin," he said, taking all the bags she had and managing to situate them where he could carry them all. Robert stood, waiting. Once convinced that Aisha was taken care of, he told her he would call her tomorrow and left.

"I can carry a bag," Aisha said, then glanced over at the empty reception desk.

"Don't you worry one bit. I got it. And that desk will be fine," Carl said, moving to the elevators. Aisha followed.

"Gotta help my favorite resident." Carl pressed the elevator button. While they waited, he continued. "Some folks sent you some flowers. Pretty flowers, too. I tried to save them as long as I could. I said, 'I know Mrs. Benjamin would like these….'" Aisha felt the impulse to tell Carl to call her by her first name, but she liked the sound of Mrs. Benjamin. She had not heard it since the kind nurse with the repaired cleft lip called her it at the hospital. With the elevator doors opening and them getting on, Carl continued, "Umm hm, I put them on the desk and watered them and kept them. I just threw them away, tell you the truth. All the residents asked about them. 'From your sweetheart, Carl?' some said. 'Nope,' I'd say." The elevator reached its floor and the two got out and turned in the direction of Aisha's apartment.

Aisha opened the door and Carl lugged her bags in, asking was there a place she'd like him to put them. Aisha, first looking around the place as if she had never seen it before, put on a forced but kind smile and said, "No, Carl, right here is fine. Thank you." Carl, taking his cue once again, nodded his head in almost a bow and, when his eyes came back up, he said, "It's good to have you back. Don't hesitate to call downstairs if you ever need anything when I'm here." Aisha thanked him and stood in the same place for a while after Carl left. When she did start moving, she retraced the whole of the apartment, as if looking for something lost, as though, by her cautious steps, she might find Aaron. She ended up in the master bedroom, going in the walk-in closet. She sat down near Aaron's side. His scent was still in the apartment, but it was strongest in the closet. She began picking up his shoes, lifting them a little, touching them, running her hand over some. She picked up his prized first pair of Air Jordans, inspecting them, putting her hand in one, bringing it to her face, looking at its wear, seeing where he had cleaned the shoe, in her mind seeing him cleaning them with a toothbrush and thinking about Pop Pop. She had never seen him clean them before, but he had told her so many stories it was as though she had been there.

Clutching the shoe to her chest like a baby doll, Aisha lay down. With images of Aaron in her head, she fell asleep on the closet floor.

Chapter 21

Aisha awoke in the morning feeling nauseated. She got up and ran to the bathroom to vomit in the toilet. After flushing, her head remained in the bowl with her eyes closed, feeling the coolness of it on her face. It occurred to her at that moment that she had not had her period yet. No, she had not. She had to be pregnant. She was on birth control, taking the pills faithfully because she and Aaron wanted to wait. But miracle babies happen and she had not had her period. She needed a miracle. With the thought "I'm pregnant" in her mind, she got up just as she was and put on Aaron's first pair of Jordans.

The daytime doorman, who was not Carl, called a cab for her and once it arrived the driver took her to the nearest convenience store, as she requested. The cab idled in front of the convenience store and Aisha didn't move. She had to be sure. She told the cab driver to take her to a bigger store. There would be more options for pregnancy tests there. Though there began to bud in her a developing fear of going out in public amongst strangers, she never wanted to feel alone as she did in the hospital bed before Biggums came, when she had those peculiar feelings about life to start and then death to end, death now not being as peculiar anymore, a constant thought for her. If she had to, she would schedule a doctor's appointment.

Going in the bigger store and finding the aisle she needed, Aisha surveyed the shelf with all the pregnancy tests. Which one would she choose? She could not determine which one would be the one, the right one. She read the labels over and over, picking up a box and putting it down and picking up the same boxes all over again. After a while, she realized how long she was taking, seeing her state from outside herself. She snatched the most expensive product, tried to look as normal as she could in line, paid for it, and left.

Back in the apartment, Aisha immediately returned to the master bathroom and began tearing open the box. In the middle of tearing, she realized she had not read the directions yet, so she proceeded to do so, holding one of the applicators in her hand. When she finished reading the directions carefully, she followed them step by step then waited.

The color that appeared was not the one she wanted, not the color of miracle, but she tried another one. Same result. She tried another and another and another. She would try every applicator in the box if she had to until she could not squeeze one more drop of urine out. After five applicators all showed no, she took a break. She drunk some water then lay on the bed. Falling asleep for a time, she hoped, in the last moments before slumber, that when she awoke she would have her result. Going to sleep with those hopes did not work for Aaron, in the hospital. Everything that had happened to her was all a dream, some terrible too true feeling nightmare. When she awoke, Biggums would not be sitting in the chair by the hospital bed she lay in, she told herself, but she knew this was a foolish lie. It was too much to ask, too much to hope for. But then, before she fell asleep, lying in her and Aaron's bed, she felt that a new life growing in her was not too much to ask. It could happen.

When she awoke, she stumbled back to the bathroom to finish off the packages. Yet there was not one positive test result. Negative pregnancy tests strewed the marble bathroom floor. Aisha stumbled out of the bathroom, crunching the applicators between her toes, and collapsed back into the bed.

Something that felt like hope, the same feeling that inexplicably kept her from all darkness, all destructive and deadly thoughts, a vestige of her old self, maybe, nudged her out of bed in the early morning. It was a curious feeling because she felt there was no reason for it, though she did not reject it as she did not reject the sadness. She went to the master bathroom, gathered all the applicators, and threw them in the trash. She washed her hands. As she washed, she thought of Carl and the flowers he mentioned in the elevator the night before. Did he bring a stack of mail to her? Was she imagining it? Did he really come up to the room? Who cared for her? Who was there for her? The water continued to run over her hands hanging limply under the flow. She stared at herself in the mirror.

Carl did come. Abandoning his post like the night before, he came up at the beginning of his shift to deliver Aisha's mail to her. In trying to make her feel welcome, he had forgotten all about the mail. He had begun gathering it for her once the mailbox could no longer contain another piece. He knocked on the apartment door loudly, loudly because he felt the stack he carried had to have some good news in it, his favorite tenant needed it, one half of his favorite tenants. On the elevator up, he thought about how the pair was among the few residents who talked to him without even a hint of condescension in their voices. There was no latent superior vibe, masked by a friendly smile, a smile perhaps that they gave their dogs. No, they loved their dogs, so maybe not the smile they showed their dogs. Anyway, he missed talking to Aaron about sports, jiving with him about which women he would do in the building. He missed seeing the light in their eyes when they came in the building together and greeted him, but most of all he missed the way they looked at him when they spoke.

Aisha came to the door after Carl's persistent heavy knocks. He handed her the stack of mail, which Aisha grabbed between both hands, nodded as he had the night before, and left without saying a word.

It was this wordless exchange that Aisha contemplated ever happening while standing over the sink. Realizing it had happened, she dried her hands and walked out the bedroom, through the hallway, turning, and then towards the kitchen. Now in the kitchen, she saw the stack half-intact, half-spread out on the counter. She gathered the bundle in her arms again and carried it to the study. She did not sit at one of her favorite reading chairs. She sat at Aaron's desk, on his side of the desk. Dropping the stack down, she noticed her twentieth-anniversary copy of *Don't Cry, Scream*, a poetry book by Don Lee, now known as Haki Madhubuti. She and Aaron had gone together to hear him speak at his charter school. Aisha respected what the author had done in the community, and she thought Aaron would like him and his story. He did. She had forgotten that Aaron mentioned to her that he had been glancing through the book. Aisha pushed the book aside so fast it almost fell on the floor.

For hours, she sat reading all the thoughtful cards and letters that people sent. Something like happiness and gratitude filled her. The cards came from a variety of people from all the circles that Aisha moved in—from her track teammates in high school and at Harvard, neighbors from the neighborhood she just left, teachers from her school, old colleagues that had moved on to a more healthy school environment before the arrival of Dr. Haywood, Dr. Haywood herself, to members of organizations she had worked with, Phillips Brooks House Association and the like around Harvard, and even one from her resident tutor from freshman year in Grays Hall. But one card from a near stranger stood out.

It came from a woman who lived in Adams House with Aisha. The woman was a class below Aisha and, like Aisha, but for different reasons, was well known throughout various circles at Harvard. Their lives intersected because they lived in the same dorm, were both black, and had been around one another enough times in both the dining hall, parties, and various black student hosted events to know each other. They had never had a full one-on-one conversation and never got to assess each other's characters up close without the distraction of others seated at the dining hall table, Kaii amongst them, always seemingly at Aisha's side, but Aisha privately had respect for the woman. Still, they could not have been more different and other than casual and rather insignificant meetings, they were strangers. Aisha read the note the woman wrote on the card:

> *I heard about your accident and wanted to tell you how sorry I am*
> *to hear about your loss. I want you to know that I really admire you.*
> *You really care about people. For many of us the chance to climb over*
> *the blockades of being black and a woman in white male-dominated*

sectors seemed too great to pass up. But you always knew what was right for you. I'll be thinking about you and your family.

After finishing, Aisha decided the woman's card would be the last one she would read for that night. Her eyes were heavy.

She returned to bed thinking about all the kind words that were written to her and their meaning. What did they mean? Why were they being so kind? What had she really done? She did not deserve their praise. The person she thought she was she was not. She was living but did not deserve to be. She was nothing, no one. Why had all those people sent cards?

At some point, again, something inside of Aisha began fighting off her dark thoughts. She started thinking about Dr. Haywood and her school. Before falling back to sleep, she determined she would call Dr. Haywood in the morning.

Chapter 22

"Where you been, Ms. Bowerman?"
"What happened to your face?"

Returning to Richard Wright Academy, Aisha heard this expression more often than she could bear. She heard it from older and younger students, same expression, some she had once taught, and some she had not. The accident engulfed her world, so it felt like the whole world should know about it. But riding the buses on the way to the school and coming at an earlier time than Dr. Haywood suggested, it became apparent to her that the entire world did not know. The world went on. This realization, and the kids asking her the same questions—the word of the tragedy not long enough to reach every student, some taking the first opportunity ever to speak to her by saying, "Where you been? What happened to your face?"—affected Aisha greater than the sympathy she received from the students she knew. Those she knew expressed their sympathy in silent, reaching looks, some silent for the first time around Aisha.

The world did go on. Aaron had died and she was suffering, but things kept moving. The people on the bus sat staring blankly ahead in their thoughts or no thoughts or ignoring the person screaming all their thoughts to everyone on the bus or the man who she saw notice her scar, and nod to her out of some kind of recognition. The sights were all the same, the sounds the same. Dr. Haywood still had her same gold pendant and crisp navy blue suit, the same familiar expressions to passing students and the same tone with faculty. Who and what was she in this big world that continued to revolve even as hers had stopped? She was trapped with her pain, and though time moved and the days passed, everything for her in the sadness remained the same. Life and death, what did it mean?

As Dr. Haywood led Aisha into her office, she thought that she could not go on.

Sitting across from Aisha, Dr. Haywood noticed the faraway look in Aisha's eyes.

"It looks like all your visible wounds have healed well."

"Yes," Aisha said, "all accept this scar on my cheek."

"It doesn't look bad, Aisha."

"The kids keep asking about it. I didn't care about it until today."

"Don't let it bother you." There was silence before Dr. Haywood spoke again.

"Aisha, I don't think you are ready to come back."

"But, I need to. I felt—"

"What? What did you feel?"

"I felt like I needed to come down here. I want to teach and be around the kids. I also want to remodel the library. What do you think?"

"That sounds like a nice idea."

"It would be in Aaron's honor. We can start whenever you're ready."

"That sounds good. Maybe that's why you came down here." Aisha knew the look on Dr. Haywood's face, but she didn't say anything. Dr. Haywood continued.

"I am so happy to see you here, up and appearing healthy. I've thought about you non-stop. I've been praying for your spirit."

"Thank you," Aisha said, lowering her head so that her eyes were no longer in contact with Dr. Haywood's. She felt like a little girl, a little lost girl. Dr. Haywood continued.

"Aisha, you're a gifted teacher, my best. And in my long career, one of the best I've had the privilege to work with." Aisha did not raise her head, just moved her hands back and forth against each other a little. "And we need you, but not now…I don't think now is the right time. You, better than most, know what our students need. And right now you cannot give that." Dr. Haywood waited for a response from Aisha and, seeing there would be none, she continued.

"Have you seen anyone?"

"No," Aisha said, thinking of Robert, hoping Dr. Haywood would not begin to sound like him. She felt like she was slipping away again. No one could understand.

"That's all right. It's not the best thing for everyone," Dr. Haywood said. Aisha lifted her head.

"But everyone must grieve the loss of a loved one," Dr. Haywood continued. "In your own way you have to allow yourself time to heal."

Heal. What a strange word. What was it and how did one go about it, this healing? How do you allow yourself to heal? What is the way?

"Could I still come around? Help out some?"

"Of course; whenever you feel up to it. I'll make room for you. Just give me a call on my cell phone when you feel like you want to come in."

"Thank you." The two fell silent again.

"Aisha, how are you feeling? I'm asking you as a friend now and not your principal." Aisha could see that Dr. Haywood really meant it, really wanted to know. If she let it all out, Dr. Haywood could take it. The horrible things she had on her mind would not shock her. It would not turn her away or cause Dr. Haywood to think of her differently. This Aisha knew. Dr. Haywood had seen it all, all the insidious shapes of human suffering. She knew full well the visceral hold over souls it held. What the cost of conditioning was. Aisha knew well Dr. Haywood's understanding of the human condition, had seen her in action with others. Yet, as much as she wanted to open up to her, to let it all out, the only thing she had strength to say out of her mouth was, "We were so beautiful. Aaron was. I don't know what to do." Dr. Haywood waited to respond, taking Aisha's words in. She replied, "You have to go within. Grieve Aaron, mourn him, but you must go on living."

"He was perfect. When we got together, it was perfect…" Aisha dropped her head again. The floor began to wobble some and she could feel her temples, hot and pulsating.

"I'm glad I was able to meet him. He was a good person. A good man, but Aisha…" Dr. Haywood paused. Aisha lifted her head to see why she had stopped. Hearing someone else talk highly about Aaron made her feel a bit of goodness.

"…You cannot make him a saint." After saying this, Dr. Haywood stared at Aisha for a moment and then stood. She walked around her desk and hugged her. Aisha hugged back, but the more she squeezed, the less of a grip she felt she had.

Leaving the school, she heard from yet another one of the rare students she did not know and had never spoken to directly. "What happened to your face, Ms. Bman?" Maybe, she thought, she would get her face fixed before she came back to the school to help. Maybe there was something to what Robert suggested. She could not stand the students asking her questions about it. She was in no way ready to answer them. She had no answers herself. Each time she heard those words, it created an external existence for her hurt. She had no control over it, either. Having no control inside was bad enough. Maybe she should get her outward appearance to look as much like before as she could. She decided that she would not return until she had surgery on her face to have the ugly scar removed.

Two days later, however, Aisha was back on the bus, heading to Richard Wright and to death, confronting her again, so soon.

Chapter 23

She heard the commotion as soon as she turned to walk up the block. "Shot! Them kids. They shot them kids!" People running around in circles, all the neighborhood out, unintelligible shouts that Aisha tried in vain to focus on as her walk picked up. Jogging now, adrenaline flowing through her legs, making them feel light, strong, blood rushing to her face, feeling it in the scar. More people, a crowd ahead, a big crowd. Frenzied and wild looks, lost looks, horrified stares. People paralyzed. Now closer, screeching, screaming, louder, louder, sobs and more screams. "Back away, get away!"

Aisha was right on the scene. She saw some of her former students holding each other, crying, many faces she knew. She forced her way through the crowds. The people moved easily for her, as though she could help—"It's Ms. Bowerman." She came to a clearing with pools of blood on the pavement, two children, a boy and a girl, lying side by side, lifeless. She did not recognize them. Dr. Haywood with them, trying to cover them, doing what she could. Her suit jacket over the girl, blood smeared all over her cream blouse, someone else's clothing over the boy. A sixth grader Aisha knew, Gwendolyn. Gwendolyn is smart, a handful. Why is she by Dr. Haywood? She's helping her. The children lying there and all the blood and all the sobbing, sobbing behind her. Dr. Haywood is calm. So is Gwendolyn. She keeps looking at Dr. Haywood. Sirens in the back, closer, closer. I believe this time.

Dr. Haywood looking up at me, back down to the children. Someone hurry; please hurry. Sirens. Please save them, someone, please, save them.

Chapter 24

Both children died. Raven called Aisha at home to tell her. She would be picking Aisha up for the protest she was organizing. It would precede the vigil.

Raven drove Aisha home from the scene. She spotted Aisha standing and staring. Only the blood was left; the children, Dr. Haywood, Gwendolyn were gone. The ambulance gone; the children whisked away. Now police were there, trying to disperse the crowds gently, many people standing and crying, the police gently trying to disperse them. Aisha did not cry. She just stood, staring, as if the spectacle were still before her, standing in the same spot that she had parted the crowds to get to. A police officer, seeing her as an easier target—she wasn't crying and she was alone—asked her gently if she would move along. Please go home. Aisha turned to look at him as if she did not know what language he spoke. She no longer was like him. The police officer restated himself in a kinder way than he had done before, trying to keep his posture upright and defeat from his face. "Miss, please, you would help us out a lot if you return to your home." It was then Raven spotted Aisha. She put her arms around her and said, "I got her" to the officer. Aisha turned to see what was touching her and recognized Raven. My friend. They walked away. Raven led, still with her arms around Aisha. Eventually, after walking in silence for a time, Raven said, "I'm going to take you home."

On the ride home, Raven talked very little about what had just happened. She said what she had pieced together from scattered reports, those initially conspicuous truths that often run and hide for fear later. The target was a guy named Toby who lived across from the school. He grew up in the neighborhood, but went away for a while. When he came back, he liked to mess with the kids getting out of school, told them to stay in school, joked with them. Who knows why? He was beefing with some guys in the neighborhood. Their names whispered. Toby didn't get hit. He left the scene. Dr. Haywood was outside, supervising the dismissal as she always does, so she was right there when it happened. She was the first one to run over and help. Gwendolyn was walking with them but didn't get hit.

Raven was going to organize a protest tomorrow in the neighborhood, get everyone together. She and Kiki had been talking about it, with all the killing going on. The last time was right after the accident, though she caught herself and did not say this part to Aisha. It was the last time she and Kiki agreed on anything or really spoke. Now, often they just walked past each other in the apartment without saying anything. It no longer felt like home. Kiki and Tyeisha are gone a lot. It was affecting Norrell.

Kiki says she has changed. The married man she's seeing has come between them. "He don't love your ass. You just a side piece. And you gone let this nigga come between us!" But Raven felt like the married man loved her. He told her he loved her all the time and he treated Norrell real nice; buys her pretty things. He never hits Raven and buys her anything that she wants. They take trips together. Kiki wasn't always acting like this. At first she liked him. At first she was happy that she found him and that he treated her nice, not like her baby's daddy or Kiki's baby's daddy. But now, Kiki and her baby's daddy have been better. She asked Aisha did she remember them talking about her letting him see Tyeisha. Aisha did not respond, but Raven talked on. Kiki had started talking to him, started talking to him differently and things were getting better with them. Well, at least he was coming around again. They were more like friends. Tears started flooding Raven's eyes, making it hard for her to see driving.

"We don't even act like nothing no more; no friends, nothing. We like strangers. I don't know what's going on, Star. She my best friend. But he's the best man I've ever had. Ain't nothing else out there. I know it. I been out there. He's better than everything else. I don't know why she trippin' like she is. Why should I let him go? Huh? Why should I?"

Aisha didn't hear much of anything Raven said, but Raven's tears brought her back to the car. She gave Raven her hand. Raven squeezed it tight. Neither said another word the rest of the way. When they arrived in front of Aisha's building, Raven wiped her eyes, and, as Aisha stepped out, said, "I'll call you later, girl."

Raven organized a large group in the community to protest all the shootings in their neighborhood. They made up signs that read, "Stop the Killings" and "When will the killing stop?" with pictures of deceased children and other young victims of stray bullets, with only their ages and names and no other words. There were other sorrowfully and woefully created signs. Kiki closed her beauty shop to participate, encouraging her stylists to join in. Two of them came and each was given a sign.

Aisha was also given a sign, and when the marching began, she circled with the others in front of Richard Wright Academy. She kept circling, her mouth closed, her legs feeling weak, her arms not feeling strong enough to hold up the sign of wood and poster board. But she kept circling, not looking around, only at the back of the protester in front of her, watching her shoulders heave up and down, up and down, the back of her sign thrust up and down, up and down. Angry words in the air. The chants became like a lullaby for Aisha. She slept and walked, feeling nothing but her legs moving and an occasional cool breeze on her face.

After about thirty minutes, news teams began showing up, vans with men hopping out, setting up equipment, and reporters scrambling into position. There was resurgence when the news teams arrived. Aisha noticed the shoulders of the protester in front of her perk back to life like in the beginning. Aisha remained the same. A cameraman approached. Circling back around and sensing the cameraman there for the first time, Aisha turned her head away from the shoulders of the woman in front of her. She looked into the dark, lifeless lens and felt a rush of indignation. She took a few more steps then stepped out of the circle. A few steps outside the circle, she dropped her sign and picked up her pace. She felt like running, wanted to run away, but she didn't know if her legs could handle it. A cameraman saw her in his peripheral vision but kept the camera on the circling protesters. A reporter saw her and thought the separation was strange, but then focused again back on the story.

Aisha walked for miles. She walked until the rage in her head ceased to push her forward for weighing her down. Her repaired arm started to throb so she stopped and looked for the nearest bus stop.

◆   ◆   ◆

For the next two weeks, Aisha didn't leave her apartment. She also did not pick up the house phone when it rang. Somehow, she put together a semi-coherent e-mail to all those close to her, saying she was okay and please not to worry about her. She could not talk. Please do not be alarmed. Do not send anyone.

But there was cause for alarm; Aisha was slipping.

Despite the e-mail, her loved ones called non-stop. Robert called often to see how she was doing, once reminding her that their yacht had to be stored for the winter. Before that, Raven called, asking why she had left, and Kiki followed that call up saying she hoped that Aisha was all right. Isaac called saying he was just checking in and that at some point he and Katie wanted to send a car for her to have dinner with them at their home. Biggums called multiple times, apologizing for being out of touch, in the earlier messages not saying why, but then telling the answering machine he couldn't take looking at Aisha in that way. He wasn't doing so well. He was back to work. He wanted to know if she wanted to play Scrabble with him and his mother. He had been with her a lot lately, had even won some money the other day in Indiana at the casino.

Aisha couldn't speak, but she could listen. Listening to the messages helped her feel human. Hearing them prevented insanity from overcoming her.

Kaii was also among those who called. Her calls, even more than the others, helped. All of Kaii's calls were the antithesis of Aisha's gloom, each one outlandish and colorful. And although Aisha's face would not form a smile, something inside her laughed a little.

After a series of interconnected messages, Kaii's final message went like this: "You have got to be shitting me. I swear if you don't pick up the phone I will tell Marvin Martin where you live. He's in Chicago now. He found me on Facebook. I don't know why I accepted it. I'm trying to be nicer nowadays. If you don't pick up the phone, I will tell him where you live and make him come sing to you. He will do it *with* pleasure. The only reason he friend requested me is so he could ask about you and your hotness. He's longed to be with you and your hotness. I will pay your doorman off and assure him that Marvin is not a stalker, serial killer, or mercilessly driven hit man, but only the most tone deaf person on the planet who has no clue how badly he sucks. He will be at your door, singing to you. I'll make up some great lie why you need it, want it, and he'll be at your door with his little round glasses and ridiculous French beret. He will sing his heart out, with all hopes that it will bring you out of the apartment and unite you two. He'll know you're there because I'll tell him. I'll convince him and eventually if you don't come out, he'll flick you off like he did everyone in the audience that night at Lowell Lecture Hall. He'll stomp and storm away, just like that night, and it'll all be because of you. This will happen or you can call me and hear about the open ticket I bought for you to come stay with me. Do not have me waiting long, or the nasally monotone maestro, Mister I'm-going-to-try-to-sing-because-I'm-smart-and-everything-else-has-worked-for-me-in-my-sheltered-life, even-not-having-to-be-black-even though-I-am-black. I said I was trying to be nice. Sorry, it's a process, but he will be at your door, embarrassing you out of your apartment. That's all I got."

Sometime after Kaii's last message, Aisha called her back. She did not tell her about the shooting at the school because bringing it from her mouth would make her relive it more than she already had been in her mind. She put on her best voice. And, after speaking to Kaii, she e-mailed the same list, telling them she was going to California.

Privately, the thoughts of starting a new life in Los Angeles consumed her.

In a separate e-mail, Aisha gave Robert all the information and authority to do whatever he needed to do with all her things, toys she cared about once only because Aaron was attached to them. Robert could have the yacht. She could not see herself stepping foot on it again, and as she stepped foot on the plane to see Kaii, she romanced the idea of never stepping foot in Chicago again.

Chapter 25

Aisha already felt better driving from LAX in Kaii's new car. She made herself feel better. The sunshine that was supposed to be shining warmed her and seeing Kaii, hearing her speak in person, warmed her. While driving, Kaii commented on Aisha's improved appearance, careful to leave it at that, not bringing directly what in her mind she was relating it to. Aisha agreed, but then pointed to the scar on her face.

"I want to have it removed. Could I do it while I'm here?"

"Are you kidding me? This is like the cut and tuck capital of the world. Botox beauties abound. Uh, yeah, I think you can get it done here."

"Okay."

"It's too bad you can't enjoy this In-N-Out burger I'm about to have. Seriously, I've been thinking about it since I left the house. I am trying to watch my weight. Before I was hired to the show, I ballooned to whale size. It was just ridiculous. Even more so because everyone is so thin out here. Ugh, I hate it! So, I'm watching my weight, but I still treat myself every now and then. I mean, you gotta live. And I'm looking good nowadays."

"You are; really good! I was just about to say it."

"Thanks, and it's helping. I'm starting to get some attention from boys again."

"Are you dating?"

"If you want to call it that. It's ridiculous out here in the land of string-bean bimbos. I don't care how much I eat properly and exercise, I'm going to be a curvy bitch. That's it. If they don't like it, someone will!"

"You're right!"

"Thanks, girl. Yeah, I tell myself that. Keeps me up. Easier to say it than to live it. But Star, I love what I do and I got to be in LA to do it." Kaii slapped Aisha on the thigh.

"Look at us, two Midwestern girls in La La land. They're not ready for us!"

The first thing Aisha did when she got settled in Kaii's apartment was stash an envelope full of money and a short, two-sentence note in Kaii's dresser. She did not put it all the way to the back of the drawer, but close to it, tucked in between the second-to-last row of panties.

How to live, to go on living, why living, did not weigh on Aisha as the days began to pass living with Kaii. With Kaii's help, Aisha quickly found a good doctor to remove the scar. During the first week of healing, Aisha laid around Kaii's apartment, watching Kaii's large collection of movies. She watched them all day, taking naps in between. When Kaii came home, she would join Aisha, not caring or commenting that she had already watched all the movies, many times. Watching the movies with Aisha, seeing her excitement about the ones she had not seen, a welcomed sign, was like watching the movies for the first time. It felt like they were roommates again, back in Harvard's safe bubble.

For the first couple of weeks, the two talked about nothing but movies and the movie industry. Not a word of anything remotely close to Aisha's life was discussed, just movies and Hollywood, as though they were critics doubling as entertainment journalists. Kaii followed Aisha's lead, careful not to disturb the comfortable routine they had seemed to fall into.

Aisha was not trying to forget. She was forgetting. She pretended that life as she had once lived it never was. The process of the scar healing, now a barely discernible mark to the naked eye, became in her mind the removal of an unsightly mole, or a birthmark. The staple marks on her arm were from an accident falling out of a tire swing when she was a little girl. She saw herself swinging and falling from a tire that never existed. She would begin a new life in Los Angeles.

In the evenings, she and Kaii walked trails in the Hollywood hills together. It was Aisha's favorite time, them talking about happy times. She felt her legs getting stronger, giving strength to her new life, ready to carry her on through it. Seeing the clouds of smog hanging over the city did not even disturb her. She viewed it with the casualness of the local weatherman announcing smog levels for the day, something that was and should not be thought about.

Kaii never brought up the accident with Aisha. She seemed to be doing well and why mess up a good thing. But when Aisha mentioned to Kaii about trying to be an actress, she began to observe her friend more closely. She realized, as the two began to go out, to bars, to clubs, around the city visiting with various people that Kaii had befriended or were acquaintances with, that Aisha was taking the transition too easily. Aisha never mentioning anything about Aaron or teaching or the accident did not feel right. Upon meeting new people, she'd say, "I'm getting into the entertainment business. Acting. What did I use to do? Does it matter?" She'd smile the most beautiful and believing smile. "All that matters to me is now." The smile looked like her own; it made them let down their guard, believe her. It made them smile, too. These were people who it was hard to make smile genuinely. None of it felt right to Kaii. Aisha was talkative now, talking about everything and nothing that was her. When out, she borrowed a piece from here or there, from Kaii, her reading, from places Kaii did not even know. She did not know this happy person who was staying with her, who looked in the mirror and commented on her own beauty. How natural she seemed! What was going on? Should she say something? Was this a part of her process? Would she one day soon change back to the quiet and unassuming person, the grieving widow teacher, as abruptly as she had made this shift?

Kaii resolved that she would wait as long as she could before saying anything. Aisha seemed happy, certainly looked and sounded better, even if wasn't her. And she was not harming anyone with this strange new alter ego. She would wait.

♦　♦　♦

Some of Kaii's new industry friends invited her to a party in the hills. She had been to the home before. It was gorgeous. The first time marked

Kaii's invitation into new circles in the film industry. The second marked her continued acceptance. Kaii talked excitedly about the party with Aisha, all the people that would be there and what it would be like, forgetting, for the moment, about her friend's transformation. But when Aisha brought two sexy new outfits into Kaii's bedroom to compare which she should wear, Kaii remembered. She reluctantly picked which dress she liked the best, looking for the least revealing, but having to settle for the color she thought was more the old Aisha.

Kaii dressed slowly, so slow that Aisha shouted at her to hurry up. When Kaii finished dressing and went to get Aisha in the guest bathroom, she found her back in front of the mirror, admiring herself. Kaii stood in the doorway, not saying a word.

"What?" Aisha said. "Stop being silly. Are you ready?"

"You look beautiful," Kaii said.

"Thank you. So do you! Let's go, girl!" Aisha swung her hand bag out in front of her as though she were trying to hold on to something that was pulling her and then put the bag on her shoulder. She led the way, even though she didn't know where she was going.

At some point during the party, Kaii and Aisha got separated. Kaii was well into a conversation with a filmmaker whose work she admired when she realized it. So she excused herself from the conversation. It was hard, but she said she had to find her friend. Kaii kept running into people she knew, feeling bad for having to cut them short. Where was Aisha? She was not in any of the open areas in the house, or by the pool, so Kaii began checking rooms. She walked around, opening a couple of doors, revealing people who had escaped for privacy, but Aisha was not among them. When she opened the third door, she saw Aisha sitting down amongst a group of people Kaii did not know. Cocaine was on the table, some lines ready. Aisha was talking as though it was she who had been to the house before. She acted as though she knew the scene, had battled to get to that point, and knew well what was for her and what was not, who she was in the city of angels. Kaii moved in smoothly. She observed one of the men motioning for Aisha to go for a line. Kaii watched as Aisha, without hesitation, brought her head down to the mirror.

"Okay. No," Kaii said in a loud voice, causing Aisha to look up and everyone in the room to look at the woman who had just entered the room, unobtrusively at first, curiously. "Star, let's go." Kaii's interruption was then met with a host of disapproving comments. Someone told her to relax, which made her even angrier. When she saw Aisha looking at her with wide-smiling eyes but not moving, Kaii forced her way beside the man and woman sitting on either side of Aisha and grabbed her arm, hard. "Not tonight, guys. Sorry, we got to go." Kaii's powerful grip pulled Aisha's out of the room, through the crowds of the party, and outside. She kept pulling her, stopping once when Aisha's shoe fell off, and continued until they reached the bottom of the driveway. Stopping there, Kaii spoke.

"Did you do a line?"

"Yeah, what's the big deal? Why are you acting this way?"

"What? Who are you?"

"Kaii…Why didn't you join us?"

"How fucked up are you?"

"Huh? Don't be silly; I feel great."

"How can you? Star, what is this all about?"

"What? Trying some cocaine? Kaii, stop being silly, you've done it before."

"No. Fuck the coca; I'm talking about you!"

"Me? I'm fine; this is all great."

"No, you are not."

"Kaii…" Aisha smiled and reached for Kaii.

"No, I don't even know who you are!"

"Why are you saying that?"

"Aisha, honey, you're scaring me." Tears began to form in Kaii's eyes.

"Don't cry. What are you doing? Come here. Don't cry." Aisha said, reaching for Kaii again.

"No. Why am I crying? Huh? Why am I fucking crying? You haven't cried once since you've been out here. You haven't mentioned Aaron or the accident or anything about the Aisha that I know, the one I thought I flew out here."

"It's me. You've comforted me. I feel alive again."

"No, you don't. It's all this, the fucking line you just did. Honey, this isn't you. Where is all this coming from? Tell me. What are you doing?"

"I'm just trying to be happy."

"Star, honey, I know, I know what you've been through. But happiness doesn't come this way. All this, sweetie…" Aisha had grown quiet then, looking more like her old self, suddenly.

"…you didn't survive the accident for all this. God left you here for a reason."

"God?" Aisha said softly.

"Yes," Kaii said.

"God?" Aisha said again, louder this time. She looked Kaii directly in the eye. "I don't know God. And God doesn't know me…You don't even know God! Why do people believe in something they don't even know exists? What tells you there is a God, huh? What?" Her voice had grown loud. "Tell me, since you're so sure you know what I'm here for."

"Because of faith."

"Faith? That's just something that people use to make themselves feel better. We're all insignificant, expendable. You die and the world keeps going. The people who make it are the ones who just remove themselves from all the shit of the world and believe in themselves. Why stay around misery? Why look back? There's nothing but forward and then you die."

"Oh, girl, no it isn't. It just isn't like that."

"Like what? When you brought me out here, I woke up. And it feels good. You need to wake up, too. Forget the past. Forget all the pain in the world. Life is about having a good time and enjoying the time when you're here. Because when you die, it doesn't matter, anyway. The lights go out. I have a way out, so I'm taking it."

"But…what… where?"

"Anywhere but where I've been. The answers aren't there. You're telling me about God. Where is God? Huh? Since you know him so well. Where is God when children are dying, hurting, neglected every day. Huh! Getting shot and dying! Where is God when little girls are raped? I've seen it! Where is God? Has he seen it, your God? Why does it go on? These horrible things all over the world to innocent people. Where is God in the Congo? Huh! There are faithful women there, right? Right! And they are raped and outcast. They are raped and burned with their babies in their arms, their village turning their backs on them forever. Forever! Where is God here? Where is God in that?"

"I don't know. There isn't. That's evil."

"So, where is God? Where is goodness? Kaii, goodness always loses. You're good. You do the right thing for your entire life—for what? To have everything taken from you. Children dying right in front of you. Everything that was ever good, gone."

"But you have to believe they're all in a better place, Star."

"A better place? A better place. Why can't I go. Huh? There is nothing but sadness here. A better place? There is no such thing. A myth to make people feel better. When you don't care about heaven and hell, you live free. Heaven and hell are here. I'm done with hell on earth; I'm free. I'm freeing myself. My heaven is here and it doesn't involve God."

Aisha's chest heaved up and down. Her eyes were wide and her bottom lip quivered. Kaii began to speak in a voice barely audible.

"I think it's time for us to go home."

Part III

The first thing Aisha did when she returned to Chicago was look for a pretty sankofa bird to send to Kaii. She found it after going to a few African stores throughout the city. Aisha wrapped the bird up in nice gift-wrapping paper and put it in a pretty box, along with a short letter:

Kaii,

Thank you for having the courage, for loving me enough to confront me. Thank you for sending me back home. This is where I am supposed to be. I guess I was trying to cover my pain with unreality, trying to escape without really realizing it. But that screaming woman, screaming at you at the bottom of the driveway, still feels real. I didn't know she was in me, but I needed to know. I am hurt and confused beyond words. I do not know where to go from here or how to live. Aaron and I were supposed to grow old together, watch each other's eyes change colors. Our story was not supposed to end this way. I often saw us telling our grandchildren the story of our love, how hard it was to get right, but eventually we got it right and it was beautiful. They were supposed to be able to see how beautiful our love was, how enduring, without me even having to say a word. Nothing ever in my life felt so right. So now doing anything without him feels wrong. Waking up each day feels wrong.

At least in California I didn't have thoughts about not waking. Kaii, I'm sorry, but it's the truth. Please don't be concerned about that. I could not hurt you anymore than I already have. I've done enough harm. I don't know how to live or how I'll live, but this bird

I'm sending you with this letter is a promise. I promise you I'll fight this sadness and I know I said I wouldn't, but I will reach back to find some goodness in this. Still, things have never been this dark. I could have never imagined the darkness I'm living with. Please know that I love you.

Your Girl,

Aisha

Writing to Kaii helped Aisha. At least she had the ability to write a coherent letter. There was a time before where the darkness of her words overwhelmed the page each time she attempted to bring the pen to it. She did not feel far from those days, now only shifting into a kind of new madness. But at least she could write a simple letter from her heart.

When Aisha's mind began thinking of the balcony again, taking a step outside, perhaps falling over the edge, seeing herself moving into position and falling, she called Biggums back. While she was gone, he had left many desperate-sounding voicemails. When Aisha spoke to him, she tried to be as positive as she could, reassuring him that she would join him and his mother for a game of Scrabble soon. All those close to her had left messages, cheerful and concerned messages awaiting her return. Isaac and Katie's messages restated their desire to have her over for the holidays. In one message, they mentioned having a surprise for her. What could the surprise be? The fantasy, the prospect of maybe a miracle still sung in her. It excited her so much she committed to the nearest night they could have her.

Isaac and Katie had a beautiful home in Winnetka, a suburb just north of Chicago. Aisha found herself trying to control her thoughts of her and Aaron's last visit there and their plans of getting a nice, single-family home of their own. Still, everything about Isaac and Katie—their affection for one another, indicators of the collective past around their home, the vintage Harvard chairs, future heirlooms, and the baby as their heir, pictures of Aaron and Isaac youthful, laughing, drunk, happy—reminded her of what might have been.

While there, Aisha tried mightily to rediscover, conjure up elements of her Los Angeles alter ego, to no avail. She did manage to smile pleasantly and not remain silent in a way that would project her sadness intensely throughout. At one point during dinner, Aisha looked at Katie and remembered the wonderful day of conversation, the day Aaron proposed to her on the water, her thinking of them surely becoming great friends. But now, Katie didn't have the same look in her eye. Things were different. Where had the feeling gone? It was all Aaron. Aaron. Where was her surprise? She looked for it when she first entered their home and periodically throughout dinner, preparing to see some sign of it. But dinner ended without even a mention of it.

With the night at an end and the car waiting for Aisha outside, she had given up hope on the surprise. Maybe it was just them getting caught up in the moment of the message. She certainly would not ask about it. Though she wanted to, it would not be proper. It might expose her desperation. All in all, despite the reminders, which convinced her she would not be returning soon, could not return soon, she enjoyed their company. She especially liked hearing Isaac talk about Aaron.

The Chicago air had finally taken on a familiar feel, though still not as cold, it was cold enough not to bother Aisha all that much. As she put on her heavy winter coat and prepared to go outside, Isaac told her to wait just a moment. He left the foyer and disappeared around the corner, coming back with an envelope. "For you," he said, handing it to her.

"Aaron told me how much you liked letters. How you thought the advance of technology was ruining opportunities for intimate communication, or something like that."

"Yeah," Aisha said, blushing, remembering her old self, the kernel of truth hidden in old ideas, ideas that had no relevance to her life anymore. Yes, she once felt that way. Not all founded or unfounded. The reaction of her face allowed Isaac and Katie to laugh. Aisha laughed too, a light, natural laugh.

"Well," Isaac continued, "there's a little note in there."

Aisha again thanked them for the evening and hugged them one more time before leaving.

Walking to the car she wondered what the note was. It must be something from Aaron. What else could it be? Yes, Aaron wrote something to her and gave it to Isaac and Isaac's been holding it, waiting to give it to her personally. She entered the car, half greeting the driver as she was so caught up in her musings. An impulse to tear open the envelope was curbed by a greater desire to read the note settled at home. Thoughts of the note's contents warmed Aisha the entire ride. She maintained a calm smile until she was in her bedroom.

Sitting on the bed, she opened the envelope carefully and pulled out the note. Something else fell out as she removed it from the envelope, but she didn't look to see what it was for her eyes were already reading the note's words.

Star,

I can't describe to you how much I miss Jamal. I won't even go into it here because I know you understand.

Just when I was getting to the point where I thought I knew it all, that there wasn't much I could learn from our business, what's more friendship, Jamal showed me how to open my mind again and not to be afraid to take big risks. It's harder to do when you already know a lot and have a lot. I never thought I would have to fight off the feeling of being comfortable. I grew up well off, but I was never comfortable with just that. When Jamal and I first met, aside from my fascination with him being able to dunk a basketball, and him knowing all about Illinois hoops like me, his hunger is what most drew us close. I identified with it, though admittedly, his was deeper, but I tried to match it anyway. We competed. We learned from each other, took away each other's best parts. As a result, it helped to make us very profitable in our business. We went our separate ways, which hurt me at first, but we did well on our own. I did so well, so soon, that I became afraid to lose what I had gained. But Jamal changed all that when he came back to Chicago—even before that, when he was still in New York and we began talking about the possibilities. He was still hungry and he brought that with him. But not only that, he brought an approach to the market that will not only keep us relevant, but significant for many years to come. With all of me, I wish he were here to celebrate his triumph. It's going to happen. I gave him a hard time about it, but I can see it. He loved this business. We fell in love with it together and now everything I do in it will remind me of him. I'll do it in honor of him.

It's still early yet. This is only the slow beginning. But I am confident this thing will be a watershed. He called it, Star. You can expect more checks like this in the future. Later, when the time is right, we'll sit down and talk about other matters. Jamal's rightful stake is yours. As a friend, I owe him so much more. I miss him terribly, Star. I am going to do right by you and Jamal's legacy. All that he'd expect from me and more.

All Good Things to You,

Isaac

Aisha read over the note again. It was not at all what she had been expecting, but her disappointment was momentarily checked by Isaac's kind words. She could feel the care he put into the letter. She also could feel the control in it, what he held back. It made her think about what his nights were like. What did he tell Katie in their private time? Did he lose himself around her? How had these months been for him? It wasn't like her months. He lost a friend, but she lost a husband and a friend. She lost her family. She had nothing to fall on. Who could she lean on? No one.

Aisha continued to hold the letter in her hand. She looked over at her bedroom reading chair and looked at Aaron's pants, still there, slung over the top. She remembered joking with him about bringing the habit to their new home and him quoting some rap lyric in response.

Still holding the letter, she looked down to see that the thing that had fallen, what Isaac had referred to in the letter, was a check. She placed the letter on the bed and picked the check up, turning it over. Again, millions of dollars to her. Aisha looked at the sum as if it were zero, nothing but zeroes, as if it were nothing.

Chapter 27

Biggums did not grow up in the cozy bungalow where Aisha sat looking at pictures stacked along a little shelf built into the wall. There was his Cook County correctional officer graduation picture, his uniform and hat too big for even his hefty size, the hat covering the top of his eyes; a picture of Biggums with his younger brother and sister, which was an older picture; and a picture of Biggums with his niece, his younger brother's daughter, the little girl sitting on top of his shoulders with the cutest smile, hunched over, covering his eyes. It felt like it should have been his childhood home, but Aaron had told her that Biggums moved around a lot. He had spent the longest time in Aaron's neighborhood.

A compilation of Frankie Beverly and Maize, which Biggums had made for his mother, sounded from the stereo. Biggums tapped his feet to it as he set up the Scrabble board. Aisha liked the feel of the place and thought, "It must feel good to have this place."

Biggums's little sister sat on the opposite side of the room from Aisha, asking Biggums questions to which he responded in exasperated expressions. "I don't know, Shanice. Around 91st and Halsted or something. I can't remember. Don't you have something to do in your room?" She had already asked Aisha many questions, which Aisha tried her best to answer. She could not bear to wear the full "I am fine" mask any longer. It was hard work just to want to live. But in Biggums's mother's home, it did not feel like she had to. Still, his sister's questions were difficult for her. They brought up things that were no more, things that Aisha no longer knew how to deal with. Was it her mind's mission to send her to a place she could not return from?

Aisha did not embrace the sadness as she had in the beginning.

But there was a new kind of misery, a treacherous taunting, the talking increasing. It told her that her life was not worth living. What was it all for? Look at your life. Look at it. All the things you know, all that you have seen. You cannot survive this. How can you go on?

Sitting in her apartment in this perpetual struggle, a war within herself, fighting but losing, she called Biggums and asked him about the Scrabble game. Now she was sitting in front of the Scrabble board, her, Biggums, and his mother, a small woman with a happy childlike face and glasses that seemed to fit it perfectly.

It was Biggums's mother's turn to lay down the first word. She had come back from the store and selected the closest letter to A; Biggums and Aisha had both picked O. She laid her tiles down, using all of them. A bingo on the first play, her word: "furnace."

Biggums laughed and said, "You're going to do us like that, Mama? Out the gates?"

"Yes, I am," his mother responded. Her play and the lively look in her eyes moved something in Aisha. "Golden Time of Day" played on the stereo and, looking at Biggums intently rearranging his tiles in his tray and his mother looking at the board and her refreshed tiles for possibilities, Aisha realized she was in the presence of true Scrabble players.

As a result of the constant back and forth, the talk about Scrabble between Biggums and Aisha—though not actually having the opportunity to play while Aaron was alive—Aisha learned that, growing up, it would be no strange sight to see Biggums and his mother locked in a heated Scrabble battle. It was their family tradition. Aaron said Biggums began to shun the game when one of his uncles started calling him a white boy for him liking the so-called "game for white people." It was bad enough that Biggums was ridiculed for the way that he spoke, so in an effort to become what he thought to be blacker, he began embracing the youthful militancy around him, the rage and the cool, and those things alone. He rejected the look his mother made for him as a schoolboy. He would only speak properly when he could use it to his advantage, only around the girls that actually enjoyed him speaking that way, which were few, and he rejected their Scrabble games. Aaron remembered the moment he noticed this conscious shift. He addressed it directly when Biggums joined the Black Stones. Aaron said to him, "Oh, you hard now, huh? You gang banging? All well, Stone. Stones run it? GDK… that's you, dog? Man, you trippin'. BBA, ain't enough? You and Wayne's ass trippin'. What y'all need to be Stones for? You was cool without that, for real. These other niggas don't know no better, but you do."

This all occurred to Aisha as she made her first play. She called out her score. "Thirty." It was not as much as Biggums's mother's seventy-four points, but a respectable start. Aisha was glad Biggums was playing with his mother and, in that moment, she was glad to be a part of the tradition. It felt like they were all old friends, as if she had grown up with Biggums, too. Aaron had been in that bungalow, too. She felt closer to him around people he was close to. Biggums was there with Aaron when the South Side was all Aaron knew.

Playing Scrabble in Biggums's mother's bungalow became routine. Every Sunday and Monday evenings, which were Biggums's off days from his second-shift duty at the jail, Aisha would wait eagerly for him to pick her up. Soon she'd be arriving in front of the board and the letters, words, beautiful strategic words, the accretive nature of the game, building, linking, working with the best with what you got and if unhappy with the selections, starting all over, trading letters or a letter in, taking a step back for the potential of greater success. Playing the game triggered the competitive need in her. Once, way back, it was satisfied by her studies and on the track, but when she stopped running she learned she had to fill the space it left. Her college studies were not challenging enough, so she began volunteering at the local Cambridge schools, in juvenile jails in Boston, teaching one of the institutionalized teens to read, one of the hardest non-family challenges she had faced up to that point. With the eschewing of one passion, one that was thrust upon her, as soon as she began taking her first steps, his face, his dream, her love, her hatred, dream no more, lead to the discovery of another.

But all that was gone. All that she had once thought was hers or saw herself doing for the rest of her life, no longer had any place in her life. She was nothing, a nothing. She could add nothing, only take away. Only away from what once brought fulfillment, now chaos, pain, into the pit of pain she fell, falling but not dying, nails digging into the pit's walls, clawing, but not climbing, and unable to cry.

A simple board game and some music, rubbing the little brown tiles with yellow letters on them in between her fingers, laying them down, hearing her voice call out the score, winning, helped. It hinted to happiness in some faraway place. It even made her smile. Seeing how similar Biggums was to his mother, their quirky mannerisms, the way they said "bye" and the look when they contemplated, even, brought forth occasional giggles.

◆　◆　◆

Aisha spent Christmas day with Robert and Susan in the suburbs. They bought her a cellular phone as a gift and asked her to please carry it around with her. They would pay the bill. Aisha thanked them for the phone and told them she would carry it with her, but refused for them to pay. Why should they pay? She told them she was feeling better and it was the truth.

That night she was back with Biggums. On the Scrabble table were Christmas cookies and candy, green and red colors. Biggums stuffed handfuls of both in his mouth. His family was there, his mother's brothers and sisters and their children, and every so often they checked to see who was winning. Aisha was winning.

New Year's Eve was spent in front of the Scrabble board. Aisha brought the New Year in with a win and a smile that left when she remembered how she had felt, only a year before, what she had been doing. Biggums's mother left after Aisha's New Year's win. It occurred to her, having been there often enough to see more, that Biggums's mother liked going to Indiana to the casino more than she liked playing Scrabble. She was not enjoying it the same as Aisha enjoyed it.

After New Year's Eve, Aisha began recognizing it more and more,

Biggums's mother leaving, sometimes cutting their Scrabble nights short and asking her son, "You coming with me?" "Naw, Mama." Still winning, Aisha began seeing Biggums's mother throwing games for her son, leaving spots open because the way they always sat put Biggums directly after his mother. It was their routine, their new tradition. But it, too, could not stay. It, too, revealed the woes of the world, all that surrounded that Scrabble board. Who was happy? Where was happiness?

She's a nice woman, but she leaves our games for the casino and she throws the game for her son. I was winning, but she doesn't want me to win. She wants her son to win. He sees it and does nothing. He takes the wins. And now, I can see Ronald looking at me differently. No, Ronald. No. I see it but I do nothing. He's confused and lonely, sad, like me. He hasn't moved out of the basement apartment yet, even with money. He hasn't really spent any of the money that Aaron left him. Same old clothes, same shoes that curl up at the toe. He's like me. He's looking at me differently. No, Ronald. No.

Before it could get any worse, before Aisha could see deeper in the lives of her Scrabble partners, before Biggums's affection grew anymore, his delusion, his confusion, Aisha stopped all communication. She stopped all communication with everyone. She retreated to her apartment, having resolved it better to only have to fight herself and not everything else. There was too much in the world and now she saw it all, all the bad, the bad lurking around every corner, bad on the streets, in lavish lifestyles, and around friendly board games. She could not handle it. How vulnerable she was. How utterly lost and no one could understand. No one.

So she lived with herself, never going outside, only occasionally to the balcony to peer over it. Why was she even born?

In the first week of isolation, she did not eat and only left her bed to take sips of water from the sink. Against her own will, she did it. Using her own hand as a cup, she sipped. Sometimes, much to her mortification, she gulped down big swallows of water. The water tasted like poison to her. But, of course, the water had the opposite effect. She wasn't even strong enough to not drink. Why couldn't she die? Everything she tried fell apart, so why go on?

Then, as inexplicable as the sips of water, Aisha began eating. First, she went through all of the sugary snacks that were left over from her and Aaron's sweet days. When she had devoured all the sugary snacks, looking at all the leafy green things in the refrigerator disgusted her. So she signed up for a grocery delivery service. She still did not eat meat, the taste for it was never there, but now the taste for anything green was gone. She wanted to eat nothing that was alive, nothing colorful, unless the color was artificial. The sugary artificial flavors appealed to her the most and she subsisted on that, binging on it and going to bed, snacking on it in front of the television. She watched shows that were easily accessible: count downs, the best this, the worst that, videos, videos of rich people, what they had, what they bought, what they liked, the biggest this, the most rare that, the best of everything, the worst divorces, who gave up the most, celebrity nightmares, celebrity marriages, everyday people catapulted to overnight celebrity, people sick of themselves seeking out celebrity as if it were the antidote. It reminded her of herself in Los Angeles, her behavior, so she turned the channel to news stations and current events. Accidents, death, shootings, death, stabbings, death, sports, her father, her hatred, the weatherman speaking of cold temps in warm places, warm temps in cold places, reoccurring disaster with no explanation, reporting it with a plain face, as if it all was common, weather records broken constantly, flooding and earthquakes and war, bombs blowing up innocent people, and more looming terrorism, fear— all of it worsened her in a way that she did not want. So she turned the channel. What could bring her peace?

Chips and sitcoms. Potato chips, rippled ones, salty and sour ones, those with sprinkles of sour cream and onions, biting, crunching, chewing, contented. Looking at the screen and chuckling with little bits of chips stuck between her teeth, teeth and gums, her tongue getting the bits loose and chuckling, only chuckling, bag after bag of chips gone, barbeque and flaming hot, finger licking. Once she looked at her hands and remembered a time when she looked at similar red stains on the fingertips of her students. She felt like them without the innocence, without the automatic hope, the daring dreams despite the blight. For Aisha nothing felt right, nothing contented her but program on program off, crunchy, cheesy chips, triangles and circles becoming mash in her mouth.

This went on month after month. She lived for junk food and humorous shows, things light and devoid of any responsibility. Not peace, but a numbing, a contented numbness. It took her away from the chaos of thought. It dulled the pain. Better to be one with the sadness, become it, than to challenge it. Better to be numb and secluded from the mad world.

During this time, everyone that loved her made efforts to establish contact. In the beginning, Biggums called incessantly, each message and its pronouncement changing. Aisha responded to the messages each time by entering a text message on the cellular phone Robert and Susan gave her for Christmas. "I'm okay. Don't worry about me. Love you." Biggums decided to come downtown. When he arrived, he was turned away by the doorman who was not Carl. All the doormen knew of Aisha's orders: they were not to let anyone up, save for the delivery man. Eventually, Biggums's messages stopped. Raven and Kiki called separately and together. They had reunited. Raven had quit the married man and was doing work in the community. But none of this moved Aisha. They received the same text message. Everyone kept receiving the same text message.

By summer's arrival, with the numbness not as gripping, not as intoxicating, Aisha felt the need to step completely outside of the apartment. But she did not dare leave her apartment, settling instead for sitting out on the balcony. The urge to fall from it was gone. Months in the numbness kneaded the pull to see what the other side was like into a quiet suppression. So Aisha would sit with her bag of chips out in the air, watching the traffic pass by on Lake Shore Drive below. Watching the water and the marine activity did not cause her to want to go back inside. She started reading while sitting on the balcony. The sunlight radiated off the pages, silently penetrating, covertly attacking the numbness.

One day the day doorman, who was not Carl, Demarco, who over the phone Aisha had gotten to know far better in her reclusive state, perhaps better than Carl, informed Aisha that she had a special delivery, which she had to sign for. Aisha allowed the deliveryman up, quickly signed for the package, and closed herself back into the apartment. The deliveryman was the first person to see her in months. She did not mind so much that he saw her and others she loved had not. He was a stranger and with strangers there is no history, no spaces where deep emotions lie tucked away, able to spring forward, outward, in an instant. No love. Love hurt. Loving and the embrace of death, while having to still live, went together. Love caused confusion and with the deliveryman, things were clear.

Aisha had gained weight. Her breasts had gotten bigger, a manifestation she once wished in her genes, but so had her stomach. In front of the mirror in the bathroom, she would admire her now bigger breasts, wondering if Aaron would like them; probably. Then she would force herself to look down at her stomach and put her hands on it. What a bulge. She never thought she would see it like that without a baby in it. But that bulge was not a baby's bulge. It was soft. It moved when she jumped. She had jumped once in front of the mirror, fascinated with the strange mass below her now bigger breasts. It jiggled. The rest of her body remained about the same. So this is where she would gain weight, in her breasts and in her stomach.

Walking to the couch with the package in hand, Aisha wondered if the deliveryman noticed her new size, but not in terms of attraction and not in a sexual way. She had not been touched since the accident and she had not touched herself since Aaron had moved in and vowed not to touch himself. With Aaron gone, she could not touch herself. She did have the urge at times, but it made her think of him in that way, see him, and that was too much. No, she wondered if the deliveryman noticed her size simply because he was the first person she had seen since shutting herself off from the world. What did she now look like in the eyes of others?

The package was from Isaac. She opened it to find another note, two CDs, and a check greatly larger than the last. In the note, Isaac said he hoped she was doing well. Her text message responses at least let him know that she was okay. He said she was welcome at their home at any time, with them anywhere at any time. Things were going well at Colossus and he anticipated more gains, huge gains.

He included Dave Matthews Band CDs because they were some of his favorite pieces of music. It was happy music. The note went on to say that he played the CDs all the time in college. Aaron would pretend he didn't like it, but Isaac caught him bobbing his head once. He called him on it, but of course, Aaron vehemently denied it.

Aisha let the bigger check lie where she had placed it and got up to put one of the CDs in the player. An up-tempo sound and an assortment of instruments blared from the speakers, and eventually a voice. Aisha sat on the couch and let the music play.

Listening to song after song, she could tell it was indeed happy music. Isaac's note, again, brought her a hint of happiness, but the money that came with it was like an invasion of a superpower country into a village long forgotten by time. What would she do with all of it? It just made things more complicated. Robert had helped her put the first check away in secure places, places she received statements from that remained unopened. Apparently, the economy was changing. Forecasters feared a recession or worse. These were Robert's words to her in the messages he left. The messages increasingly seemed to be more concerned with the mountain of money she had in secure places and less concerned with her. Maybe not; his voice didn't sound ugly. But the large sum had changed him. The first check, the surprise, was larger than Aaron's estate and it must have seemed to Robert, given his tone in some of his messages, that the accident was a distant memory. Not to Aisha. It had not yet been a year and she lived with it every day. She would live with it every day for the rest of her life.

Now that Isaac had sent her another big check, what would she do with it? Who could she trust? She could trust Robert, but maybe not with such large amounts. Maybe people who are not used to such large amounts, but still really cared about them, could not handle them. Telling Robert about this new check might make him more than infatuated, crazed maybe. No, no, no, she just did not know. How do you have that conversation? Was it just her or was she really seeing a difference? Her mother loved Robert and she loved Robert and Susan was a kind woman, but Aisha just did not know. Maybe when, if ever, she reached out to the outside world again she would ask Isaac to help her with it. Why did it have to come to her? She did not care about it. But then, she did. The money was an extension of Aaron. He had worked hard and believed in what he did for a living. Aisha could see his face, the flames in his eyes when he talked about his business; the money he made was just a result, like making beautiful music for yourself because you loved it, but also having millions of adoring fans, like the band that played from the stereo. How valuable music was. Isaac said it himself. It made him happy. The sound playing from the speakers made people happy. Could there be a price for it?

Chapter 28

Biggums began leaving messages again around the end of the summer. He had not called in months and, as time passed, Aisha hoped he was okay, though she knew there was nothing she could do. She was glad to hear from him again, and the emotion she experienced from hearing his calm and balanced tone, a wholly different kind of voice, consistent with each message, made her consider picking up the phone and reaching out to him. She had to see it. It sounded like he had grown, but was that growth possible, in that short of a time period? What was behind it? Was it just another fleeting period of levity that led back to depravity? Biggums said he would like to tell her in person what he had been up to, his story. She liked stories, especially ones with happy endings. Happy-ending stories used to make her cry. She had not shed a single tear since Aaron's funeral. Tears used to flow from her eyes easily, in sad moments and in happy moments. Her inability to cry had bothered her in the beginning, but the numbness had made her lack of tears feel normal. But Biggums's voice, the resurrecting power of remembrance and the peculiar quality of his voice, the ring of its authenticity—not so much in his words, because in his messages he spoke briefly, confidently and vaguely—caused her to consider the problem of tears again.

One day Biggums left a very specific message. It said, "I'm glad that you went away, Star. Neither of us was in the right mind or spirit to be of any benefit to one another. You pulled away at the right time and I'm thankful for that. It was providence. But I've been feeling in my spirit that you all locked up away isn't right anymore. I would like to see you as a friend, for the sake of our friendship and my friendship with Jam. I'm in a whole other place now, a place that I have never been and I am so thankful I'm here, so grateful for where God led me."

Shortly after Aisha listened to the message, she sent Biggums a text message telling him he could come by whenever he was free. He should only let her know well in advance.

Biggums came the next day.

Biggums's weight loss was the first thing Aisha noticed when he walked through the door. His face looked slimmer and healthier. Hugging him did not even feel the same; big portions of back were gone. What had he been into? What would this meeting be like? She flushed with insecurity, an aftershock of the panic attack she had when she realized that Biggums was downstairs, on his way up. She composed herself as best she could but still felt terribly out of sorts. Yet Biggums did not look at her with an evaluating eye, but a caring eye, one of understanding. She could see it and it eased her tension.

"Ronald, look at you! You look great!"

"I feel great. I can't even remember feeling this good. Maybe back when me and Jam first met, when we used to play baseball." The two sat down, Biggums on the love seat, Aisha on the couch.

"Did he ever tell you I used to play baseball?"

"Yes, he told me."

"Yeah, I used to be really into it. I'd memorize all the category leaders from both leagues and everything. I felt good back then and I didn't even know it. Gave it up for nothing." Biggums looked through Aisha to another time, his smile removed for a moment, then coming back.

"But that's all the past, living and learning. I didn't come over here to talk about that. I came over here to invite you to go to church with me."

Aisha began to say something, but seeing the look in her face change, Biggums cut her off.

"Hold up, before you say something. I know what you're about to say. I know, and I feel you. But let me tell you why I'm asking before you respond." Aisha nodded her head. She could do that.

Biggums smiled, then began telling Aisha about the time they were apart. Much of that time he ran around with women. Going to the nightclub became a hobby, then a habit. With the help of Aaron's trust fund money, the servers began to call him Big and he liked it so he started going by it. Big, he introduced himself as Big to the women. They liked it and had no problem calling him it. He found out quickly that money made people do things that they would otherwise not. He could make them do things that he wanted. No one would have called him Big before. Big, as if it were his real name. Big, as though his mother called him by it.

He still worked at the jail so every month he blew every bit of his allowance. By day, he was Ronald T. Biggums, the Cook County correctional officer who was still just as involved in practical jokes as every other officer in the County, though his fellow officers did notice his developing swagger. They noticed now him pulling up in a new car, noticed pretty women in the passenger seat, then taking his new car and coming back to pick him up. The word began going around that he was selling dope on the side.

But of course he was not. He was just blowing every bit of the money that Aaron left for him. He blew it in places that made the money seem like more, made him appear big, in places around people that would call him Big. And in the beginning, living a lie felt better than the truth, better than any truth he had ever known. The girls did things to him he had always fantasized about, things he had heard Aaron talk about before he settled with Aisha. He did not tell Aisha the details. He did not tell her that his motto became "good food and good pussy," but he told her his story in a way that she would understand where he had been. He told the story in an even tone, in the same way as the messages he had left. He described the times with no excitement or disappointment in his voice. It was his truth.

He told her that going through all of it helped him to see. He called himself Big, but he was really being small. It was small of him to use Aaron's money in that way. Small of him to buy his niece anything she wanted, but never have any time to spend with her anymore. Small of him to give his mother money to blow, like him. Small of him to blow up in the club fighting over a small thing, risking his job and his life over a small thing, fighting as if he were fifteen again. Aaron was right—he knew better back then—but then after the club incident he laughed about it with his so-called friends, but later on that night, when alone, he felt small. He woke up the next morning, Sunday morning, and was in the mood for a piece of his motto. None of his girls would pick up the phone, so he decided to get up and satisfy the other half of his incessant hunger.

While driving down 95th street, he saw a beautiful woman walking toward a church like an eagle flies. He saw another one and another one. This was enough for him to turn around to go back home, shower, put on fresh clothes, and visit the church. Biggums went into the church smiling, happy he had stumbled upon such a treasure chest of women. Walking past the pews, he found a pretty young lady to sit by. Sitting down, he opened up his church bulletin and feigned great interest in it. He did not have the nerve to speak to the young lady right away and by the time he had built up the courage the minister started his sermon.

The minister's sermon pulled Biggums in so much he decided to put off asking the young lady he sat by for her number. He returned the next Sunday, intent on getting a number from one of the church girls; church girls got down, too. They got nasty; he was no fool. But again, the minister's words and the feel of the place took away the feeling that he had brought with him.

He went back to the church the following Sunday after having a particularly bad Saturday night. Out of nowhere, the girl he took home drunk began hitting him and screaming and acting as if she had not been all over him all night, like she had not been all on him every Saturday. Now that he had taken her home and was about to get down, though he had hardly taken her clothes off, had not even touched her, she was acting crazy. What kind of blackout drinker was she? Blacking out while still being awake? Waking up while being awake and not liking what she saw? Hitting him and screaming at him as if she wasn't just all over him in the car? He had to stand up and step away from her, talk calmly to her from a distance. "I am not going to harm you. You came home with me, remember? We were in the club. You told your girls you were going with me. You've been on me for weeks. I'm Big, remember? Big?"

Driving her to wherever she lived, he couldn't get her out of his car fast enough. With her gone, on his drive home, he thought about getting up and going back to church the next morning. This time he would go with the intention of gaining clarity in his life.

And he did. The pastor cared about his congregation and the community at large. And while sitting in service for the eighth straight week, he felt something visit his spirit. It told him to invite her.

Biggums told Aisha he was not trying to bring her along on his journey; this was no recruitment. He had been down that road before with people he knew who had found religion. This was not that. They were on two distinctly different paths. This realization came to him in their separation. But the salience of the feeling that came to him in the sanctuary, it not leaving when he left, actually grew stronger. It was not a thorn but a consistent feeling that he figured would not get right until he asked Aisha to join him. Just once; that was all he was asking.

Aisha saw the new light on Biggums's face that gave it a gentle glow. She was opposed to religion. Growing up, she had never stepped foot inside a church with her family. The closest thing to religion she and her mother had was practicing yoga together after her father left. It helped to bring them closer, helped them both, in their own way, to recover from the trauma.

In college, she had gone to church occasionally with friends. The families that she worked with invited her a few times. Kaii, who grew up in a very religious household, would sometimes come into her room after a wild party night and ask Aisha whether she would like to go to church with her. In Senegal, she participated in religious rituals, but they were unlike American traditions. Yet when she graduated from college all her participation in religion ceased. She was too busy working with the children who lived in neighborhoods with churches on every other corner. It frustrated Aisha to see all the churches. For as many churches as there were, for as many members, where were the movements? Where was the widespread impact? Shouldn't it spread beyond the walls of the church? If there was so much goodness happening within those walls, why didn't it spread? Organized religion had been around so long, shouldn't it by then have gained mastery at reaching people, helping people so they could help others? How was it helping her students' communities? Who was it reaching? Wasn't the goal of religion to teach and to reach as many people as possible, so that the world would be a better place? For people to use those teachings to spread joy, love, and happiness? Shouldn't goodness be as visible as the many churches that take up plots of land all over the city?

She had met many great people who were not religious. Aaron was not religious. He shared with her stories of corrupt churches in his neighborhood, him seeing it and Grandma Benjamin not seeing it, and Pop Pop muttering but going along with it until Grandma Benjamin died. Aisha admired James Baldwin and, other than being a preacher as a child, he and Aaron's stories of their neighborhood and its religion seemed to be about the same. All this and more, how women were treated throughout the world in the name of religion, the many heinous acts performed throughout history in the name of religion, finally pushed Aisha away from it. She vowed she would never step foot in any church again. What was the point?

But seeing the look on Biggums's face made her curious. Was it the church that had brought about this obvious change? Whatever it was, she hoped it would last. She told Biggums she would consider it. Although, as she said this, it occurred to her that she had not left her apartment in six months. Had it really been that long? She told Biggums that going back out into the world might be a challenge. Biggums looked at her and replied, "You'll be all right. I'll be with you and will be praying for you until then." Something about the way Biggums spoke now gave Aisha a comforting feeling. What had he been up to?

Aisha did not immediately call Biggums. She mulled over the idea of finally leaving the apartment and joining him at church. When she eventually called him, Biggums was there to pick her up promptly for that Sunday's service.

Standing patiently in the apartment, Biggums waited until Aisha was ready to move.

"It's going to be all right, Star."

"I'm a little scared. I don't know if I can go."

"Here," Biggums reached out his hand. Aisha took it. "Will you pray with me?"

"What do you mean?" Aisha asked. Biggums laughed. His full laughter filled the room, the energy of it going through Aisha's hand.

"You know, get down on your knees, close your eyes, pray."

"Oh."

"So? Are we just going to stand here holding hands?"

"Where?"

"Anywhere, right there," Biggums said, pointing at the couch. He let Aisha's hand go and walked over to it. He got on his knees. "C'mon, it ain't going to hurt. Have you prayed before?"

"No. Well, not like this."

"That's cool; maybe then this can be a beginning." Biggums smiled big and bright. "It's not hard. You just humble yourself and open up your heart." Biggums waved her over again. Aisha walked over to him and thought of Aaron. She had seen him doing the very thing that Biggums was trying to get her to do. It was new to him, to her, her seeing him like that, but it began to become more frequent. She never asked him about it. She asked him about everything. Why not that? What was there to ask? At the time, what he was doing seemed obvious. But why? Why then? He was mostly like her, after all, so she did not understand. And she did not ask. He never talked about it, either, only his allusions to God in a joking way, a secret of his or something. But they had no secrets. Why did Aaron never ask her to pray with him?

"C'mon," Biggums said, pulling at her hand gently. "I don't know how slow you're going to be walking up out of here." Biggums smiled again and Aisha moved to her knees. Biggums closed his eyes and clasped his hands. Aisha looked at what he was doing and closed her eyes, but she left her hands free. Biggums began to pray. "Father God, thank you for speaking to me. Thank you for bringing me to this apartment. This is my friend. You know her. God, I ask that you allow us to leave this place without stress or worry, and that we return in the same way. Amen."

Aisha opened one of her eyes and turned slowly to Biggums to see what he was doing. He was smiling at her with both eyes open so she opened her other eye quickly. Biggums stood up. "So we're ready," he said. "You can take my arm, if you like."

Holding Biggums's arm, they walked out of her apartment, down the hallway, and onto the elevator. How was she feeling? She was fine. She continued to hold Biggums's arm down the elevator and out the elevator past Demarco, the doorman who was not Carl. He smiled and nodded. Aisha gave him a little wave with her free hand and smiled.

The church was big, but not huge. Aisha surveyed it as they approached. They had not parked in the parking lot but on one of the side streets east of the church. Aisha felt confident enough to let go of Biggums, so she did. There were people around; all the churchgoers walking toward the church alongside of them and in front of them, some crossing the street in between traffic, all headed in the same direction.

As she and Biggums walked, almost to the church now, they crossed a set of train tracks. Aisha looked at the cars to her left slowing to cross over the tracks. She took in every moment, out again in fresh air, on the solid ground, the hard concrete, people all around, and she felt fine. Again, although in a different way this time, she observed the world had not changed. She certainly had, though. Walking up to the nice man who greeted them at the entrance of the church with a genuine smile, then past him into the church, being given two programs and then moving, her following Biggums into the sanctuary, being directed by the ushers and finally sitting, Aisha knew she had changed. What type of change? The sadness was there, not as intense, but there. The intensity was gone and with it, feeling. She felt nothing.

Aaron, I love you. Why do I feel you are farther from me? Can you see me? Can you see me here with Ronald? Is this a special place? Ronald's looking good. Why did I feel closer to you when I was hurting inside? Now it's this blank feeling. At least when I hurt I knew I was alive. And being alive meant you and me even when I lost you and me. At least desiring death gave me purpose. Now what? I'm here with Ronald. Now what? Now I am not who I was before I came out. I am not who I was before I had to shut myself in, or who I was with us or before us. This blankness, the blank feeling, is the ugliest feeling, unfeeling. I want to feel you again. Where are you?

Aisha caught herself staring ahead at nothing. She lowered her head and began to read the program in her hand to try to ground herself to something in the moment. Biggums seemed to be enjoying himself, not worried about her. Reading the program kept Aisha's attention. It was well thought out, well written; as Biggums talked about, it detailed much about the surrounding community and the issues that needed to be addressed in it. It talked about things that were happening in Chicago that were relevant to members of the congregation: this representative will be here to talk and answer questions, this informative event is happening on this day, activities, counseling, art, singles ministry meeting downtown, food drives, prayer for the sick and shut in. The sick and shut in? The pastor's notes page took Aisha's attention away from her thinking about her shut-in time. She spotted the words "Relief for Haiti, Flooding," and began reading the entry only to be pulled from the page by the sound of music. She looked up and saw young girls in all white matching dance outfits. They started to dance in the center of the church, dancing mostly with their arms and hands. What was the name for it? She asked Biggums. Right, liturgical. It reminded her of her school, her students, the things she used to do with them and Dr. Haywood. The girls were spinning, enlivened, their arms telling a story. Could she teach again? The school year had already begun, but aside from that, no she could not. How could she teach? How did Dr. Haywood go back? She had to go back, but Aisha could not. How could she? What could she teach? All that she knew and thought she knew was not helping her. All of the knowledge she had, schooled in one the finest universities in the world, all the books she had read—how was it helping her? Some of her knowing added to her distress, to her state, but none of it took it away. What was the point of it all? She used to think much of the mind but its power had become less impressive.

The girls finished up their routine to a round of applause. Right after the applause stopped the choir began to sing. Aisha looked at Biggums. His eyes shined as he looked with a contented face at the choir, tapping his hand on his thigh, tapping, tapping, then standing up and clapping his hands to the rhythm of the music. Others who were moved by the music stood, too. It was all nice to Aisha, sitting there among all the people, out, hearing the mighty choir sing, watching Biggums, a new person. It seemed quite odd to Aisha that she had spent so long in the apartment alone. Still, she could go back. There was nothing for her on the outside, but this church was nice, being there, in the moment, was nice. Aisha put her head down and finished reading the pastor's page.

The choir stopped singing and the pastor announced it was time for offering, "For the Lord loves…" "A cheerful giver," the congregation replied. Aisha leaned over and whispered to Biggums. "Did you know about this place, before you came?"

"Yeah, it's legit. He's got a great reputation in the area."

"And they really help the community?"

"Oh, yeah," Biggums said, still matching Aisha's low voice with a serious nod. "Before I even came here I was always hearing stuff." Biggums prepared his offering and so did Aisha. She wrote a large check, but did not feel cheerful. Everyone in the church, including Biggums, raised their envelopes in the air. Aisha's envelope remained in her lap. She watched everyone in the church bow their heads and close their eyes as the pastor said a prayer for the offering. She watched the pastor closely, critically. When the basket came around she quickly tossed her envelope in it.

When it came time for the pastor to preach, he announced the title of his sermon: "Our Brothers with Records and Our Records of their Wrongs." He began preaching, and as Aisha listened to his sermon, she found the pastor to be not only well spoken, but well informed, reflecting the words she had read on the pastor's page. He was passionate and funny, turned a tough subject into laughter. "Now I'm not saying that everyone belongs back on the outside being loved. We got to love some of these brothers on the inside. Now, c'mon now, pastor know, some of these Negroes are just crazy…"

Aisha thought about her discussions with Aaron on the same subject. So, although she could appreciate the pastor's stance, nothing really stood out for her until the pastor began to get more serious, seriously talking about love. He preached about deep love, loving people through the unthinkable, the mission of love, and what it required. And then, this from the pastor's mouth, "For love to exist, records of wrongs cannot, y'all hear that? Look inside yourself; wipe those records clean." It jilted something in Aisha, unsettled a piece of her that had been set even deeper after the accident. As quickly as it was unearthed, exposed to the light, it was sent barreling back, deeper, yet this time with an even more pernicious partner, digging into the core of her and scorching her to unfeeling.

So consumed was Aisha with what was once again set free in her, it moving around disturbing things, after church was over she could only say to Biggums, "Thank you for bringing me." There was so much she wanted to say, so much on her heart, but she feared it would come out like babble.

Sitting in the passenger seat of Biggums's car, riding back to Museum Park, Aisha's emotions overflowed. She turned her head to look out the window so Biggums would not see her face, for she knew it would betray her. She glanced over at him once and saw that he still glowed, bobbing his head and tapping his hand on the steering wheel to the music that played.

As they arrived at Museum Park, Biggums spoke for the first time during the car ride.

"I ain't going to bother you, Star, but whenever you want to go to church with me, I'll come pick you up. I'll be in that joint every Sunday, for real." Aisha smiled and nodded. Biggums swung the car around the circular drive of Aisha's building and parked, leaving the car running. He and Aisha both got out. Biggums made his way around the car, arms wide for a hug. When the two finished hugging, Aisha said softly, almost to herself, "I can't go back to the way things have been."

"That's good," Biggums replied. "Star, Jam used to always say to me how strong you were. That's one of things he really loved about you. Matter of fact, that's one of the first things he said when I first heard about you. That, and how you seemed to understand him. He kept saying 'she understands me.'" Aisha dropped her head down. She liked hearing about Aaron, but everything Biggums said sounded like lies. She did not feel strong. She felt as far from strength as a person could possibly be.

"We're going to make it through this. Star, you got too many gifts." Biggums bent his head down so Aisha's dropped eyes could see a part of his. "You're going to make it through this. You have to." Aisha nodded an unbelieving nod and Biggums hugged her again, repeating the same words to her. When they parted, Biggums went in one direction and Aisha in the other.

For three weeks, after going to church with Biggums, Aisha fought with herself in the apartment. Aside from occasionally ordering foods that were alive, she fell back into the way that had given her comfort in seclusion. Yet, despite this, she could find no comfort. Again, she felt pain. It ached in her, bit by bit it nipped at the pieces of sanity she was able to salvage. It haunted her all around the apartment, projecting images of what her next steps must be. As the days passed, the vision she had leaving church with Biggums months before increasingly became clearer. She had to complete the journey to Haveton, alone.

Going to Haveton was a big trip then, all the dreams, all the years, all the mystery, all of Grandmother Johnson's letters—which she had begun reading again in the apartment with new eyes—but now? No, she could not do it. She could not go. Taking the trip felt like destruction, an end rather than a beginning. But there was that feeling. She had to end all she knew. She had to leave Chicago, something had to be destroyed, something had to die, and, after many months of wanting to die, wishing for it, she was afraid.

Yet, on a warm day in early November, Aisha resigned herself to it. She'd rather die than go crazy in the apartment, living as one who had lost their mind. She had no choice. Going online, she bought a bus ticket. Afterwards, she quickly packed her bags then took a cab to the Greyhound bus station on Harrison Street.

Before getting on the bus, Aisha asked the bus driver which route they would be taking to Haveton. She found out that they would be traveling the same highway where Aaron lost his life. She had suspected this. And, as she walked through the bus to find a seat, she could think of nothing but that morning, the vividness, the scene. She chose a window seat, sat down, and pressed her forehead against the cool glass window. She could feel the sun on her face. It was one o'clock. It would be dark when she arrived. What was she doing? She had no plan. Back then, Grandmother Johnson was expecting her. Now, no one knew she was coming and no one knew she was leaving.

If something happened to her, if she should die, how long would it take them to find out? What would they say? In her obituary the money would probably stand out the most, not how much she loved teaching, children, not her and Aaron's love, them happy in her old apartment on South Shore Drive, surrounded by the steaming serenade of the noisy radiators in the winter. Not how she would kiss the milk from Aaron's mouth when he came home, not the misery of her losing him and all that was simple and wonderful about their connection, but the millions and Colossus and its gains, the result of Aaron's discovery, the risk he took and won would be mentioned, not the risk they took for love. Now she had nothing to lose. All that she had seen, so much to be seen in the world, she had seen a lot of it, though there were endless amounts more to see. Weeks before in the apartment, as she struggled with the idea of Haveton, she pondered taking other trips instead. Why Haveton? There were other challenges, weren't they? Why not take on other great challenges. Mountain climbing? Yes, she could climb a mountain. She had once read a wonderful short story about a British mountain surveyor, one of the first expeditions to measure the heights of the Himalayas. He wrote sanitized letters, lies, back home to his wife, even as the trek, its demands and its revelations, pulled them farther apart. But who could she write to? Who knew her and loved her for all of her like Aaron once did? After climbing the mountain, descending it, then what? Another mountain? Who did she have to write home to, go home to? She could travel to the most beautiful places on earth, but she'd be alone, perhaps adopting family and friends, maybe even some real, but still alone, the wonders of the world making her feel more so. Who would ever be able to know her like Aaron did? There was so much. Mom is gone, too.

Mom, I'm going down here to see about Daddy. I really don't want to. We'll be traveling down the same road. Did you see me that day? See Aaron, now? Why didn't I see Aaron by my side when I awoke? Why can't I remember? How did I get from the truck to sitting on the pavement? I can't remember anything but the after, seeing his hand. Who pulled me from the truck? The EMT was right, Mom. I listened to her. I did not want to see Aaron in that way, but why did I see the two children in the street? The puddles of blood? Why did I see that and not Aaron? They are killing each other. What does it all mean? Mother, do you know? Who knows?

"Hello," said an old white man with bushy eyebrows and an old black baseball hat with a red truck on it as he sat down next to her.

"Hi," Aisha said.

"So, where you headed?"

"Haveton, Missouri."

"Really? I'm heading to Sikeston," the man replied. Aisha nodded her head and turned some toward the window.

"So, you going to see family?"

"Yes."

"That's good. I came up here to visit my daughter. She works up here in the big city. My name is Samuel Tranks."

"I'm Aisha."

"Nice to meet you, Aisha. What's your last name? Maybe I know some of your people. We got family down around Haveton. You got any family anywhere else in the region?"

"I don't know. This is my first time going to visit."

"Really? That's good. Family's important. So what's the name?"

"Johnson."

"Oh, there's a lot of Johnsons. Ralph Johnson and family?"

"No."

"How about Walt Johnson?"

"No. Those names don't sound familiar, sorry."

"That's all right, Aisha. You seem like good company. Glad to be riding away from the big city with you." Aisha smiled and nodded her head slightly. Samuel Tranks returned a kind smile and settled into his seat more. He was going to continue talking. It always happened that way on charter bus rides. It had been so long she had almost forgotten about it. In college, before she bought her first car, she used to take rides to visit Kaii in Indianapolis. She liked visiting Kaii. Kaii was born and raised in Indianapolis and it seemed like she knew the entire city and the entire city knew her, blacks and whites equally. But more importantly, Aisha got the feel of home when she visited Kaii. Kaii was rooted in a strong, loving community.

On her bus rides to visit, Aisha always attracted the strangest people who felt it was all right to sit next to her and talk. The most memorable was an older, skinny black man with a pockmarked face, who bragged how he couldn't stand black women. He asked Aisha if she was biracial and when she said yes, he looked justified, as though he knew, as though castigating black women sitting beside her was then okay. She wasn't all the way black. As the man went on, Aisha could hear whispers from the black women on the bus. Without seeing them, she felt them cutting laser beams into his head with their eyes. Still, no one confronted him. Where was the proud and loud black woman who could not stand him talking so freely, the one who could cut him to pieces with her words, her rhetoric? Aisha felt all of that churning inside of her, but she had remained silent. The man looked crazy. Eventually, and thankfully, he changed topics and began talking about his love for *Star Trek*. He talked the rest of the ride to Indianapolis about *Star Trek* and all of its derivatives, obscure and little known facts. He was a "Trekkie".

Samuel Tranks talked but not in a strange way and not about strange things. He talked about his family who began not far from the banks of the Mississippi River. Aisha liked listening to him. He had a soothing, slow and kind voice that took her out of her head.

Hours passed and Samuel Tranks continued talking. At some point, Aisha realized that the bus could be approaching the area of the accident. But at a quick glance, nothing looked familiar. So she decided that keeping eye contact on Samuel Tranks was more important than being rude and trying to locate the place of the accident. She liked Samuel Tranks; his stories about family were happy stories.

Much of the trip had passed when Samuel Tranks finally asked Aisha about herself. She told him the truth, half of it. She told him she was a teacher. She taught the little ones, first graders. She was going to Haveton to see her father, whom she had not seen in nearly twenty years, and her great grandmother, whom she had never met. Aisha tried her best to appear happy, again wearing some variation of her Los Angeles alter ego. But Samuel Tranks saw the hurt in her face. There was more to the story, he knew. But he did not ask Aisha any more than she wanted to offer. This pleased Aisha. However, when she was finished, he asked, "Will they be waiting in Sikeston for you?" Aisha wanted to lie, to say yes, they would be, but they would not and she could not lie to the kind man. Receiving the true answer, Samuel Tranks paused, and for the first time in the trip pondered, briefly. Then he spoke. "How are you going to get to Haveton? As far as I know, the bus doesn't run to there." Aisha was aware of this. Her ticket was from Chicago to Sikeston. This time, she had not even looked at a map. It was too painful. Instead, when buying the ticket online, she tried to access her long-term memory. Out of all the cities that came up in the scroll box, she recalled Sikeston was the closet to Haveton. So she clicked on it, printed her ticket, and left.

It had to be spontaneous, as it had been before. She would not be controlling because she had begun to realize how little control she had, anyway. She would face the trip as she had been living her life after the accident. Whatever came, however it came. Out of the protection of the apartment, she would face death if it were there to meet her again.

But Samuel Tranks heard none of this. Aisha told him she thought she might be able to get a cab or something, which was the truth, she did.

But in saying it, she realized the logical part of her mind did not work as well as it had before, since logic had little to do with the circumstances of her present life.

"Darling, Sikeston ain't the big city. Takes more time and planning to get from one point to another down here. A bluebell like you shouldn't be alone, trying to figure it out in a strange city. My wife will be waiting for me when we arrive to Sikeston. We'll take you Haveton."

Nothing in Aisha told her to refuse the offer or act as if she would be okay without it, so she looked Samuel Tranks in the eye and simply said, "Thank you."

Chapter 29

In the Tranks's car, surrounded by the black night, Mrs. Tranks asked Aisha whether she had a phone number. They said she should call, because they did not know Haveton well and they were getting close.

Haveton was about fifty miles southeast of Sikeston. What did she do to deserve the Tranks's kindness? Aisha dialed Grandmother Johnson. She did so easily, though she had dreaded it before. It was better to reach Haveton, just reach it, then to have to hear bad news over the telephone that may have prevented her from going. She would rather get the news in person. Whatever was there, just get there and face it. But listening to the ringing dial tone then was easy. It would make her and the Tranks's travels easier. They had been so kind and she did not want to be any more of a burden.

Many rings, Aisha looking out the window into the darkness, the Tranks in the front seat patiently waiting, then a voice. It was as if Aisha knew the voice. She announced herself; Grandmother Johnson, ecstatic, praising God in a hushed and serious tone, thanking God, but still listening, allowing an opening to listen, willing to talk to the Tranks to lead them to her doorstep.

After getting directions from Grandmother Johnson, Mr. Tranks handed the phone back to Aisha. She spoke a hello into it, to which Grandmother Johnson replied, "Oh, yes. God is able. Mercy, mercy. Thank ya! Oh, yes. I have told him the direction he must go and he understands. With the will of the Lord, I will see you soon, dear."

The Tranks followed Grandmother Johnson's directions precisely. At the end, they arrived at what appeared to be a white house with its front and side porch lights on. Aisha saw its features better than the little one-story houses they had passed in route to the destination. It was nothing like the South Side. Those little houses were much smaller and meek looking than the blocks and blocks of sturdy bungalows and other buildings on the South Side. But as the Tranks pulled up the long gravel driveway, Aisha saw that Grandmother Johnson's house had multiple stories to it and, unlike the little homes they passed in Haveton, differentiating character. Pulling up, the partially illuminated white home was to her left. To her right, shadowed in the darkness, maybe two hundred feet from the driveway, there appeared to be a big barn.

"Nice land your folks have here," Mr. Tranks said. "We'll wait for you," he continued as Aisha gathered her things.

Aisha exited the car and walked up to the side of the house, which was the nearest lit up entrance to where they had parked. Before she was able to reach the porch, the main door opened and a figure, Grandmother Johnson, looked through the fancy barred screen door. She appeared to be hopping up and down, though barely leaving the ground, maybe not at all, and clapping her hands. Then Aisha was at the door. Grandmother Johnson opened the screen door some, Aisha opening it the rest of the way.

Grandmother Johnson stepped back into the entrance of the house, whose walls were lined with pictures. She held out her arms bent at the elbows, raised with clenched fists. She had on a long nightgown that touched the floor. It covered a frail frame. Long, silvery hair hung down her back.

"What a God! My great grandbaby! The Lord answers prayers. Mighty God, mighty God!" Grandmother Johnson unclenched her fists and moved to hug Aisha. She hugged Aisha tight. Aisha could feel her frailness, just bones and breasts. Her breasts were the only thing on Grandmother Johnson's body that had some fullness left. Aisha kept hugging and feeling. Grandmother Johnson kept hugging back, saying, "My God! My God!" drawing out the "y" sound in my. Still in the goodness of the embrace, Aisha remembered the Tranks out in the car, waiting for her. She slowly let go of her hold on Grandmother Johnson, stepping back and mentioning it to Grandmother Johnson. "Oh, yes.

Blessed assurance; what a God!"Aisha turned around to head outside the door, but before she exited, she turned back to Grandmother Johnson as if to see if she was indeed real, if it all were real. Grandmother Johnson's smile illuminated her entire face. She glowed, too. It was as though Aisha could see her aura. She felt a calm come over her and she stepped outside.

Mr. Tranks stood by the car with Aisha's bags by his side. Aisha smiled at him and said, "Everything is okay."

"That makes me happy, good," Mr. Tranks replied. "Here's our number. Call us if you ever need anything." Aisha hugged him and thanked him. Then, going into her pocket and pulling out some money, she swiped three times at what she had in her hand, three hundred dollar bills.

"Oh, no," Mr. Tranks said. "I cannot accept anything from you, darling." Aisha insisted, pressing the money into Mr. Tranks's unwilling hand. It would not close around the bills.

"Please," Aisha said, staring at Mr. Tranks. "Please, take it. I have money. Please, for your grandchildren, anyone special." Mr. Tranks looked at the earnestness in Aisha's eyes. The surety made him reluctantly accept the money. Aisha hugged him again and then went around to the other side of the car to thank Mrs. Tranks and say goodbye to her.

She waved at them until the taillights of their car disappeared from her sight. Grandmother Johnson was still standing in the same spot when Aisha reentered the house, offering to help her with her bag. Aisha smiled and said that she had it. What grace this woman had.

"Oh, yes. The Lord answers prayers. Well," Grandmother Johnson said, clasping her hands with a smile and a shrug of her shoulders, "let me take you to your room."Aisha followed her, looking around as they went through the house and made it to the staircase. There were pictures everywhere, on every wall, and dolls, many, many, dolls and knitted things. As they climbed the stairs, Grandmother Johnson taking her time, being very careful, Aisha thought about how everything seemed old, as though nothing had ever disturbed it, moved it from the original places, the items set for decades. The only thing that appeared new was the computer. Now upstairs, a strange feeling of familiarity came over her, as though it were all something she had dreamed. Entering her room, she could see there were dolls in it, too.

"Did you make some of these dolls?" Aisha said, picking one up.

"Yes, many of them, precious." Aisha looked around the room.

"Grandmother, have I been here before?"

"Oh, yes, when you were very little. You, your mother, and your father came from California to see me. I gave you a little monkey."

"That was you!"

"Yes," Grandmother Johnson said with a delighted, childlike smile on her face.

Aisha had loved her nameless monkey to tatters. Mr. Monkey was the only name he had gotten, which she moderately approved of. She did not name him and did not feel the need to name him, but her parents tried to. They constantly tried to name him for her. He needed a name, but Aisha did not feel like he did. Though, eventually, she accepted the offering up of Mr. Monkey. She approved the name to satisfy her parents, since both of them seemed to agree on it, but in her mind, her monkey remained nameless.

She always assumed the monkey came from her father. And after her mother died and after she discovered the letters, in letting go of her father, forgetting him, she let go of her monkey, throwing it into the trash after all of their years together and not thinking of him again until that moment with Grandmother Johnson. She had not even told Aaron about it, though he knew much about her childhood. Her monkey had been a constant fixture in her life, first a plaything, then a silent and inactive friend, a faithful remainder of her childhood that sat on her bed, holding its special place.

Smiling at Grandmother Johnson, who was now sitting on the bed, and at the unearthing, the revelation, Aisha looked at her and said, "You must be tired."

"Yes. But your coming has filled me up with the glory of the Lord." Aisha sat down next to her.

"Grandmother, how old are you?"

"Ninety-eight, with the help of the Lord. I've outlived all of my children except for three. Your Aunt Martha and your Aunt Catherine. Martha still lives in St Louis. She is a retired teacher. Catherine lives in New Mexico with her husband George. And Charles, who lives in Memphis. Charles comes to check on me, the most."

"Is Charles my grandfather?"

"Oh no, your grandfather was the first to go to the Lord, many years ago, when your father was a baby."

"Is my father still alive?" At this, Grandmother Johnson's face perked up.

"Oh, yes, he'll be overjoyed to see you. Life has been hard, but the Lord is able. We must stay encouraged. He does not live far from here."

The letters had come to life. Grandmother Johnson was all that Aisha had imagined her to be. But then, right then, she wanted to go see her father. She asked Grandmother Johnson whether she could borrow her car, the newer silver Chevy parked by the house. A serious look came over Grandmother Johnson's face.

"It would be best if you went in the morning to see him." Undeterred, Aisha looked at Grandmother Johnson with a stern face and said, "I've come a long way, Grandmother, and I understanding waiting, but this can't wait. I'm not going to be able to sleep." Grandmother Johnson stared at Aisha, the two of them silent, Aisha so determined she'd walk in total darkness to get there if she had to.

"All right, precious. The Lord will be with you."

Before Aisha drove away, she sat and got comfortable with Grandmother Johnson's car. She had not driven since her outing with her students before the accident. But sitting there, she was not concerned with the driving. Driving she knew she could do.

Something made Aisha look back over at the house. When she did, she saw Grandmother Johnson looking out the window at her. She put the keys in the ignition, started the car, and pulled it slowly down the driveway.

In the pitch-blackness of the country, still driving slowly, Aisha focused on the landmarks that Grandmother Johnson gave her before she left. They were simple directions, but the darkness made it hard. Her head and her pounding heart disturbed her motor skills and her attention as she moved along the strange, dark road. At some point, it seemed she was not riding to her father at all, but towards oblivion, the old thoughts of her demise circling. But there came another landmark and she heard Grandmother Johnson's reassuring words in her head. Aisha concentrated on the instant love she felt from her and the words "he'll be overjoyed to see you." It buoyed her, keeping her above the overwhelming spirit of loss and despair, which made the short trip seem endless. There was bleakness, but her mother was with her. Aaron was with her. They would be going along, too, into the little house by the church that Aisha was then pulling up to.

Stepping out of the car, and with each step, her progress felt protected. She felt strong, as though nothing in the world could prevent the moment from happening, not even herself. She climbed the few wooden steps that led to a junky porch. She could make out a few items out of the clutter, a tire, a wheelbarrow, a long pole of some kind—did she see a football? She turned to the door, took a breath, and knocked. Her hand came down hard. The sound of it did not seem to be of her. A voice, a raspy sound that she had never forgotten, raspier now, came through the door.

"Who is it?" the voice, her father's, said powerfully, almost angrily.

"Aisha," she said.

"Who?" returned the voice, her father's, so strange to hear. There were footsteps and the porch light coming on, then the door opening fast, and there he was. They were face to face. Nothing was said by either. He looked different, not how Aisha remembered. Maybe it was the long beard and unkempt hair. But in his eyes, beaming at her, focused, silent, she saw him. Those eyes gazed at her, unblinking, his mouth closed. Aisha opened hers.

"Do you know who I am?" was all she could say.

"Do you know who I AM?" he returned, breaking his still pose with an animated gesture, something not right about it, unlike how Aisha remembered seeing him move. But his voice and those eyes…

"You're my daddy," just came out.

"That's right. That's right; and you Daddy's Isha. I knew you would come! I knew this day would come! I knew you would come find me! Poppa and Daddy's Isha. I knew I would see you again." He hugged her. He was thinner than what he used to be, but Aisha could still feel the muscles in his back.

"I love you, Isha. Always have. Poppa and Daddy's Isha." She remembered the expression "Daddy's Isha," but she never called him "Poppa." The strange, growing stranger, and the familiar.

"I love you, Isha. Never stopped. I knew you would find me." Aisha held tight, her senses working to the max of their capabilities, a strange smell on him, and in the air. Had she smelled it before? Then a strange voice from inside. "Speedy, who is it, Speedy?"

"It's my daughter. She came back." They let each other go. He smiled at her, all his teeth still there, the life in his smile gone.

"C'mon in, Isha. I knew you would come back. I prayed for this day." Him saying the word "prayer" made her think again of Grandmother Johnson. It felt nothing like her words.

They moved into the house; Aisha stood. The house was in shambles, junky like the porch. And who was the woman? She looked bad, worse than her father did.

"Lil Bit, this is my daughter, Isha."

"Oh, Isha! Hey, Isha!" The woman stood and shook her hand as if they were both dignitaries. What was that smell?

"C'mon, Isha, let's go out back," Speedy said. "Lil Bit, me and Isha going out back."

Aisha followed her father through the house. She had a vague feeling that she had been to that house before as well. But as feelings from the distant past came back to her, all the clutter around the house made it difficult to retrieve a specific memory.

Speedy turned on a light in the back, stepped through the back door, and down some stairs.

"C'mon, Isha." Aisha made her way down the stairs so that she, too, was standing on the grass in the backyard. She closed her jacket tight; the night was cold.

"I always knew you would come back, Isha. I love you. Daddy loves you. C'mon, let's walk."

Aisha wondered where they would be walking to, but as she walked with Speedy, it became apparent they would walk the backyard, round it.

"You remember we used to walk like this?" Speedy asked. She did not. She remembered the track, and always running around it; sometimes her father jogged around it with her, talking to her, cool downs, only walking at the end of the workout, but not for long, never in the way they were rounding the backyard.

"I said, 'When Isha come back to me we gone walk like we used to.' And here you are. I love you, Isha, always have. Now all that with me and your mama," Speedy paused, "all that's the past. Things didn't go how I wanted them to. But that's life. But the most important thing is you here with your daddy now, in Haveton. This your home. You a Johnson." They continued to round the backyard, Aisha watching her footsteps and her father closely because there were objects in the dark that he knew better than she did. He steered her clear of them with fluidity, as though he had actually planned this walk. He had.

They continued to round. While walking, her father asked her nothing about her past, her life, said nothing else about her mother, asked nothing about how she had gotten to Haveton. All at once, she felt like a little girl, quiet and obedient, and like a wild woman capable of screaming unceasing questions at him, her voice booming in the darkness. She desperately wanted to tell him all she had been through without him, all the things she had done. But most of all, she wanted him to know what the last year had been like for her, the result of her trying to get to Haveton to see him. She wanted him to know her pain.

Yet as they walked, beginning yet another circle of the backyard, and Speedy beginning to repeat himself, the same sentiment repeated in varying ways, Aisha started to sense his pain. Adding hers to his didn't feel right.

As they ended their walk and started walking back towards the house,

Aisha looked at her father. Her father, a stranger, a man hurting deeply like her. More than her. More than her? Yes, she could see how far she had come through his presence, his pain. It showed in his gait, moreso in his gaze, in his garbled and raspy words, all at once intelligent, familiar, and incomprehensible. It showed in the shabby-looking woman's smile.

Aisha reentered the wrecked front room and sat down. Her father and the woman smiled at her with saddened, glossy eyes. "Glad you here, Isha…best day of my life." Really? Did he really mean that? How could he? How?

Dark thoughts began to fill Aisha's head. All was decay, slow death, and loss. All was loss and sadness. The air still stunk of that peculiar smell and though her father and the woman continued to smile at her, silent, lifeless smiles, just smiling because it seemed like the right thing to do, they were waiting for something, smiling, waiting for her to leave. It was time for her to go.

"I'm staying with Grandmother. I drove her car over here." Aisha stood up. Speedy stood up quickly with her.

"All right," he sung. "I'll be there in the morning. Got a lot of good people for you to meet. You and I, that's right. Best day of my life." Aisha had already begun walking out the door. The woman said goodbye to her in the same excited way that she had said hello. Halfway out of the door, Aisha hesitated before turning to give the woman a quick wave. Aisha walked back onto the junky porch and back into the night. She heard Speedy behind her. When she reached the car, he spoke.

"You know your way back?"

"Yes."

"Yeah, you got it. You smart. Got that from your daddy. It's in the Johnson blood. Remember I used to read to you. In the offseason, me and you."

"Yes."

"*The Poky Little Puppy.* Your favorite little book. What's he gone find here, what's he gone find there…" Speedy laughed. Aisha remained silent. She could not speak or move, the strangeness of the moment, her life, her grasp of its range, its fullness, was slipping away. What was there to hold onto? Memories? She did remember *The Poky Little Puppy* and her father reading to her, but she remembered her mother reading to her more. She remembered reading more to her father, him listening, correcting her when she began reading more advanced books and then not having to correct her anymore, not listening anymore, things becoming worse, and then him gone.

"I love you, Isha. Always have." This time when she looked in his eyes, looking hard, she saw sincerity behind the sadness, love, as he said, hidden behind all the pain.

"I love you, too," Aisha said, taking her eyes away from his. Not looking at him again. She closed the car door and drove away.

Back on the dark road to Grandmother Johnson's house, Aisha thought about all that had just occurred. Did she love him? He was practically a stranger. What did he know about her that wasn't in some far away time, almost a lifetime ago? Her mother had once said to her, "Lashawn was a good father, but he was an awful husband." Aisha had not forgotten any of the remarks, the few remarks, her mother had made about her father. They were always prompted by Aisha's questions. She'd wait until she thought the opportunity was right, her mother seeming to be in a good place, and she'd ask.

Despite the life her father was living, the haze that hung over everything, she saw that he was truly excited to see her. But all the happiness felt strangled. Was that love? Did she love someone she had not seen in twenty years, only to be pushed away, out the door, feeling like she had intruded on something, anxiousness for her to leave after that many years? Love? What kind of love leaves, never to return? Nothing good could come from returning to a love long dead.

Aisha pulled up to Grandmother Johnson's white house with the feeling that she had done it many times before. When she entered, she found Grandmother Johnson sitting asleep in a chair. Aisha spoke softly to her and placed her hand on her shoulder, giving the gentlest of nudges. "Grandmother…Grandmother." Grandmother Johnson opened her eyes suddenly and easily. Smiling and taking Aisha's face between her hands, she said, "By the Lord's grace, my great grandbaby has returned to me." Aisha felt her body relax as Grandmother Johnson let go of her face.

"Now, did you see your father?"

"Yes. He was happy to see me like you said. He'll be here in the morning."

"That's a blessing. Let us go to bed."

Grandmother Johnson rose slowly and led the way to the bedrooms. Placing both feet on each stair before advancing, she began singing softly.

"Morning by morning new mercies I see; All I have needed Thy hand hath provided, Great is Thy faithfulness, Lord unto me…"

Arriving at her room, Aisha hugged Grandmother Johnson tightly.

"Yes. Bless you. Good night, precious. If the Lord allows, I will see you in the morning."

Chapter 30

Awaking to the sound of birds, Aisha listened to their happy chirping. Their merriment fascinated her, as though it were the first time she had ever heard such a sound. The harder she listened, the more it seemed she could understand their language. "Good morning. Good morning to you. We are happy and free. Yes, we are happy and free."

When the birds no longer held her interest, she examined the room. Flowery patterns covered the walls. There was a dresser with a mirror atop it and a little chair beside it. The sun, announcing its presence, cast its light through the window. With various dolls being brightened by sunshine, Aisha began to think of her monkey, how she used to carry it everywhere, and how she had forgotten about it so effortlessly.

Someone was knocking at the door downstairs. Aisha didn't move on the first set of knocks, but on the next she rose and found it was her father.

"Morning, Isha. You sleep good?" he said, removing his hat and walking inside with the confidence of someone who knows a place well.

"Yes."

"That's good. That's good. This is a happy time." He took a few steps. Both were silent for a moment then he began talking.

"You see all these folks?" he said, pointing at the pictures on the walls. "These your people. All the way back to slavery. You're from a long line of teachers and doctors. We don't make no dummies."

"You see him?" Speedy pointed to a yellowed black and white picture of a man with a dignified pose. "That's your Great Great Great Grandfather Willis Johnson. Slave born. He was literate, freed himself, and taught other freed slaves to read."

"This man in this picture here," he said, pointing to another old picture, "this your Great Great Grandfather Cyrus. He married this woman, here." He pointed to another picture. "You see her light skin? Didn't know that, did you? That's right. You got it on both sides. Can't change history. Part of life." Speedy flashed a sly smile through his beard.

"Good morning, children," Grandmother Johnson said from the stairwell before emerging from the bottom step fully dressed. Aisha and Speedy both greeted her.

"Good morning, Grandmother, I was just showing Isha the family, family history and all that." He turned to Aisha. "Everybody can't chart it like us. Especially black folks. Being a Johnson is something to be proud of."

"My children, here with me," Grandmother Johnson said, clasping her hands together. "What a God, yes, a blessing."

"Grandmother, we're not about to hang around. I'm about to take Isha around to meet some good people."

"Good, father and daughter together, yes. Let me prepare breakfast for you before you go."

"No, thank you though, Grandmother. We'll be all right. I want to get to folks before they get to stepping."

"It's no trouble. It won't take but a minute."

"I know. I know. I appreciate you offering. If it was another time, you know I'd take you up on it. But we're going to gone on ahead and go. I'll bring her back to you."

"Well, okay," Grandmother Johnson said, looking a bit disappointed. "Maybe when you come back, precious, you could help me on the computer. I'm learning it. I can show you."

"Aw yeah, Isha can help with that, sure?" Aisha looked at Speedy then back to her grandmother.

"Yes, Grandmother. It would be my pleasure."

In the car, as Aisha buckled her seatbelt and prepared to pull off, Speedy spoke up. "I see you're still quiet, like your dad. Not much for talking, are we? Only with people we love." To hear him speak with such authority and truth about her unsettled Aisha. Questions, there were so many.

"I'm a diabetic. You need to know that. You got a history of that on the Johnson side." Aisha had pulled away slowly and Speedy motioned for her to make a right out of the driveway.

"And, Isha, when you came last night, I saw your face was looking funny. Had that funny look on it and all that."Speedy's voice changed. He turned away from Aisha, staring ahead as though he were the one driving.

"Last night you came in on a party. I like to party every now and then…you know."

"No, I don't know," Aisha said firmly.

"Crack," Speedy said, his head slightly bowed, as though the word disgusted him. There was silence.

"That was the smell?" Aisha said, almost to herself. Speedy did not respond. She continued, addressing her father more directly this time. "Here? How does it get here?"

"Just like anything else. Finds its way," Speedy replied.

"What else?" Aisha said, her voice more soft.

"I done done it all, Isha. No needles though. Drank."

"How long?"

"Long time. What you came in on last night I didn't start until I got back from the Persian Gulf."

"You were in the military?"

Speedy continued to stare out the front window."Yeah, done done a lot, Isha. Said when I saw you again, when you came to me, I wasn't going to keep nothing from you. But we 'bout to see some good people," Speedy said changing the subject and turning to her again. "Yeah, they gone be excited to meet you, yeah. Just keep on up the road, we on our way."

Aaron had helped Aisha better understand street drug culture. When she started teaching, she saw signs of it all around her. After the school day, in the night, she looked forward to her telephone conversation with Aaron and his responses to her questions. His love helped her become a better teacher. The subjects they discussed were serious but somehow he made them light. He made her laugh, and while she laughed she learned.

During their fractured period , the period they did not speak, when Aaron was swept up in the grief of Pop Pop's death, after it finally settled in, and him getting swept up in the fastlife his business allowed greater access to, Aisha would think of his lessons. She would think of him when she saw little boys, students she did not know, running wildly in the streets after school. He was once one of those boys. No supervision, until Pop Pop came along.

Aaron rarely talked about his mother, but when he did, it was all about good things. Although once, only once, when he came for Pop Pop's funeral, he told her everything. Back in her apartment, he cried in her arms. Through his sobs and fractured memories, he told her about his childhood, the scary times, the empty times, his mother's never-ending hard time, a nightmare Aaron learned to survive in. That night and Aisha's early years teaching forever removed her naivety about pain enmeshed with poverty.

Her father smoked crack.The crack epidemic was over, but the end of a drug epidemic does not end all the need. Where there is need, there are drugs. They never go anywhere, in private places, on public corners, in pockets of corrupted forgotten worlds. When it becomes comedy in the world, talk of crack heads, and junkies, caricatured, the need remains, uncured.

Someone, somewhere, like her father said, finds it. It finds its way, and they embrace it like the first hit, like when it first hit the world. It was never new, but some never knew, never know. It finds them, holding on, comforting, often never letting go until the end.

Aisha and Speedy pulled into the parking lot of what appeared to be a newer subsection of homes. The homes were all connected, still one level like the older, small single-family homes. The rest was nothing but open land and sky, electric and telephone poles the tallest objects.

Parking the car, Aisha observed that the subdivision contrasted with the rest of the town landscapes. It looked urban. They both got out of the car. Without saying anything, Speedy began walking. Aisha did not question him. She trusted him, not with her heart, but with her life.

They walked up to one of the homes and Speedy knocked. A little girl opened the door, her face dark and radiant, shining, beautiful. The doorknob was above her head. She could not have been any older than four.

"How's Poppa's baby? Yeah…" Speedy picked the little girl up and stepped inside. Timidly, Aisha followed. The place was smaller than Speedy's house, but it looked more spacious because it was well kept. It would have looked even more spacious if it was not for the huge television toward the back of the room to Aisha's left. Its screen was black. Sounds from a radio filled the air. Sitting on the couch directly to Aisha's left was a pretty, fair-skinned girl, who appeared to be around the age of twenty. She stared at a book, sucking her thumb. There was a toddler on the floor, scooting, with the same shiny face of the little girl who opened the door. A lean man sat at the kitchen table in the next room and a middle-aged, tall, and robust woman sat on the love seat to Aisha's right against the wall. The radio was sitting atop an end table next to the middle-aged woman. Speedy spoke to this woman.

"Hey Aunty Meta, Candy Cane, where Angie?"

"Speedy, you know she at work."

"Well, I got a surprise for y'all." As he was saying these words, the lean man from the kitchen table looked over and got up. He was walking toward Speedy and Aisha, past Speedy to her. He was special. He hugged Aisha. At first, Aisha's arms remained at her side, but she slowly brought them up to hug the man back, lightly.

"Sugarman," Speedy said.

"Sugarman, get off of her," said the robust woman, sitting down.

"Well, Sugarman done beat me to it, this Isha."

"Get out of here, Speedy!" said the same woman who had told the man to get off of her, getting up from her seat.

"Sho is, she came on down, happy day."

The lean special man they called Sugarman still held on to Aisha. Aisha held him back and, out of the corner of her eye, she could see the young woman, the thumb sucker, had removed her thumb from her mouth and had taken her eyes from her book to see what was going on.

"Sugarman, c'mon, get on off her," the woman said, prying Sugarman off Aisha.

"I ain't never seen him do that before. Sugarman likes women, but not all and not right away." Now the woman had her arms open to hug Aisha. She did.

"Hey, girl, I'm Meta or Aunty Meta, whichever." They parted.

"You already done met Sugarman. This baby here crawling at my feet is your niece Celestia." Her what?

"That one right there, Speedy holding, is your niece Sheilah."

"They mama, your sister Angie, is at work. She an assistant manager at the McDonald's over in Caruthersville. This one here is Angie's best friend, Candance. We call her Candy." Candance, making eye contact with Aisha for the first time, waved with the wet thumb hand.

"When did you get into town?" Meta asked.

"I got in last night," Aisha replied, the words coming out automatically, taking in all that was before her. She had a sister with two children, her nieces?

"And Speedy got you up early to show you off, huh?"

"That's right. She got a lot of good folk to meet."

"Well, y'all gone head. We'll be here. Isha, you make sure you come back around to talk to me. Angie gets off at six o'clock. I know Speedy ain't told you nothing. This Angie's house; we'll be here."

Aisha smiled and nodded her head. Below her Sheilah pulled at her shirt, so Aisha looked down.

"You're pretty," she said.

"Thank you, Sheilah, you're pretty, too," Aisha returned. At this, Sheilah smiled, put her hand by her face, and twirled.

"A'ight," Speedy said. "We out the door."

Stepping into the cool air, Aisha felt lightheaded, her legs unsteady.

"I have a sister?"

"Yeah," Speedy said, not looking at her again.

"How old is she?"

"'bout ten years younger than you. Somewhere around there."

Aisha looked at Speedy and said nothing at all. He returned a different look, also saying nothing.

At the beginning of her Haveton tour, she thought about nothing but her sister. There was another person with her DNA in the world, other people that she never knew about. She had beautiful, shiny-faced nieces. They looked like they had been well taken care of. Who were these people, Meta, the thumb sucker, Candance, Sugarman? All of them, in their own way, seemed to know her.

The day passed as Speedy took Aisha around Haveton. She met cousins, friends, and Speedy's partying friends. On the way to each destination, both rode in silence, Speedy's directions sufficient for verbal communication. Still, upon each new visit, Speedy would enliven. It seemed everyone whom they came across respected him. It was as if they did not see what Aisha saw or looked past it or did not care. One of her second cousins, nicknamed Horse, told her that Speedy had been his hero growing up and he'd never forget the time Speedy flew him out to Oakland to see a game. He had met Aisha then. He told her this when she said, "Nice to meet you." He responded, "Meet you? We already met!"

But it was not interactions like these that stood out for Aisha. The reactions of the people at most of the places they went exposed a side of her father that she already knew. Who she did not know was the man who inhabited another world with his so-called partying friends.

Finally, they visited the last partying friend. The man lived in a grey home no bigger than Aisha's living room in Chicago. Upon entering, the man stared at Aisha in a way that made her feel uncomfortable. Speedy saw this and quickly said, "Hey, this my daughter." The man gave her father a strange look and replied, "Your daughter? Nigga, you got kids? I thought you shot blanks!"

Aisha dropped Speedy back off at his home around two o'clock in the afternoon. Now alone, riding back to Grandmother Johnson's house, Aisha thought about her Haveton tour. It seemed as though she had met the entire town. Each time they would return from the car to see someone Speedy would tell her of each person. He would just tell the facts and nothing more, except in the case of Jimmy the general store owner and his ex-wife Anna. Speedy and Aisha had stopped to meet both, but only Jimmy was available at the small store. After leaving the general store, Speedy told Aisha that Jimmy and Anna were of the few white people that remained in Haveton. The rest had all eventually moved to a newer neighborhood built right next door, named Haveton Heights. They were also the only people from the town who were not family that were able to come see him play, and with their own money. During that time, they were on their second marriage to each other. Speedy knew the story well, because he had heard Anna tell it so much. Their first marriage lasted three years. They divorced for about a year and remarried each other; that marriage lasted seventeen years. Speedy hoped Anna would be home, because she told the story better than he did. It was hers. But when he saw she was not home, he said, "Probably in Caruthersville. She work at a donut shop. You see that?" He pointed to a home. "That's where Anna stay. She got the original house. And that right there," Speedy said, pointing to what looked to be a garage with living quarters on top, "that's where Jimmy stay. It used to be his shop, but when they split, they couldn't decide who was going to keep the land, so he just built a place on top of it. It's all the same lot. You see? Arrangement been kept all these years. Not for them, but for the kids. Jimmy don't ever talk about it, but Anna's told me out her mouth. And they don't talk or nothing. About the most they say to each other is who has to pay what on the light and water bill each month because they split it. 'You owe thirty-three fifty this month.'" Speedy started to chuckle. "That's about all they say to each other. But for the kids. One place to see both. Right here mama, right here daddy, right here grandmamma, right here granddaddy. Not a bad way to live."

Aisha found Grandmother Johnson crocheting when she entered. Grandmother Johnson praised God, hugged her, and asked her whether she had ever crocheted before. Aisha said, out of all the things she had done, she had never even sewed a stitch.

"It's easy, watch now." She sat down what she was working on and picked up a fresh piece of yarn. With the needle, she made a swift move, all one fluid motion, while saying, "You just make a loop and pull it on through…here, like this!" She showed Aisha once again, then gave Aisha her own yarn and needle to work with. Aisha tried the technique many times, but found it to be not as easy as Grandmother Johnson made it look. "Hold your fingers like this. Like this, make the loop, and pull it on through." When Aisha did finally get it right, she set the needle and material down. Her concentration on it had exhausted the rest of her energy. How much newness and revelation could she take? Summoning some reserve energy, she asked Grandmother Johnson if she would like her help on the computer. "Oh, yes!" she replied, looking like a child who had just been offered a sweet treat. Aisha delighted in seeing this face, its childlike quality, the wisdom and innocence together.

Grandmother Johnson took great satisfaction in Aisha helping her on the computer. As they worked, she told Aisha she had finished her high school education as a much older woman, well after her children were grown. As a girl, there was not much time or opportunity for schooling. "In Haveton, you worked in the fields. Planted cotton in the spring and picked it in the fall. But all of our children went to school. Lacy was intelligent, but unlike his brothers, he liked the field. But he respected education and we decided that I would work with the children. With his land, he made more than enough to provide for us. Our children all graduated near the top of their class. I remember when the two oldest were in middle school and there was a big test coming up, a state examination. They came on the radio, 'Don't teach your children at home. You don't know how!' But I thought that was nonsense. I stayed up with them, drilling them, and they came home from school and said, 'Mama, we scored the highest in the county!'" Aisha enjoyed hearing Grandmother Johnson talk, especially when it was straight talk. But in the middle of Grandmother Johnson's words Aisha interrupted her, saying, "Grandmother, why did my mother start writing to you?"

"Well, it was a long time ago and my memory isn't as good as it used to be. I don't know the exact reason. It was before she left your father."

"Do you still have her letters?" At this, Grandmother Johnson's face lit up.

"Yes!" she replied, rising immediately and walking away to get the letters. Aisha rose from the computer station and walked to the dining room table. After a while, Grandmother Johnson returned, walking slowly and carrying a box.

"I'm sorry, Grandmother. I wasn't thinking. I could have gotten those for you," Aisha said, getting up and taking the load for the rest of the way.

"That's all right, child. The Lord has blessed me to live alone. I'm used to it." She moved to pull out a stack of letters.

"You're old enough to see. I've arranged them by date. Yes, oh yes, what a God." Aisha sat down, looked at the stack of letters in front of her and then up at Grandmother Johnson. Grandmother Johnson put her hand on Aisha's shoulder and then walked off toward the kitchen.

The aroma of the meal being prepared wafted to Aisha's nose. It was five thirty. She had been reading for two straight hours. Her mother's letters were full of wonder. There was also pain, but the pain brought clarity. The letters took her away from the table in Haveton to a time she did not know and times she did, although not from the perspective she read. As the letters got later in chronology, Aisha began remembering some of the instances that were written about. Yet, the fullness of the details had her reliving the experience as if she had never lived it before, adding deeper meaning. She read the letters fast, though not missing the subtlest or slightest detail. Letter after letter, she opened and read each, folding it back neatly and placing it back in its envelope, back in its place, and on to the next. With still more letters to go, Aisha reached a shorter letter from her mother. It was the point that her mother decided to finally keep Aisha away from her father.

Dear Mother Johnson,

I have decided, finally, that I do not want Lashawn in our lives. I need to be safe and beyond my safety, Aisha needs consistency and stability. Lashawn loves her, I know, but his lifestyle, the things he does, his erratic behavior, I do not want her anywhere around it. I believe her childhood should be as free as possible from the ugliness of adult life. It will come one day, I know. I'm going to have to let her go , but not now. So if he ever asks where we are now, please tell him you do not know. I don't know what this will mean for Aisha. She loves her father and she is beginning to resent me for his leaving. But she's smart. I have to trust that this will pass. She knows things were not right between us. Aisha is my child and I have to make the decision that I believe is right for her and hope that one day she will understand.

Well, that's that. I'm healing well. Thank you for your loving kindness. I've mentioned it before, but I think I am reaching a point where I can begin dating again. But I'm going to take it slow, more for Aisha's sake. The men that come into my life need not come into hers. I don't know; we'll see. Dating isn't a high priority for me. My greatest concern is that Aisha grow up with the best of opportunities that I am able to provide her with, an abundance of healthy challenges, and to see as much beauty in the world as she can.

You have helped me so much over these past years. I cannot comprehend your strength, but maybe one day I will. Please, if Lashawn ever asks you if you know where we are, say no, please. That's final. I know I'm asking you to lie and that may not agree with you, but you know what I have been through. I must move on and raise Aisha in a stable, healthy, happy environment. Her happiness is mine. I will continue to write you, letting you know how things are going with me and how she is growing. Of course I'll call, too, but letters are lovely. Aren't they?

With Love,
Rose

Aisha finished this letter, folding it and putting it back in its proper place as she had done the rest. Grandmother Johnson began bringing delicious-smelling dishes to the table. Many of the dishes were meatless. What wonderful-smelling collard greens and what variety. How long had it been since she had a meal like this?

Having finished a good portion of her mother's letters and having read all of the letters Grandmother Johnson sent to her mother, Aisha understood to an even greater extent how well her grandmother knew her. She watched as Grandmother Johnson moved from the kitchen to the table, watched her setting the table. This woman had seen nearly a century and been widowed for over two decades. In her living, she had seen the cycles of life, the ups and downs, steps backward and forward, progression and stagnation, the Great Depression and personal ones. She witnessed oppression spawning invention, oppression preventing it, invention with support, innovation, contention, and domination. How did she survive it all? How did she survive all those years with that awareness? And she still was open, loving, when having lived most of her life with her most immediate world believing she was less than, less than white men, white women, a man, her men, treating her in varying ways in the same way of those who hated them whom they hated. Almost one hundred years? Look at her still walking upright, able to take care of herself, now alone, though having already raised children in a world that was cruel to them, hated them. How was Haveton? What kind of man was Grandfather Lacy? She had him for so long and now he was gone. Now death any day is a normal, expected thing. How do you live that long and see all that she's seen, death any day now, and set plates on the table with a smile?

When everything had been set up, Grandmother Johnson sat down and said a prayer. Both fixed their plates and began to eat. The food tasted as good as it smelled. Its steam rose, falling delicately on Aisha's face. She took bites and observed Grandmother Johnson eating. They ate in silence until Aisha spoke up.

"Grandmother, do you know I have a sister?"

"No. You do?" Grandmother Johnson replied, putting her fork down and looking at Aisha, waiting for her to say more.

"Here in Haveton. Her name is Angie. You don't know her?"

"No." Grandmother Johnson's face grew grave. "I did not know." Both women fell silent. This time, it was Aisha who waited for Grandmother Johnson to speak. She did not want to continue looking at her while waiting, so she put her fork to her plate and played with her food some. When Grandmother Johnson did begin to speak, Aisha lifted her head.

"Did your mother tell you that you were named after your father's mother?"

"Yes, I was told when I was younger." Grandmother Johnson pushed her plate forward and folded her hands on the table.

"I didn't know her well, your grandmother. She used to be around here with your grandfather, Hankey. But you know there were a lot of little girls who liked my boys and I didn't pay them much mind. But then Hankey got her pregnant and she had your father. Your grandfather was a young father and I did not want that life for him. But that is the way it went. And just when I was getting used to him being a father early, the Lord took him from us. We loved your father, and we had big plans for him and Hankey. Hankey was my baby. After he went home to glory, I did not treat your grandmother in the way that the Lord would have wanted. We didn't have much to do with her. Your father had two lives, one with us and one with his mother. We helped raise him. He loved coming around us and playing with all his cousins. He got that name from them. They began calling him Speedy because he would be out there beating all the older boys in foot races." Grandmother Johnson abruptly stopped her speech and got up from the table, slowly walking out of the dining room. When she came back, she was carrying a large photo album and a few picture frames stacked on top of it.

"Did your father show you a picture of Hankey?"

"No. I guess we didn't make it to him."

"Well, here he is," she said, stacking the three framed pictures up in front of Aisha. "Handsome, isn't he?"

They stared at the different pictures, three different perspectives, one of him in a suit, a shot from the waist up; one of him wearing overalls, chasing a little boy, her father, which her grandmother pointed out when she saw Aisha's eyes fall on the picture; and the third of her grandfather posing by his car.

"It was hard on me, losing him. But even as I fell short, unworthy of his goodness, the Lord was with me."

When enough time had passed, Grandmother Johnson brought the photo album over to Aisha and began turning through the pages. The sound of the sticking pages filled the air.

"This is the only picture I have of your grandmother, here," she said, pointing at the picture in the album, "with Hankey." Aisha stared at the two. They were posed outside of the very house Aisha sat in at an angle where a part of the big barn could be seen in the distance. Aisha stared hard and long at that picture. It made her think of her and Aaron.

"Your father should have some more pictures of her." The two fell silent again.

"I never asked your father if he had any more children. When he came around, he would only talk about you. I don't get around now as much as I used to. But when I used to be busy about the town, I would look in the faces of the children I saw. I would look for a resemblance. The Lord has allowed me to have a long life, yet I am imperfect. Only God knows why we do the things we do. When your father comes, I never ask him much about what he does. The Lord will bring him to me when he wants to." Grandmother Johnson laid her hand atop Aisha's hand and continued talking. "Be encouraged. When your mother died, I told him where to reach you. I gave him a picture of you by your dorm at Harvard. Your mother had sent it to me right before the Lord took her."

"How did he respond?" Aisha asked. Grandmother Johnson waited a moment before speaking.

"He said thank you. He said if I had anymore pictures I could give him, he'd take them. Then he went home."

"Did he ever ask you if you knew where I was before then?" Again, Grandmother Johnson waited, then looked straight at Aisha and said, "No."

"Precious, he's a good man. He helps me around here whenever I need it. I pay him some money, but I know he would do the work without it. He likes the land. He was raised on it. The Lord handles all. Bring your sister here…my lost great grandbaby. The ways of the Lord are mysterious, oh yes. He wants us to know his greatness."

The idea of bringing her family together lifted Aisha's spirits momentarily. She and Grandmother Johnson resumed eating in a comfortable silence. Aisha appreciated her efforts to comfort her about her father's absence and his lack of communication even when he knew where she could be found. But Aisha had long since overcome the hurtful feelings associated with this. Once upon a time, she was a well-balanced and successful woman. She became that without him. Yet, now she was dealing with a far greater pain. The move she made to tie her whole life together was the same move that unraveled all the right that she had ever known, all the beauty she had built up in her, the work from herself and her mother. She was fortunate to have had such a loving mother. What kind of mother does Angie have?

In these thoughts, Aisha realized the time, remembering the time Meta said Angie would return home. It was then twenty after six.

"Grandmother, may I use your car again? I'm supposed to meet my sister, Angie, at her house at six o'clock."

"Oh, yes! Go ahead, sweetheart, anytime you want to use it, go right ahead. I don't use it much, anymore. The Lord has finally begun to take my strength, but I've been blessed with walking on my own and in my right mind. Thank you, Jesus! The Lord allowed me to buy that car new at ninety-two, and with the help of the Lord, I was able to take care of the payments. When Lacy died, I had to do things on my own, manage the farm, our land, new siding on the house, but the Lord made a way… Oh! I'm sorry child. I'm just talking. I'm just so happy. Go on, precious, my beautiful grandbaby, the Lord will be with you."

Smiling, Aisha got up from her chair and picked up her plate.

"I'll take care of that, precious, I got it. You go on. Grandmother loves you dearly."

Still smiling, Aisha walked over and hugged Grandmother Johnson very tight. "I love you too, Grandmother."

Aisha arrived at Angie's house and knocked at the door. A different woman opened it. She had the same clear and radiant skin as the little ones, Sheilah at her legs. Her sister. She opened her arms wide to hug Aisha. Aisha embraced her, feeling a hard, round bulge, the kind she had once contemplated having.

"I was hoping you would come back tonight. When Aunty Meta told me, I was so excited! I couldn't believe it! C'mon, c'mon in!"

"Thank you, Angie. I'm happy to meet you."

"Girl, I know! C'mon, we were waiting on you to start dinner. You see, I'm eating for two now."

"Yes, I see. I felt it."

"With the girls I found out what I was having, but this time I want it to be a surprise." Aisha followed her sister in, smiling down at Sheilah who, still by her mother's side, had turned around quickly to look at Aisha. Celestia was on a cushy-looking blanket on the floor, some toys around her. Sugarman sat on the couch where Candance had sat, although on the opposite side. The huge TV was on, which he watched. Aisha almost expected him to get up and greet her again, but he sat, not even turning. Meta was in the kitchen preparing dinner.

"Speedy take you around?" Meta asked.

"Yes, he did."

"Sit down, Isha. Let me have your coat," Angie said. Aisha took off her coat and handed it to her sister, then sat down next to Sugarman. Feeling the vibration of someone sitting down next to him, Sugarman turned and saw Aisha. He hugged her, laying his head on her shoulder for a moment, and then went back to watching his program.

"They told me Sugarman liked you," Angie said. "Candance called me at work this morning right when you left and told me you were here with Speedy. I didn't believe it! I was like, 'Girl stop lying,' but…you hungry? We were waiting on you. Aunty Meta said you would be here."

"No, thank you. I just ate." A strange feeling came over Aisha. Her sister had never sat at the table she had just sat at. She had probably seen

Grandmother Johnson many times in town, but did not know her love. "Please, start. I'm sorry I made you wait."

"Uh uh, don't even worry about it," Angie said, picking up Celestia from the floor. "I'm just happy you here. But let me get the girls to the table. I gave them a little snack, but I know they ready to eat." As she spoke, Meta had called Sugarman to the kitchen table. It appeared he was also ready to eat.

As Angie got the girls settled at the table and Meta served the plates, Aisha sat down on the other couch near the stereo, where Meta had sat earlier in the day. From the spot Aisha sat, she could look right into the kitchen and be a part of dinner. She leaned her body so that it showed her interest in what was happening in the kitchen. A family dinner. Growing up, she had longed to be apart of such a sight. When she would eat at other people's houses and they ate together, in the way Angie, the girls, Meta, and Sugarman ate, Aisha secretly wished she had a family that would do the same. Compared to those she grew up around, her and her mother's life was different in many ways. The very makeup of her household—its mix of races, first three then two, and her mother's unorthodox beliefs, like raising Aisha vegetarian, a conviction Aisha resented at times when she was younger because it made her stand out even more, though by that time there was not much she could do about it—made her feel different.

Once Angie saw that her children were comfortable, busy at finishing their food, she asked Aisha about her trip. Where did she live, what did she do for a living, and what did she think about Haveton? Surprisingly, Aisha answered the questions with relative ease, not exposing the hurtful truth that remained behind them, yet at the same time not being disingenuous. She was impressed with the way it all came from her mouth, half-truths flowing, and nothing more necessary. Angie and Meta listened to her every word intently. Meta, however, was quiet, different from how she had appeared earlier. Angie asked all the questions. She asked Aisha, "What was going to Harvard like?" at the same time rising to get up from the table and passing Aisha while still talking, apparently going to get something. Sheilah looked curiously at the direction her mother went. Angie came back with a picture of Aisha. It must have been the same picture Grandmother Johnson gave her father. "I had Speedy give it to me so I could make a copy." It was indeed. While Angie returned to the table, Aisha stared at the picture, her smiling by the red brick of Grays Hall. Her mother died not long after the picture was taken. Aisha kept staring at it, looking at the smiling girl as though she could not believe it was her. How was going to Harvard?

Aisha looked up from the picture and saw her sister's beautiful chocolate skin shining, her eyes bright with anticipation of Aisha's answer. Meta too, looking on, waiting. They waited with curious and excited looks, a real wanting to know, and not the cynical, facetious, envious, or perfunctory expressions others showed after having asked the same question. She had grown used to the question being asked by those who felt the need to. Out of all the times she had to answer, only once in a great while she would get pleasing reactions, ones of admiration, support, or gleeful disbelief, somewhere underneath the thought 'if you can, I can.' But mostly Aisha saw many did not know how to feel when confronted with the knowledge of where she had been schooled. Most, however, knew they should feel something, should say something, so they did, and it often came out flat. No questions following it, no looks like Angie and Meta.

For years, others' discomfort around her answer of having gone to Harvard, discomforted her, so much so that at one time she was reluctant to tell people where she went to school. She'd say it fast, or when people did not hear her correctly, thinking she said Howard, she'd hesitate to correct them, sometimes leaving it incorrect. No shame in Howard. Once she moved to the South Side of Chicago to teach, she was at once removed from those that felt more readily compelled to ask the question of where she had gone to school and those whom the answer to the question left no shock. Teaching in Englewood, the question of Harvard rarely came up. All that mattered was her working to lift her students up, helping them learn to lift themselves and helping them to know that rising, climbing, was possible, and discovering dreams, their own dream places, was also possible. Growing up, she did not dream of going to Harvard. She happened upon the possibility and it seemed like a good thing. Sitting on Angie's couch, like teaching on the South Side, the place was so distant it seemed she had never been.

But that night, fulfilling the air of expectation from the on looking eyes that looked like hers, not in color but in their shape and even the sincerity, the earnestness, Aisha took them back to Harvard with her. She told them about the wonders, gave them the full picture, as full as she could paint it. She could see they truly wanted to hear about it. And as she told of it, she realized she enjoyed the telling.

Despite losing her mother at its beginning, it was a beautiful time in her life. She told Meta and Angie about Kaii and how loving and supportive and funny she was. She would not have made it without her. Together, they made Harvard a playground. While many of their peers were silently or openly struggling with the stress and pressure of Harvard's competitive atmosphere, so convicted were they to be the best among the best, she and Kaii focused on having the best experience. They focused on fun and the best elements of the place beyond books and intellectual discourse. Certainly, they were interested in both, but more on falling in love with each other, liking the unveiling of commonality, personality, and perspective, each other's spirited openness, each other's love of laughter, laughter and happiness wherever they could find it, in whatever shape and color it came in. Together, their friendship helped them enjoy the extraordinary elements of Harvard, smiling through the experience together.

She told them, in her time, Harvard was one of the rare places on earth that the daughter of a billionaire sat equally next to the son of migrant farmers, with their backgrounds unknown unless exposed. Their backgrounds mattered, were important, only in the exchange of culture and how it contributed to the collection of thought or the pursuit of truth. Certainly, there was exclusion, those that sectioned themselves off for status, the homogeneity of status being of the utmost importance. There were those who would section themselves off regardless of where they were in the world, but mostly for Aisha its diversity welcomed inclusion unlike any place she had ever seen. There were the many wonderful speakers she heard up close and how easy it was to see them, Nelson Mandela being the greatest. How easy it was to confer with esteemed professors in their field, walk right up and, for a time, be privileged with the intimacy of the up-close imbibing of their knowledge. Daily, she sat with the children of world leaders, those who aspired to lead the world themselves, those who looked to follow a great something else, or those in the line of pioneers, those students who looked to pioneer, and those who had already pioneered. It was the place where two loves for her became clear, teaching and Aaron.

The flow of Aisha's description was disrupted with Aaron stuck in the forefront of her mind. She had tried, hard, but she could no longer keep him separate. Her speech faltered when she was struck by the vividness of a memory. She saw the night she and Aaron took a walk down JFK, over the bridge, crossing the Charles, and entering into the athletic complex. Aaron had already said goodbye to that daily walk and at the time of them walking together that night Aisha was contemplating saying goodbye. She had told Aaron that she was thinking about quitting track. He teased her, saying she was just trying to be like him.

That night was a special night, a warm spring night, their time together on campus coming to an end. The moon shined big, lighting the ivy-covered walls of Harvard Stadium, which towered over the rest of the buildings. They had begun the walk with no intention of walking to the athletic fields, but they ended up there. They ended up in front of Lavietes Pavilion, and Aaron tried the doors on the gym with a trick he used to use that no longer worked. The two then walked to Gordon Field House and tried every door, jerking at them, until one opened easily. They entered and walked to the track and on the track, around the track. Aisha began to jog, urging Aaron on with her legs. They jogged together, talking about the first time they had met in that very place, their first impressions, not speaking about how far they had come in that short time, but both feeling it as they strode around the embankment of the track, and picking up speed and more speed, and more, not racing, but matching each other's stride until they moved swiftly, slowing only when they realized what had begun. Each smiled and with each slowing stride, their laughter grew. What were they doing? Walking now, Aisha told Aaron that she sometimes hurdled in high school. She was good at it and won every time she ran the event. Still, she enjoyed the sprints the best. With the moon shining on part of Aaron's face, he feigned disbelief. "Why you lying? You didn't hurdle." At that, Aisha picked up a hurdle and walked with it until she found its mark on the track. Without saying a word, Aaron picked up a hurdle, looked to see what mark Aisha set her hurdle on, and set his up. They set up two more and when they were finished, Aisha backed up to get a little start and took off. She glided easily over the hurdles, one, step, step, step, two, step, step, step, three, step, step, step, four. Her jeaned legs scraped one of the hurdles only slightly, each time her lead leg effortlessly showed the flat soles of her shoes. Turning around from the hurdle, her chest heaving a bit, she saw Aaron's face smile in the moonlight. In that moment, he told her she was beautiful for the first time.

So sitting there in these thoughts, with happy times at Harvard with Aaron, how early, how brief, how beautiful, Aisha's speech about her alma mater began to fail. But even in her failing, her tripping over words, speaking harder, clumsily, choppy, the flow gone, Angie and Meta's faces remained warm. Even through her ineloquence, their faces remained warm and inviting, until Aisha felt it best to stop.

"I can tell you loved it, Isha," Angie said.

"I guess I did. I don't think about it much now."

"I want to go to college. After this one…"Angie said, resting her hand on her stomach. "…I'm going to try." Sugarman began to shake his head side to side, not saying no, only shaking his head side to side. Celestia imitated him, holding her spoon in the air with a small clump of mashed potatoes in it.

"You can do it," Meta said, speaking up for the first time. Aisha, now at a loss for words, feeling strange for how much she had spoken, shook her head slowly but demonstratively in agreement. "Just keep believing," Meta continued, "and after you have this baby, that's it. You got your family. Just got to change your living, change your thinking, and keep believing."

Was it that easy? Aisha thought. Perhaps it was, once for her it was, but now? Now her challenge was something else, something greater, which made those three changes seem impossible. She had tried, had not given in fully. She was there, in Haveton, and felt good to be sitting with her sister and Meta. She felt more alive with less active pain, yet she could still feel the sadness's power over her. It defined her.

"Okay," Meta began, "been here long enough time for me and the Sugarman to gone home."

Angie stood up and took Celestia out of her high chair, motioning to Sheilah.

"Meta, do you need a ride?" Aisha said. "I can take you wherever you need to go."

"Thank you, Isha," Angie said, still standing holding Celestia, wiping her face. Aisha smiled.

"C'mon, Sugarman, c'mon; we riding with Isha."

Everyone said their goodbyes, hugs all around. When Aisha hugged Angie, she hugged her tight and told her she would be back tomorrow.

Meta did not live on the outskirts of town like Grandmother Johnson, so the ride was short.

"Usually in the summertime me and Sugarman walk," Meta said as they arrived at the house. Meta gave a wave of her hand, inviting Aisha inside. It was an old home like Speedy's, although far more orderly in appearance. Aisha could tell from only looking at it in the dark. When Meta turned on the lights, Aisha noticed that the ceiling in the center of the living room had collapsed. A sight to see, it looked as if the roof intended to cave all the way in at that exact center point, but changed its mind, remaining there, sagging. Meta noticed Aisha staring at the sagging ceiling.

"It's been like that for years. I don't think it's going anywhere anytime soon. Me and Sugarman will deal with it when it does."

I can fix it, Aisha thought.

"Gone head, Isha, sit down." She did, watching Sugarman move around freely, a different kind of look to him in his own home.

"He's my baby brother. My mama only had two of us. I takes care of him and he takes care of me. A simple life; easy living.

"I probably looked the same way you did coming through Angie's door when I found out I had a brother. I didn't know, just like you." And with that, Meta began to again look like the woman Aisha had first met that morning. She spoke freely to Aisha, as though she had been waiting to have the conversation for a long time. They talked well past midnight, Meta talking the most. She spoke of her life, which was connected to Speedy's life.

Meta rarely got to talk with anyone anymore who could understand, who would listen, who, in their own way, could match the substance of her years, the span and depth of her experience. She told Aisha she talked to Sugarman all the time, but he couldn't understand, or at least he could not to reciprocate. He could not ask her questions like Aisha asked, which she appreciated, which made her talk more. But who knew what happened inside of him. At times, his eyes stared with such a gaze it seemed as though he had deep understanding of life. Those looks helped her get along. She told Aisha how she talked to Angie and Candance a lot, but knew they were young and would listen only so much, could only comprehend but so much. The stories she chose to tell them, though vivid, were distant, unreal to them because nothing in Meta's current life reflected them. But she had lived it. It was all real.

She told Aisha that her grandmother, who was Speedy's mother, and Meta's mother were great friends, close like Angie and Candance. Meta's mother never wanted any children. She let Meta know this constantly. Growing up, she felt her mother's hatred far more than her love. She hated Meta's father and Meta favored her father in appearance and, in addition to her father's likeness, a man she saw only a few times in her life, her mother sensed that Meta liked women. She would say to her, "Stop acting like a damn dyke. What the hell wrong with you?" She knew even before Meta knew fully. "Mamas have intuition. She could smell it on me."

Speedy was like Meta's big brother. And her big brother was the town hero. Surely, everyone would say, by the way he moved on the field, God had made him to play the game of football. Because Meta was so tall, Speedy would encourage her to play basketball. She said that Grandmother Johnson did not know her, but she knew Grandmother Johnson. The whole town knew her and loved her. 'Mother Johnson' is what they called her. But Meta knew her before she was known as Mother Johnson.

There used to be a basketball hoop on the side of the Johnson's barn. There were a few times where Speedy would coach her on how to play the game. What she remembered most is how dreamy he was, how he told her she could be the best woman player in the world. She remembered how excited his eyes looked, how much he believed what he was saying. Meta could not stand throwing the ball at the basket. Seeing it fall in rarely, in many tries, brought her no joy. She did not like the game, but when she was with her big brother, she enjoyed doing anything he wanted to do. He made her feel special.

Halfway through high school, Speedy's mother moved from Haveton to Chicago. Meta remembered the day Speedy's mother told her mother she had to get out of the town. Speedy decided to stay because Haveton was what he knew and all his friends were there and he wanted to win the state championships for Haveton, which he did. But he did not stay with the Johnsons; he lived with his mother's parents, the Williams. He won state championships in football and track. After high school, he and some of his teammates went to Lincoln University in Jefferson City, Missouri. Meta never got the opportunity to attend one of Speedy's track meets, but the whole town knew he turned down an invitation to the Olympic trials to play professional football. What she did remember was the one college football game of Speedy's she attended. Like his high school games, Meta really did not know the rules well. What she remembered most about the action on the field that day was Speedy running up and down the field and the opposing team falling at his feet, trying to tackle him. But she had seen all that before. What interested her most was the bag of popcorn a stranger sitting next to her gave to her and its buttery goodness. And the atmosphere, what an atmosphere, all the fans, parents, alumni, and students, all cheering passionately. And the bands, the halftime show, what a performance, the sun reflecting off the shiny brass instruments, the synchronization, and the drum majors. She remembered setting her popcorn down, standing up in the stands and trying to imitate the drum major and majorettes. Meta stood up while telling the story and tried to recreate the moment by dancing. Sugarman took the opportunity to do a dance himself, keeping it going far too long, doing his own dance well after Meta had returned to her seat. "Okay Sugarman, sit on down," Meta said, turning in her chair to him then turning back to Aisha and continuing her story.

Meta told Aisha that her mother followed Aisha's grandmother to Chicago after a couple of years. The year was 1973 and Meta was thirteen years old. Between the period of thirteen and fifteen was a dark time. Her mother's abuse grew worse. One of the happy moments Meta remembered during those years was when she had the opportunity to see Speedy play on television. She wished that she could walk through the television and once again be in the stands away from her mother, and she would stay there. "Country folk should have a plan when they move to the city. It'll swallow you up easy if you don't." It happened to her mother, no plan. And when her relationship was strained with Aisha's grandmother, things began to fall apart. Aisha's grandmother had found a good man and, as a result, Meta's mother did not see Aisha's Grandmother as much anymore. They did not go out partying and drinking like they used to when Meta and her mother first moved to Chicago. And it seemed to Meta that her mother took all her aggression and frustrations out on her. When she could no longer take the abuse, she ran away.

After three days of wandering, hungry, walking down the street in delirium, not knowing where she would go, only that she would never return to her mother, she came into the hands of the philosopher pimp, Plato. He pulled his red El Dorado with white leather interior over and began talking to her. He knew she was hungry, knew she needed shelter, and he made Meta feel like he was the only one who could provide it for her. He was her only option and best option. At the start, and for most of the time, Plato treated her real kind, kinder than most ever had. He flattered her about her height and her body. She was one of the finest, strangest things he had ever seen and he would take care of her. He brought her to live with the rest of his ladies. After a while, she became known as Gooney Girl because of her striking height, large breasts, small waist, and big behind. She liked the nickname. The girls called her it with affection. She liked the fact that she had a nice place to live and food to eat and she was not being hit. And being around all the girls was fun. Plato took a long time before he suggested that she turn her first trick. He had already taken her virginity. She felt it was the least she could do for all that he had done for her. He was gentle with her. He made her feel like no one ever had. So when he suggested that she turn her first trick, she did so willingly.

Quickly, she became one of Plato's favorites. Not his bottom bitch, because she was too young, but one of his favorites. The tricks could not get enough of her, either, but Plato would not put her out in the street as much as he did the other girls. She was special, privileged. So the times she strolled up and down Madison Street, the times she laid down in the fanciest hotels, the times she laid down in the filthiest of motels, bending over in cars, she did not mind. Plato did not hit her like her mother did and the times he cursed at her did not cut like when her mother cursed her.

But of it all, what Meta enjoyed most of all were all the girls. She loved being around them. She found them all to be beautiful, each in her own unique way, even as she saw that beauty changing, fading, with each passing day on the street. When they were not working, they stayed together in a big house on the West Side of Chicago. They were all at once sisters and lovers, selling their bodies so they could stay together. So they could be touched by Plato, clutched by Plato. They shared him. Sharing him was all right, because everyone got his attention. When Meta was not working the street or getting special attention from Plato, an act that never ceased to feel like duty for her, turning tricks duty for her, she was under one of the girls. They did everything together. During the good times, Plato would take them to the amusement park or to the movies. Occasionally, they would go to a fancy restaurant, where they nearly always were asked to leave. What a scene they caused! They caused a scene wherever they went, but it did not matter, because they were together laughing and trying to love one another the only way they knew how.

Aisha could see Meta's fondness for the girls in how her eyes lit up in telling of those times. Even with the sadness alongside it, she could see her understanding. She talked of how she loved to hear the girls tell funny stories about the tricks, them consoling one another when a trick turned out bad, and consoling one another when Plato hit one of them bad. She enjoyed watching the way they all popped up, came alive, when Plato blew his funny sounding horn, watching each girl's unique shuffle toward him, toward that sound. She could still see it. Sometimes, she still heard that horn.

Meta made the sound of Plato's horn for Aisha. She did it over and over until the sound rang in Aisha's ears. Meta made the noise as if she liked bringing it from her head through her mouth, momentarily losing herself in it. Sugarman came over close to Meta, staring at her mouth. Had he not heard her make that sound before? He put his hand on Meta's shoulder and brought his face close to her, looking at her making the sound of the horn. Meta did not move him, just kept making the sound. Aisha confirmed it then; Sugarman was mute. He wanted to imitate the sound, she could see it, but could not. When Meta stopped making the noise, he backed away from her, sat down on the couch, and began rocking a little and listening to Meta continue to talk.

She told Aisha that the end of the seventies marked the end of the good times. In the eighties, things changed on the street. More girls and tricks were being arrested. The stroll started to be less profitable and Plato started to take more of his frustrations out on the girls. He started using drugs more heavily. He still had not hit Meta, but things around her got scarier. Vicious and violent acts around her and brought against the girls became routine. The danger that had always loomed in the seventies seemed like nothing in the eighties. It was all danger in the eighties; every time you turned a trick, you feared your life. The tricks changed; there were more lowlifes than ever. The atmosphere of the house changed, more frowns than ever. All their pasts were now before them, living it out again in the present in newer ways, but the same feeling, the dreaded feeling, the feeling to want to run away again. But where? Two of the girls, Violet and Sapphire, turned up dead, brutalized and butchered. Those were the stories the girls told mostly then. It became a fascination talking about it, so maybe they could talk it away or take it away. Then it happened. Plato came to the house mad about something, about something Meta will never know. And for no reason at all, when Meta walked up to greet him, to show him affection, he hit her, punched her hard in the mouth. He did not knock her down, though, and he did not hit her again, though he hovered over her. Seeing her half her height, bent over and blood dripping from her mouth,must have satisfied him, because he walked away. While Meta braced for other blows, she felt around in her mouth. He had not knocked her two front teeth out but back. Horrified, just reacting, she reached back in her mouth and pulled her teeth back in place. They stayed, thankfully. Still, she was in pain and she was the only one home. All the girls were out and there was no one there to comfort her. What was she going to do?

The girls knew Meta brushed her teeth many times a day, but none of them knew why. None of them knew why her teeth were so important to her, because none of them were from Haveton and she never shared anything about Haveton with them. Why talk about the home you left, the mother she left? Her mother use to let her sleep with her bottle in her mouth and it eventually rotted her baby teeth. It made her self-conscious. She saw that her neighborhood friends' teeth did not look like hers. And no matter how she tried to clean them, they would not get better. Looking back, her friends in the neighborhood were nice children. They never made fun of her, so when she started school and the name-calling from other children began, she was not prepared for it. "Blacky Big Foot with the nasty teeth," they called her. They made a song about it and would sing it around her in groups, taunting her. She prayed for her baby teeth to fall out fast and vowed that when they did, she would have the prettiest teeth in the whole world. She would grow up to be the prettiest girl in the whole world. A part of her prayers were answered. She did not know if she was the prettiest girl in the world, though she felt pretty, but her new teeth came in straight and white, which she made even whiter.

At this Meta laughed, showing Aisha her pretty teeth now somewhat tinted by Plato's blow. After he walked up to her and hit her for no reason, Meta knew it was time for her to go. All was in ruin, anyway. Plato had long stopped taking care of the girls and their medical needs, and Meta knew if she stayed she could stand to lose more than her teeth. So, quickly, she packed a little bag and left. On her journey back to the South Side, to find her mother, she reconnected with Speedy.

For a little over a week, she dared not try to eat anything solid. She stayed in a rundown motel, far away from the West Side and Plato. He would not find her there. For a week, she just drank milk, because she figured milk had to help her teeth some, and slept. When her money ran out she called her mother, but her mother was no longer at that number. She had been gone eight years. Eight years had gone by without her even thinking about the time. How quickly the time had gone by. She had thought about her mother during that time, but not enough to want to see her or to ever go back to her. But after seeing all the horrible things she saw on the street, her mother's flare ups did not seem as bad. She missed her. She did not realize how much she missed her until all turned bad. To find her mother, she went to the only other place where she might obtain information about her whereabouts. She was confident that Aisha's grandmother still lived in the same house. The last time she saw her, she had been living a good life. She had a home and security. It was hard for people to leave that kind of comfort. When Meta made it to the home and knocked on the door, Speedy opened it.

Sitting there, listening to Meta, Aisha could not believe all that she was hearing, how open this woman, Meta, was in sharing her life, the seemingly sincere tone of her voice, her steady, reflective, gaze. Strangely, through the telling, lost pieces of Aisha's life had been found. In the oddity of the night's conversation, having reached the point where her father once again emerged, Aisha began thinking about her life in conjunction with Meta's. When Aisha was six, they moved from California to Chicago. She remembered her mother telling her that her father had gotten a good job offer in Chicago and that his mother, her grandmother, lived there, and he wanted to be there with her. Aisha remembered asking her mother, "Daddy doesn't play football anymore?" and seeing her mother's expression change. "No, not anymore, honey," her mother replied. Looking at her mother's face then, she remembered feeling real hurt for the first time.

Meta continued with her story. At the door, she saw at once that something was troubling Speedy, but she knew nothing of Aisha and her mother at the time. Sitting down with him and talking to him, he mentioned nothing of them. They both said very little, actually. Looking back, Meta realized how much they were alike in that moment. They had both lost something. Sometimes she wondered what would have happened if they had been open, talked, as she was talking to Aisha. What would have happened if they had hugged each other and talked about their troubles? Until she and Speedy were reunited again, finally, in Haveton, Meta thought about that moment often. So much could have happened, but little did. Speedy told her that his mother had recently died and he was staying with his stepfather until he went off to basic training. "I can't sit in no office. I got to get out of here, see what else is out there…" He told Meta that her mother had moved back to Haveton and into Meta's grandmother's house, the very house with the collapsed ceiling that Meta and Aisha sat in. Speedy did not ask where Meta had been or what she had been up to. The only vestige of the big brother she knew showed when she stood up to leave. The silence had become unbearable. He gave her a couple hundred dollars. She thanked him, hugged him tight, so close she could feel the soreness of her mouth on his shoulder, and left.

Meta ended up in Saint Louis, closer to Haveton, but not quite there. She struggled with money for a while, barely getting by, until she began working for herself. After a year or so of working independently in the streets of Saint Louis, she became a Madame. Staying so close to Plato all those years had taught her to hustle and how to get women to do what she wanted. It was all she knew, although she did it differently, better, she thought, than how she had seen it done on Madison Street. She remembered the occasional fancy hotels, the occasional businessman that braved the West Side of Chicago to live on the edge, to find something to break up the boredom and sameness around him, to feel alive. So Meta became a master at the illusion of the dangerous but sexy girl, the exotic pretty city girl. She made a lot of money providing the fantasy. And she was proud at how professional she was, how well her enterprise ran and how well she took care of her girls, never once cursing them or hitting them. But at some point in the early nineties, she was struck with a fit of conscience. She missed her mother. What was her mother up to? How had she been living? So, finally, she called her mother. It was then she found that she had a brother. His name was Dennis, but her mother called him Sugarman. Talking to her mother and hearing the news of her brother, hearing the glad in her mother's changed tone, the hardness removed, she had to go back to Haveton to visit.

Arriving in Haveton, reuniting with her mother, and meeting her brother, Sugarman, exacerbated Meta's fits of conscience. She thought about her girls in Saint Louis awaiting her return. They probably ran away from families, as she had. Maybe some should stay away, but should they be with her in the way that they were? No. They weren't really a family. Her mother had grown sickly. Seeing her and spending time with her spirited, speechless brother made her realize what true care was, or what it needed to be, the beginning of it, at least. She was needed in Haveton. She was needed not only by her mother and Sugarman, but by her childhood friend, Angie's mother, Tanya.

Meta told Aisha that when Speedy came back to Haveton, he and Tanya partied together in some pitiful attempt to relive their youth in Haveton, those glorious carefree days. They smoked crack together. Meta did not know who introduced who to it. Maybe they both knew it before. All she knew is when they got their hands on it, they liked smoking it together. They would go for days and days until the money ran out or the product or both. Then Speedy would go on his way, but

Tanya had to stay. She was already badly addicted when Meta came back to Haveton. And being addicted in a small town is worse than in the big city. The droughts were more frequent, longer. Cocaine affected women differently. Meta said she had seen it. Something in their chemical makeup made it harder for women. How many times had she seen it bring them down? But it was not the drug that eventually brought Tanya down, it was A.I.D.S.

Speedy and Angie were lucky, as far as she knew. She had asked Speedy outright years ago, then had Angie tested. They were both negative. In talking about Angie, Meta's posture changed, her tone grew more serious, more so than talking about her own trials in the streets. Angie and Candance were her little nieces, the dearest people to her next to Sugarman. Meta knew Candance's mother as well. Candance needed Meta's attention, the same as Angie did.

In time, Meta's mother died. She was a tough woman. Meta nursed her until the end. Witnessing her mother's reduction to helplessness, and the innocent helplessness of her brother, Angie and Candance, them needing her, helped Meta to put her past life working the streets of Chicago and as the madam of the suites in Saint Louis behind her. She resettled in Haveton, tending to herself, Sugarman and the others as best she could. In the beginning, it was hard work; so much in her had been unresolved and when her money started to run out old temptations and habits resurfaced. But she fought against it and, after a long battle, won. Ironically, it was only when she had spent her last dime of her former life on treatment for her mother, for Tanya, and on things for the girls, again relegated to the food stamps of her childhood and Sugarman's Supplemental Security Income checks, did she begin to feel balanced. It would not always be that way, she promised herself. But while she resolved what else she could do, she would take care of the people in the place she knew. She and Sugarman would take care of each other, him teaching her things and her teaching him things. And she would watch Angie and Candance grow, give them an outlet from their homes, so they did not have to run away and unlearn lessons from the streets. Any direction but hers and their mothers' would do. But circumstances can trap you and make you feel trapped, especially when where you come from is all you know, all you can see. Despite Meta's stories and warnings, she realized the girls had to go through their own experiences. Now, Angie was going to have another baby, a blessing, but then a burden, too.

But Aisha coming down could be nothing but good. Good for Speedy, good for Angie, and, Meta admitted, good for her. She realized that she had not ever talked the way that she had that night. And despite Speedy being absent from Aisha and Angie's life, who was the worst off, Aisha who had him fully for some years as a child or Angie who never had him fully but in flashes? Meta could not say. Like with her and Sugarman, family had been brought back together. They all had something to learn from one another, some part to share that would help each one of them become whole, another side to see. For better or worse, to know your family is to know yourself. No simple task. It's the task for a lifetime.

Chapter 31

The next morning, Aisha and Grandmother Johnson had breakfast together and went to Grandmother Johnson's church. Grandmother Johnson's little, but well-constructed, newly constructed, it appeared, brick building hosted the Pentecostalist. At the beginning of the service, Grandmother Johnson pointed to their minister. "He's our pastor, right there. And there's his wife. He built this church himself. I will introduce you after service." She patted Aisha's leg, nodded her head seriously, then reached into her purse and pulled out a peppermint, placing it in Aisha's hand. Aisha immediately took the wrapping off the peppermint and popped it into her mouth.

Grandmother Johnson and her church was a scene, people stomping and hopping and running back and forth. She thought of Aaron and something he once said to her. Though Aisha was nonreligious, she was no stranger to various places of worship. She could not remember how it came up. Maybe it was nothing at all. She and Aaron had arbitrary conversations all the time, but she remembered telling Aaron she had gone to Harvard Hillel after multiple, stimulating conversations with her entryway mate, Samantha. They had cultivated an in-passing relationship and study break relationship and one of their conversations led to Samantha inviting Aisha to the Hillel. Never one to turn down a new experience, Aisha accepted. "You been up in the Hillel?" Aaron said when she told him. "Superstar, you crazy! How you gone be like "uh uh" to religion and all up in the Jewish joint? Isaac's my best friend, and I never went up in the Hillel. Hell, he didn't, either!" Aisha smiled for a moment thinking of this thought. She looked to her left and wished that Aaron was there with her and the smile went away. She turned to look at Grandmother Johnson, who had stood up, clapping her hands and moving her legs ever so slowly and cautiously. Aisha wondered, had this always been Grandmother Johnson's religion? What had been there before the new brick church? Where did the people in the town go when it was being built? Where did they have to run around then, flailing, gesticulating to the music, and when it stopped all going back to their seats, except one woman on the floor, being fanned? How peculiar.

After church, Grandmother Johnson made it her point to introduce Aisha to the minister. During the service, she wondered what motivated him to build a church in the small, lonely town, her critical lens on its highest magnification. But meeting him, he seemed like a sincere man, and she trusted Grandmother Johnson's judgment. But what if he was not sincere and the church was the only place Grandmother Johnson had to go? Would she still go?

The two left the church with Aisha driving.

"Grandmother, do you mind if we stop to see my dad?"

"Oh, no, child; I expect it. Go on. I'll wait for you in the car."

Knocking on Speedy's door, it felt like it would be the last time she would do so. She had seen enough. She had learned some things, but the sadness was still there. It was not her place to be in Haveton. She felt glad that she had visited, but the longer she stayed, the more she was reminded that Aaron had not made it down there with her.

Speedy came to the door without a shirt. Strange. Aisha remembered the configuration and look of his chest hairs. He was far skinnier, but the chest hairs had remained the same.

"Daddy's Isha; look at you. You coming from church with Grandmother?"

"Yes."

"C'mon in, C'mon in. I knew y'all were over there. You know, I can hear the music and all that. I gets over there sometimes."

"Daddy, Grandmother's in the car." Speedy stepped onto the porch and waved to Grandmother Johnson.

"Aw, okay, yeah; what y'all gone do today?"

"I think I'm leaving today. I have to get back."

"Aw, naw, you gotta go? I sure wish you would stay." Aisha remained quiet, the chest hairs beginning to bother her. She wished she did not have any recollection of them. She wished that she did not know this place.

"Well, let me throw some clothes on. I'm gone ride with y'all. There's some place I want to take you. Step on in, Isha, yeah; have a seat."

Aisha went in and sat down. Speedy began talking to her about her leaving, but Aisha could not focus on his words. All the clutter distracted her. She remembered the same man in an orderly home, orderly except for the yelling and fighting. Back then, she thought that is just what they did; orderly, her room, mommy and daddy's room, other rooms, her playroom, a room for Speedy's awards. She used to examine them, read their inscriptions, the years, for what team, what feat, what sport. Sometimes, she walked in there by herself and sometimes she would go in the trophy room with him. He liked being in there with her and liked when she read the inscriptions to him. She could tell by his smile.

"Daddy's Isha gone win more awards than this one day. Ain't that right?" Aisha would nod her head happily.

"Isha, I named you Star, 'cause you are." And he would always pick her up, lifting her up high over his head. She could always see it coming. She liked the times he did it in the trophy room. She liked being lifted up higher than the awards.

But now, where were the awards? Lost forever, heaped under all the garbage, objects that had no meaning to her, that were unfamiliar to her.

Speedy came out of his bedroom clothed in a slight variation of what he had worn the day before. Aisha almost asked him about his awards. What happened to all the trophies that once had their own room? Where did it all go? But instead, she kept quiet and walked to the car. She knew the answer. She had gotten all her answers.

On the ride to Grandmother Johnson's house, Speedy informed Grandmother Johnson that he would be showing Aisha some more of Haveton, a part she did not see on her first day. After dropping Grandmother Johnson off, Speedy directed Aisha to make a left out of the driveway instead of making the right she had become accustomed to making. Again, neither of them talked, the only sounds were Speedy's directions. "You going right, on up here." Aisha noticed the landscape changing; wilderness up ahead. Speedy instructed her to turn off the road to go toward it. She hesitated for a moment. "Gone on, Isha, it's all right. It's a path, you see?" She did see it. She turned off the road. The change in the ride was jarring, very bumpy. Speedy did not seem to mind. The path they were on was rocky, larger rocks, not like Grandmother Johnson's gravel driveway. Aisha began to worry about the stability of Grandmother Johnson's car.

"Where are we going?"

"You see them trees up ahead?" Aisha nodded.

"It's where I use to run around as a boy. They tried to come in here and develop it. Take it away. What we riding on used to be trees. They didn't know what they were doing. Gone on ahead, Isha."

There was a clearing through the trees. Aisha slowed the car to an almost standstill. The fit was tight.

"Been a while since I've been back here. Stop the car, Isha; we can get out here."

They both exited the car and walked through between the canopy of trees, Aisha taking her time to appreciate its beauty, slowing her steps, both she and Speedy walking slowly.

"Yeah, these trees, they know everything," Speedy said, almost to himself, not looking at Aisha.

As they continued to walk, they came to another clearing, an outlet from the trees. There was a flat bridge up ahead. Speedy pointed to it.

"We gone walk on up there. That's Cooper's Crossing."

They both walked onto the bridge. Aisha looked over its side at the running stream. How long had it been since she was surrounded by nature? How very long she'd been working in the midst of man's manufacturings. The sound of the running stream below relaxed her. Looking down at it, she felt glad Speedy had brought her out there, although, she still did not quite know what his intentions were. Perhaps it was as simple as standing on the bridge, Cooper's Crossing, and appreciating it. He seemed to be.

"Isha, keep your back turned. I'm about to piss off the side of this bridge." Not thinking much about what he said, Aisha obeyed his order. Speedy continued talking.

"Yeah, I do this every time I come out here. If you was a boy, we'd be pissing together." He chuckled. "We used to do it together as kids. I did it with my uncles. The bridge wasn't like this, though. Wooden and rickety, with rickety rails on both sides. Never gave way, though, none of it. Us little guys used to climb up the sides and piss off of it. Pissing tall, we called it. If you were brave, you'd climb all the way to the top."Speedy began to laugh.

"A'ight, I'm done, Isha." Aisha remained turned.

"Isha, c'mon. There's something else I want to show you."

Speedy began walking and Aisha followed him off the bridge and away from the stream. She wished they did not have to leave its serenity. It was the closest she had been to water since she and Aaron last were on the lake together. It made her realize how much she missed staring out into the water. Speedy continued to walk in silence, his face sobering. Aisha felt his energy changing.

He stopped at an ordinary-looking place, it not at all possessing the character of the first two areas. They had taken a curve on the path and the land bent so that there were valleys now on each side of it, although there was no stream like at Cooper's Crossing. Speedy walked to one side, his feet right at the beginning of the small valley's descent. He looked down at the land. He was silent. Then, he pointed and spoke.

"Right there, down there, is where your granddaddy died." The gravity of the moment fell upon Aisha. She did not know what to say, but "how?" came out of her mouth.

"Driving. Him and some of his boys came through here. Car turned over. Everyone got out but him." Both were silent for a time, just staring at the spot. Then Speedy started speaking again.

"I used to drive through here too, flying." Speedy paused then turned to Aisha.

"Isha, what you got going on in your life?" It was the question Aisha had been waiting for him to ask, but it was the wrong time.

"I feel like you have something going on in your life. What are you doing? Why you leaving? Why don't you stay down here with your poppa? We need each other. I can get you a job working in the store with Jimmy. Jimmy would do it for me. Wouldn't pay nothing, but you don't need nothing down here." Speedy continued to stare right at Aisha. How did he know? He knew nothing. Why had he taken her there? Why was he looking at her in that way, asking her to stay? Aaron had died the same way her grandfather died and she walked away from it. Tell him. When Aisha did not speak, Speedy took his eyes away from her and looked back at the little valley. After a moment, Aisha spoke.

"I've taken this year off—"

"See. See. Stay on down here with me. We got a lot of catching up to do. We need each other." Aisha let his words remain without answering, considering how odd they sounded. The spot, another accident, Aaron, something was not right, his revelation, too familiar, too central to her life. It was not right.

"Okay. I'll stay," she said involuntarily.

On the ride back, Speedy talked more than ever and Aisha heard but she could not listen, so riddled was her mind.

"…but that's what I do, little handiwork around town, Kennett, Caruthersville. Me and my partner Roy raising a hog right now. Keeps me busy. Don't need the money. Got a hundred percent service connection. Live off that little money. They found all kinds of shit wrong with me when I got back from the Persian Gulf. They didn't know that I was fucked up before I went. I wasn't going to tell them. Yeah, the war affected me, being in that desert and all that, you know. War is war, but Desert Storm wasn't nothing like what these boys going through now. IEDs, going through them hostile cities, not knowing who's the enemy, and your man getting his arm blown off, legs blown off, blown away in front of you. And then, y'all got to come home like that. Naw, didn't go through what these boys going through. I seen war, but not like those boys, not like the boys in the World Wars. 'Nam, you know, you on the ground depending on your man, your man next to you; helps you stay alive. Y'all both helping each other to stay alive. In the foxholes, jungles, desert, death right there, facing the enemy face to face, but not knowing who your enemy is, where he coming from, is the worst thing. I didn't go through none of that, but I deserve my check. I served my country twice. On the battlefield and the football field. That's service. I'm gone tell you what, Isha, ain't nothing like football. You and your teammates. It ain't nothing like war, but it's the closest thing to it without someone dying, without you having to worry about your man next to you dying, you dying. But it's as close to death as you gone come. We out there, trying to hit the hell out of each other. That pain. That's why people love the game. Nature of man all on display. Closest thang you get to war. Out there, hitting the hell out of each other, protecting each other from that hell coming. Hell coming for you, Isha. It's out here. And I hear them talking about the sport, it's too violent, changing this and that. Fuck that, they need to pay us for our service. Our pension plan ain't shit. The old timers don't get paid shit and we led the shit. We broke our necks and now everybody realize how good a game it is. Why the hell you gone change it? We choose it. Ain't nothing better. And these young boys now getting paid millions. But they still facing hell, that hell still coming for 'em. You better believe that and hitting the hell out of someone else keeps them away from it, takes them away from it, takes the hell out of them, because it's hell out here. Especially in the city. I know, Isha, I used to be back and forth between here and the city, visiting your grandmother. You didn't know that, did you? I know about Chi-town. Wouldn't be alive if I had stayed there with Mama; too much to get into. And I liked getting into it. Even football can't take you away from that. Don't matter what you do on the field, that hell's coming and it'll catch you. Look at that boy from Denver, football can't keep you from that. It's the hell coming. The field can only keep you so far away. Everybody understand football, but they can't understand that. And more gone keep dying…fast or slow, fast or slow, hell's coming…" Speedy stopped talking for a moment. Aisha was pulling up to his house.

"Happy you here though, Isha. Don't mean to be talking so negative.

I get that way. But I'm happy. I'm glad you staying down here with me. You all right, Isha? You all right? I'm gone tell you, I never stopped loving you."

"I love you, too," Aisha responded automatically. She smelled the liquor all over him as he hugged her and got out of the car.

"All right, I'll be over to see you and Grandmother in the morning."

"All right," she said, again speaking automatically.

With only the smell of her father left in the car, her mind let go. A curse. The accident, Aaron, her grandfather. She should have been the one driving. She should have been the one who died, not Aaron. So convinced of this idea was she, so spellbound by the idea of a curse and death, hers and Aaron's, her grandfather's, how it all happened, that immediately upon entering Grandmother Johnson's house it all spilled out of her.

Grandmother Johnson listened, watching Aisha's mouth move fast in a fantastical and frantic way. All in a flurry, Aisha told Grandmother Johnson about Aaron, their relationship, how much he loved her, the drive to Haveton and the accident, and how she did not deserve to live, the sadness, the money, all the money, a curse. She did not deserve it, because she did not deserve to live. She should not even be here, because Cooper's Crossing, but not Cooper's Crossing, but the place not far from it, the place where her Grandfather died. Was she cursed? She was cursed! Are curses real? They must be. Look at her grandfather, how it happened. Look at her father, look at her, something went wrong! Look at the blood! The blood! Something went terribly wrong. She was not supposed to be there. Aaron was. Something went wrong. And she could not cry. She was cursed.

Grandmother Johnson took both of Aisha's hands in her hands and closed her eyes tight, tilting her head slightly upward. "The devil is a liar! He's a liar! In the name of God...in the name—of—God, we rebuke you Satan! You will not destroy this child! O, mercy, mercy! My God, fall fresh. We do not believe these lies. Release her!" Grandmother Johnson opened her eyes and brought them down at Aisha. "Look up and live, child! Look up and live! The Lord is calling you to submit. Let your burdens go. Give them to God. Precious child. My precious grandbaby, you are a gift. You are God's child. He loves you. Give it to him. All your burdens. Give it all to God, right now. For his glory. He wants us to. He wants you to. Be encouraged! The Lord has not forsaken you; he is with you, with us always." Grandmother Johnson stood up powerfully, without caution. She walked over to the end table and picked up a Bible.

"Read this," she said, pressing the Bible into Aisha's hands. "Read this, precious. Study it. And pray." Aisha felt an energy coming from Grandmother Johnson. Her hands pressed firmly on top of Aisha's hands, pressing Aisha's hands firmly against the Bible. Grandmother Johnson's energy, her eyes, looking alive, strong, stronger than what Aisha had already seen, caused Aisha to nod her head. Yes. She met Grandmother Johnson's stare. She nodded her head again. She would do what she was told. Grandmother Johnson hugged her, said she loved her, holding onto her for what seemed like an eternity. Aisha wanted to stay in that position for that long. But eventually, Grandmother Johnson let her go. When she did, Aisha felt drained, as though a thousand sleepless nights had just fallen upon her.

"Grandmother, I'm tired."

"Yes, child, go and rest."

Chapter 32

As soon Aisha awoke, she began reading the Bible. She slowed her reading down deliberately. She took the scholar's approach, reading it critically, taking notes as if she were writing her thesis again, going to Widener library to find some unpopular and unpopulated spot to immerse herself. However, Haveton was not Harvard. In Haveton, she was pulled away far more easily from her studying.

While she read the Bible, a book she had avoided, only having read isolated scriptures here and there, her relationship grew with her Haveton family. As she discovered original sin in the paradise of Eden, completing the foundational stories in Genesis, the story of Joseph being her favorite, she coordinated Thanksgiving dinner at Grandmother Johnson's house. Angie, her nieces and Meta, Sugarman and Candance came. Speedy showed up early. His beard was gone, clean-shaven. He helped Grandmother Johnson prepare the meal.

At the dinner table, Grandmother Johnson beamed, hardly eating. "The Lord has provided. Look at my children…" Speedy devoured the food as if he had never eaten before. He looked more like Aisha remembered him with his beard shaven. Candance looked far prettier without her thumb in her mouth. Angie's personality made all the newly acquainted more comfortable. She beamed like Grandmother Johnson and the girls. The girls had fallen in love with all the dolls around the house. Grandmother Johnson gave each one a doll. Sheilah sat her doll on her lap while she ate. Angie stuck Celestia's doll next to her in the high chair. Meta looked on, pleased. She politely brought up times past that she and Grandmother Johnson both knew well, other Haveton families and well-known Haveton events. She brought up Grandmother Johnson's well-known accomplishments and firsts in Haveton for blacks.

Her flattery made Grandmother Johnson giggle and start encouraging everyone else at the table, giving praises to God for all she had been able to do. Aisha wished Aaron could be there with her. The feeling of family reminded her of Aaron and her mother. Maybe they could see it all. Maybe they were helping with all the love that was in the atmosphere.

As Aisha continued reading the Bible, she learned about Moses, learning details beyond what had been projected to her over the years through popular culture, how it all came about and about his brother Aaron. The name stuck out so much to her she had trouble not being distracted by it, not connecting her Aaron with that Aaron, an absurd feeling she worked to dismiss. Yet the name attracted her deeper into the story, the brothers, freeing the Israelites, the parting of the Red Sea, and Moses climbing Mt. Sinai and receiving the Ten Commandments, and the encounter with the golden calf, Aaron helping with its construction, him building an altar for it. Aaron was deviating from what he was supposed to do, what the story had called for, had prepared her for. This bothered Aisha; she had to tell herself, "This Aaron is not your Aaron. He is not here. Is he here? Where is he?" Had Aaron read the words she was reading? He did not like his name. He went by Jamal, but she called him AJ. Biggums called him Jam. Had his mother called him Aaron? She did not know. A simple question, what did his mother call him and how was he named? Did she get his name from the Bible? Maybe something that stuck out to her as a little girl? They had never talked about his name. Who could tell her about it now? When she saw Biggums again, she was going to ask him about Aaron's mother. Did he remember her and, if so, what did she call Aaron? Moses's order of having brother kill brother, as a result of the calf incident, and sister kill sister disturbed her. She did not know there was so much violence in the Bible.

As she learned all of Leviticus's rules, she learned of the rules in Haveton, became accustomed to the routines while developing her own. Speedy did try to get her a job at Jimmy's store, but Aisha told him she was well prepared for her time off and she did not need the money.

Instead of working, she spent her time with Grandmother Johnson, helping her learn more about her computer, crocheting with her, and learning more about her life and her family's history. She also spent much time with Meta and her nieces. She helped Meta watch her nieces during the day while Angie was away at work. Eventually, them sitting in front of the huge TV all day motivated Aisha to drive to Caruthersville with Grandmother Johnson, who delighted in such small trips, to buy children's books and games. Angie had a few books at her apartment, but not near enough to satisfy Aisha. Those few books had little power by themselves. They needed more company.

As she shopped, she looked over each book. Many of them she recognized. Those she threw quickly in the cart. The books she was not familiar with she glanced through more carefully. Grandmother Johnson reading titles of various children's books, reading parts of them aloud to herself, proud of her reading voice, tickled Aisha. What fun it was gathering books with Grandmother Johnson. Now the lonely books at Angie's house would have so much company! It would take good numbers and wonderment to compete with the TV.

Aisha was satisfied when finally the books had formed an impressive mound in her cart. It took a good bit of time to load and unload the books. Grandmother Johnson pointed out that it would not be wise to give the children all the games at one time. Aisha agreed. She would introduce a game at a time, but the books she would present all at once.

Seeing Sheilah excited about the books filled Aisha with joy. Together they stacked most of the books against the wall in the front room, the rest they took to the girls' room. Aisha had to take a few books from Sheilah's arms as she walked, for fear that she might trip. Meta was also enthusiastic. She took right to helping Aisha read with the girls, even taking time away from her stories. "I done seen it all a hundred times, anyway."

By the end of the day, their passionate reading session had won over Sheilah. This became clear to Aisha when Angie came home. Sheilah raced to her, taking her hand and pulling her toward all the books. She picked up her favorite story of the day and asked Angie to read it to her. Aisha had done something right. Something she did had worked. In this moment of realization, looking at the entire scene, all the books scattered around, Meta's smile, Sugarman with a book in hand, mimicking, it occurred to Aisha that in her excitement to get the books she had neglected to get a proper place for them. How did she forget? The books looked homeless without shelves. They needed shelter. She had to give them a home as soon as possible; tomorrow she would go back out with Grandmother Johnson and find them proper homes. Then something else occurred to her. Her father liked handiwork. Surely, he could build bookshelves. She could take him to buy the materials and he could build the bookshelves. Yes, this could help him to be productive and take him away from the other routines of his life.

Speedy's other routines saddened Aisha. He continued to go about life just as he had before she arrived. Once, Meta said she could see a difference in Speedy since her arrival. Because of this, Aisha naively thought her presence could eradicate his addiction, his "partying," as he called it. How foolish of her to think such a thing. How could she help him? She could not help herself. She, herself, was battling, struggling, so how could she, an embattled one, bring clarity to someone else? For that matter, how could anyone else, any adult, save another adult without them wanting to be saved? Speedy did not want to save himself. It was as if he had given up, long ago lost hope. But Aisha, more than any other time after the accident, wanted to get better. She could see small improvements, in her mind, in her mood, but the sadness was still omnipresent. It felt like no matter how hard she worked, no matter what she turned to, regardless if she lived a vice less life, shunning the extremes she now had seen her father succumb to, the sadness would always be there.

But living with Grandmother Johnson helped; talking with her, her hugs and exhortations of love, going to church with her, which she still found silly, but not all of it, helped. Spending days with Meta and Sugarman, her nieces, and at night and on the weekends with Angie, and often, Candance coming over with books of her own, reading with her thumb in her mouth, helped. It all helped but did not heal. And nights were the hardest. She would curl up and think of Aaron, wishing he were there with her. It hurt. And seeing her father's pain hurt her. But going to the hardware store together, picking out the materials, him building beautiful bookshelves, small children's bookshelves and a beautiful adult bookshelf, and painting them together, playing with paint, and the laughter in the air, and eating together while waiting for the paint to dry, and then stacking the books on the shelves together, all of them, Angie, her nieces, Meta, Sugarman, Candance, Speedy, and Aisha, and Speedy picking up a book and reading to his Sheilah and Celestia, helped.

Aisha's appreciation for Grandmother Johnson's entreating of her to read the Bible grew significantly over time. She was reading again, her love of reading revived. Every day she read with Meta and the girls. Oftentimes, Candance read with them, although not aloud. She sat reading her own book, sucking her thumb.

At night, after Aisha had eaten dinner with Grandmother Johnson and after returning from spending time with Angie after work, she would settle in her room with the Bible. Reading it then was best.

When she reached the story of Gideon and his three hundred men, the trumpets and jars they carried, them not having to kill, but instead blow the horns and break the jars to victory, she ceased to read the Bible like a scholar. Instead of dissecting it line by line and analyzing how its words could affect her life, affected others' lives, how it was supposed to lift her from the sadness, she started reading it like she were a child. What a great story! Yet upon reaching the violent story of Samson, Aisha was forced to grow up again, to remember. Inside of her, there was an adult who knew, knew how little she knew, and a child who loved the exaltation of discovery for the sake of whatever beauty there was to be found. It was as her mother had intended and how appreciative she was of her childhood, swept away and in love with books, newness, and innocence. Both adult and child sat comfortably alongside each other as she read.

Surrounded by all Grandmother Johnson's dolls, one of them right beside her, and all the crocheted things, a few of her own completed needled projects in the room, she read of Ruth and Naomi. She was glad to have reached the story. Up to that point, it seemed to her that women were too-often depicted as the betrayers and the catalysts for it all falling apart and not the heroines she knew they could be, heroes just as often as men though in a woman's way. This fact helped her to see the book for itself, compelled her to see through it to the writers of it. Men wrote the Bible. God's hand could not have written in the skewed fashion in which the Bible portrayed women. But the book of Ruth redeemed some of its power for her. It was only a slice of the words, a quiet story, but to Aisha it was one of the truest stories. From Ruth came the line of David. Aisha thought of Angie, what was growing inside of her. Women were not just the deliverers, they were also the shapers, indeed, they too were the great shapers of greatness and in that, great themselves, could be great themselves, were great themselves. The kind of women who lay down at the threshing floor, *the lord bless you, my daughter; you have not run after the younger men, whether rich or poor. Yes, but there was so much more.*

Aisha could not help but think about Grandmother Johnson when she read about Elijah ascending to heaven in a chariot of fire. What was it like to anticipate your own death, death a very likely possibility any day? How much harder is it when you cannot see the chariot coming down from the heavens to take you away? Grandmother Johnson talked about death every day, comfortable with the idea of it. Not in a way that Aisha had been comfortable with the idea of it, wanting death to take her. No, but in a way that Aisha could not comprehend. Her mother died early, unexpectedly; Aaron died early, unexpectedly. But Grandmother Johnson was the opposite. Man's life had a line, an end point, a clear limit. Grandmother Johnson was at that limit, the any-day limit, any-year limit. How many more years, one, two, ten, twenty, certainly not many more than twenty? How did one exist, how was one to exist when closer to a century of living? What then was there to look forward to? What were you supposed to do, living when everyone around you is expecting you to go? Expectation with such confidence, such willful ignorance.

Everyone knows that death comes, but no one knows what is truly on the other side. Regardless, it seemed Grandmother Johnson was quite comfortable with the idea of the here and the hereafter. And because of that wisdom, that existence that Aisha could not comprehend, Aisha saw herself somewhat like Elisha. A curious thing, his request, asking for double Elijah's spirit. Aisha wanted that, the wisdom of Grandmother Johnson's years, plus some.

Job asked for death the way that Aisha had once asked for it. The book of Job was the hardest for her to read. For him to lose everything, going through those horrific trials, his pain brought hers into perspective. Not lessening it, but giving her a lens to view someone else's great pain. Someone else had felt the way she felt. Yet it all was restored for Job, even greater than before. But his pain was so great, so long, and the restoration happened so quickly. Aisha had to go back and read how it was written that God restored it all for Job. What had she missed? Why so simple after the complex matrix of catastrophe he endured? What was it? Then she found it, a word from God, an order. God asked Job to pray for his friends. In discovering this, Aisha realized that she had forgotten the second part of Grandmother Johnson's entreating. She had been reading the Bible diligently, but not praying. How was she supposed to pray? Was it as simple as opening your heart, like Biggums said? Reading the Psalms of David confused Aisha regarding prayer. Should she pray like David? David knew God. How perilous his life was; many of the Psalms were about him on the run, praying to God to protect him, praising God. In the Psalms, he sounded like Grandmother Johnson, the way he thanked God with such high reverence. When you know God, do you talk this way? And what is the proper way to pray? Is there a proper way? Do you pray for your friends, like Job, or do you praise God and ask him for your protection, your deliverance, like David? Both?

Aisha resolved not to ask Grandmother Johnson. There was a reason she did not offer to teach her how to pray, unlike crocheting. Aisha resolved to try it and figure it out on her own.

In the meantime, she began talking with Grandmother Johnson about her Bible reading. Grandmother Johnson did not ask her about it, never once, and Aisha did not want to discuss it with her until she had become very familiar with the text. Once she finished reading the book of Proverbs, its tenants of knowledge, wisdom, understanding, and discipline, she felt better about discussion. She knew she would have to go back and read it again, for she had stopped reading it like a scholar. Reading it in that way would have taken too long and did not feel organic. She may have missed some things, but that was okay.

After her beginning talks with Grandmother Johnson, seeing how fervently and passionately Grandmother Johnson believed in the book, how much she enjoyed talking about it, and in reflection upon her own reading, Aisha finally understood why religions had been formed around it. No wonder it was so celebrated. No wonder people followed it, tried to figure out its teachings and unpack its stories. The Bible's influence on all the books she had read that were written by Western writers was clear. For many years, she, herself, had not been conscious of the great influences of the book in her life or its influence on the country she lived in. She felt ashamed, silly, for ignorantly shunning it for all those years, for having never read it as a complete work, only picking through it critically. She limited herself. She had not read the Bible all those years for fear that reading it would somehow cause her to lose her good sense. That in some way it would limit her, bring rigidity to her life or, better yet, a word she learned reading the Bible, religiosity. Foolishly, she believed that by reading it fully it would make her accepting of all the folly and fallacy, those elements in the world that at one time made her pick up the book and critically pick at scriptures. But reading the Bible independently did not ensnare her into the net of religion, lure her, or convert her into something that was not right for her life. She had seen it happen to others, others like her who did not grow up with religion and those who did, each embracing the Bible's words and becoming rigid, dogmatic, mean, and judgmental, succumbing to religiosity or losing all religion, falling out of it and becoming cynical, mean, and judgmental.

Having made her way to and through the stories of Jesus, his righteous words, unlike anything she had ever read, and setting the Bible down to reflect, Aisha realized that all of those who had become rigid or cynical, mean or judgmental, had not become that way because of the Bible. Reading the Bible in the way that she read it did not cause that. It must have been something else, other things that caused rigidity or disillusionment or cynicism after having read it. Something else must have accompanied the reading. It could not have been from reading the Bible alone, because if she knew anything well it was books, stories. Finally, she had made it almost completely through the Bible and in that, in her reading, it became apparent to her that it was one of the greatest books ever written. Certainly the greatest she had ever read. None even rivaled it. But she could not say it was the greatest ever written, what would be the point in that, anyway? Would that not also be being rigid? A useless debate. When she finished, she would read other religious text not of the West. The world was not the West, this she knew, for she had spent time in Eastern places and embraced the humanity of its people. Just as she had not read the religious text of her own culture, she had not read theirs, either, but she would. Life had forced her to witness, up close, the mark of ultimate limit. Still, her breath came freely. So her instances of self-inflicted limitation had to end.

Chapter 33

One cool evening in March, Aisha went to visit Speedy. Typically, she made sure not to visit him at night. Their first encounter was at night and it had been unpleasant. Now that she knew what the nights meant for him, or had a much better idea, she did not want to see him, catch him again, in that way. Curiously, often during the day he was fine. Aisha mentioned this to Meta one day, hoping it was some sign of his healing, only for Meta to respond, saying, "Yeah, it's his willpower. He the most functional user I done ever seen. Amazes me every day." This quieted Aisha.

Still, inspired by her reading and motivated by restlessness, she decided to give a nighttime visit another try.

For a while, things were fine. She sat there in Speedy's wholly unchanged den, scattered junk and disarray. She had gotten to know the entire place, yet had not spotted a single trophy. There were a few old pictures of her as a baby, pictures of women she did not know, family she did not know, pictures of her grandmother, and a few articles from the army, the press had found him even there, but not one trophy.

Right around the time Aisha felt ready to go, felt that she should leave, Speedy said to her, "C'mon, Isha, take your poppa on around here. It's not too far. Gotta go holla at my man." Aisha looked at him. He looked fine, calm, so she went along.

Speedy had to direct her again. He had stopped doing it when they got together at other times because Aisha had learned the area. As he directed her, Aisha realized that she was quite familiar with the area she was in and the turns she was making. She knew the street they were turning down. And when they arrived in front of the house that Candance lived in, a strange feeling came over her. She should have known. She was stupid, too trusting. She wanted to turn around, talk Speedy out of it, but she could not. Adding to her frustration was the fact that the run had landed them in front of Candance's house. In the months Aisha had been in Haveton, she and Candance had talked the least, partly because Candance, like Aisha, did not talk much. She knew Candance mostly through Angie and Meta and when they were all together. She had never been inside Candance's home because Candance had never invited them in whenever they dropped her off.

Aisha and Speedy walked up to the home, the house of his "main man." Aisha saw Speedy growing in excitement, his gait changing. It was a small house, a Haveton home like all the rest. A man, maybe his "main man," answered the door with a stern look that eased some when he recognized Speedy.

"My man Fred, this my daughter, Isha."

"Yeah," Fred said, turning his head and yelling over his shoulder. "Candance! Speedy here and he brought your girl."

He turned back around with the same hard look, not changing it when he looked at Aisha. There was no acknowledgement in his face, even though he had just acknowledged her with his mouth. She followed Speedy in, entering into the dimly lit front room.

"Sit on down, Isha, we'll be right back," Speedy said, putting his arm around Fred's shoulder and walking away with a bounce in his step. The way Speedy moved now agitated Aisha, made her angry, the whole situation. She sat in virtual darkness and disbelief. She waited for Candance to appear because she had been called for, but there was no sign of her. Then a light came on. Candance stood in the way Aisha had grown accustomed to seeing her, a wet thumb and a book in her hand. Of course, it was one of those books that, over time, had begun to annoy Aisha. Seeing Candance reading as much as she did made Aisha want to give her a five, a high five. She liked high fives. She used to give them to her track teammates and her students. What bothered Aisha was the sameness of the books, the lack of variety. Candance only reading books with black figures on the cover: black figures from the same period in the same poses, naked black figures intertwined between silky sheets, the sexy, scantily dressed, well-endowed black woman, the sexy shirtless black man with rippling abdominal muscles, the blacks sitting atop fancy motorcycles in stylish leather biker suits, the blacks leaning on fancy cars, their cars, this is the car I drive in this book, the I-am-a-black-professional blacks, the black gangsters hard and menacing. It was not all bad; this she knew. Aisha understood, it was entertainment, like action movies. Entertainment was needed and it was new. Blacks now had more outlets to tell entertaining stories. But with all her heart Aisha felt reading should be more than just entertainment. She had read through many of them and finished them feeling empty, even after the ones with so-called moral lessons built in. Where was the enlightenment? Where was deep feeling? How did people lose the desire, the ability to see themselves as others that did not look like them? It was just as bad as seeking only things that did not look like you. No one looked like Aisha growing up. None of the characters in the books her mother introduced her to looked like her. She had not read one book about a character that looked like her, the product of black and white, until she had become a young adult. Still, in her reading, she saw herself in other worlds, the protagonists of different colors, cultures, and of different times. Even when, as a teenager, she discovered the sisterhood, the black women writers of the seventies, her favorites, even after she read as much of their work as she could find, she never lost the love of seeing herself in stories that appeared to have absolutely nothing to do with her and her world. In them, she found much of herself. She had learned that beautifully written words are not written for a particular color or particular culture, but for the demonstration of human freedom.

But sitting in Candance's front room, waiting for Speedy, Candance only able to say, "Hey, Isha" and Aisha only being able to wave sadly in return, the book Candance was holding did not matter. Aisha thought nothing of it. She could only think of Speedy in the back, what was occurring, and how strange it felt to be sitting in Candance's front room in silence, she and Candance, who was now sitting; not being able to look at each other.

Speedy came back just as the awkwardness between her and Candance rose to its highest pitch, just as Aisha felt like she would get up walk out and leave Speedy there. He came back looking like a child who had gotten exactly what he wanted, except he did not proudly display the object of his affection as a child would. Aisha could see no signs of it. The man, Fred, looked the same, hollow faced, expressionless, cold. Aisha could not stand up fast enough. In a quiet voice, quieter than she had greeted Aisha, Candance said, "Bye, Isha." Aisha returned the same wave, although that time she had to turn around because she was walking out the door. That time, she and Candance made full eye contact, Candance's eyes saying, "Now you know."

In the car, Speedy talked about anything but what had just transpired. Babble inspired by what he possessed. Aisha's anger steadily grew as she neared his house. When they arrived, she could feel the full heat of her anger. Before Speedy got out of the car he turned and looked at Aisha. "I'll see you tomorrow morning, Isha, okay?" She refused to turn and meet his glance but when he said okay, she turned to him, fury in her eyes.

"Love you, Isha."

"Love you," Aisha quickly and unwittingly mumbled back.

When Speedy slammed the car door, Aisha felt like she would spontaneously combust. Fire, all over her. She had helped him, allowed herself to be part of it. And Meta, why hadn't Meta told her about Candance? It was important, something that affected her, and Meta knew all along. She told her everything else, but conveniently forgot to tell her that.

In these thoughts, Aisha pulled out of Speedy's driveway and sped to Meta's house.

Meta opened the door sleepily when Aisha arrived.

"Isha, what's going on?" Aisha stepped inside as Meta stepped back.

"Why didn't you tell me my dad got drugs from Candance's house?"

"Huh, girl, what you talking about? Slow down," Meta said, rubbing her eyes.

"Candance's house. My dad just took me over there. I took him to get drugs."

"Oh, from Fred, huh?"

"Yes, Meta, why didn't you tell me?" Meta sat down and waited for Aisha to do the same before she spoke.

"Wasn't no reason to tell; it never came up, and you never asked."

"But you knew."

"Yeah, I knew. I know everything that's going on in this little ol' town. Me and Sugarman know all the business," Meta laughed.

Sugarman must have been sleeping. Meta's smile irritated Aisha. She was at a loss for words. The passion pulsing through her veins made her feel even more alive. Rage, I can feel! Meta continued talking.

"Now, Isha, you know what Speedy do," Meta paused "What? You mad that he took you over there? Did he ask you for money?"

"No."

"I didn't think he would. He won't. Don't be mad. Speedy gone be himself. He just getting comfortable around you now. What, you went over there tonight?" Aisha nodded her head.

"So you was his ride. You were there. If it wasn't you, it would have been somebody else. Or he would have just walked."

"What about Candance?"

"What about her?"

"I don't know. I mean, how did she get in that situation?"

"What do you mean, she?" Aisha dropped her eyes and shrugged her shoulders.

"What, being with Fred?" Meta said. "He her family. They been boyfriend and girlfriend since way back before her mother left."

"Her mother left? Why didn't she go with her?"

"C'mon, Isha, you done seen some life now."

"I know, I know, but I hate drugs. Why always drugs?"

"People gone do what they gone do."

"But there's so many other things he could do!"

"I know that and you know that, but we done lived whole different lives. All he done seen is Haveton and the cities he go get them drugs from, and that's the street life. The street life ain't much different from city to city. Game run the same everywhere. Some places just got more of it. So that's what he learning. That's all he know. Who gone tell him something? Who gone show him different? Me? Tuh, they look at me as a crazy old woman taking care of her crazy brother, collecting government checks like the rest."

"They don't see you in that way," Aisha said.

"Yeah, they do. And that's all right. Long as they know I love them. But they ain't bad kids, Isha. Fred ain't bad. They take care of each other. But you see Angie don't never go in there. You see that, don't you?" Aisha nodded her head.

"She seen what drugs did to her mama and she can't stand to even be around it. She ain't never even smoked no reefer. But she know it ain't Fred's fault. Just don't want to go up in there."

Meta's poise calmed Aisha, her pulse regular now, her body cool. She felt closer then to Meta than at any other time. How strange things were, her in the tiny town, sitting comfortably next to a woman who a year before she knew nothing about. But they knew of her, had heard about her. They had welcomed her as she was. They had opened up to her. Should she open to them more? Was it time? What a strange thing, how quickly circumstance, openness, and close quarters accelerate affection. She cared for Meta. Meta should know her story.

Aisha had been able to convincingly cover up the most hurtful parts of her past since she had been in Haveton. Grandmother Johnson was the only one who knew her real story. She had been able to lie and tell half-truths about her love life when they asked her. She had lost someone special she told them without going into any greater depth. At times like those, it was apparent how far she had come. Before, she would have fallen apart. She was not hurting as much as before; still, the sadness was there. The nights were very hard, especially since she no longer had her Bible reading sessions. Maybe she would start reading it again. But it alone would not take the pain away, just cover it. On regular nights, nights like then, her sitting with Meta, she would curl up in bed hoping to dream of Aaron. She did dream of him, but the dreams were infrequent. When they came, they were unbelievably vivid, as though he were really there with her. He felt real to talk to, real to touch. She could never make sense of the conversations they had, but the feeling, his face, his eyes, his hugs. She wanted to stay, be where he was, stay where he was, but she always woke up. Awake, she'd feel good about receiving another special night, but shortly after sadness would return. Always reminding her that those dreams, what she felt in them, were no longer her life.

Aisha and Meta sat quietly. Aisha looked up at the sagging ceiling and said, "Meta, I'm going to fix your ceiling soon. The weather is getting warmer."

She had asked Speedy about it, the details about fixing roofs and if he knew someone who could do it well. He told her he definitely knew someone, asking her if Grandmother was thinking about getting her roof fixed. Aisha said no, but again, left it at that, and so did he.

Meta laughed at her statement and, as if on cue, said, "Girl, you ain't rich. Don't be going and trying to do that. Me and Sugarman all right. It's like that tower. What's that tower? Yeah Pisa, it's leaning to the floor but it ain't gone fall in. Keep your little money, no need for us all being broke." Aisha smiled; how strange life was.

She told Meta her story.

Chapter 34

Weeks passed from the night Speedy's supplier was revealed, but Aisha saw no change in Meta. It made her happy. She had been monitoring Meta, yet found nothing about her behavior different. She hoped it would continue. She knew she had not changed, other than the monitoring, which did not make her feel good but she could not help it. Having all the money added yet another level of complexity to her life.

Aisha never doubted her vulnerability in giving Grandmother Johnson her full confidence. Finally, she saw the full extent to which her mother confided in Grandmother Johnson, trusting deeply personal parts of her life, even before her father. And living with her, Aisha saw for herself the nature of Grandmother Johnson's character, her virtue and integrity. She saw it in how the town's people expressed their respect for her. She was known by all as Mother Johnson, with no exception, even to those residents of Haveton Heights. With Aisha going here and there between the two towns with Grandmother Johnson, she saw the reverence, felt the honored looks she was given when she was with her. Millions did not move her. Aisha revealing her wealth mattered nothing to her. Doing what she thought to be God's will was the only thing that mattered. Grandmother being a good person was clear to Aisha, but her consistently bringing up God and this business of God's will was not clear. What was it with people's belief in God? She was not against it. If it helped them to be better people, then fine, but she could not understand it. Still far more than any other time in her life, the word "God," the idea of God, kept coming up, kept standing out. And not only from Grandmother Johnson's mouth, she started to see it in other places.

Aisha's Haveton routine consisted of crocheting with Grandmother Johnson, going to the little church all throughout the week, and teaching Grandmother Johnson various elements of the computer, now the internet, Biblical resources on it. She and Grandmother Johnson had their daily chores and sometimes ran errands together. When she was with Meta and her nieces, sometimes Candance coming by, the three of them together with Angie during the evenings after work, they read and played with the kids, playing card games when the kids occupied themselves. When the kids were asleep, they played cards listening to music, gossip seemingly flowing along with the beat of the music; Aisha enjoying music again.

She enjoyed her routine, but it needed something else, a book club. She had never been a part of a book club. She always had an interest, but never seemed to find the leisure time. In Haveton she had plenty of leisure time and the idea of the book club excited her. It would give her a chance to introduce some of her favorite books. Maybe they would become their favorites, too? But, also, Aisha's irritation with the books Candance read had reached its threshold, the books and the thumb sucking. She figured if she could not stop the thumb sucking—even Meta could not, she told Aisha that she had tried, talking about her and reprimanding her, but nothing worked so she stopped— at least she could introduce her to a variety of great stories. She would not strip the joy away from the books Candance liked reading but would introduce her to something new, perhaps bringing some balance. When Angie, Meta, and Candance all agreed with her suggestion, she was ecstatic. The first reading she offered up was *Their Eyes Were Watching God.*

When the books came in the mail, Aisha took one book out of its packaging and held it as if she were being reunited with an old friend after long separation. She had read the book many times at different stages in her life and each time she read she found something different in it, it meant something different to her. She felt she had gained full understanding of the book when she read it the last time, a few years before, in Chicago.

Once again, she held the book, looking at its cover, and the times were different for her, far different. Stroking the pages against her thumbs as though the book needed relieving after its treacherous journey through the mail system, Aisha wondered what her reading experience would be like then. Staring intently at the title, there was the word again, God. Before she had never given the title much thought, but then she wondered. Why God in the title? What did Zora see?

God popped up again when she made a daytime visit to Speedy's house. After much curiosity in the blue book with the sunken and blended in blue words on the cover, that day, Aisha picked it up, sat down, and began reading it. She had consciously gone into Speedy's room and removed it from around all the clutter with the intention of bringing Speedy's attention to her. Maybe her reading it could get them to talk about it, for all he had said when she asked him about it previously was "yeah, that's the big book," and continued to listen to his favorite talk radio programs. He sat that day doing the same, listening to his talk radio and barely turning his head to see Aisha as she sat down, making as much noise as she could. Once she started to read, she continued her efforts to attract his attention, pathetically clearing her throat and shifting loudly in her chair. She'd read a paragraph then look up from the book to see if he were looking over at her. She did this over and over until the book's words drew her in. She found it so interesting she dismissed her original intentions and continued to read the book for her own interest.

She left Speedy's house with the book, fascinated by the literature of the brotherhood of anonymous alcoholics. She read it throughout the rest of the day, however she did not finish. Their book club meeting was close and her excitement about rereading her favorite book was too great. Still, she had read enough of the blue book to see how it could be valuable. Again, the word God was practically on every other page. Just the same, God was practically on every other page in one of her favorite contemporary works of fiction. It was about a former slave who in turn became a slave master. In it, the author used the word to highlight the spectral usages, the deviation, and the absurdity, of how God was used in the world. This was Aisha's understanding of the word. How smart of him, she thought while reading it. But Zora's usage of God had to be different and certainly the authors of the stories written in the "big book" were not using it in this mocking way. What is the way?

On the day of their first book club meeting, the gang sat in Angie's front room like they normally would. Looking down at the cover, Aisha began to have similar thoughts about the title until Meta kicked off her lively conversation about the book. Aisha sat back, quiet, save for her laughter, letting Meta lead and Angie and Candance compliment her with their commentary. They picked up things it took her many reads to get! And how light, how funny! They started comparing the hog Speedy was raising with his friend Roy to the mule in the book. Their jokes and imitations of Speedy, imitations of what the hog must have been thinking being raised by Speedy, all of them getting in on it and it just building, had Aisha bent over nearly on the floor, grabbing her stomach in laughter.

Chapter 35

On a warm April spring day in Haveton, Aisha was reading the next book club selection when Candance called her. Angie was having the baby. She scrambled to her feet, told Grandmother Johnson the news, and headed to pick Meta and Sugarman up from their house.

The three of them arrived at the hospital and were directed to the maternity ward and Angie's room. It was a big hospital room, a single, not at all what Aisha had expected. She had only seen births on TV and, at the outset, she expected more drama, a much more confined space, and not the casual atmosphere she found. Candance was sitting with the girls, watching the cartoon about the yellow sea sponge and his friends. Angie was lying on the bed, sitting up somewhat, looking quite comfortable. "Isha, stop looking all nervous," Angie said as the three newcomers got settled in the room.

Time passed and Aisha watched Angie intently. Except for the rising contractions, it was like an ordinary day for the four women, only the setting being a hospital room. They all talked and joked and entertained the girls after they grew tired of entertaining themselves with the items Candance brought in their book bags. The day turned to afternoon, then early evening, and things began to change.

Angie refused the epidural anesthesia when the contractions began to strengthen in intensity. Things moved quickly from there. Candance and the nurse stood on both sides of Angie's bed, helping her push when the big contractions came. Angie screamed and wore a look of pure anguish and determination with each push. Candance started to speak louder than Aisha had ever heard her, encouraging Angie, cheering her on, "Breathe girl, breathe! That's it! A couple more!" All the action compelled Aisha from her seat and moved her to a vantage point where she could see the process occurring. She could see hair that was not Angie's hair. "I see hair!" she shouted. With the hair followed a head, a big hairy head, then a peek of brown forehead. Angie gave one final awesome push and scream and the doctor pulled a big baby boy out. As it came out, the entire room let out a collective "whoaaa" at his impressive size. He was alert already, trying to open his eyes, not crying, wise looking, as though he were returning to a familiar place. Aisha stood, amazed. The doctor gave the baby to Meta first as she checked on Angie. Candance wiped Angie's forehead, praising her for her strength and telling her how her son looked. Angie smiled wearily. Aisha's legs grew weak. She had to sit down. How amazing. She watched the afterbirth fall to the floor and it looked to her like one big beautiful mess. All was beautiful. How beautiful, what an energy!

On the ride home, Aisha followed Candance back to Angie's house. Angie and the baby would stay in the hospital overnight. During the drive, Aisha reflected on what she had just been a part of and the fulfilled, but exhausted, utterly spent look on her sister's face after she had delivered the baby. She had a new level of respect for her sister, for how she handled it all. She saw women, herself, differently. How wonderful an experience, how exhilarating, the most amazing event she had ever witnessed. How many others were like her, felt the way she felt? There had to be many. Did they not carry this experience around with them? Did something not change in them after seeing it? How could something so common be the most amazing sight she had ever seen? And how, other than its depiction on TV, which felt nothing like the real event, being there, could she have been oblivious to this wonder for so long? Being a woman, she had thought that she understood it in her being. Yes, she did, the power. But in seeing it, standing their watching her sister bring forth life, usher life into the world, having watched that big beautiful boy grow over the months, she had been there, and she had that ability. Did she have that ability? Aisha thought of Aaron and began to be brought down. But Meta speaking up again after silence, talking about having to think of a name for the baby, lifted Aisha back up, pulled her out of her brood and put her back in the hospital room and out of head. Better to think of it apart from her. "I know! What names do you like?" Aisha said, feeling good to finally be able to speak.

After putting Sheilah and Celestia to bed, Candance, Meta, Sugarman, and Aisha sat in Angie's front room, listening to the radio and talking, still high from the delivery. At some point, the song "My Life" came on the radio. It made Meta stand up, close her eyes, and start to sway.

"Whew, y'all, this song, this song. Every time I hear it…took me through some thangs," she said, slowly snapping her fingers, eyes still closed, swaying side to side to the music.

Aisha watched Meta's large frame moving, her seeming to be in another place. She focused on the song. Why did it take her away, what made her stand up and sway that way? Aisha had heard the song before. It was a good song, but something about the way Meta moved, eyes closed, her finger snaps the only part of her that seemed to be in the room, made Aisha listen more closely. At first every part of the song sounded the same, the words, but then, as Meta swayed, now Candance swaying in her own way and Sugarman off beat, for the first time the word he stood out to Aisha. Who was this *he*, the *he*, the *him* Mary J sung so soulfully about? Who was this *he* that she sung about with such passion, such yearning, such belief, such feeling, a feeling Aisha began to feel herself only to have the song end.

"Umph, that's my song! That girl is bad. I wish I still had my tape. I would play that again," Meta said, sitting down.

Aisha wished she could play the song again, too. She looked at Meta's glowing face and began to feel tired, sad again. What was it?

Aisha got up and hugged everyone in the room, telling them that she was going to bed and she would see them tomorrow.

On the road to Grandmother Johnson's house, Aisha thought over her life, looked over her life as the songstress had sung. She thought about her sister giving birth, her once hoping for a miracle she knew little about. She wanted to know.

She arrived at Grandmother Johnson's, parked the car, and got out. But she did not go toward the house. Instead, she began walking toward the pasture. The spring night air was cool, but pleasant. Aisha passed the great barn and into the pastures behind it. At some point in the middle of the open field, she stopped and looked up at the stars, then down, out, at the darkness ahead. Slowly, she crouched, getting on her knees. She looked out at the darkness ahead and when she felt the sadness starting to come on, she brought her head to the grass, resting her forehead against it. She opened her hands so that she could feel the sprouting blades of grass between her fingers. She closed her eyes and was still. She stayed there, breathing and being still, just breathing and feeling the grass between her fingers. Breathing, being still, breathing and being. I feel something, a feeling, keep breathing, yes? Yes. This stillness, I feel this, keep going, yes? Yes, now, still, be breath, be, what is in me, still, what—still—feel? Yes. I feel thankful, yes, thank you, my breath, thank you, my life, oh my life, my life, oh thank you, thank you, thank you, thank you this…a feeling beyond her, all over her, pushing tears from her eyes. She wept, shaking and shuddering into the earth.

When the water no longer flowed from her eyes, only remaining as residue on her cheeks, Aisha kept her head and hands on the grass, breathing. She waited and then stood. The darkness now looked like light. Taking a step, she started walking toward home in perfect peace.

Epilogue

The next morning Aisha rose, aware still of the profound immensity within. Yet, with each passing second, she felt its presence beclouded with the cares of the day, of yesterdays and tomorrows. Still, now she knew. What she felt was real but so was the bed she sat up in, Grandmother Johnson's dolls, and her feet touching the floor. Living, how to reconcile what can be seen with what cannot? It occurred to her then, like all other great conundrums she had known, she would need to work as hard as she could in order to reach the highest place of understanding. But what work? What works? How would she know what to do so that she would continue to know that feeling?

Aisha stood up from the bed. She heard Grandmother Johnson's bathwater running. It was early. She looked around for a pen and a piece of paper and, upon finding what she needed, wrote Grandmother Johnson a note telling her she was going for a walk. Setting the pen down she proceeded to put on some comfortable clothes and immediately after left the house.

Outside, she turned left and began walking past the big barn to the pasture where she knelt the night before. Where was the spot? It was hard to tell. A slight smile came to her face and she did a spin, her arms coming up and out as she twirled. She then left the pasture, walking down the driveway and turning to walk toward town. At some point, she began to jog alongside the road. The morning was cool but the warming of her body made her feel more comfortable. How stiff she was, muscles, joints, ligaments, all tight. How about her wind? She was winded. She was heavy but all of that could change. She knew how to change all of that. She kept running.

Running became her morning routine, running long distances

at a pace that pushed but did not press. She ran from Grandmother Johnson's to Meta's, from Grandmother Johnson's to Speedy's, from Grandmother Johnson's to Angie's, helping her get Sheilah, Celestia, and the baby, Adriel, ready for their day before Meta and Sugarman arrived.

On her runs, after the initial pain of her body coming back to life subsided, after she stopped thinking about her body mostly on her runs, listening to it, focusing on its feel, pushing through the soreness during and after, mostly after, how it hurt, all the little hurts, and the rediscovery of her flexibility, everything firing properly again, lucid thoughts came to her. After the business of Meta's roof being fixed was resolved, she thought about Angie and Candance. She could pay for their schooling. I could help them go to college full time, although with contingencies. How am I going to live now with all of the money? I have to observe myself with it, learn myself, and know myself fully with it. I am the same, but I am also much changed, everything has changed. I have to learn more about it. Aaron is with me. He taught me a lot about it. But I have to care about it in my own way. I must learn it so I can care more for others and help others without harm. It's vast. I have to be open to its growth, it growing even greater to support the growth of my visions. I have to be able to see who really does not share my vision though professing that they do. I have to able to see the beautiful truth in other's visions. Easy, take your time. I have to take my time. She could reach out to those who could help her speed up time, the network of beautiful people she knew, Isaac to start. He continued to update her as he said he would. The other day he said she was sounding good. Still, she had to take her time. Anything of impactful substance takes time and deliberate attention to grow great.

Like Biggums and Raven, look at how their relationship is growing. It began from a simple request, Biggums asking her for Raven's new phone number. He had the same calm voice and he did not rush to call her and they did not rush to go out on a date. They were both busy doing new things that made them happy, Raven organizing and working in the community, still working at Richard Wright with Dr. Haywood in her absence, and Biggums still going to church, now coaching the church's youth baseball team. Raven called her and told her that she thought she was in love, real love, despite Biggums not being like anyone she had ever dated, him not being at all who she had seen herself being with. Biggums called Aisha expressing the same sentiment, saying Aaron would be proud of him because of Raven's age and maturity, them laughing, real laughter again, laughing over the phone with Robert and Susan and Kaii. Kaii was hired to a new show and wanted to come to Haveton to meet all the people she had been telling her about before the show started. Aisha was laughing, laughing and not feeling bad about feeling good, not feeling guilty anymore.

When Kaii came to Haveton, she brought the force of her personality along with the allure of Hollywood. She and the ladies, Angie, Meta, and Candance, got along as if they were long friends, as though Kaii were a Haveton regular.

Kaii settled into her room at Grandmother Johnson's, into conversation with Grandmother Johnson about the Bible and her life, as though she had done it all before. Aisha quietly watched in delight. Kaii even handled meeting Speedy with grace. She was a gust of good wind into lungs that were already being filled with freshness, new breath.

Kaii happened to visit around the time of the Johnson family reunion, which occurred every two years. Most of the Johnson family attended, coming from all parts of the country, back to Haveton and the land that spawned the many branches.

Aisha had talked to some family members over the phone when they would call to check on Grandmother Johnson. "You're Speedy's daughter?" She knew her Uncle Charles from his visits but all others she had never met. So many cousins, so many relatives, and they all embraced her. Aisha watched how they embraced her father, looking past his affliction as he moved around, all at once being dignified, worldly, helpful, a hero, and over indulgent, careless shrinking, a mess. Aisha had to shrug her deep contemplations off. It was not the time.

It was the time to celebrate the coming together of family, stories, laughter, good eating being prepared in the barn and shared live music, and their biennial theme, which that year happened to be "Healthy Living." Various family members spoke on the aspects of their lives that contributed to healthy living. There were doctors, a dentist, and some educators. Aisha was impressed how it was all put together and how eloquently and passionately her family members spoke. She wished she had been able to be at the reunions when most of the elders were living. But what a time there was before her, Kaii and Meta, Sugarman being fully accepted, and Angie and Candance fitting right in, mingling as though they were family. Angie was family and Aisha took it upon herself to have her by her side as often as she could, facilitate the introductions of them meeting new faces, making sure Angie got some attention, some recognition and praise for her accomplishments, as everyone enlivened about what they had heard about Aisha. She did not need the attention. She needed to bring ease to strained situations. And she did. She could see it in Angie's beautiful smile.

At the reunion's end, that night, after Grandmother Johnson went to bed and after Kaii and Aisha talked about the weekend, rehashing their favorite moments, back in her own room Aisha thought about Angie's radiant smile, Kaii's smile, Meta's smile, and Candance smiling without her thumb in her mouth. How powerful women's smiles were! They could singularly lift spirits and lighten moods. Struck by this, Aisha picked up a pen and piece of paper and tried to fashion an acronym. After scribbling and crossing out, thinking, scribbling and crossing out some more, she came up with something: sisters in movement, illuminating and loving eternal. Yes, that's it! Maybe she could start an organization called s.m.i.l.e. There surely were others with the name, but hers would be different. It would be composed of beautiful women who wanted to make the world happier, of women who were happy themselves, balanced themselves, who would work to bring balance to imbalanced places, adding their areas of expertise under one beautiful umbrella. She had the start of it right there, Kaii sleeping in the next room! It could begin in Chicago. She had to eventually go back.

Aisha smiled to herself about her fanciful thinking. Then she thought of Aaron. No, she could not leave out men. Men had to be a part. How to bring them together equally? She could start by inserting the word souls in place of sisters. The soul. Why was there little talk of the soul? Why is the talk hushed, loud only on Sundays, some Saturdays? Designated days, designated times, was not the point. Be careful, Aisha. It was all new. She was new. She had to be careful to reflect the firming of her feelings through her acts. Words came easier, could come masterfully without understanding, could lose their meaning, be meaningless, be misconstrued, misinterpreted easier, but to act, to be...

Every day Aisha missed Aaron. Good days and bad days, him being gone hurt. Seeing her father struggle, continually not living up to his potential, giving in and not letting go, hurt. And there was nothing she could do. Despite her revelation and her slow healing, the hurt would always be there. There would always be times when there was nothing she could do. There was much she could do. But in solving the great mysteries of life, fixing the hurt for good, there was nothing she could do.

She could pray.